Night Wolf

A Novel of Viking Age Ireland

Book Five of The Norsemen Saga

James L. Nelson

This is a work of fiction. Names, characters, places and incidents either are the product of the author's imagination or are used fictitiously. Any resemblance to actual events, locales, organizations, or persons, living or dead, is entirely coincidental and beyond the intent of either the author or the publisher.

Fore Topsail Press
64 Ash Point Road
Harpswell, Maine, 04079

ISBN- 13:978-1534879683
ISBN-10: 1534879684

To Steve Cromwell, with gratitude for your fine work in creating the look for this series, and for all your kindnesses over the years.

Shape-shifter: Closely associated with the berserks, those who were *hamrammir* [shape-shifters] were believed to change their shape at night or in times of stress, or leave their bodies (which appeared asleep) and take the physical form of animals such as bears or wolves.

From *Glossary – The Icelandic Sagas*

He always went to sleep early in the evening and woke up early in the morning. People claimed he was a shape-shifter and they called him Kveldulf (Night Wolf).

Egil's Saga

For other terms, see Glossary, page 309.

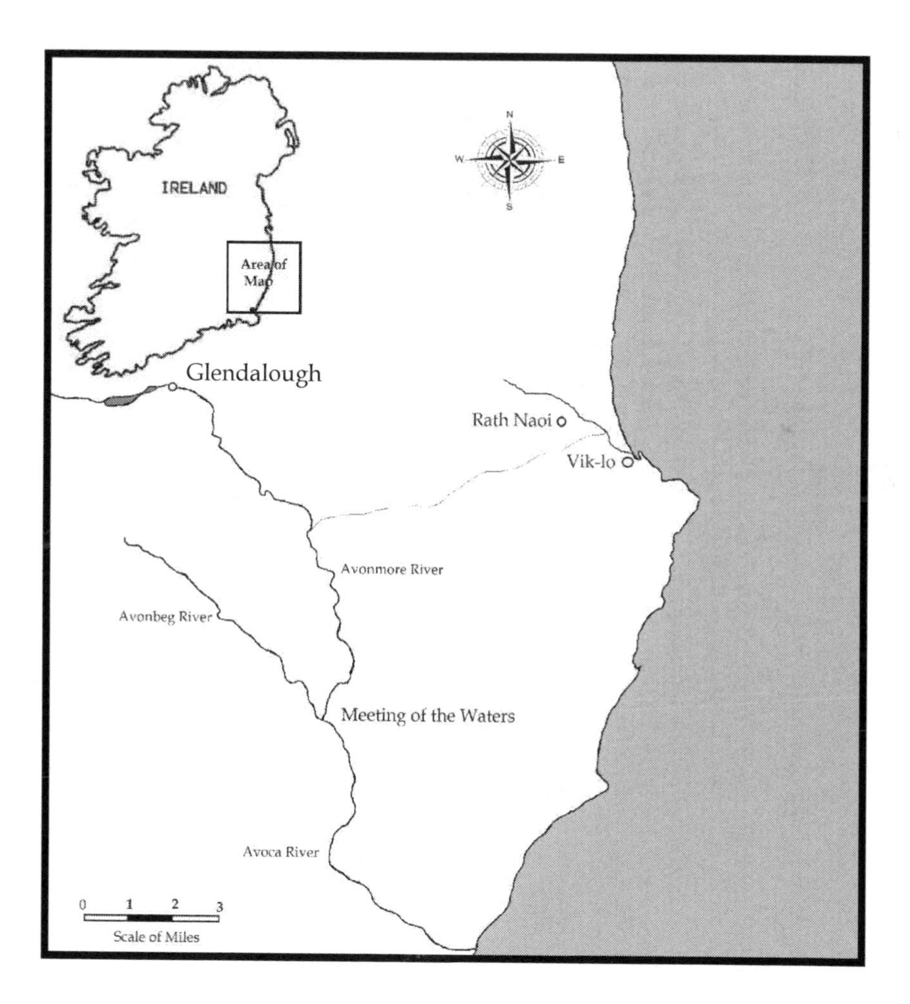
IRELAND
Area of Map
N
W
E
S
Glendalough
Rath Naoi
Vik-lo
Avonmore River
Avonbeg River
Meeting of the Waters
Avoca River
0 1 2 3
Scale of Miles

Prologue

The Saga of Thorgrim Ulfsson

There was a man named Thorgrim Ulfsson who was the son of Ulf Ospaksson, who was known as Ulf Quick-wit. Thorgrim was also clever and he was a skilled warrior as well, and so he was looked upon as a leader of men. If he had one fault, it was that he would sometimes grow foul-tempered as the sun went down. During those times his anger was such that people would not dare be near him. Some people thought that he was a shape-shifter, and that earned him the name of Thorgrim Kveldulf, which means Night Wolf. In his younger days the wolf spirit frequently came over him, but as he grew older he found it happened less often, and he was generally glad of that.

As a young man Thorgrim had gone a'viking with a local jarl named Ornolf the Restless. For many summers they raided around England and sometimes as far off as Frankia. The raiding was good in those days and Ornolf, who was already wealthy, grew wealthier still, and the men who sailed with him likewise gained much plunder. But of all those men, Thorgrim was Ornolf's favorite, and so he offered his daughter, Hallbera, to Thorgrim as his bride. This was a match that Thorgrim was happy to make. Thorgrim gave Ornolf fifty silver coins as a bride-price and Ornolf gave Thorgrim a bountiful farm as a dowry.

Thorgrim and Hallbera made a good marriage and they were happy. Thorgrim gave up raiding to tend to the farm and to his family, which soon consisted of two sons, Odd and Harald, and a daughter named Hild. Odd, the oldest, was a serious boy who worked hard and diligently. Harald, too, was a hard worker, but he dreamed of going a'viking as his father and grandfather had. Harald took care to learn from Thorgrim all he could about the use of weapons, and he sought out any others who could also teach him. When his chores were done, Harald would often sneak off to a secret place in the woods where he would practice with sword, ax, spear and shield.

Many years passed and Thorgrim continued to grow in wealth and reputation. Odd married and Thorgrim gave him the farm that Ornolf had given as a dowry. Then, after Thorgrim had passed forty winters, Hallbera found she was again with child. Hallbera was no longer young, and she died in childbirth, which broke Thorgrim's heart.

Thorgrim's father-in-law, Ornolf, wished to once again go a'viking, this time to Ireland, and because Thorgrim found he was no longer happy on his farm with Hallbera gone, he agreed to go with him. Thorgrim took Harald, who was fifteen years of age. Harald was not overly tall, but he was very strong, and he soon earned the nickname of Broadarm. Having studied the use of weapons so long and diligently, he was a good warrior, if not quite as clever as his father.

Ornolf and his crew sailed to Ireland aboard Ornolf's ship *Red Dragon*, and there they had many adventures and won and lost several fortunes. Ornolf was killed in a battle against a Dane named Grimarr Giant who was lord of a longphort called Vík-ló. After Harald killed Grimarr, Thorgrim was made Lord of Vík-ló and there he and his men, as well as those who had followed Grimarr, spent the winter building ships for the spring's raiding.

When spring at last came, an Irishman named Kevin mac Lugaed, with whom the Northmen had been trading, arrived at Vík-ló to suggest that his men and Thorgrim's men join together to raid a monastery at a place called Glendalough. This Thorgrim and his men agreed to, and they were joined by another army of Northmen led by a man named Ottar Thorolfson whose nickname was Bloodax.

Thorgrim and Ottar went to Glendalough by rowing their ships as far up the rivers as they could. Glendalough was indeed a wealthy monastery, but before they reached it they were met by a great army of Irish warriors, with whom they fought. Thorgrim was betrayed by Kevin, who switched sides even before the fighting, and by Ottar who slipped away in the night. Ottar and his men made off with all the ships, save Thorgrim's ship *Sea Hammer*, which was holed. Ottar wished to go to Vík-ló and claim the longphort and the wealth there for himself and leave Thorgrim and his men behind to be killed by the Irish.

The Irish soldiers did great slaughter among Thorgrim's people as they tried to escape, and in the end only Thorgrim and ten of his men were left alive. The Irish tried to burn *Sea Hammer*, but through a clever trick Thorgrim made them run off before the ship was set on fire. Then Thorgrim plugged the hole as best he could and he and his remaining men sailed the ship down river to a place of safety where they would fix it properly. Thorgrim vowed that he would get revenge on those who had wronged him.

Here is what happened

Chapter One

I, maker of the sword's voice
Heard two loon birds fighting
And I knew that soon the dew
Of bows would be descending
Gisli Sursson's Saga

Six miles downstream from Glendalough, Thorgrim Night Wolf found the place on the river where he intended to beach *Sea Hammer*, his longship. He had noticed the spot on their voyage up, had tucked the location away in his mind. That was a week before.

He had had no notion then that he and his men might find themselves in need of a place where they could hide their ship and make repairs so that they might carry out a desperate and unlikely escape. That thought had not occurred to him, and yet he had seen the place and noted it and remembered it. The gods, perhaps, whispering in his ear. Thor wishing to come to his aid. Loki, playing a trick to prolong his misery.

The spot was on the south bank, which meant little on a river that was fordable in so many places, but still it put them on the shore opposite the monastery and the encampment from which the horse soldiers would come. The riverbank was heavily wooded on both sides, so the Northmen could not be seen from a distance, could only be discovered if someone hacked their way through the forest to the water's edge. There was a gravel sandbar that reached out into the stream, perfect for beaching a ship. The wide curve in the river that had deposited the gravel there also helped hide the ship from anyone upstream or down.

"There," Thorgrim said, loud but not very loud. The gravel bar was two hundred feet down current, and Thorgrim spoke to let the handful of men at the sweeps know that their labor would soon be over. He held the tiller himself, keeping the ship midstream as best he could.

Forward he saw heads turning to look, not many, as there were not that many heads aboard to turn. Harald, his son. The massive Godi, pulling the oar opposite Harald. A warrior named Olaf Thordarson, who had been with them since leaving Dubh-linn, and another named Ulf. Ten men in all, including Starri Deathless, wounded in the first fight with the Irish and left aboard *Sea Hammer* when they had launched the attack on Glendalough. Ten men out of more than two hundred who had sailed from Vík-ló on this raid.

"Harald, get some lines ready to run to the trees ashore," Thorgrim called. Harald nodded and pulled his long oar inboard and laid it across the sea chests that the rowers used for benches. The loss of Harald's oar did little to slow *Sea Hammer*'s progress downstream. It was the current that was driving the ship, not the rowers. The men at the oars were concerned mostly with keeping the vessel in the middle of the river, keeping her from turning sideways, and making a bit of headway when needed to give the steering board some bite.

And that was fortunate, because ten men, ten wounded, exhausted, dispirited men, and two prisoners, one a woman, were not about to move sixty-five feet of oak and pine longship through their own strength of arm.

"Give a pull! Unship your oars!" Thorgrim called next and the men still at the oars, five to larboard and four to starboard, leaned back for one last pull, then slid their oars in and laid them out as Harald had done. Thorgrim gave a twist of the tiller and *Sea Hammer* slewed sideways, coming up onto the gravel not bow-first but with the round part of her bilge sliding up into the shallow water in a way that would allow the sandbar to most effectively support the injured vessel.

The ship gave a slight shudder as she touched and Harald leapt off the sheer strake and onto the sandbar, ropes in hand. The water that ran an inch deep over *Sea Hammer*'s deck boards rolled to the larboard side like a small tidal surge.

Another ten minutes and we would have been on the river bed, Thorgrim thought. Dead men's tunics stuffed into a two-foot hole in the ship's bottom would not stanch a leak in any meaningful way.

Sea Hammer was the only ship of nine left after Ottar, the lunatic, and his men had abandoned Thorgrim's warriors to the Irish in the predawn hours before battle. *Sea Hammer* had been left behind only because Ottar's brother, Kjartan, who had turned against him, had cut a hole in her to stop Ottar's stealing her as well. Thorgrim and the handful of men who had escaped the butchery that the Irish had doled out found her run up on the riverbank and half sunk.

Then the Irish had found her, too. Twenty of them, mounted warriors, too many for the Northmen to take on. As Thorgrim and his men watched from the cover of the trees, the Irish made ready to burn her where she lay. That, for Thorgrim, was too much. He was willing to die, indeed he preferred to die, before suffering such a final humiliation.

In the end that sacrifice was not necessary. Thorgrim's prisoner, his male prisoner, was an Irish warrior named Louis, and Thorgrim sent him to warn the soldiers off, to tell them there were sixty Norse warriors coming up river. Thorgrim then made a show of force with the few men he had, and that had been enough to make the Irish ride off. But he knew they would not be gone for long, and they would not come back alone.

With the sound of the horses' hooves growing fainter, Thorgrim led his men back aboard *Sea Hammer*. She was badly holed, true, but she did not have to voyage far, just a ways beyond where they might expect the Irish to come looking for them.

"We need something to stop up that hole," Thorgrim said after peering at the damage through the clear water that flooded the hull. He straightened and looked around. There were dead men all over the shore. Most were his own men, those who had been left behind to guard the ships. They had given their lives in that effort, but they had not been enough to stop the near three hundred men under Ottar's command.

Not all of the dead, however, were Thorgrim's men. "Find some of Ottar's dead," Thorgrim ordered, "strip off their tunics and bring them to me. Just cut them away." Thorgrim was tormented by the memory of the men who had died because of his misjudgment. He was tormented by the fact that he had no time to give them a proper funereal. He could not stand the thought of leaving their corpses, naked and bloating, for the ravens and the wolves to feast on.

The others nodded their understanding and climbed back ashore to find the corpses from which to strip clothing. They shuffled, they limped, they moved with obvious pain. They had all been wounded in some manner during the fight: a slash from a sword, a wound from the spear of a mounted warrior, a hard kick from a horse. They were wounded, but they could still move and that was why they lived. Those too wounded to run had been hacked down on the field.

One by one the men returned with the bundles of cloth that just that morning had clothed living warriors, and Thorgrim knew he had another decision to make. A harder one. He took the tunics and once again ran his eyes over the shore. His men had died fighting. The Choosers of the Slain had been among them already—they must have been; it had been hours. What need had they of weapons? They were in the corpse hall now, or they never would be.

"I need four of you to find helmets to bail the ship," Thorgrim said, gesturing toward the river water that had flooded into *Sea Hammer*, a foot high at its deepest. "The rest of you, gather up all the swords, shields, mail, any weapons you can find and get them on board."

"From Ottar's men, Lord Thorgrim?" Ulf asked. "Or from all the dead men?"

"From all the men. They have no use for weapons now," Thorgrim said, and his tone did not welcome discussion. "And do not call me 'Lord'," he added. "I'm not the lord of anything. Not a dung heap, nothing."

I am not a lord because I am a fool, he thought.

Once again the men climbed over the side and spread out along the shore. Starri Deathless limped after them, his wound graver than the others, and greatly aggravated by the day's events. He had been there when Ottar's men arrived, had taken up arms despite his agony, and fought until he had collapsed. But for Starri, the torment of having to stay still was worse than the torment of having to move.

"Starri," Thorgrim said as Starri was swinging a leg painfully over the ship's side. "Stay aboard, listen for the riders coming back. None of the others will hear them before you do."

Starri nodded. His hearing was legendary. He brought his leg back inboard and climbed up onto the foredeck, leaning against the tall stem. The elegant, sweeping post terminated ten feet above with a carving of an angry, vengeful Thor looking out past the bow. Now Thor and Starri together faced the land beyond the riverbank, alert for any sound of danger.

Thorgrim draped the cut tunics over the sheer strake and kneeled down into the water in the ship's bottom. He took up one of the tunics and shoved it into the hole, jamming it as tightly into the corner as he could, then reached for another.

He heard the sound of someone climbing aboard and then the splash of water. He looked over his shoulder. Harald was there with a leather helmet in hand, already scooping water from the bilge and throwing it back into the river. Thorgrim had guessed that he would opt for that job. As much as Harald liked to play the man, Thorgrim did not think he would relish the idea of stripping mail from the corpses of the dead.

"Harald," Thorgrim said. "Wait until I've plugged the hole before you start bailing."

Harald flushed. "Oh…yes…of course," was all he managed to say. Harald was always eager to be foremost in everything, and sometimes he got ahead of himself.

Two more tunics, and the hole was as filled as it was going to get. Thorgrim had no doubt water would stream though it, but not as fast as they could bail, not for a while, anyway.

"All right," Thorgrim said. "Start bailing."

Harald went right at it, filling the helmet and flinging the water over the side. He had been voyaging for several years now. The Norse longships were the finest seagoing vessels on earth—fast, nimble, flexible and seaworthy—but they were still essentially just big open boats, and Harald, like the other mariners from the North countries, had considerable experience with bailing.

Harald was joined in his efforts by Thorodd Bollason, who flung water with great vigor despite the deep gash on his upper arm, left in the wake of a stroke from an Irish sword and bound with a blood-soaked bandage. Two others, Vali and Armod, joined in, and it was not long before Thorgrim could see the level of the water dropping against the ship's side.

He looked up river and down, judging the strength of the current. He heard the sound of something falling on the deck, felt the shudder in his feet, and looked up to see Godi dropping a great armload of mail shirts and swords and axes over the sheer strake forward. More men were behind him, similarly laden. Their faces were grim and Thorgrim guessed that they, like himself, understood the need to do what they were doing, but were not happy about doing it.

Thorgrim looked out at the beach. The men were back scouring the dead for weapons, but the two prisoners just stood watching, arms folded. They were enigmas, a man and a woman, both clad in mail and wearing swords, of which they had been relieved. They had come walking down the riverbank and stumbled into Thorgrim and his men. They were Irish, as far as Thorgrim could tell, but he had the sense that they were trying to escape from something, or someone.

The man carried a sack over his shoulder, which Thorgrim had correctly guessed carried a small chest with a hoard of silver, gold and jewels inside.

Thieves? Thorgrim wondered. Perhaps, but they were dressed and armed better than any itinerant bandits that Thorgrim had ever seen. Nor did it matter at that moment. Whatever they were, they would not be idle.

"Harald!" Thorgrim called. "Tell our new friends there to find some helmets and get to bailing."

Harald nodded and called to the two ashore, addressing them in the Irish tongue. He had picked up much of the language during their time in that country, motivated by a desire to speak with the various Irish women he had met, for better or worse.

Grudgingly, the prisoners found helmets and climbed aboard and soon they added their efforts to the bailing. Thorgrim felt the vessel shifting underfoot as the water level dropped and the keel came up off the bottom. More water went over the side. *Sea Hammer* rolled more upright.

"Night Wolf," Starri called from forward. "Riders."

Thorgrim nodded. "That's all we get," he called. These horsemen might have been the Irishmen coming back with more men, or they might not have been, but either way Thorgrim knew they could not risk waiting to find out. He looked over the side. The ship seemed to be floating, and high enough that they could get her off the shore. "Shove her out, let's be gone!" he said. The men gleaning weapons ashore left off and put their shoulders to the side of the ship, and Harald leapt overboard and did likewise.

With a minimum of grunting and cursing, *Sea Hammer*'s bow slid off the gravel beach and, before climbing aboard, the men who had pushed her off turned her so she was pointing downstream. The current took her and swirled her away and Thorgrim steered as best he could until the oars were out and the ship was making way. They were around the bend and lost from sight before any of the mounted warriors appeared on the shore astern.

For two hours they worked their way downstream, rowing and bailing, until at last *Sea Hammer* came to rest on the sandbar that had stuck in Thorgrim's memory.

Harald crossed the gravel to the trees beyond, uncoiling the rope as he went, and soon had the ship tied fore and aft. On Thorgrim's orders the yard was lowered to the deck, the parrel binding it to the mast untied, and the heavy spar was set to rest on the larboard side.

That done, the vantnales were cast off to free the lower ends of the shrouds and the mast was unstepped and set beside the yard. This was no easy task with so few men, and those few in such bad shape, but it would greatly help in hiding the ship. More importantly, the weight of the spars on the larboard side lifted the hole to starboard out of the water, and so the ship was no longer in danger of filling.

Thorgrim pulled the soaked tunics from the rent in the side and was finally able to examine the hole more closely. He knelt on the deck and leaned into the damage. In his mind he saw the shattered planks cut back to where they were still solid, the holes drilled in the new pieces, the clench nails set in place. His thoughts traveled to the space beneath the deck boards where the spare strakes were stored away. In his mind he sorted through them just as he had with his eyes when they had first come aboard.

Sea Hammer was Thorgrim's ship in every way. He built her, he and Aghen Ormsson, the skilled old shipwright who made his home at Vík-ló. All through the winter months Thorgrim and Aghen had worked side by side, shaping *Sea Hammer* and the other ships, *Dragon* and *Blood Hawk*. They had discussed every step, argued about some things, readily agreed on others. They had selected wood, shaped the strakes, laid out the keel and the frames and the mast steps. While every man in the longphort had had a hand in the building, the creating was done by Thorgrim and Aghen alone.

And so Thorgrim had no doubt that he could make his ship strong and whole again. Not just strong enough to live on the Irish river, but strong enough to survive the open sea. And he knew it would not be a simple task.

He also knew that it would not start that day. The sun was sinking in the west, and even as he looked at the damaged strakes, Thorgrim felt exhaustion wash over him. He recalled, with some surprise, that it was only that morning he and his men had been fighting for their lives against the mounted Irish warriors, that it had been just after dawn that he had seen his men, his shipmates, hacked down around him. It seemed like half a lifetime's worth of horror and rage and grief had been shoved into those dozen hours of daylight.

He gathered his men and set a watch, and despite his exhaustion he took the first shift himself. The others crawled off to sleep and Thorgrim took his place on the afterdeck, his eyes turned out toward the darkening shore, his ears sharp for any sounds that were not the normal sounds of the night.

The details of the shoreline faded with the setting sun, and as they did the ghosts appeared, the images of the men he had lost that day: Agnarr, Skidi Battleax, Bersi, Sutare Thorvaldsson, all those men who had put themselves under his command, all those men who had followed him, and he had led them only to their deaths. In his mind he could see them all still alive, and some he could see at the moment their lives had ended, cut down by the Irish swords and spears.

He had led men before. And he had seen slaughter before. But he had never seen his own men butchered in that way. And he had never felt so entirely responsible for having led men to a bloody end.

In the younger days, and even when they had first come back to Ireland, the men he commanded were Ornolf's men, not his. He might have been leading them, but the ultimate responsibility had rested with Ornolf, not him.

He reminded himself that the other chief men, Skidi and Bersi and Kjartan, had also agreed to take part in this raid. They had wanted to, and so had their men. And that thought did nothing to lift his burden.

"Never again," he said, softly to himself. The men under his command might still meet with bloody and violent death, but not because he had been played for a fool.

The hours passed, and somewhere beyond the thick clouds Thorgrim knew the stars were wheeling in place, and at last he woke Godi to take the watch. With a grunt Godi hefted himself up, stood and stretched. Thorgrim gave one last look around. All was quiet. Some of the men were snoring. He lay down on a fur on the deck and closed his eyes. He was not sure sleep would come to him, and if it did he was wary of what dreams it might bring, but in the end exhaustion won the night and he slept, deep and dreamless.

And then he awoke and he knew something was wrong. He opened his eyes to the gray light of *rismál*, the hour of rising. It was quiet, no sound of alarm, but he knew something was wrong. He sat up just in time to see Godi stepping toward him, moving sideways, his eyes never leaving the riverbank.

Chapter Two

A generous prudent man of shields
Who brought plenty to landed Temair,
Against iron-tipped spears a buckler
From the forge-fire of the land of the sons of Mil.
The Annals of Ulster

Lochlánn mac Ainmire, formerly Brother Lochlánn, novitiate at the monastery at Glendalough, led his twenty mounted men-at-arms back to the *dúnad*, the soldiers' camp, just outside of the monastic city. They rode hard. They did not know if the Northmen were coming in pursuit. And whether they were or not, Lochlánn was desperately eager to round up more men, return to the river, and crush the heathens before they could escape. But for all that, the ride back was a blur. He was aware of none of it.

Louis…damn him…Louis…son of a bitch… Those disjointed curses echoed through his mind as he rode. Rage, confusion, fear—it all swirled around in some unholy brew and it would not let him think.

Louis de Roumois…

A fellow novitiate. A Frank, a former soldier, a second son exiled to the monastery by his family, as Lochlánn had been. But then Louis had been lifted from that unwelcome circumstance and set at the head of the men-at-arms, charged with defending Glendalough against the heathens, and he had taken Lochlánn as his aide. He had given Lochlánn a purpose and a new life. He had taught him how to be a soldier and showed him how to fight the heathen.

Louis, you son of a bitch… And then Louis had murdered his second in command, a man named Aileran, and run off with the wife of Colman mac Breandan, the nominal head of Glendalough's defense. And now Colman was dead, too, and Lochlánn had no reason to think that Louis had not killed him as well.

Except that Louis insisted that he had not.

There at the river. Lochlánn was preparing to burn the heathens' ship to the waterline and Louis de Roumois, of all people, had come out of the woods, arms spread to show he meant no harm. Lochlánn drew his sword and might have cut Louis down on the spot if he had not been so stunned.

Then Louis had begun to talk, the words calm, forceful, with a hint of pleading, the Frankish accent so familiar. "Lochlánn, I must say two things, and you will listen to me, and then you can kill me or not, as you wish," he said.

Lochlánn was still too stunned to reply.

"The first thing is that Colman sent Aileran to kill me," Louis said. "Colman was paid by my brother, I think. It is very complicated. But I killed Aileran because he was going to kill me."

"So you *did* kill Aileran?" Lochlánn said. A stupid question, but he had not recovered his wits.

"Yes. Because he was going to kill me. The next thing is that there are sixty of the heathens coming up the river, not far now, and they'll kill you all if you don't flee."

Lochlánn squinted at Louis. The other men at arms began to move around Louis's flanks, ready to block any attempt at escape. "How do you know this?" Lochlánn asked.

"Because they sent me. They want you to flee. They don't want to fight. They just want to leave."

Lochlánn's reply was on his lips. *Why should I believe a murderer like you?* But before he could speak he saw movement on the edge of his vision. He looked up. Two hundred feet downstream, the heathens were coming out of the woods, weapons in hand. Coming toward them. Just as Louis had said.

"Go," Louis said. "Go now. There's no reason for you and your men to die."

Lochlánn hesitated. He shook his head, not in refusal but in hope that doing so might help order his thoughts. But it did not. "Come with us," Lochlánn said.

"No," Louis said. "The heathens have Failend. They'll kill her if I go with you."

Failend… Colman's wife. That name brought another thought into Lochlánn's head.

"Colman is dead," Lochlánn said. "Did you kill him?"

There was a look of surprise on Louis's face, and it seemed genuine. "No," Louis said. "How was he killed?"

"His throat was slashed. In his own home. I found his body. It looked as if he had been digging up a hoard, but if he was, someone stole it."

Louis had no reply to that. For the first time since his appearance on the riverbank he seemed as dazed as Lochlánn. Then Senach, who was second in command of the small detachment of riders, made a sound in his throat, a low warning sound. Lochlánn looked up. The heathens were still advancing through the shallow water, ten men at least, and likely more in the trees.

Louis saw Lochlánn's eyes move downstream. "Go," Louis said again. Lochlánn slid his sword back into its scabbard.

"You men," Lochlánn called to his soldiers, "let us mount up and go. We've had fighting enough for today." And that was true, though Lochlánn had already decided they would ride back to the *dúnad* for more men and with luck return in time to kill the rest of the heathens and to take Louis de Roumois prisoner. If your task was wiping out a nest of vipers, you did not suffer a few to live that they might strike again.

He turned to Louis, who was also starting to back away. "I'm not done with you," he said, and at that Louis visibly bristled.

"You mind how you talk to me, boy," Louis said, the calm all but gone now, the anger rising up. "You knew nothing before I trained you, and you hardly know more now."

Lochlánn's men were moving back. Not fleeing, but returning to their mounts, and Lochlánn took a step back as well. He pointed at Louis. "You killed Aileran and you admitted as much. If you had to kill him or not, I don't know. You ran off with Colman's wife. These are things you must answer for. In the eyes of the law and of God."

Louis shook his head. "Go, boy," he said. "Go and see how the world of men really works."

And that was the last that Lochlánn mac Ainmire had seen of Louis de Roumois. He and Senach and the others mounted up, kicked their horses to a gallop. They had been riding for nearly an hour when the steeple on the big church at Glendalough came into view, and Lochlánn's mind was no more settled than it had been standing by the river.

In truth he had not known Louis for so very long, but in that short time he had come to love him as he loved no other man, not even his brother. Certainly not his father. And that made him all the more desperate to take Louis prisoner and to find out the truth and to drive a sword through his heart if Louis had indeed betrayed them.

Lochlánn slowed his tired horse to a walk and he heard the men behind him do the same. Senach gave his horse a kick and drew up by Lochlánn's side and for a moment they rode on like that without speaking. Senach was only a few years' Lochlánn's senior, but he was a man-at-arms by training and had considerable experience in combat. Still, he did not seem to resent Lochlánn's having command. Lochlánn's father was a Lord of Superior Testimony, wealthy and influential. Lochlánn could read and write. That seemed enough by Senach's lights to qualify him for leadership.

Just a few weeks before, that would have been all the qualification Lochlánn could have mustered, that and some remedial training as a young man. But since that time he and Senach had fought side by side in several ugly battles. And despite the fears that had kept Lochlánn awake in the nights leading up to the mayhem, he had acquitted himself well. Every warrior among them would have to say Lochlánn was an able fighting man.

"These men," Lochlánn said, giving a slight nod toward the mounted warriors behind them, "will they ride back to face the heathens again? Do they have the strength still, or are they too tired?"

"The horses are too tired," Senach said. "We'll need fresh horses. The men? If you lead them back to fight, they'll go. They'd be more afraid of seeming backward in their courage."

Lochlánn nodded. "Good," he said. He was ready for more, but he understood that he might feel more driven for this fight than the others did.

They rode up over a rise in the land and saw the dúnad spread out beyond them, or what remained of the dúnad. At the end of the fighting that morning there had been three or four hundred men there. Some were the *bóaire* and the *fuidir*, the small-time farmers, those who were not freemen, who had been called up for the military service they owed their lords. Others were the household guards and the men-at-arms that the various *rí túaithe* maintained. But already they were melting away, the farmers back to their sorry plots of land, the men-at-arms back to their lords' halls. The heathen had been driven off; no one was eager to remain.

"Damn them for fools," Lochlánn said. "Do they think the threat's gone? Will they just abandon the dúnad?"

He looked over to Senach for an answer, but Senach just shrugged. They rode on for a moment more, and then Senach said, "We did great slaughter among the heathens this very morning. All their ships are gone, save for the one we nearly burned, and that one had a great hole in the side. I guess they don't see a need to tarry here."

Lochlánn made a grunting noise. There was reason enough for the army to remain. They did not know where the heathens had gone, if they had returned to the sea or if they were just a few leagues down the river, biding their time. Louis de Roumois had said there were sixty at least within striking distance of Glendalough.

What's more, Lochlánn and his men had failed to take Louis prisoner. That, Lochlánn realized, was the thing that bothered him most of all, the chief reason it angered him to see the army breaking apart like a sheet of ice on a spring lake.

They came to the edge of the encampment where a group of soldiers were folding tents and taking down a rather impressive pavilion that no doubt belonged to the lord whom they served. Louis reined to a stop.

"You there," he said, and the man nearest him left off what he was doing, straightened, turned, and looked up at Lochlánn.

"Yes?" the man said.

"Who is the lord of the highest standing in the dúnad now?" Lochlánn asked. "Who has command here?" With Colman dead and Louis run off, Lochlánn did not know who to turn to for instructions, or who might have the authority to order more mounted warriors to accompany him on his renewed attack on the heathens.

The men-at-arms who followed him now had been Colman's men, Louis's men. They knew Lochlánn and respected him and were willing to obey his orders. They, like Lochlánn, were seething at the thought of Louis de Roumois's killing Aileran, a man they had loved. Some might even resent his killing Colman, though Colman was not much loved by anyone. When Lochlánn had ordered those men to follow him, they had obeyed, and gladly. But there were no other men whom Lochlánn might call up to fight.

"Lord of the highest standing…" the soldier repeated, frowning and looking around. "I guess it's Lord Niall mac Oengus, who I serve. Me and these men. I can think of no other."

Lochlánn nodded. "And where is your lord?" he asked.

The soldier pointed to a cluster of men down the road. "That's him, yonder, on the big black gelding," he said. Lochlánn thanked him and spurred his horse on, his weary men following behind.

Niall mac Oengus was in discussion with two other men who, judging by their clothes and their obsequious looks, did not appear to have the level of authority that Niall enjoyed.

"My lord!" Lochlánn called as he rode up. "My Lord Niall?"

Niall turned on his horse and eyed Lochlánn and the men trailing behind him. "Yes?" he said. Whatever Lochlánn had to say, Niall did not sound terribly eager to hear it.

"My lord," Lochlánn said, pulling his horse to a stop. "I am Lochlánn mac Ainmire; I lead the house guard of Colman mac Breandan," he said, which strictly speaking was not true. Actually, in no sense was it true. But the truth, Lochlánn felt, was too complex to explain, and he did not care to raise the name of Louis de Roumois.

"Colman's dead," Niall said.

"Yes, lord," Lochlánn said. He waited for Niall to continue, to explain how that was relevant, but when he did not, Lochlánn continued. "Lord, there's a band of the heathens down by the river, still. Some who escaped us this morning. Sixty or so. Lord, if you could provide me with three dozen mounted warriors, I'll ride them down and kill them all. We should not suffer any to live."

"Sixty heathens?" Niall said, and he did not sound impressed. "We killed near three times that number today. What harm can sixty heathens do? Let the wolves get them."

"Lord, they are the wolves," Lochlánn said, trying to keep the frustration from his voice. "They must be killed, or they'll be back." He considered telling Niall that Louis de Roumois was with them, but he did not. He did not know what response, if any, that news might bring.

"Look here…Lochlánn," Niall said, speaking in some odd imitation of a fatherly tone. "It costs me a damned lot of silver to keep these men in the dúnad. I've lost six of them in the fighting, and with so many others killed, hiring more men-at-arms will come at a dear price, I can tell you. And the Lord knows what's happening back on my lands while I'm gone. Sixty heathens? There's naught they can do. Let them go. You fought well today, you and your men. There's nothing more needs be done."

With that, Niall tapped his horse's flanks with his heels and rode back to where his men were breaking camp and stacking their sundry gear on wagons. Lochlánn heard the sound of Senach hacking up phlegm and spitting on the ground. "*You fought well today*," he said in a mocking, singsong tone. "Damned whoremonger, as if he knows how we fought. I didn't see him in the thick of it."

"The dumb ass," Lochlánn agreed. "But we'll get no men from him." He turned in the saddle and looked at Senach. "Let's find Father Finnian."

Father Finnian was one of the priests at the monastery at Glendalough, as far as Lochlánn understood. The man seemed to come and go in a way that no others associated with the monastery did, and he seemed to have influence and authority far beyond what Lochlánn would expect from a simple man of God. There was quite a bit about Father Finnian that Lochlánn did not understand.

It was Finnian who had put Louis in command of the men-at-arms, and it was Finnian who had brought Louis and Lochlánn together. Father Finnian, Lochlánn was sure, would understand the dangers of leaving the heathens alive. And Father Finnian wanted Louis taken prisoner and the truth of all this discovered nearly as much as Lochlánn did. If anyone would be willing to round up more warriors, and able to do so, it would be Father Finnian.

But they could not find him. Lochlánn led the men and their drooping horses back to the monastery at Glendalough. They asked after Father Finnian, but no one had seen him. They looked in all the places that they might expect to find him, but he was in none of those places.

At last, dispirited, sore, exhausted, Lochlánn dismounted and sat on the low wall that surrounded the monastery. He hung his head, too weary to hold it up. Senach sat beside him and the others sat or sprawled around, while the horses contented themselves with the monastic grass.

"You know," Senach said at last, "we never saw but ten or so of the heathen dogs that Louis the Frank said were there. Less, maybe."

Lochlánn straightened, but he did not feel the weight come off his shoulders. "Yes, so?" he said.

"Maybe ten was all there were. Maybe Louis was lying about there being sixty. He's not one I would trust, damned Frankish cur. Maybe he wanted to scare us off."

Lochlánn considered that. "Maybe you're right," he said. The two remained silent for a while, and then Senach spoke again.

"You know," he said. "Me, these men, we were Colman's men. And he's dead. We have no lord we answer to. Same with you."

Lochlánn nodded. He waited for Senach to continue, which he did.

"Every one of us, we want to see that Louis de Roumois dead. Aileran was our captain. Our friend. We have weapons. We have horses. We have you as captain now. What keeps us from going after these sons of bitches on our own?"

What, indeed? Lochlánn thought.

It was an incredible idea. Too incredible, really. It was not something he could do. Lead these men in hunting Louis down? Senach was right about one thing. They had what they needed and he, Lochlánn, had a fair amount of silver hoarded away, silver sent by his father and silver won in gambling and silver taken from his father's hoards when his father was away. He could pay for what they might need.

But there were other considerations. Lochlánn had no authority to do any such thing. In the worst case he could be considered an outlaw. He was under the discipline of the abbot; he had obligations to the monastery.

"No," Lochlánn said. "It's a mad idea. I couldn't do it."

"Of course," Senach said. "Of course not. Foolish of me to bring it up, really. I'm sure you're eager to get back to your life in the monastery, the sexts and the antiphons and all that. Prayer. Working in the kitchen. All that."

Lochlánn nodded. He had changed his mind. Even before Senach had finished speaking, Lochlánn had changed his mind.

Chapter Three

[U]ncertain is the witting
that there be no foeman sitting,
within, before one on the floor
Hávamál

Thorgrim watched them approach, the men coming out of the trees and stepping down onto the sandbar that ran right up to the shore. Not twenty men as he had first guessed, but more than that. Twenty-five at least. They were spread out in a line, weapons in hand. Their leader, or the one Thorgrim took to be their leader, was in the center. A big man, an ugly son of a bitch.

Godi, who had been coming to rouse Thorgrim, stopped where he was. He held a battle ax in his hand, but smart man that he was, he held it low and at his side. Godi understood, as Thorgrim did, that there was no need to show aggression until it was clear that aggression was the right response.

Thorgrim hopped down from the afterdeck and walked forward, his movements awkward with *Sea Hammer* rolled partway onto her larboard side. He glanced at his own men, sleeping in various places around the ship. He had to get them up, get them to arms, without provoking the Irish into attacking before the Northmen were ready. He was just considering how to do that when he saw one man, then another and another, stir, cast off their blankets, reach for weapons. It was the instinct of fighting men in the field. Something was wrong. They could feel it.

As Thorgrim's men stood, weapons in hand, the Irish halted their advance. The sight of a Norse ship run up on the sandbar would have piqued their interest, though they could have had no idea of what sort of a fight they were walking into.

Looking for easy pickings, were you? Thorgrim thought. *You'll not find them here.*

He reached the place just aft of the ship's beam, then stopped and considered these new arrivals more carefully. Even in the uncertain light of early morning he could see they were an ugly lot, clad in dirty, torn, stained tunics, long cowls hanging down their backs, or leines with ragged hems and brats of coarse cloth over their shoulders. Some wore pointed, soft leather shoes, though most were barefoot.

And they were armed. Not armed like Norsemen or even Irish warriors. They carried polished clubs and long knives and axes, axes made for splitting kindling rather than skulls. A few carried spears. The one in the center of the line, the big one, carried a sword. It was a Norse of Frisian blade and it was in bad shape. Thorgrim guessed the Irishman had found it, or taken it from the hand of someone he had killed. The man to his left, a smaller man with a lean and sinewy look, and a shock of red hair, carried a sword as well. Neither held their weapons with the confidence of men long used to them.

But for all that, the crude weapons, the tattered clothing, Thorgrim could see that these were not men to be dismissed. They were tough, hard-looking men. Men who eked out their existence through remorseless violence. They were bandits, savage men, outcasts, and there were a lot of them.

Harald stepped up to Thorgrim's side, even before Thorgrim could call to him. That was good. Thorgrim knew he would need Harald's unique skills. In this situation, talking rather than fighting was their best hope, and Harald was the one among them who could talk to the Irish.

"Father," Harald said, his voice low, his eyes on the line of Irishmen halted two perches away. "That Irishman…the prisoner…Louis, he wants a sword."

It took Thorgrim a second to register this change of subject, so focused was he on the bandits come from the trees. He glanced over and his eyes met Louis's. He could read a lot in the man's face: determination, defiance. Concern. But no fear.

And there was a touch of anger as well, and Thorgrim guessed that the man, this Louis, was not happy about having to ask for a weapon. All of that Thorgrim considered to be marks in his favor. He shifted his eyes to Thorodd Bollason who stood beside Louis and held Louis's sword and belt. Thorgrim gave Thorodd a brief nod. Thorodd handed the weapon to Louis and there was relief on Louis's face.

Thorgrim turned his attention back to the Irish, who were advancing again, slowly, tentatively, like approaching the edge of a cliff with the wind at your back.

"All of you," Thorgrim called to his men, keeping his voice low, his tone neutral, speaking just loud enough to be heard the length of the ship. "Take up your weapons. Shields, too. Move slowly. Make a line along the starboard side, here." It was like facing off against a pack of wolves. No sudden moves.

Thorgrim heard the shuffle of his men doing as they had been ordered, but his eyes were fixed on the bandits, the leader in particular, because what he did would determine what the others did, and that would determine what the Northmen did to counter them. Harald stepped away and in a minute he was back with his shield and Thorgrim's as well, which Thorgrim took, slipping his arm through the strap and taking firm hold of the boss.

The others moved, calm but quick, and soon they were lining the side of *Sea Hammer*, manning the ramparts on their makeshift fortress. If the Irish attacked, they would have to climb over the high side in the face of the Northmen's weapons, or wade through the river to get to the lower, larboard side.

Thorgrim glanced quickly down the line. His men were in mail because they had slept in it. They were armed with swords and battle axes and they carried shields. They were warriors, trained and experienced fighting men. But they were no more than ten in number, and they were injured to a man. All except their prisoners, the man and the woman, who were also mail-clad and taking their place in the defensive line.

We can't beat these sons of whores, Thorgrim thought.

If the Irish attacked, then many of them would die at the Northmen's hands. Maybe most of them. But in the end the Irishmen's numbers would prevail. If the circumstances had been different, if his men had been in better shape, if Starri Deathless were not struggling just to stand upright, then Thorgrim might have been more confident taking the fight to an enemy that outnumbered them more than two to one. But as things stood, he did not like the odds.

But if the Irish did not attack, if they went away, then they would be back. In the dark hours of the night, on a day of thick fog, sometime, they would be back. A stranded vessel guarded by just a handful of men, perhaps holding a hoard of looted silver, would be too tempting to ignore. There would be no peace; there would be no chance to set *Sea Hammer* to rights, with those bastards dogging them.

This must be settled now, Thorgrim thought. He turned to Harald.

"Bid these bastards come closer and talk," he said. Harald nodded.

"But don't call them 'bastards,'" Thorgrim added and Harald nodded again. He turned toward the line of bandits and called out to them in their own language. Thorgrim could see the look of surprise on the big man's face, and others as well.

The Irishman with the sword, the leader, took a half step forward, then stepped back again. He looked left and right, clearly unsure as to how to proceed. Behind him, the smaller man, the one with the red hair like dying embers, stepped up and said something in a low voice. The big man looked annoyed. The smaller man spoke again. The big man looked even more annoyed, but together they stepped away from the line, approaching *Sea Hammer* with all the boldness they could muster.

They stopped a rod short of the ship's side. Thorgrim was about to tell Harald what next to say when the big man spoke first, his voice insistent and louder than it needed to be. The words seemed rushed, though Thorgrim could never really tell with the Irish.

"He says, 'give us your weapons and your mail and any silver you have and we'll let you live,'" Harald translated. Thorgrim smiled.

"That's kind of them," Thorgrim said, but he could feel the anger building in him like thunderheads on the horizon. He had work to do. He did not need this distraction.

"Tell him that we are warriors and they are dumb oxen. Tell him they can attack us if they wish. They're more than twice our numbers. They may beat us. But most of them will die trying, and him, that big bastard, he'll be the first. I will personally put my sword through his heart. Ask if he thinks that it's worth it."

Harald translated the words. The big man frowned. He glanced back at the others. His choice was simple: attack the Northmen and die, or back off and face the humiliation of retreating before an inferior enemy. He had built this trap himself and walked right into it.

Once again the smaller man stepped up and spoke to the big man, too low for any of the Northmen to hear. The big man turned back to Thorgrim and shouted out again, holding his sword up as if showing it off.

"He says they have killed many Northmen and they will kill us, too," Harald said. "He says he took his sword off the last Northman he killed."

"Does he sound confident, at all?" Thorgrim asked.

"No," Harald said. "I think the other one, the one with the red hair, told him what to say."

Thorgrim nodded. *Time to end this*, he thought.

"Tell him we are both leaders, he and I, and leaders don't let their men die for no reason. Tell him we'll fight, just the two of us. If I win, they leave. If he wins, we give up our weapons and silver, and then they leave. Tell him any man who has killed so many Northmen as he has shouldn't fear one more. And speak loud enough so that all his men can hear."

Harald translated. The boy had a powerful voice to match his frame, and the words carried easily across the spit of sand. Thorgrim needed no translator to interpret the play of considerations on the Irishman's face. He had seen oxen led to the slaughter, their expressions confused and slightly suspicious as their dull brains registered that something was wrong. That was how the man looked. This was not a fight he wanted, not one he had anticipated. But neither could he see a way out of it.

The smaller man was speaking again, but the big man waved him away. He took half a step forward and spoke again.

"He says he's not fooled by your tricks," Harald said, "that you have mail and a helmet and shield."

Without a word Thorgrim took the helmet from his head and tossed it aside. He handed the shield to Harald, unbuckled his sword belt and set it down, then shucked the mail shirt off his head. He felt the odd, buoyed feeling that comes with taking off mail after having worn it for so long. He picked up Iron-tooth and drew it from the scabbard. He stepped up on the sheer strake and hopped down onto the sand. He heard Harald drop beside him.

"Tell him we are even now," Thorgrim said. "Tell him if he agrees to what I said, then now is his chance to drive his fierce sword through my neck."

Harald translated the words, still speaking loud enough for all to hear. The big man frowned. He was trapped. If the lead wolf showed weakness the rest of the pack would tear him apart. It was the way of things.

Then Thorgrim saw the change of expression on the man's face, the confusion and anger hardening into resolve as he understood that a fight would not be avoided, and that his only chance at life now was to kill this Northman in front of him. The Irishman looked determined, but he did not look frightened. He had had a lifetime of fighting, Thorgrim imagined, and had probably faced worse odds than he was facing now.

Nor were the odds necessarily against him now. The man was very big, five inches taller than Thorgrim, two stone heavier, and appeared strong like a bear. He did not seem like the sort who had gained leadership because he was clever. That meant he was brutal and tough enough that hard men feared him.

Thorgrim began circling around the Irishman, Iron-tooth held low. He would let his enemy move first, gauge his skill. But the big man, as Thorgrim had guessed, was not one for subtlety. He lifted his sword over his head and took a step in Thorgrim's direction, a battle roar building in his throat. But Thorgrim held up his hand and the man stopped in mid stride, his blood-lust turning to confusion.

"Harald, ask him if he agrees to my terms," Thorgrim said.

Harald translated, still making his voice carry over the strip of sand. The Irishman replied, the sound more like a howl than a word. He took another step and slashed at Thorgrim and Thorgrim stepped back, letting the blade swish past.

"He agrees, Father," Harald said.

Thorgrim continued to circle, stepping sideways, his eyes on his opponent, watching his face, his weapon. The Irishman held the sword high, ready to chop rather than slash or thrust. Thorgrim still held Iron-tooth low and at his side, inviting an attack, making the man angry with his seeming nonchalance.

The Irishman swung again, a fast, hard strike, the weight of the sword negligible to one so strong of arm. Thorgrim leapt back as the blade came down. He heard the swishing sound as it cut air, and as it passed he darted forward, driving the tip of Iron-tooth into the man's side an inch deep, leaving a painful wound, an enraging wound, but not a deadly one.

How long do I toy with you? Thorgrim wondered. That was really the question here. How long should he let this fight go on? Too brief and the rest of the bandits might think he cheated somehow and attack Thorgrim's men, their leader's agreement notwithstanding. Too long and they might think Thorgrim and the rest were weak, and likewise attack.

The big man had stumbled backward, away from Thorgrim and his fast blade. He pressed a hand to the wound, lifted it up to see the bright red blood on his fingers. Thorgrim saw the pain and the rage in his eyes, the expression of an untrained fighting man about to launch a savage and ill-conceived attack.

And that was what the Irishman did. He let out a roar, or it might have been an insult; Thorgrim could not tell. He lifted his sword and charged, though he still had wits enough to use his longer reach to slash at Thorgrim before he charged into the arc of Thorgrim's blade.

In that instant Thorgrim made his decision. *Time to end it.*

He did not give it any conscious thought, he just knew. As the Irishman's blade came sweeping around, Thorgrim made a counterstroke with his own sword. He had no doubt as to what would happen when the man's ugly, nicked and much-abused weapon came in contact with Iron-tooth's fine steel.

And it happened just as Thorgrim imagined. The two blades hit with a dull clanging sound, their motion checked for a heartbeat, no more, and then the Irishman's blade snapped in two. Thorgrim had a glimpse of the broken end flying off to his right. The Irishman stumbled, his face all confusion and surprise. And then Thorgrim saw the first expression of fear as the man realized what had happened—and what would happen next.

Thorgrim let the momentum of his stroke carry Iron-tooth back over his shoulder. His arm stopped, the blade cocked for a backhand blow. The Irishman straightened, his eyes wide, but there was no time for any reaction beyond that. Thorgrim swung Iron-tooth back and caught the man in the throat. He twisted as he fell, the spray of blood preceding him to the sand and making a red line that ran in a ragged trail for ten feet from the spot where he hit the ground.

The Irishman did not die instantly, but close enough. His feet kicked some, his fingers dug into the sand. He made an odd gurgling noise. And then he was still.

"Stand ready," Thorgrim called to his men. He did not know what the Irish would do next, if they would be furious at their leader's death and look for vengeance, or abide by the agreement he had made in his last moments on earth.

He looked up. The outlaws had moved in closer during the few moments of the fight, apparently to get a better look. Now they stood motionless, staring down at the unmoving, dirty heap that was once the man who had led them. The smaller man with the red hair was closest, having come forward to join in talking with Thorgrim. He was the first to move, stepping up to the dead man and looking down at him with no discernable expression on his face. He put his shoe against the man's shoulder and pushed and the dead man rolled over on his back, his eyes open and staring blankly at the gray morning sky, his throat a wash of blood.

The red-haired man pulled a dagger from his belt, bent down and cut the dead man's purse away, not bothering to look to Thorgrim for permission, or even acknowledging the Northmen's presence. He straightened and turned, heading back toward the line of men farther up the sand spit.

"Wait," Thorgrim called and the man stopped and turned. Thorgrim turned to Harald. "Tell him they can take their leader's body," he said. "Tell him we won't stop them from giving him a proper funeral."

Harald said the words. The redheaded man listened. His expression did not change. When Harald finished, he shrugged and spoke.

"He says they'll leave him for the crows and the ravens," Harald said. "He says no one much liked him anyway."

Thorgrim could not help but smile. *Loyal sons of bitches, aren't they?* he thought. And then another idea came to him.

"Tell this fellow that he and his men should join with us. Tell him they should come fight with us."

Harald registered a flash of surprise, no more, and then he rendered the words into Irish. The Irishman cocked his head and considered Thorgrim with a curious expression. He did not have the same dull, bovine look as the former leader. This one looked clever. With his red hair and the freckles on his face and his small but powerful-looking frame he seemed more the fox than the oxen. He considered Thorgrim's words for a second before responding.

"He wants to know why they should join with us," Harald said.

"Tell him because we have real weapons. Swords, shields, mail. Enough for all his men. They'll have no need of those ridiculous clubs and knives. And we'll teach them the use of these weapons."

Harald translated. The red-haired man looked more amused than tempted. He spoke again.

"He says he's very impressed with all the Northmen's fine weapons," Harald said, "but I don't think he was serious. He wonders what we mean to do with these weapons."

"Tell him we mean to return to Glendalough and sack the monastery there, a thing he would not dare do on his own," Thorgrim said. "Tell him we'll divide the plunder evenly with him and his men if they're with us."

This time Harald's surprise was so great that he could not immediately recover. He looked at Thorgrim, eyes wide, mouth open. And that was no wonder. Thorgrim was improvising like a skald at a feast, creating his plans even as the words left his mouth.

Chapter Four

The miserable man and evil minded
makes of all things mockery,
and knows not that which he best should know,
that he is not free from faults.
Hávamál

Aghen Ormsson was the first to see the ships returning to Vík-ló, but that was hardly a surprise. Aghen was a shipwright to his core, to the heartwood of his strong if aging body. When there were ships at the longphort, they were foremost in his thoughts. When they were away, his thoughts went with them, and his eyes turned toward the sea, waiting their return.

It had been weeks since Thorgrim Night Wolf, Lord of Vík-ló, had sailed to the south with the intention of raiding the monastery at Glendalough. With him had gone nearly all the men from the longphort, the crews of the ships *Sea Hammer*, *Blood Hawk* and *Fox*, around two hundred men in all. Kjartan Thorolfson, captain of the fourth ship, *Dragon*, had left the longphort days before, bound to where, no one knew.

Only thirty or so were left at Vík-ló, about half of them women. The men who remained behind were mostly those who were injured or sick or were too old to go a'viking. Some were skilled artisans who could not be spared, such as Mar the blacksmith. Some, such as Aghen, were both.

In his younger days Aghen had spent many summers raiding. His father was a ship builder, but Aghen, like all young men in his native Norway, dreamed not of building ships but of sailing them beyond that bright line on the horizon to whatever fantastical places and great wealth awaited those who were bold enough to take it.

He had made half a dozen voyages under the command of a local jarl, raiding in England and in Scotland, and sailing up the wide rivers of Frankia. Some of it had been good, some had been nightmarish, but through it all, it was the ships, not the raiding, that had grabbed young Aghen's imagination.

He loved the sailing. He loved the play of wind and water on the lean oak hulls; he loved seeing how different ships behaved in different conditions, how a beamier ship would take the seas one way, a narrower ship another. When there were repairs to be made, it was Aghen, raised as a shipwright, who was called on to do the work, work for which he clearly had a gift.

So, after returning home from his sixth summer a'viking, he set aside his sword and his shield and took up chisel and saw and joined his father in the shipbuilding trade. Together they earned a reputation as two of the finest shipwrights on the Oslofiord, and when his father died, literally fell dead with an auger in his hand, Aghen continued on alone.

At that time, many raiders were returning from Ireland with tales of the fine opportunities to be found in Dubh-linn. Others spoke of the quality and the abundance of Irish timber. Soon Aghen, who still had some of the young man's desire to sail beyond the horizon, took ship to Ireland and set up shop on the banks of the Liffey. He remained happy at his trade, but he found Dubh-linn too big, too squalid for his liking, so he moved again, this time to Vík-ló. And he was happy there. Mostly.

Vík-ló had been lorded over by a brute of a man named Grimarr Knutson, known as Grimarr Giant. Grimarr had not been so bad at first, a hard man but not an unjust one. Not the sort Aghen could befriend, but the sort he could respect, and that was good enough, but it did not last.

Grimarr's sons, his beloved sons, had been killed at Dubh-linn. Grimarr seemed to go mad with grief, like a wounded and cornered bear. And like such a beast, he lashed out wildly in every direction, trying to mitigate his hurt by inflicting hurt on others.

Then Thorgrim Night Wolf and his men had arrived. They came limping in from the sea, their ship on the verge of sinking after running afoul of a floating log. And the ship they sailed, which they called *Far Voyager*, was the same ship in which Grimarr's sons had sailed for Vík-ló. It had been painted black, and various other changes had been made, but still Aghen recognized her immediately. He said nothing. He did not think any good would come of Grimarr's knowing.

And when Grimarr did eventually realize that Thorgrim was sailing his sons' ship, and that Thorgrim was the one who had killed them, he reacted just as Aghen guessed he would. The two men left a long and bloody trail of corpses in their wake.

Aghen never understood entirely what had transpired. It had come down to a great fight, Grimarr Giant and his men against Thorgrim Night Wolf and his, and then an army of Irishmen as well. When the blood had stopped flowing, it was Thorgrim Night Wolf who stood as Lord of Vík-ló.

And that was a good thing, as far as Aghen was concerned. He and Thorgrim had worked together to repair *Far Voyager*, and Aghen had already formed a favorable opinion of the man. And that good opinion only grew stronger as the winter months passed and he and Thorgrim built three new ships from the keels up.

Thorgrim Night Wolf loved ships the way Aghen loved ships, and his skill and understanding of the trade nearly rivaled Aghen's own. They had discussed every aspect of the building, the properties they wished to impart to the vessels, the tricks they would use to make them strong and light and flexible. They had not always agreed, but they had always respected one another, and by the time the ships had been rolled down the muddy banks and into the river, Aghen was proud to call Thorgrim friend.

And for that reason he was delighted now to see the sails of Thorgrim's fleet far off on the horizon, standing in toward Vík-ló at the mouth of the River Leitrim. It was *hádegi*, midday, and Aghen was down by the water as he so often was. He had spent the morning moving some of the spare timber out of the weather and sharpening and oiling his tools, but in truth he did not have very much to do. He was a shipwright in a longphort that had no ships.

He stood on top of the earthen wall that enclosed the longphort and looked out over the water, off to the south where he had last seen the fleet sailing away. The distant ships appeared as tiny spots of color, no more. He squinted, not against the sun, because there was no sun, but to help him see better. He looked for a long time, until he was certain. Not part of the shoreline, not the flash of whitecaps. They were sails, he was certain. He had seen sails so many times from a great distance that he knew their look.

His first instinct was to alert the longphort of the fleet's return, but he did not. He told himself he wanted to be certain, though in truth he knew he just wanted to enjoy the moment. He had known the joy of standing on a ship's deck and seeing his home slowly resolve out of the ambiguous shore. To stand on the shore and see the ships rise up out of the sea was nearly as good.

For the better part of an hour Aghen watched the ships come on, saw their sails changing from barely discernable points of color to genuine rectangles, pitching and rolling with the ships they drove through the dull gray sea. Eight of them. Which was cause for some concern, since Thorgrim had sailed with only three.

Aghen climbed down the rough ladder from the wall and walked up the plank road to where the two dozen or so sundry shops and homes were huddled together. Some were built in the wattle and daub style of the Irish, some in the timber style of the Norse, but none were particularly grand or luxurious.

The largest and most substantial of the buildings were the twin halls near the gate at the far end of the longphort, one built for Grimarr Knutson, the other for his second in command, Fasti Magnisson. Both men were dead now and the halls stood empty, though Aghen guessed they would soon be filled again by their new occupants, Thorgrim Night Wolf and Bersi Jorundarson and their households.

Halfway down the plank road stood the home and shop of Mar the blacksmith. Aghen found Mar at work on his anvil under the thatch roof that covered his workspace in the trampled yard.

"Mar!" Aghen shouted, waited for a break in the clanging of iron hammer on molten iron, then called again. "Mar!"

Mar, whose hearing was not good after so many years of enduring the ring of iron on iron, looked up after the second shout. "Aghen! What news?"

Aghen stepped through the gate in the wattle fence. "The fleet's returning," he said. "They are some ways off still, but I see them bound for the river mouth."

"Ha!" Mar shouted. "That's good news. They'll have weapons in need of repair, and ships too, and they'll have silver to pay for it."

"It might be good news," Aghen said. "Or it might not. I can see eight ships, I'm nearly certain."

"Eight?" Mar asked.

"Eight. I think *Blood Hawk* is one. She had that red-and-black-checkered sail. But she's far off and my eyes are old."

Mar nodded. "Well, maybe they've taken more plunder or met with others who wish to join us here." Mar was a jovial and optimistic fellow, as Aghen had observed blacksmiths often were. He wondered if all that pounding worked the unpleasantness right out of them.

"We should tell the others," Aghen said. Mar nodded and set his hammer down. They continued up the plank road, calling into the houses, spreading the word, giving warning.

By the time the handful of people remaining in Vík-ló had gathered by the water, the fleet was considerably closer, making for the river mouth and visible from the shore, not just the top of the wall. They could see the individual ships, and even the patterns on their sails were discernable to the younger eyes.

"*Blood Hawk* for certain," said Valgerd Unnson, a man of twenty years who'd had the bad luck to break his leg a week before the fleet put to sea. Actually, it was not so much bad luck as Valgerd's famous bad judgment, in this case his decision to try to balance on the top of the palisades at a time when he was so drunk he could barely stand on the plank road.

"I can see her checked sail," Valgerd continued, shielding his eyes from the dull sunlight overhead. "And *Fox*, with the black stripes, to the east of her."

"What of *Sea Hammer*, do you see her?" Aghen asked. "Her sail was red stripes, bold red stripes."

"I know what pattern her sail had, Aghen," Valgerd said, "and I don't see her. But she might be astern of the others."

Aghen frowned. Thorgrim Night Wolf would not let *Sea Hammer* sail in another's wake. Nor was there another ship that could outpace her. *Sea Hammer* was their pride, he and Thorgrim, the last ship built, the culmination of all they had learned about the quality of the wood they had taken from the high country, the best use to be made of the tools and materials at hand. They loved *Sea Hammer*, both of them. Thorgrim would not let her fall astern of another vessel.

"Those other ships, I have no idea," Valgerd said. There was a murmur of speculation among the others, but Aghen remained silent. No reason to waste time and breath guessing when an hour or so would reveal the truth.

The ships were still half a mile off when they began to lower their sails and stow them, then run their long oars out of the row ports for the final pull to the shore. By then Aghen knew for certain that *Sea Hammer* was not among them. He felt sick, his stomach rebelling against this knowledge. It seemed impossible that his beloved *Sea Hammer* was gone. He could barely tolerate the thought of it.

As long as Thorgrim still lives, Aghen thought. They could build another ship, he and Thorgrim. A better ship, if such a thing was possible.

One of the approaching fleet led the way in, but Aghen did not recognize the ship. She was longer than *Sea Hammer*, but not by much, driven by sixteen oars on each side. She had a great dragon's head on her high prow, which her captain had not bothered to remove—or had left there on purpose to show that he did not come with peaceful intent.

Whoever he was, the captain of this longship leading the others in, Aghen could see him now, standing on the foredeck, clad in mail, a cloak flapping at his shoulders. He was a big man—the carved dragonhead was only a few feet above his own—and he was broad as well, the size and shape of some great rune stone set as a monument at a crossroads. His ship was no more than twenty yards from the muddy shore, and still the man stood motionless, staring ahead as the rowers pulled hard.

Somewhere aft an order was given. The men on the rowing benches gave one last pull, and then the oars disappeared like a turtle drawing its legs into its shell. The momentum from that last stroke carried the ship the final feet to the shore. Her bow ran up onto the muddy shallows and two men appeared as if by magic and set a gangplank over the bow and down to the riverbank. Only then did the huge man stir, stepping up onto the gangplank and down to the shore, the boards bending under his weight.

Aghen studied him close. He had never seen the man before, of that he was certain. He was not the sort one might forget. He was as big as Grimarr Giant, bigger perhaps. His hair was yellow and long and hung in two braids down either side of his head. His beard was the same straw color as his hair and covered half his face and hung down to near his belly. A deep, ugly scar emerged from the beard and ran up to the corner of his right eye, like a snake slithering out of hiding.

No one among the thirty or so residents of Vík-ló who had gathered on the shore spoke; no one moved. The big man stepped up the bank and his eyes swept the longphort, and behind him the crew of his ship came down the gangplank as well. Like their captain they were wearing mail. Unlike him they were carrying shields and had weapons drawn.

The next two ships came gliding up to the shore and ran aground on either side of the first. One was *Blood Hawk*, the ship commanded by Bersi Jorundarson, but Aghen could not see Bersi anywhere aboard her. Indeed, as her crew stood and took up their shields Aghen realized that he did not recognize any of the men aboard her.

This is not good, he thought. *Not good.*

His eyes moved back to the big man and the forty or so others under his command who had formed up in a line behind him. They seemed a small crew for so large a ship, but they were more than all the population of Vík-ló, and they were warriors and they were armed.

Finally the big man's eyes moved from the longphort beyond the river to the knot of people who stood watching his arrival. His gaze swept along the crowd as if he was seeing them for the first time. For a moment his expression did not change. And then he did the one thing that Aghen would not have expected: he threw back his head and he laughed.

His laugh was loud and ugly and had a barking quality to it. He laughed hard and when he was done he spit on the ground and wiped his mouth with his mail-clad sleeve. "This is it?" he roared. "This is all the people of Vík-ló? Old men and cripples and women?" Behind him some of his men laughed as well.

"Who are you?" someone shouted from the crowd. The big man took a step forward, and there was surprising menace in that one small move.

"I am Ottar Thorolfson and I am known as Ottar Bloodax. Of all the Northmen in Ireland, and all the Irishmen as well, none are more powerful than me!"

"Where is Thorgrim Night Wolf?" Aghen demanded. This Ottar might indeed be the most powerful man in Ireland. It was not hard to believe. But Aghen, having seen more than fifty winters, was too old to be intimidated by such as him.

Ottar Bloodax's head jerked around and he stared at Aghen as if the name of Thorgrim had been an insult to him, or a threat.

Aghen met his stare and returned it. "Why do you sail Thorgrim's ships?" he added.

Chapter Five

Hail, ye Givers! a guest is come;
say! where shall he sit within?
Hávamál

The sandbar in the bend of the Avonmore, that half acre or so of dry land, had been no more than an isolated and unseen stretch of sand and gravel on a forgotten part of the river at the time they ran *Sea Hammer* aground. That was why Thorgrim had picked it. Now, it seemed to Harald Broadarm, it was more like a town, a miniature longphort, Dubh-linn writ small.

The Irish bandits had numbered twenty-six men in all, not including their dead leader, whose name Harald never did learn. When Thorgrim had objected to his corpse being left on the sandbar where he fell, a few of his former subjects hefted him up and waded out into the river with him and tossed him in. Harald watched as the dead man was tumbled and rolled by the current until he was out of sight downstream.

The new leader, the sinewy, redheaded man, was named Cónán, or so they learned. With the former chieftain now bobbing away out of sight, Thorgrim and Cónán faced off over the ragged trail of blood drying on the sand. Harald, the translator, stood by Thorgrim's side.

"Your men will be willing to join with us?" Thorgrim asked by way of Harald. "They won't resent me killing their leader?"

Cónán glanced back at his men, but there was no uncertainty in his face. He turned back to Thorgrim and spoke.

"He says he's their leader now, and they'll do as he says," Harald translated. The man's confidence only strengthened Harald's earlier impression that Cónán had been leading all along, whatever the dead man had thought. Harald had the idea that the dead man's challenge to Thorgrim had been more the result of Cónán's goading than any desire of his own for such a fight. And he guessed that the fight had ended the way Cónán, at least, had hoped it would.

Thorgrim nodded. He and Cónán were looking into each other's eyes, each man taking the measure of the other, like combatants in the first few steps of a fight, sensing out one another before making any bold move.

"Tell Cónán," Thorgrim said, "that he should make no mistake about who leads here. There'll be much advantage to him and his men if they join with us, but I command. No one else."

Harald nodded. He could hear the hardness in his father's voice. He suspected that Thorgrim blamed much of the late disaster on his own willingness to consider the council of others. He would not be doing that again. Harald translated the words. At first Cónán did not reply, and when he did he spoke slowly and deliberately.

"He says they will not be servants and they will not be slaves," Harald said. "When we are raiding or fighting, you lead. When we are not, you do not command his men."

Now it was Thorgrim's turn to consider the words. Finally he nodded. "Good," he said. "It's agreed." He held out his hand and Cónán grasped it and they shook.

Then Cónán was speaking again. "He says you mentioned weapons?" Harald translated. "And training?"

At that Thorgrim had Cónán summon his men and explain to them what they had agreed upon, but to keep any talk of raiding Glendalough to himself. Harald listened as Cónán spoke, making certain he told it the way Thorgrim had instructed. There seemed to be little reaction among the bandits beyond nodding heads and some low murmuring that Harald could not catch. Cónán apparently had spoken the truth. They took Cónán as their new leader and would do as he told them.

That done, Cónán looked past his men to the trees on the shore and called, "Come on out, then!" Harald frowned. He turned to his father, ready to warn him, ready to alert him to some trick, when he saw a dozen or so women come hesitantly out of the trees and down to the sand. He heard a stir run through the watching Northmen.

"They bring their women with them when they go raiding?" Thorgrim asked. Harald relayed the question.

"Cónán says they have no home. They're outlaws, always moving," Harald said. "If their women did not come with them, they would have no women. And what good would that be?"

Harald had to agree with that. Cónán spoke again. "He says," Harald translated, "when the women are with child they find some farm where they can live, but otherwise the women stay with their men."

Cónán issued a few more orders and soon the women were making fires and bringing bundles of their few sorry belongings out of the woods. Cónán turned to Thorgrim again.

"He says the road to Glendalough is about a half mile that way," Harald said, pointing toward the north. "He says he thinks we are well hidden here, but he will send men to watch the road, and others to the south, to see we're not caught by surprise."

Harald paused as Cónán added more. A smile played on the Irishman's face. "He says he heard the heathens met with great slaughter at Glendalough and that there might be men-at-arms out looking for the last of them."

Thorgrim made a grunting noise which suggested that he was not amused. "Tell him to get his breakfast and we'll get ours and then we'll set to work."

And they did. The Northmen ate the dried fish and bread that was still in *Sea Hammer*'s hold. The Irishmen ate whatever they had found or killed the day before. Then, at Cónán's command, they gathered at *Sea Hammer*'s side.

"Tell Cónán we have chainmail. We have swords and axes and shields for them," Thorgrim said. Which they did. In a pile by the mast step were all the weapons and armor they had managed to glean from the dead men left in the wake of the fighting, before the sound of riders in the distance had convinced them it was time to go.

"Tell him to have his men sort through them," Thorgrim continued, "take what they want, the mail that will fit them. Then we'll start training."

Harald nodded. He would do as his father said, of course, but he did not think this was a good idea. Not at all. He knew what his father was thinking, and he thought he was wrong.

Certainly the few Northmen in their band, the remnants of *Sea Hammer*'s crew, could do little by themselves. They could not even row the ship for very long. Without more warriors they could hope for nothing save getting away, and probably not even that. Vengeance, plunder were out of the question. But Harald did not think asking these half-wild men to join with them was a very reasonable solution.

But he also knew, with absolute certainty, that arguing with his father's decision would be a much worse idea.

All of them, all the Norsemen, were still stunned by what had happened, staggered as if they had been hit on their heads. Harald felt a constant sickness in his gut; he felt like he was in a fever dream, coming in and out of reality.

Two days before there had been hundreds of them, a powerful Norse army sweeping upriver to Glendalough. Brothers in arms, unstoppable as a tidal surge. And now they were all gone, all save for these few. Instead of three dozen shipmates, they had only the memory of the horrors they had witnessed, the butchery that would not leave them.

Harald could feel it like it was heavy chainmail, pressing him down, and he was sure that the others could as well. And he knew that his father felt it in ways none of them could understand.

Thorgrim took all the blame on himself. Harald was sure of that, even without asking, and of course he would never ask. But he knew. Despite the fact that Bersi and Skidi and the others had readily agreed to join the raid on Glendalough, despite their all having been betrayed by Kjartan and Ottar and Kevin, despite Thorgrim's having done everything a man could do to keep his warriors alive, right up to the moment he was knocked to unconsciousness, Harald knew that he put the blame on himself. And he would be avenged. Even if vengeance did nothing to better their circumstance, he would be avenged.

And Harald would not question his decisions.

So the Irishmen poked through the pile of weapons, and those who could find mail shirts of their size slipped them awkwardly over their heads, regarding them as if they were kingly robes of finest fur and silk. And well they might have been.

Mail was not something that ragged outlaws could ever hope to own. Even most Northmen made due with leather armor, and only those who enjoyed wealth or good luck could expect to wear mail. And so as the Irish sifted through the weapons, donning the mail and taking up swords—also luxuries for which they could never have hoped—Cónán made sure, in a dozen subtle ways, that his men understood that it was he who had put such gifts in their path.

He is a clever one, Harald thought, not for the first time.

With the weapons sorted out, the training began without delay, because Thorgrim knew, as did Harald, that their situation was precarious. Eventually they would be discovered. Eventually they would find themselves once again fighting their way to safety, and the sooner these undisciplined bandits could be turned into something resembling warriors, the better.

It was awkward at first, with Godi drilling the men by giving instruction to Cónán by way of Harald. But then, to Harald's surprise, the prisoner, Louis, had stepped forward.

Failend had claimed Louis was her bodyguard, but Harald was fairly certain there was more to it than that. Louis was young and handsome and carried himself with a somewhat regal bearing, and did so naturally, as if he was born to it. He had nothing of the grizzled old campaigner about him, though he seemed comfortable enough with weapons and had shown no fear that Harald could see, despite all that had happened.

He no longer stayed by Failend's side like a she-wolf with her cubs. He seemed to have accepted that neither he nor Failend were in any immediate danger from the heathens who had captured them. He did not know about the plan to return to Glendalough. No one did, save for Thorgrim and Harald and Cónán. They had kept it that way.

"Pardon me," Louis said, interrupting Godi in mid-sentence. The Irishmen stood in a line and were armed with swords and shields, holding the weapons with the same sort of awkward unfamiliarity as they might hold an illuminated manuscript, while Godi tried to show them the proper way.

Godi stopped and turned to Louis, his eyebrows raised in question.

"Pardon me, but I have considerable experience in training such men as these," Louis said, his eyes moving between Godi, whom he apparently thought was in charge, and Harald, the only one of the Northmen with whom he could speak. "Men who know nothing of the use of weapons. And I speak their language. Might I be of help?"

Harald stepped closer and asked, "Why do you want to help? You are our prisoner."

Louis shrugged. "I have nothing else to do. Besides, even I, a lowly prisoner, can see we might need to fight soon. If that's true, I would prefer we win."

"Even if we're fighting the Irish? Fighting your people?"

"I'm not Irish," Louis said. "I'm Frankish. None here are my people."

Of course, Harald thought. Failend had told him that when they first met, but it had slipped his mind. Suddenly things came a bit clearer. All along he had felt that Louis's accent was not quite right, but Harald was still enough of a stranger to the Irish language that he could not tell for certain. Louis had never seemed very loyal to the Irish anyway, or shown much desire to get back among them, and Harald had wondered why.

"Very well," Harald said. "If you think you can train these men, have a go." He turned to Godi, who had been listening but not understanding. "Louis will be helping with the training," Harald said. "He knows the use of weapons, it seems, and he speaks the Irish language."

Godi, whose frustration with his charges was evident and building, did not protest. Louis stepped up beside Godi and pulled his sword. He launched into a simple talk on how best to hold the weapon, so unfamiliar to the outlaw band. He showed them a thrust and a parry. He grabbed the most likely looking of the outlaws and demonstrated the moves in faux combat.

Harald watched for twenty minutes, and during that time he did not once feel the need to step in. *This Frankish bastard knows his business*, he admitted to himself. He was just starting to wonder if he was needed there at all when he heard his father calling to him.

Thorgrim Night Wolf was concerned with making his ship whole again, nearly to the exclusion of any other worry. No sooner had the arrangements with Cónán and his men been made than Thorgrim turned to the gaping wound in *Sea Hammer*'s side. Harald found him now with a small saw in hand, carefully cutting away one of the damaged strakes back to a place where he could scarph in a new piece.

As Harald approached, Thorgrim straightened and leaned back with his hands pressed to his waist, grimacing as he stretched. He nodded toward the Irishmen training on the sandbar.

"That prisoner, Louis," Thorgrim said, "he seems very helpful. More helpful than I would expect an Irishman to be with…what do they call us?"

"Fin gall?" Harald offered.

"No, the other thing."

"Heathens?"

"Yes, heathens," Thorgrim said. "More helpful than I'd expect him to be with heathens."

"He's not Irish, actually," Harald said.

"No?"

"No. He's a Frank. I never did think he talked like an Irishman."

"Hmm," Thorgrim said, looking over at Louis. He was trading practice blows with one of the outlaws, moving slow and deliberate. "That makes more sense."

"Still, I don't know if we can trust him," Harald said. "I think he's playing a double game."

At that Thorgrim smiled, though there was little mirth in it. "We are all playing double games," he said. "All of us. Some play in the open, some play in the shadows. Now, about that other one, the woman…"

"Failend?"

"Yes, Failend. You said she's a healer?"

"That was what she told me. A very experienced healer." When Harald had first taken Failend prisoner, it had occurred to him she might be of use if she was skilled in the healing arts. He'd asked her then, and as good luck would have it, she'd assured him she was.

"Hmm," Thorgrim said again. "I don't usually think that one so young would be a very experienced healer. But maybe she is. Ask her to take a look at Starri. See if she can help him."

Harald swallowed his frustration, nodded, and said he would do as Thorgrim asked. There was nothing else he could say. What's more, Harald loved Starri. They had fought together in many fights, big and small. He would do anything to help Starri. But still it annoyed him to be sent on this task while there was real work, men's work, ship work and training with sword and shield, to be done.

If any of these other ignorant bastards bothered to learn the Irish tongue, Harald thought bitterly, *then I would not be called on every time there's need to speak to an Irishman.*

Harald left Thorgrim to his shipwright work and trudged across the sand to where Failend was sitting by herself on top of one of the sea chests that had been hoisted out of *Sea Hammer*. She was idly running a whetstone over the edge of her dagger, but in truth she seemed to be doing so more to look busy than through any pressing need to sharpen the weapon.

"Failend," Harald said as he approached. The girl looked up, tossing her long, brown hair behind her. She had stopped wearing her mail, apparently concluding as Louis had that the Northmen were no immediate threat. She was dressed now in a blue linen leine, a wool brat around her shoulders that was pinned in place with a silver brooch that glinted dull in the muted light. Even when she had been wearing mail, Harald had noticed how very lovely she was. Seeing her now in more feminine clothes reminded him that she was indeed a beauty, her skin smooth and white, her hair thick and luxurious.

"Yes?" Failend said.

"You told me, back when first we met, that you're a healer. We have one of us who's badly wounded and I would ask you tend to him."

"Ahh…yes," Failend said, sounding not at all sure about that suggestion.

"Is there a problem?" Harald asked. He guessed that this Irishwoman, this Christian, would not care to heal a heathen fin gall.

"Well, it's just that all my herbs, my tinctures and such, all those I left back in Glendalough," Failend said. "I don't have all I might need."

"You should look at him, all the same," Harald said. "Maybe there's something you can do. Maybe we can collect the herbs you need."

"Very well," Failend said, standing and sheathing her knife. Harald led the way across the sand to where Starri lay on a pile of furs, his eyes closed, his back propped up against a sea chest.

"Starri," Harald said, softly so as not to startle him. "Failend here is a healer, and she's come to look at you." Starri opened his eyes and looked up at them, though he did not seem entirely aware of what was happening.

Starri Deathless was a berserker. He wanted nothing from life but to die in battle and join Odin and the other fallen warriors in the corpse hall. But he was also a wild, reckless, brutal fighting man, and every battle seemed to end with Starri still alive amid a pile of men he had sent to the corpse hall ahead of him. Harald envied Starri's complete lack of fear, even while recognizing that it was really a form of madness.

On the voyage upriver, on the way to Glendalough, Starri's luck had nearly changed. The Northmen had been surprised in their camp by Irish warriors and had beaten them back after a short, hard fight. Starri had launched himself into the fray with his usual lunacy, but this time an enemy spear had found him, the iron point tearing clear through his shoulder just inches from his heart. No one thought he would even live through that night, but he had, and since then he had been suffering agonies as he slowly recovered.

While the rest of Thorgrim's men and the others had fought their way upriver and launched the raid on Glendalough, Starri had remained in his sick bed, which for him was the worst agony of all. When Ottar Bloodax had come for the ships, Starri had stood and fought, battle axes in hand. In doing so he tore the half-mended wound open again, reversing what little gains he had made.

Now Failend knelt by his side and gently lifted the blanket off Starri's torso, exposing the bandage pressed against his wounded chest. The linen was soaked through with blood that was dried around the edges but still wet where it pressed against the torn flesh. She took the edge of the cloth between her fingers, using both hands, and pulled gently. The cloth peeled back and then stopped, plastered as it was to Starri's skin.

Failend made a little noise in her throat and tugged harder, but still the bandage would not come. Harald could see her press her lips together and then she gave the bandage a yank. Starri gasped and Harald gasped and the linen tore clear, revealing an ugly wound, ragged and bloody and covered in pus.

A second later the smell of the rotting flesh hit them. Harald clenched his teeth and he saw Failend turn her head and make a choking sound. Starri groaned louder and shifted his head side to side, just once, then lay still.

"Is it bad?" Harald asked when he had recovered his wits.

"Let me look," Failend said, sounding very much as if she did not want to look. She turned her head back toward Starri, leaned a little closer in, made another gagging sound. "I see," she said at last. She stood and took a step back.

"Yes?" Harald asked.

"Well..." Failend said. "It's a terrible wound, I can tell you that. The spear...it was a spear, wasn't it?"

"Yes, a spear."

"Well, the spear went right through his genuflect, do you see?"

"It did?" Harald asked.

"Yes. Through the genuflect, and it seems to have done great hurt to the monstrance. The worst I've seen."

Harald nodded. This did not sound good. "We had a thought to bleed him," he offered.

"Bleed?" Failend said, as if considering this approach. "It seems like he's been bleeding quite well on his own."

"Yes, but is it the right sort of bleeding?" Harald asked.

"That's difficult to say, at this point," Failend said. "We'll have to see what sort of humors are left in him. But I had another thought. Those women with the bandits, maybe one of them has the herbs and such that I need. To replace the ones I left back in Glendalough. Would you mind if I asked among them?"

Harald shook his head. "No, not at all. Anything that might be of help to Starri."

Failend turned and hurried across the sandbar to where the Irish women were making their camp. She stopped and spoke with the first of the women she came to and was directed to another. A moment later Failend and the second woman were crossing back toward them, the other woman with a basket on her arm.

"This is Cara," Failend said. "She's the healer to these…fellows."

Harald nodded his greeting. Cara was ten years Failend's senior, he guessed, and she had a seriousness about her that spoke of the hard and precarious life that the outlaws lived.

"This is my friend Starri Deathless," Harald said, gesturing toward Starri, who seemed to have passed out. "He's badly wounded," he added, but Cara had stopped listening even before Harald got to Starri's name. She knelt down at Starri's side and looked close at the wound. She leaned in and sniffed it and made a soft noise like disgust, though her reaction was not nearly as violent as Harald's and Failend's had been.

"We were thinking we might bleed him," Harald said.

"Bleed him?" Cara said, reaching for her basket. "Bleeding is to balance the humors, not for a wound such as this. He's bled quite enough, I think."

"Yes," Failend said, "that was what I thought as well."

"The flesh is rotting," Cara continued. "The wound was not well tended. The dead flesh will have to be removed."

"Removed?" Harald said, suddenly afraid that Cara was suggesting he do it. "By…you? Or Failend?"

"No, by my barber-surgeons," Cara said. She reached into her basket and withdrew a clay pot with a cloth bound around the top. She removed the cloth and spilled the contents into her hand: a tangle of white, squirming maggots in a clump the size of a small stone. Harald clenched his teeth together.

"Yes, just so," Failend said, and Harald could tell her teeth were clenched as well. "I have maggots of my own, of course. Back at Glendalough."

Carefully, two or three at a time, Cara placed the maggots in Starri's wound. When they were all there, a writhing presence in the black, red and greenish rent in the flesh, she pulled a ball of spider webs from her basket and laid that across the wound, then laid a clean bit of linen over it. She stood and faced Failend and Harald.

"That must stay on for a day at least, and then we'll see how things fare. I'll make up some broth and he should be made to eat. That would be your advice, would it not, m'lady?" she said, addressing the last to Failend.

"Pray, call me Failend," Failend said, "and yes…maggots and broth, just as I was thinking."

Thorgrim arrived before any more was said, crossing the sandbar and brushing wood chips from his tunic. "How does he do?" he asked.

"Good," Harald said, "or better, anyway. Failend and Cara…this is Cara…they've done good work by him. Set him up well. Cara used…she did good work."

"I'm glad to hear it," Thorgrim said. Harald knew that his father was uncomfortable around the sick and wounded because he knew little of their treatment and it made him feel useless and ignorant. Thorgrim turned to the women. "I thank you for your help," he said, nodding respectfully so they might understand his meaning, if not his words. He turned to Harald. "If you're done here, get some of our men and set up a ridge pole, six feet high, no more. We'll stretch the sail out over it and make a tent. I doubt it will go two full days without raining in this miserable land."

Harald nodded, pleased to have a task more befitting his station, not women's work such as tending the wounded, even if it was Starri Deathless. He moved off, calling to some of *Sea Hammer*'s men who were not otherwise occupied. The shoreline rang with the sound of weapons on weapons as the Irish outlaws were trained to fight like Norsemen and the air was filled with the smoke of the fires and the smell of the *náttmál*, the night-meal, cooking.

It made Harald happy. It gave him a sense of hope, of purpose, something he had not felt in some time. They were training. They were preparing. They were setting *Sea Hammer* to rights. Because soon they would return to Glendalough.

Chapter Six

Little heed to laws
The loud-mouth paid
Though money he has,
More than enough.
The Saga of the Confederates

Ottar Bloodax and his men did not linger long at the river's edge. After announcing himself as Lord of Vík-ló, Ottar seemed to feel that no more explanation was needed. Nor were the thirty or so men and women of the longphort in any position to demand that one be given. Ottar and his several hundred warriors were free to ignore them as they wished.

And that was what they did. Ottar punctuated the end of his brief introduction with a loud grunt, then headed toward the plank road, pushing past the assembled people with no further word. Most of his men followed behind, shields still held on arms, swords in hand. The others busied themselves in hauling the ships as far up the mud bank as they could and running lines ashore.

The people of Vík-ló stepped aside, making way for Ottar's column. Aghen studied the newly arrived warriors as they shuffled past, and he could see that whatever fight they had just come from, they had not had an easy time of it. There were wounds on faces, heads and hands, dark stained bandages and smears of blood only half washed away. He could see rents in chainmail and gouges in shields and nicks in the blades of their swords, deep enough that they were visible even to his old eyes from half a rod away.

"They've had some hard fighting," Aghen said in a low voice and Mar nodded.

"Plenty of work for me," the blacksmith said, but he did not sound as enthusiastic as he had before. Ottar's men did not wear the expressions of conquering warriors who had returned with their ships' holds bulging with silver. They looked like men who had seen hard use, who had accomplished little more than escaping with their lives and now wished only to be done with it all.

The last of the warriors passed by and the people of Vík-ló closed ranks again and watched them as they marched off. No one spoke. Aghen guessed that the others, like himself, were trying to make sense of this new order of things.

Thorgrim is dead? Aghen thought, Ottar's words coming back to him. It did not seem possible. He had not known Thorgrim long, it was true, but Thorgrim was one of those men who seemed to have always been there, the sort who always would. Somehow it had never occurred to Aghen that Thorgrim might not return from this raid and resume his rule over the longphort. Foolish, he knew. At his age he had seen countless men die in more ways than he could recall. But he had never considered that Thorgrim might go that way.

How did Thorgrim die? Aghen wondered. Death, more often than not, came from something foolish: a minor wound turned rotten, a fever, falling drunk off the side of a ship and drowning. He hoped it was nothing of that sort that had felled Thorgrim Night Wolf. He hoped he had been holding Iron-tooth in his hand, the blade dripping with his enemy's blood, when he had finally been cut down.

Whatever the truth of the matter was, Aghen did not think he would learn it from Ottar or his men. Ottar's reaction to the mention of Thorgrim's name told the shipwright all he needed to know about that situation.

Did Ottar kill Thorgrim? Aghen wondered next. *Did he kill him so he might set himself up as Lord of Vík-ló?*

The last of Ottar's men disappeared over the rise in the ground that led to the plank road. Aghen followed behind. He crossed the stretch of grass and dirt and mud where the longphort of Vík-ló ran along the southern shore of the River Leitrim. It was this open ground that he and Thorgrim had turned into the shipyard, where trees had been split into planks and hewn into keels and masts and yards, where the longships had risen on their keel blocks like new creations molded by the hands of the gods.

He climbed up to the crest of the slope and stopped. From there he could take in all of the longphort: the thatched houses puffing smoke from their gable ends, the rough plank road that twisted slightly east then west as it ran from where he stood to the big oak gate in the earthen wall, flanked on either side by the twin halls. The whole was enclosed by the great half circle of earthen wall topped with a palisade. Under Thorgrim's leadership that wall had been built up and repaired over the course of the previous winter. It was hard work, filthy and exhausting and often done in the cold, driving rain. But now the wall represented a real defense, and not the crumbling pretense that Grimarr had let it become.

Vík-ló was not much to look at. It was not Dubh-linn; it certainly was not Hedeby or Birka. But it was well positioned just within the river's mouth, sheltered, but open to the sea. It was secure and there were ample resources at hand. And there was wealth, considerable wealth. There was the plunder that Thorgrim had brought with him and the plunder that Grimarr had amassed and the silver and gold from Grimarr and Fasti's last raid which Thorgrim had recovered. It was all there. The men who had sailed for Glendalough had left it behind because they had intended to return.

Ottar knew that. Aghen had no doubt that he did, and that was why he had come.

He watched the line of Ottar's men move like a great serpent up the plank road, Ottar at its head, looming above the others. They reached the gate and the doors of the two halls that faced one another. They stopped there, and Aghen guessed Ottar was deciding which he would claim as his own. And then Ottar disappeared into the hall north of the gate. Thorgrim's hall.

"Making himself right at home, isn't he?" Mar said, stepping up beside Aghen. The blacksmith was still wearing his soot-smeared leather apron. Aghen had often teased him about the number of cows that had to die to make an apron wide enough to cover his broad chest and ample belly, but the shipwright did not feel particularly jovial at the moment.

Aghen shook his head. "This is not good, not good at all," he said. Aghen had lived under jarls who were benevolent and jarls who were cruel, and he could see right off what sort Ottar would be. Worse, there was no escape. In a place such as Dubh-linn one could always find passage on some ship bound somewhere. But in all of Vík-ló there were only eight ships to be found, and they were all the property of Ottar Bloodax.

"Well, who knows what this Ottar will be?" Mar said. "There was Grimarr and Thorgrim, and now him. Lords come and lords go. But we go on, eh?" Mar was trying to sound like his usual optimistic self, but he was not succeeding. He was right about one thing, however: they would go on. There was nothing else to be done. So Aghen went back to the shipyard and continued to sift through the lumber that had been stacked for future use, sorting white oak from maple from pine. And he wondered what Ottar would do next to squeeze the wealth from the longphort he had so effortlessly taken.

He did not have to wait long for an answer, as it turned out, an hour or two, no more. Aghen had worked nearly to exhaustion and was sitting on a pile of white oak boards and staring out toward the sea when he heard the man calling. Someone up at the far end of the longphort, someone with a substantial voice, though not substantial enough for Aghen to make out the words, just the tone of command. He stood with a groan and climbed up to the high point in the road.

Ottar's men were milling about near the gates by the two halls. The people of Vík-ló who had retreated in confusion and fear to their homes were now stepping out onto the plank road, summoned by the man calling to them as he walked toward the river.

"Up to Lord Ottar's hall, all of you, come along! Come along!" Aghen could make out the words now. "Lord Ottar would speak with you all! Come along!"

And the people went. Slowly, with all the enthusiasm of prisoners going to their executions, they stepped through their wattle gates and made their way up the road to the hall, a handful of people, a sorry and inconsequential force in the face of Ottar's warriors.

Aghen frowned. He wanted to ignore this summons just to show that he would not be ordered around like a thrall. He wanted to make it clear that he was not willing to cooperate.

"It's pointless," he said out loud. And it was. What did he think would happen, that Ottar would be cowed by his defiance? No, Ottar would welcome the chance to make an example of him, to show all of Vík-ló how he crushed defiance under his heel. The old shipwright sighed and headed up the plank road, his knees aching as he walked.

Aghen reached the fringes of the crowd and stopped. He could sense the uncertainty and dread; it hung like smoke over the people as they waited. No one spoke. Ottar's warriors were making a line across the gate, as if to suggest to those in the longphort that there was no way out. They did not carry shields and their weapons were sheathed, but that did not lessen the quiet menace of their presence.

The cowed silence was just giving way to muttered speculation when Ottar came out the door of Thorgrim's hall. He walked down the line of warriors, then stopped and looked out toward the cluster of men and women who had assembled there. His height was so great he looked as if he were standing on a platform, and when he spoke his voice was like a physical presence.

"See here," he called, and the crowd's soft murmuring stopped instantly. "The men who sailed from here, under the command of Thorgrim, who you call Night Wolf, they're all dead. Killed by the Irish. If they'd waited for us to come to their aide they might have lived, but they didn't, so they're dead. And now I am lord here. Those dead men don't need their halls, or their houses, or any of their silver, and so I will take that for my men.

"Now, I want to be fair about this, because I'm a fair man. We'll divide it up, all of us, my men and you people. Equal shares for all. So I am ordering you, each and every one of you, to gather up any silver, gold, jewels, whatever hoard you have, and bring it to me in my hall. There my men and me, we'll see every man here in the longphort has an equal share. Don't anyone hold out or think you'll cheat your neighbor. Go now. I want all of it before the sun is below the roof of my hall."

No one moved. No one spoke. Aghen shook his head and spit on the ground in disgust. *My hall…* All that horse shit about equal shares. Ottar had not even tried to sound like he was telling the truth. That was how little regard he had for the people of Vík-ló.

Then the man who had summoned them to Ottar's hall stepped forward again and in the same booming voice, a voice that was nearly the equal of Ottar's, said, "You heard Lord Ottar! Go now! Gather your hoards and bring them here and be quick. And don't think even for a moment that you'll cheat your new lord!"

That was enough to spur the people to action. They turned, they headed off to their homes and shops, moving quick or slow depending on how frightened they were or how enraged by this thievery. Mar was moving slow, bear-like, a deep scowl on his face. Aghen saw him coming and waited for him. Mar had amassed a considerable hoard of silver, Aghen knew. Blacksmithing was a profitable trade, particularly when you were the only blacksmith in the town.

"Listen, my friend," Aghen said. "This is a bad situation we're in, but it could be worse. You could be dead."

"We'll all be dead soon, mark my words," Mar said.

"If you try to hold out on this Ottar, you'll be dead sooner than most," Aghen said. "I beg of you, whatever silver you have, give it to him."

Mar stopped and looked at Aghen, his scowl deepening. "You're not a man I would have thought was backward in his courage," he said.

In Aghen's younger days, such words would certainly have ended with weapons drawn and blood spilled, but he was too old now for such nonsense. "I know Ottar's sort," he said instead. "He's looking to make an example."

Mar grunted, and that was all he said by way of reply. He left Aghen on the plank road and pushed through the gate in his wattle fence and disappeared into the gloom of his small house.

Don't be a fool, Aghen thought and he stared at the open door to Mar's house. With all that had happened already that day, the thought of watching Mar die was too much to bear.

Aghen turned and continued down the road to his own home, a plank-built house with the floor dug two feet down into the earth. His was smaller than most because, unlike most, there was no workshop attached to it. Aghen's work took place by the water's edge, and that was where he kept his tools and his bench.

But not his silver. That was secured in a small wooden chest and buried under the bench on which Aghen slept that was pushed up against the far wall by the hearth. He pulled the bench away from the wall and knelt on the cool earth floor. He pulled his knife from the sheath and used it to dig the dirt away.

It was not a hard job. Aghen had unearthed the chest not long before, when Thorgrim had given him two silver arm rings to show his appreciation for the work done on the new longships. Now he cleared the dirt away once more and pulled the small chest from the ground. It was heavy, as a hoard should be, but not terribly so. Aghen was not a wealthy man.

He stood and hefted the chest and stepped out into the gray light of the day. People were already heading back up the road to Ottar's hall, carrying their wealth in their arms, some struggling under the weight, and some, like Aghen, bearing it easily.

Ottar's men were swarming over the town. They were searching the empty long houses, the homes of those who had sailed with Thorgrim and not returned. But it was not just the empty houses they were searching. They were going through the others as well, the houses that were still occupied, to be sure that no one was hiding anything to which Ottar laid claim.

By the time Aghen reached the longphort's gates, most of the people had returned to the twin halls. Ottar's warriors were pushing them into a line where they could wait their chance to hand over all the wealth they had amassed to this stranger and his men. Mar was there, and the chest he carried appeared to be a substantial burden, and that gave Aghen some relief. It was, hopefully, for Mar's sake, all the wealth he had hidden in his shop.

One by one the people were ushered into Ottar's hall, bearing chests and sacks. One by one they came out, empty-handed and red-faced with suppressed fury. Mar went in and was gone less than a minute. He came out again and pushed his way through the crowd. He made a point of shouldering one of Ottar's men aside, nearly knocking him to the ground, but the man only threw a curse at Mar's back as the smith stomped away.

And then it was Aghen's turn. He stepped through the door into that hall he knew so well: the sleeping benches, the hearth, the wattle wall that divided off the back end of the building from the main room. The day was getting on and a fire was burning in the hearth and it added an orange light to the room, which was still mostly lit by the last of the day's sun.

Ottar was seated at the table at which Aghen had so often seen Thorgrim. Now the table seemed dwarfed by Ottar's looming presence; the bench on which he sat seemed barely able to hold him. A dozen armed men stood in a semicircle behind him, and at his feet was the cumulative wealth of Vík-ló, or at least all that Ottar had so far collected.

With a wave, Ottar indicated that Aghen was to place the small chest on the table, and Aghen did. Ottar flipped the lid open, poked at the collection of silver coins and rings and brooches with a massive finger. He frowned.

"This is it?" he said, looking up at Aghen for the first time.

"That's it," Aghen said. "I'm not a wealthy man."

Ottar stared at him for a moment, as if trying to see what was inside. "What's your name?" he asked.

"Aghen. Aghen Ormsson."

"You were here with Grimarr Knutson. You went a'viking with him," Ottar said, the words more an accusation than a statement.

"No," Aghen said. "My raiding days are over. I'm a shipwright. I built the ships you took from Thorgrim Night Wolf."

Ottar squinted at him, and Aghen guessed he was remembering the words that had passed between them at the river's edge. Ottar had only just learned Aghen's name and it was clear he disliked him already. But being a shipwright, and the only shipwright in Vík-ló, offered Aghen a certain level of protection. A longphort could not function if there was no one who knew how to properly repair ships.

"Shipwright, huh?" Ottar said. "Where are your tools?"

"My tools?" Aghen said. "They are down by the river. Where we build the ships."

"Down by the river!" Ottar roared and slammed his fist on the table, making the small chest jump. The volume and intensity of the outburst surprised Aghen and made him jump as well. The men on either side of Ottar took a step closer.

"Were you not told to bring anything of value to me?" Ottar continued, his volume barely diminished. "Were you not?"

"I was," Aghen said, confused, but not liking the direction in which this was leading.

"Well, your tools are a damned bit more valuable than this pathetic little box of trash you've brought me here," Ottar said. "Go down to the river, get your tools, and bring them to me."

Aghen straightened and his hands curled into fists. "I can't work on your ships if I don't have my tools," he said, forcing calm into his voice.

"I'll decide if you work on my ships!" Ottar roared. "You are nothing, you are a sorry thrall, unless I say otherwise! Now, gather your tools and bring them to me or by the gods you will live to regret it. But not for long."

Aghen turned without another word and left the hall. The crowd outside the door, the armed men, the deep shadows falling over the longphort, he saw none of it in his fury.

My tools…

Aghen felt about his tools the way a warrior felt about his sword, indeed the way he himself had felt about his sword in his raiding days. His tools were as much a part of him as his hands, just as integral, just as necessary. Until that moment he had never really appreciated the depth of that connection, because until that moment no one had ever threatened to take his tools from him, to defile them thus.

He stumbled his way through the line of Ottar's men and past the people still waiting to be called into Thorgrim's hall. Ottar's hall. He sat heavily on the stump of a tree used for splitting wood and stared off at the dull glow of the sun behind thick clouds to the west.

My tools…what by the gods do I do now? he wondered. He had given up his silver. Not willingly, but he had done it. He would not, however, be turning his tools over to Ottar. That was not even a consideration. So, would he die at Ottar's hands? Would he throw his tools in the river first? There was a boat down by the water, one of those Irish leather boats they called a *curach*. He could take that, load his tools aboard, make his way down the coast.

He got no further in his considerations. There was shout from inside Ottar's hall, the sound of furniture overturned, coins or some such spilling. Aghen heard the thrashing of struggling men. He stood, and from there he saw two of Ottar's guards pulling Valgerd Unnson, the hot-headed, intemperate Valgerd, through the door. The young man shouted and cursed and struggled, but Ottar's men were bigger than him and had him by the arms, and Aghen knew that Valgerd's broken leg was still weak.

They dragged him from the hall and pulled him in front of the watching crowd. One of Ottar's men stepped up and hit him hard on the side of the head and his struggling all but ceased. The men holding his arms forced him to his knees, and Ottar stepped from the hall, a linen sack in his hand. He stood by Valgerd and held the sack aloft.

"This!" Ottar shouted to the people who watched, silent and motionless. "This is what this whore's son tells me is all he has. And yet my men search his house and they find two chests… two chests! Filled with silver!"

Valgerd looked up. He spit blood at Ottar's feet. "The chests are not mine!" he shouted, the words more defiance than defense. Even Valgerd could see that argument would do him no good now.

"You're lying to me and you're cheating every man here!" Ottar shouted. He turned to a half dozen men standing nearby, not his men but men of Vík-ló who had stayed behind when Thorgrim sailed. "You lot, find a pole, half a rod long. Stand it up there." He pointed to an open spot beside the hall. "We'll see what become of liars and cheats."

Aghen looked away. Valgerd might well have been trying to keep some of his silver from Ottar's grasp. It would be like him to do that. But Aghen also knew that Valgerd shared a longhouse with five other warriors, all of whom had sailed with Thorgrim, each of whom likely had a hoard buried in the floor.

Speak up! Aghen said to himself. *Speak up, you damned coward!* But his lips remained closed, and all the rage and the loathing he felt would not open them. Nor would those feelings open the mouths of any other man there, every one of whom knew Valgerd's circumstance.

It took little time to find a pole and dig a footing for it and stand it upright in the open ground. The sun had gone behind the mountains and the longphort was in deep shadow. Torches were lit as Valgerd was tied to the upright shaft, cursing and shouting defiance. Then Ottar stepped forward, his massive sword in hand, ready to deliver the lesson he was so eager to give.

Aghen watched it all, and if there was any consolation, it was that Valgerd died well, as well as any man could die in that manner. He did not beg for mercy or further plead his innocence. He died angry and defiant. But not quickly.

They went at him with arrows first. Ottar's archers lined up no more than a rod distant, close enough that they could not fail to hit where they wished. They shot for Valgerd's shoulders, his legs, his belly. The arrows ripped into his body, one at a time, but the bowmen were careful to avoid any spot that would bring instant death.

Valgerd twisted and shrieked and heaped curses on Ottar and his men. Aghen turned to look at Ottar, who stood by the bowmen, his face lit by the torches that ringed the scene. He was not scowling, he was not angry. Nor was he gleeful or triumphant. He was calm as he watched and listened to the vile words Valgerd spewed at him. He was enjoying it.

Then Ottar stepped up, three quick steps, and he was in front of Valgerd. Valgerd cursed and tried to spit on him, but he could not because Ottar had stopped an arm and sword length short. Valgerd twisted against the bonds as if still trying to get at Ottar, despite the five arrows that jutted from his body. Then Ottar swung his sword in a wide arc, the stroke carefully aimed, the depth of the cut gauged perfectly.

Valgerd's tunic was split open across his belly and a bright red line appeared against the white skin beneath. Valgerd stopped struggling, stopped cursing. He sucked in his breath and his eyes went wide and then his belly seemed to erupt as his entrails, pink and gleaming wet, spilled from the wicked cut that Ottar had delivered.

Then the real shrieking began, the terrible high-pitched screams of a man who has abandoned himself to the agony. The people who were watching, and that was all the people of Vík-ló, there by Ottar's command, turned as if they had been physically struck. Ottar's own men watched as well, but they had little reaction, if any at all, like men who had seen this sort of thing often enough to be used to it.

The screaming continued as Ottar's men piled brush and branches and heaps of wood chips collected from the shipyard at Valgerd's feet. Valgerd shuddered. The last of his guts hung from the rent in his belly as the torches were tossed onto the brush and the wood chips, and the flames leapt up and wrapped themselves around the dying man. Valgerd shrieked once more, again and again, as his voice grew weaker and he began to cough. And then he stopped any noise at all, and Aghen hoped above all other hopes that the man was dead at last.

It was full night by the time Valgerd's body was reduced to a blackened and shriveled nothing and the people watching were allowed to disperse. Ottar said nothing more, gave no speech about what would become of anyone who did not do as they were instructed by their new lord. He did not have to. The point was made.

Aghen staggered off into the dark. He had no thought as to where he would go, but his feet carried him down the plank road, down to the shipyard and the water's edge. He stopped at the place where the grass yielded to mud and stared out into the blackness of the sea.

My tools… He had forgotten, in the horror of watching Valgerd die, that he was supposed to render up his tools to Ottar. He slowly shook his head, side to side. That would not happen. He was filled with self-loathing at his remaining silent as they dragged Valgerd to his death. He would certainly die before he gave in to Ottar again. How could he ever hope to reach the corpse hall if he did not?

It might already be too late. He might have already made himself unworthy in the eyes of the Valkyrie.

No, he thought. *No. I might die soon. I will likely die soon. But I will not die badly.*

Chapter Seven

Let the wary stranger who seeks refreshment
keep silent with sharpened hearing;
with his ears let him listen, and look with his eyes;
thus each wise man spies out the way.
Hávamál

Thorgrim Night Wolf sat on *Sea Hammer*'s afterdeck, using his teeth to rip meat from a beef rib, a remnant from the cow that Cónán's men had stolen and roasted the night before. He watched as Louis the Frank came toward him over the sandbar.

Here we go, he thought.

This was a confrontation he had anticipated, though he had not been entirely certain it would take place. Louis the Frank was an enigma to him. He was not Irish, or so Harald had discovered. He seemed in fact to hate the Irish. Except when he didn't. Thorgrim could not get a finger on where the man's loyalties lay, a problem that was not made easier by having to speak to him by way of Harald's interpretation.

He had learned more about Louis from the woman, Failend, than he had from Louis himself. Once she came to understand that the Northmen did not intend to rape her or kill her or make her a thrall, she became much less standoffish, as women, in Thorgrim's experience, tended to do.

She had even made the effort to speak to him, by way of Harald. She told him she was the widow of a powerful man from Glendalough and that she had been fighting with the Irish men-at-arms. She told him she fought the heathens only because they were attacking her home, that she bore them no ill will. Thorgrim agreed that she had been right to take up arms; there was nothing else to be done.

Failend asked if she might have her sword back, saying that, like the Irish bandits, she would like the chance to train with her weapon.

Thorgrim agreed and climbed aboard *Sea Hammer* to retrieve it. He came back with two weapons: the sword he had taken from her and a seax that had been recovered from one of Ottar's dead. He handed her the sword.

"Tell her she's welcome to her sword," Thorgrim said to Harald. "But tell her I think it's heavy for so short a blade and poorly balanced."

Harald translated. Failend pulled her sword from its scabbard and held it out, frowning at it.

"Tell her," Thorgrim continued, "that this one is a Frisian blade, a short sword called a seax. It's as long as her sword but lighter. Double edged, as she can see. The steel is well made. She's welcome to it, if she likes."

Harald translated. Failend smiled and held out her hand and Thorgrim gave her the seax. She took it and held it as if making ready for a fight and Thorgrim saw the delight in her face as she felt the lighter blade, the nice balance of the weapon. She nodded and spoke.

"She thanks you," Harald said, "and asks if she might impose on you at some time to show her something of blade work."

"Tell her I will, when there's time," Thorgrim said. Why he was giving the Irish woman a weapon, let alone agreeing to teach her the use of it, he did not know. But there was a passion and spirit in her that he recognized, and liked.

There was passion in Louis the Frank as well, and watching him approach, Thorgrim knew he would soon be seeing it in full bloom.

Louis had a fighting spirit, the pride of a warrior, but Thorgrim could also sense the man's turmoil. Fighting men did not care for ambiguity. They liked to have the people in their world clearly defined. Friend. Enemy. But no doubt Louis now found those clear distinctions were blurred, former certainties wiped away. Thorgrim understood. It was the same serpent with which he was currently wrestling, the one that had dragged him down to his present nightmare.

They had been five days on the sandbar and now they were ready to go. Five days of work, training, planning and healing. Five days of making *Sea Hammer* whole again. Five days during which Thorgrim worried that they might be discovered and that the Irish would bring an overwhelming force against them.

Cónán assured him that would not happen. He had men out watching the roads and the countryside. They had seen only a few men-at-arms on horseback, and those appeared to be heading back to wherever they had come from, and not hunting down fugitive heathens. Only once did a group of riders come closer to the river than Cónán's men wished them to. When they did, one of the outlaws had sent an arrow in their direction, and in the ensuing chase they had led the riders well away from the camp they shared with the Northmen.

Now they were sitting aboard *Sea Hammer*: Thorgrim, Cónán, Harald and Godi, all the men who had worked out the plan to return to Glendalough. They had told no one, not until just that moment, when they had let word filter through the camp. That, Thorgrim guessed, would be the subject Louis wished to discuss.

"Thorgrim!" Louis called as he approached, making no effort to hide his agitation. "Thorgrim!" He pronounced the name "Tor-grim" which Thorgrim generally found amusing, though neither he nor Louis was feeling very amused at the moment.

Louis stopped at *Sea Hammer*'s bow and stared down her length at the men in the stern. The ship was floating now. Thorgrim had finished scarfing in the new strakes, caulking and tarring the patch until it was all but invisible. They had pushed the ship into the river and she had leaked a bit as the wood swelled and then the leaking had stopped. It was the last part of their plan completed, the ship floating, ready to carry them and their plunder down river faster than horsemen could hope to follow.

"Come aboard," Thorgrim called, waving to Louis, knowing he would understand the gesture. Louis swung himself up over the sheer strake and stomped aft, stopping just short of the cluster of men. Thorgrim tossed his denuded bone over the side and looked up at the young warrior.

Louis spoke. Harald translated. Harald's translation lacked the barely controlled anger of Louis's words, but Thorgrim got it.

"He says he hears in the camp that we are going to sack Glendalough, and that he is expected to help. He says he will not help."

Thorgrim nodded. He was long past the point where he was willing to argue or cajole. He was not interested in discussion; he had done enough of that as of late and it had led to nothing but disaster.

"Tell him I know he belonged to the Christ temple there," Thorgrim instructed Harald. "Tell him he will show us where the silver, the things of value are to be found. If he helps us to raid the church quick and be gone, there is less chance that any of his brother Christ men will be hurt. Tell him I will not expect him to fight, or to raise a weapon against anyone." In truth, Thorgrim had not yet decided if he would even let Louis carry a sword on the raid.

Harald translated. Louis listened. He frowned. And then he spoke again.

"Louis says he's grateful for your words, but still he will not help."

Thorgrim looked at Louis for a long moment, taking the measure of the man. He guessed that threatening harm to Failend would be the most effective lever against him, but he also knew better than to make threats that they both understood he would not carry out. That was not a problem. He had other carrots, other sticks.

"I understand you're a Frank?" Thorgrim said, looking at Louis as he spoke, keeping his eyes on him as Harald translated the words.

"*Oui*," Louis said.

"I imagine you're eager to get back to your homeland," Thorgrim went on. "I guess you're counting on that hoard of silver you carry to buy your passage back. Maybe you and Failend."

Harald translated. Louis said nothing.

"I'll wager that's why you took pains to secretly bury the chest at the far end of the sandbar, there," Thorgrim continued, "when you imagined no one was watching you."

Thorgrim had often wondered how well Harald actually spoke the Irish language. He had no way of gauging for himself, of course. He wondered now if Harald would be able to translate "sandbar." But apparently he could, because Louis turned quickly and looked off in the direction in which he had buried his hoard, and where Thorgrim had later dug it up, after Louis's nocturnal activities had been reported to him.

Louis turned back and his cheeks were red and his face pinched in fury. Thorgrim stood and he raised his hands in a calming gesture. "Tell the young Frank, here," he said to Harald, "that we'll raid Glendalough with or without him. If he's with us, then he can prevent bloodshed. And I don't mean our blood. I mean the blood of the men at the Christ temple. Tell him if he joins us he gets his hoard back. If not, then I'll need silver to give to my men and Cónán's, and it will come from him."

Harald translated. Louis listened, but still he did not say anything. He turned on his heel and headed forward again, hopped over the bow of the ship down to the sand and stomped off the way he had come.

Thorgrim watched him go. He could see Louis was struggling with tangled questions about loyalty and allegiance, and Thorgrim knew he had just made those questions vastly more complex for the young man. He took his seat again. "Good," he said. "Louis the Frank is with us."

"Why do you think so?" Godi asked. "He did not look so pleased when he left."

"He's with us," Thorgrim said. "I could see it in his eyes. He has no choice, and he knows it."

And Louis was indeed with them. The sun was down and the night-meal finished when the Northmen and the Irishmen and Failend and Louis began making ready to move out. They gathered on the sand by *Sea Hammer*'s bow. The Northmen wore tunics and mail; the Irish wore mail shirts over their leines, those who had leines, and various cowls or cloaks or brats over that, to hide the armor.

Starri was there, wearing a tunic, which was more clothing than he would normally wear going into a fight. Two battle axes were stuck in his belt. He was making an effort to walk effortlessly and failing, the pain from his wound obvious on his face and in his halting gait.

"Starri…" Thorgrim said, "I'm not sure you're healed enough for this."

"I'm fit as can be, Night Wolf," Starri protested. "These women, they've put the maggots to me, and made me drink some great horrors, and now I'm well set up and ready to fight again."

To be sure, Starri had improved considerably over the five days they had remained on the sandbar. Harald seemed to think this was due to Failend's healing skills and their good luck in finding that Cara always seemed to have the herbs and poultices and such that Failend said she needed. Thorgrim agreed that was lucky, though from what he could see, Cara was doing most of the healing business while Failend spent her time practicing with a shield and her seax against any who would spar with her.

But for all the improvement Starri had made, it was clear to everyone except Starri that he was still in rough shape. Thorgrim glanced over the man's shoulder. Cara was standing there, having just changed the dressing on Starri's wound. She would not have understood the words that passed between Thorgrim and Starri, but it was clear enough what was being discussed. She met Thorgrim's eyes and gave a quick shake of her head.

"Here's the thing of it, Starri," Thorgrim said. "It's two leagues to Glendalough. We'll be moving fast, covering the distance before midnight. This Louis, the Frank, he knows where the silver and gold are found in the church. The Irishmen…you see how their mail is hidden? They'll keep guard around the church while we go in and take what we can; then it's a quick retreat back here and then off down river aboard *Sea Hammer*. If the gods favor us we'll be gone before any at the Christ temple even know we're there."

"Oh," Starri said as the reality of the thing became clear. "So…no fighting?"

"None. Just walking. Some running, I would think."

"Oh," Starri said again. "Well, you know, I wonder if I wouldn't be better use here, guarding the ship?"

"And the women," Thorgrim said. "If our camp is discovered, there's a better chance there'll be fighting here at the ship then on our raid on Glendalough."

That was all Starri needed to hear. With a sigh he turned and ambled back toward his bed of branches and furs, his step much more labored now that he had given up trying to appear fit.

Thorgrim looked out over the assembled men. They were about thirty-five in number, not a great army, but they had other advantages. The Northmen were experienced fighting men, well-versed in this sort of work. The Irish were new to their weapons, but they had learned fast. More importantly, they were tough and unafraid and inured to physical hardship, able to fight hard and to move fast overland in any sort of weather, night or day. Thorgrim knew they were cunning because men who lived an outlaw's life were either cunning or soon dead.

Cónán stood with Thorgrim, as did Harald and Godi. Cónán had not joined his men in training with sword and shield, but on a few occasions Thorgrim had seen him spar with others, including Harald and Godi. It was clear that he had had some knowledge of the weapons. He did not have a Norseman's skill, and Thorgrim did not doubt that Harald or Godi or some of the others could put him down in a fight, but it would not be an easy thing. Not like killing the bandits' former chief.

"Your men are ready?" Thorgrim asked Cónán, and Harald translated.

"He says they are," Harald said.

"Good," Thorgrim said. "Lead on."

Cónán nodded. He spoke to his men in a voice that was both soft and commanding. Thorgrim saw heads nod. Whatever he said, Harald did not feel the need to translate it, so Thorgrim figured it was of no great import. Then Cónán turned and headed off toward the trees and Thorgrim followed and the rest followed them.

And Thorgrim realized, to his surprise, that he was feeling something he had not felt in some time, and that was hope. It was far off, like a memory, like a distant shore seen through the mist. There was a time not long before, a week, maybe, that he would not have imagined ever feeling that again. But he felt it now. Just a shadow, but it was there.

It was hope driven by momentum. Moving forward. Until that moment his life had been a ship battered by the seas, driven by forces he could not control. He could affect nothing, he could only beg the gods to let him survive and bring those under his command to safety.

But now that was over, the storm had blown itself out, the ship still floated, some of the crew still lived. Now the wind had filled in and it was steady and blowing in their direction.

Thorgrim understood that he could not undo the disaster that had befallen them. But he could move on, he could make those responsible pay. He could exact revenge and that would please the gods and then maybe they would forgive him his stupidity. He knew his destination now, and they were underway again, and the rudder was biting and they were masters once more. And they were going back to Glendalough.

Chapter Eight

A great and frequent increase in the number of heathens arriving...
the laity and clergy ...were plundered by them.
The Annals of Ulster

They were making their way toward Glendalough on foot, but Louis de Roumois was thinking about horses.

As a young man, Louis had been an avid hunter, riding after fox and hind. Later he'd become a mounted warrior, captain of a troop of horse soldiers. Their chief duty had been to beat back the frequent, violent incursions of the Northmen along the Seine River in his native Frankia. All told, Louis had spent many, many days on horseback in almost every conceivable circumstance. And so he knew well what it meant to have a horse spook under him.

He knew the frightening sensation of having the massive animal on which he was riding suddenly kick and buck and rear, stumble and charge off in a panic. He knew the terror of having no choice but to hang on and try to bring the beast under control, or hope that the animal would calm down or exhaust itself before some great harm came to them both.

And that was how his entire life felt now. He was no longer in control.

He had been in control, or so he thought. After he had been lifted out of the monastic life into which he had been forced by his older brother, and put in command of the men-at-arms defending Glendalough, he had felt like his control was returning, that life was responding to the reins and the spurs. It had been a joy, his renewed career as a soldier and a leader of men. But it had been brief and then it had collapsed around him.

But still he maintained control. He and Failend, with the hoard that had belonged to Failend's late husband, making their escape, leaving Glendalough behind, making their way to some place where they might take ship to Frankia. Where Louis might begin to take back all that was rightfully his.

But control had been an illusion, as it so often was. He and Failend had stumbled right into Thorgrim and his band, the remnants of the Norse army that had come for Glendalough. And that was it. A dozen steps along a riverbank and control was gone, freedom sent packing.

It could have been worse, of course. They could have been killed. Failend could have been ravaged. They could have been taken for the slave market in Dubh-linn or over the seas. If Thorgrim knew who Louis really was, the man who had arranged for the slaughter of the Northmen, then that would no doubt be their fate. But the fact that it could have been worse did not make it any less terrible.

All these things were churning and whirling through Louis's mind as he trudged along, unseeing, hardly aware of what was taking place. They were near the front of the column, he and Failend. Ahead of them were Thorgrim and his son, Cónán, the Irish bandit leader, and the big Northman whose name Louis did not know.

They were following the south bank of the river. Louis had overheard some discussion—Thorgrim apparently thinking they should take the road, Cónán telling him there was a better approach, a more hidden way, a trail through the stands of trees that lined the riverbank. Since their conversations had to be translated into Irish for Cónán to understand, Louis was able to follow along, though he did not much care one way or another.

They had decided to take Cónán's route. Thorgrim was not so stubborn as to ignore local knowledge. And Louis could see it was the right choice. The going was harder along the trail, but they were almost entirely hidden as they made their way to the monastic city.

Louis, head down, his mind working, was not aware that they had stopped until the back of the big man loomed in front of him, like walking right into a cliff. Louis checked himself before he slammed into the man and looked up to see what was going on.

They had come to a place where the trail ran right into the river. A ford, apparently. It was full dark, but the perpetual overcast had actually broken up hours before and a tolerably full moon was lighting their way. He could hear Thorgrim and Cónán speaking softly.

Thorgrim turned and said something to Harald and then he and the Irishmen splashed out into the river, but Harald and the big man did not move, so Louis guessed the others were scouting the way. He turned to Failend. Louis was not particularly talkative, at least for a Frank, but he felt the need now to vent some of the anguish he was feeling.

He opened his mouth to speak and then closed it again as Failend's expression caught him off guard. He had expected to see a look of rage, barely suppressed, to match his own. Certainly when they had spoken earlier Failend had expressed anger and outrage at Thorgrim's plans, and his coercing his prisoners into helping. But that was not the expression he was seeing now.

Failend's head was up, her eyes bright, and she seemed alert like a deer at the edge of a pond. In the dim light it was hard to read her mood, but her mouth seemed on the edge of a smile.

"Failend," Louis said, speaking softly and stepping back, away from Harald, the only one close by who might understand their words. "I've been trying to think of some way out of this."

"Out of…what?" Failend asked. Her hand was resting on the grip of her seax, her thick hair bound behind her head with a leather thong.

"Out of the raid. On Glendalough. Some way we don't have to be part of this abomination."

"Oh," Failend said. "Have you thought of anything?"

"No," Louis said. "Have you?"

"No," Failend said in a tone that suggested she had not really been thinking about it.

"You don't…" Louis began then stopped, because the question he was about to ask was absurd. And yet, given Failend's demeanor, he still felt compelled to ask it. "You don't want to join this raid, do you?" he said at last.

"No!" Failend hissed. "No, of course I don't."

Louis nodded. They were silent for a moment, listening to the splashing of Thorgrim and Cónán, who had crossed the ford and now were coming back.

"Not that I bear any great love for the people of Glendalough," Failend added, almost grudgingly.

"No great love?" Louis said. Thorgrim and Cónán stepped out of the river and Thorgrim said something in a low voice to the other Northmen. "They're your people," Louis reminded her.

"My people?" Failend said, and Louis could hear the rising note in her voice. "They want to hang us both for murder. After they tried to murder us first and failed. My people?"

Louis was about to make reply to the effect that it was Failend's late husband, *Colman mac Breandan,* not all of Glendalough, who was to blame for that. *Colman,* who Louis could not help but think was killed by Failend herself, while he, Louis, unwittingly stood guard outside the house. But now they were moving again, stepping down the shallow sloping bank and into the cold Avonmore River and the chance to speak was lost.

They kept on for the next hour or more. Thorgrim and Cónán set a quick pace, but Louis was naturally athletic and had no trouble keeping up. It was harder on Failend, her stride being considerably shorter than the others, but she did not waver, and Louis could see in her expression a determination to show no weakness.

After some time they came out into open country and stopped. Thorgrim and Cónán told their men to take a rest, to have some of the dried meat they had brought with them if they wished, or a shot of the mead or ale they carried in skins.

Louis swung his sword clear and sat on the cool grass, and Failend did likewise. Louis took a drink from his skin and handed it to Failend and she squirted some of the liquid into her mouth. Good Irish ale, cool and savory like meat. Louis wondered where the Northmen had come by it. Trading with the Irish, no doubt. The Northmen had silver, and the Irish were willing to deal with any sort of vermin if the vermin could pay.

The irony, of course, was that the silver had been stolen from the Irish in the first place. The Northmen were robbing Peter so they could then buy ale from him.

Louis and Failend had not spoken since the river, but Louis had been hearing her words in his head, over and over, as he walked. With each repetition they raised more questions. He remembered back to the first time he had led the Irish men-at-arms in an attack against the Northmen. Failend had come along without his knowledge. She had joined in the fight, driven a sword right through one of the Northmen's necks. She had told him after she was more afraid of being bored than she was of being killed.

"Failend," Louis asked, "why are you here? Did Thorgrim tell you that you had to come with us?"

"No," Failend said. "He didn't say it. Not right out. But I think he intended that I should come. Like you."

Louis nodded. "Thorgrim knows how to get what he wants. I thought he would threaten violence against you, in order to force me to come. He hit on the next best thing, holding my chest of silver as hostage."

Even as he spoke he saw Failend's eyebrows come together and her lips turn down to form a scowl. "*Your* chest of silver?" she hissed. "That silver belonged to my late husband. And me. It is my chest of silver, and that's why I'm here. To protect it."

Louis felt as if he had been slapped. Of course she was right, strictly speaking. But she had been with him, she was his lover. They were bound away together, fleeing the false charge of murder that had been leveled at them both. The silver was their passport, and he did not think of it as hers, *per se*.

"Fine," Louis said, and he tried to sound mollifying. "That's understandable, of course. I just did not want to think you were helping the heathens with their crimes because…"

"Because what?"

"Because you wanted to. I knew it couldn't be that you came along for that reason."

"Oh course not," Failend said. "I want the silver back. Like you." She was quiet for a moment as she drank more ale and chewed a particularly difficult mouthful of dried beef. She swallowed. "But what if I did wish to come on this raid?" she asked.

Louis was stumbling around for a reply when a soft order came down the line and the men and one woman rose to their feet again. They headed out in a long column across the open ground. The night was quiet, nothing to be heard beyond the insects and the branches moving in the light breeze and the muted sounds of thirty-five armed warriors moving at a near jog.

The moonlight revealed a bit of the countryside around them, and Louis was just starting to think there was something familiar about it, that he knew where he was, when he became aware of some obstacle in their way. Thorgrim and Harald and Cónán were spreading out, approaching the dark, hulking shapes with caution. Louis instinctively rested his hand on the pommel of his sword as he followed behind them.

And then he saw what they were. They were wagons, or what was left of them. The remains of three heavy, well-appointed caravans. They had been owned by a company of players, led by a fellow named Crimthann. Thorgrim's son, Harald, had hijacked the wagons and driven them right into the middle of the battle between the Irish and Norsemen, with him and Failend and the others in the back.

Thorgrim walked around the north side of the wagons and Cónán around the south. Louis followed behind Thorgrim. The wagons had been looted and stripped of anything of value. The wheels were gone, the traces, much of the siding had been torn away. They looked like corpses that had been picked over by vultures.

They met up with Cónán on the far side of the ravaged vehicles and he said in a low voice, "We're close now. Right over that hill we will be able to see Glendalough." Harald translated and Thorgrim nodded. Louis suspected that Thorgrim already knew that. He was no stranger to this terrain.

They moved on, taking pains to be quieter as they approached the crest of the hill. A week or so earlier, when Louis was last at Glendalough, there had been a sizable army of Irish men-at-arms and the bóaire and fuidir, three hundred or so men in the dúnad. If even a fraction of them were still there, this raid would be over before the Northmen even reached the far side of the hill.

They crouched as they came to the crest. Beyond it was darkness. The monastery and the town that had grown up around it were on low ground, and they were lost in the darkness that seemed to spill from the steep hills surrounding them. Louis thought he could see a few tiny points of light, the candles that burned perpetually in the big stone church, perhaps, seen through the windows that lined the nave.

Louis looked to the north, where the dúnad had been situated. Nothing. No dull glow of a dying campfire, no sign of pavilions or tents or wagons. If the encampment had still been there, Louis was sure he would be able to see something of it, but this was just empty ground as far as he could tell.

You are damned lucky, Thorgrim, for a Godforsaken heathen, Louis thought. But he knew it was not just luck that they should find the army gone. Cónán's men, with the advantage of looking and speaking like any other misbegotten Irish peasant, had traveled regularly to Glendalough and back while the Northmen had been on the sandbar, preparing. The Irishmen brought back daily news of the defenses around the monastic town. Neither the Northmen nor the Irish bandits were going to be caught unawares.

They waited at the top of the hill for what seemed like a long time, though Louis doubted it was more than twenty minutes. In that time there was no sound out of the ordinary, no sign of life beyond the buzzing of the insects and, once, an owl hooting in the dark.

Thorgrim said something, his voice soft, and waved his hand in a beckoning gesture. He stood and moved over the crest of the hill and down the other side. The rest followed behind, including Louis, who felt as if he were being irresistibly tumbled along, like a man caught in the surf. They were here, the monastery at their feet, and nothing had come along to disrupt Thorgrim's plans, and Louis had hit on no strategy to stop this raid. Apparently they would be sacking Glendalough, and Louis de Roumois would be helping, and there was not a damned thing he could do to prevent it.

They were less than half a mile away, near enough that they could see the dark shapes of the homes and workshops that spread out like toadstools growing against the monastery's wall. They could see the monastic buildings as well: the abbot's house and the dormitory that Louis had once called home, the stables, and, looming above it all, the grand, stone-built church, a monument to St. Kevin who had brought the Christian faith to that place two hundred years before.

Thorgrim stopped and the others stopped as well. He turned and looked at Louis and beckoned him forward. Louis stepped up, huddling with Thorgrim and Cónán and Harald.

"We're here," Thorgrim said, by way of his son. "The church is there." He nodded toward the dark shape in the distance. Louis could see that he had been right; there were lit candles visible though the tall arched windows. "Now we come to the part you play."

Louis nodded.

"You know the best way to approach this place," Thorgrim continued. "You'll lead. When we're near the church, half our men will go in and half will find hiding places from which to watch for trouble. You and I will be going into the church. If we move fast, and no alarm is raised, then we can be gone before there's the need for anyone to die. Any of your fellow Christ men to die," he clarified.

He looked at Louis and his expression seemed to say, *Do you understand?* Louis nodded his head. Thorgrim nodded toward the church that was all but lost in shadow. Louis stepped off in that direction and the rest followed behind.

This is like having a tooth pulled, Louis thought. It was horribly unpleasant, but when it had to be done then it had to be done, and the best for it was to do it fast and get it over with.

He moved over the open ground and crossed the road that led from the east into the town. He considered just leading the men down the road. The chances that anyone would notice them at that hour were slim. But, small risk that it was, it was still too great, and there was a good chance that Thorgrim would think it was some sort of trick.

Instead, Louis led the near three dozen men across the road and into the tall grass beyond, then down the hill to the trampled ground that marked the outer edge of the town. He had been at Glendalough more than a year and had taken every opportunity to get away from the monastery and the life there that he found so intolerably dull, and so he knew well how to sneak through those narrow dirt lanes.

They came to an alleyway that led behind a blacksmith's shop and a bead maker's. Louis was moving with confidence now, stepping light and quick, his ears alert for any indication that they had been seen. He realized, to his shame, that he was falling naturally back into his role as a man-at-arms and had forgotten to be disgusted with what he was being made to do.

They came to the stone wall that surrounded the monastic ground, no more than five feet high, more a symbolic marker of sanctuary than real defense. He stopped and heard the sound of the men behind him stopping as well. They were well hidden in that place, both from the monastery and the town. Louis peered over the wall. Nothing. No one moving. He would have been very surprised if there was.

He turned to Thorgrim and Harald and Cónán. "We'll go over the wall here," he said. "Just those who are going to the church. The men standing guard, they should stay here. Less chance of being seen, and if there's any threat it will come from the town. There will be no one in the church," he said, and as he did, another thought came to him. He hesitated, just for a heartbeat, but it seemed Harald did not notice the small catch in his words.

Thorgrim nodded as Harald translated. Cónán nodded as well. Thorgrim looked over the wall, looked around the alley, taking in what little he could see. Louis had the notion that he was checking to see if there was some trick being played, some betrayal. But he saw nothing because there was no trick being played. Not yet.

With a quick word to his men, Thorgrim put his hands on the top of the wall and hoisted himself up and dropped to the ground on the other side, the only sound a soft thud and the light tinkling of chainmail. Louis followed behind. He backed into the shadow of the wall and crouched, as Thorgrim was doing. Then one after another the others followed, making a line pressed against the wall, all ten of the Northmen and Failend as well, with Cónán's outlaws remaining on the other side, keeping watch.

For a moment they stayed motionless and quiet, watching and listening for any sign they had been seen, but there was nothing. Louis stood and beckoned the others and they moved quickly across the open ground to the great stone church that loomed mountainous above them. They stopped again, shoulders and backs pressed against the rough stone wall.

"There's a side way in, more hidden," Louis hissed to Harald and Harald hissed to Thorgrim. Thorgrim nodded.

"Sometimes the monks pray all through the night," Louis continued. "I'll go in first, make sure the church is truly empty."

Harald translated. Thorgrim made a short reply. Harald said, "I'll go with you."

Louis nodded and the two of them left the others, skirting along the stone wall, keeping in what shadows there were, Louis leading the way. They came at last to an unimposing wooden door sunk into the side of the nave, a door for utilitarian rather than ecclesiastical purposes. Louis paused, looked left and right, then lifted the latch and swung the door in.

It moved silently for half a foot then gave a squeal. Louis sucked in his breath and stopped pushing. He and Harald stood there, silent, listening. The sharp, high note had sounded as loud as a thunderclap in the still night, but Louis realized that even Thorgrim and the rest had probably not been able to hear it.

Slowly, an inch at a time, Louis pushed the door open. It gave one more tiny squeak and then it was wide enough for both Louis and the somewhat broader Harald to get through. Louis stepped in. Harald followed behind.

There were candles flickering at the various altars scattered around the nave, and they gave off enough light that patches of the interior were illuminated, though barely, while much of it remained in deep shadow. The flames glinted on silver and gold on the high altar and on the reliquaries and the gilded and bejeweled covers of holy books on their stands.

"I see no one here," Harald whispered. He sounded nervous, but Louis did not think it was fear of being discovered, or having to fight. From what Louis knew of Northmen, Harald would have welcomed a fight. He guessed, rather, that it was fear of being in a Christian church. Fear of Christian magic he did not understand.

Good, Louis thought.

"No, no one here," Louis agreed. "Back there"—he pointed to the door to the sacristy behind the altar—"that's where the monks sometimes go to pray."

"All right, let's look there," Harald said.

"That's the tabernacle, where God himself resides," Louis whispered. "Have a care as you pass that way."

Harald's eyes went a bit wider. He looked at the tabernacle and then back at Louis. "I know nothing of these things," he said. "You go. I'll keep a watch here."

Louis nodded, his expression one of understanding and sympathy. He left Harald there, crossing the nave, his soft shoes making only a slight rustling sound in the rushes strewn on the floor. His eyes darted left and right. There was no one. The church was empty.

But not entirely. He was fairly certain of that. He had only remembered at the last moment, when they reached the monastery wall, and he knew that if he was right this might be his one chance to stop the plundering of Glendalough.

He stepped up onto the altar and made the sign of the cross. He snatched up a lit candle and crossed to the sacristy door, then gently pushed it open and stepped though. The small flame cast a circle of light ten feet around, falling on a few ornate chairs and a wooden trunk that Louis knew contained vestments and albs.

He took another half dozen steps. In the far corner he could see a shapeless hump of wool cloth and he knew it was the boy, Trian, who did all the menial and dirty tasks around the church. The novitiates and the younger monks all knew, though the abbot and senior monks did not, that he had a secret way into the sacristy where he slept nights, having no other home.

Louis took three quick steps over to where the boy lay sleeping, knelt and clapped a hand over his mouth. Trian's eyes opened wide and he began to thrash his way out from under the blanket, but Louis held him fast and made reassuring sounds.

"Shh, shh, shh, Trian, it's only me, Brother Louis," Louis said, aware that that might not be so comforting if the boy had heard rumors that Louis was a murderer. "It's all right, I'm not going to hurt you."

Trian looked up at Louis's face, illuminated by the candle, and Louis felt him relax under his hand.

"You won't yell when I move my hand, will you?" Louis whispered and the boy shook his head. Louis moved his hand and, true to his word, Trian remained silent, though he still looked frightened enough.

"You know where Brother Lochlánn sleeps?" Louis asked and the boy nodded. "And you have a secret way out of here?"

Trian nodded again and pointed to some place in the shadows behind them.

"Good. Go, as fast as you can, to Lochlánn's cell. Tell him the heathens are plundering the church, this very moment. Tell him they're led by a heathen lord named Thorgrim Night Wolf. Tell him to turn out armed men if he can. Not monks. If monks come here and try to stop them they'll be slaughtered. Do you understand?"

Trian nodded again.

"Good. Go," Louis said and Trian was up like a rabbit and bolting for his secret way out, and in an instant he was swallowed up by the dark.

Louis stood and stepped quickly and quietly out of the sacristy and across the altar to the nave. Harald was standing near one of the banks of candles, apparently seeking out the best lit spot in that frightening and foreign place.

"Was there anyone there?" Harald asked in a loud whisper.

"No one," Louis said. "Let's call the others. It was just as I hoped."

Chapter Nine

Alas, o holy Patrick
That your prayers did not protect it
When the foreigners with their axes
Were smiting your oratory!
The Annals of Ulster

Lochlánn mac Ainmire dreamt of battle. He dreamt of the close fighting with sword and shield, the jostling of men in the battle line, blows from right and left, coming fast, knocking him back.

And then he was awake and he realized that he was being jostled, hard. His right hand went under his pillow and his fingers wrapped around the horn handle of the dagger he kept there. He rolled over and his left hand shot out and grabbed his assailant by the shirt. The dagger came around, but Lochlánn had the presence of mind, half asleep though he was, to see who was shaking him before plunging the blade into his heart.

Whoever it was was no more than a shadow in the dark cell. Lochlánn jerked the stranger closer and could feel that he was pretty insubstantial, no more than a boy. He heard the stranger gasp and in a panicked, strangled voice cry, "Brother Lochlánn! It's me, Trian!"

Lochlánn pulled the boy closer still and peered at him through the dark. It was indeed Trian, he could see that now, the boy who cleaned up the church and slept there at night. Lochlánn had cuffed him around on a few occasions, back when he was inclined to do that sort of thing.

He let go of Trian's shirt and swung his legs around, putting his feet on the cold stone floor. "Forgive me, Trian, you surprised me, is all," Lochlánn said.

The past month had been a strange and violent time for Lochlánn. He had gone from novitiate to soldier, had trained with Louis de Roumois and fought at his side. He had killed men. He had discovered that Louis, whom he had worshiped, was a murderer. Or at least was accused of murder. Louis, who had gone off with the heathens.

Lochlánn had found the body of *Colman mac Breandan, enemy to Louis de Roumois, his throat slashed.*

And then Lochlánn had been dropped right back into his old life as a novice monk. He felt like he was in some great river that was tumbling him along as he thrashed to regain his footing. It was little wonder to him that he felt the need to sleep with a dagger under his pillow.

He looked up. "What is it, Trian? Why are you here?"

Trian seemed to have forgotten. He opened his mouth, closed it, then opened it again as he remembered. "It's Brother Louis!"

That made Lochlánn sit up straighter. "Louis?"

"Yes, Brother. He sent me. He found me…ah…"

"Yes, yes, everyone knows you sleep in the sacristy," Lochlánn said. "Is that where he found you?"

"Yes, Brother. He told me to come get you, to tell you that the heathens are looting the church. Even now, Brother. A heathen lord named Thorgrim Night Wolf. He says to get some men-at-arms if you can and come quick. He said don't bring monks or they'll all be killed, sure."

Brother Louis? The name was like a slap in the face. Stunning. Lochlánn did not know how to react. He still had not sorted out what he thought of Louis de Roumois, if the man was a killer and his enemy, or still his dear friend who was wrongly accused. He knew only that he wanted to find him, to bring him before the law, to find the truth.

He would welcome with all his heart the discovery of Louis's innocence. At the same time, he would rather see the Frank hanged than get away with the murder of Aileran and Colman. Lochlánn still had every intention of hunting Louis down. But he had thought the man would be many leagues from Glendalough by now, not two hundred yards away.

"Heathens?" Lochlánn said, somewhat stupidly. This would have been hard to fathom if he had been fully awake. Stepping from sleep into this new reality was perplexing at best.

"Yes, Brother. Heathens, come to sack the church."

"You saw them? The heathens?"

"No, Brother Lochlánn. I only saw Brother Louis. And he told me to come tell you."

Lochlánn nodded. It was sorting itself out in his mind now. Louis had sent a warning, and it might be genuine or it might be a trap, and Lochlánn could not know because he did not know where Louis's loyalties were. So he had to meet this new threat, the heathens plundering the church, but he had to be careful about it as well.

"Do you know the home of *Colman mac Breandan?" Lochlánn asked the boy.*

"Yes, Brother, God rest his soul," Trian said, making the sign of the cross. He did it quickly, as if trying to head off any evil spirits coming his way.

"Senach and the rest of the house guard are there. Do you know Senach?"

"Yes, Brother."

"Go to him now. Quick as you can. Tell him I want him to turn the men out immediately. Armed. Mail if they have time. I'll meet them in the alley behind Colman's house."

"Yes, Brother," Trian said. He waited half a second to see if there would be more to his instructions, but Lochlánn jerked his head toward the door and Trian bolted off.

Lochlánn stood. He was awake now, but his mind was still whirling, too much coming at him at once. He focused on the immediate concerns. Arms, meeting his men, determining what was going on. He crossed his small cell to the plain wooden chest against the wall, flipped the lid up. There were rough wool blankets and a spare robe and a cloak and a leine inside and he pulled them out and tossed them to the floor. He lifted out the false bottom he had paid a carpenter to install and set that aside as well.

He could not see to the bottom of the chest, but he knew well enough what was there. His fingers felt the rough, cool links of his chainmail shirt. He pulled that out and slipped it over his head, then pulled out his belt from which hung his sword and seax and he fastened that around his waist. There was no shield; that was too big to fit in the chest and so was left with the others at Colman's house. Lochlánn wondered if Senach would think to bring it.

Much as he longed to be gone, he took the time to put the false bottom back in the chest and the other things on top of it, then closed the lid. He crossed to the door, which still gaped open, Trian having not bothered shutting it. Lochlánn peered out into the hall. No one moving, no sound save for the muffled snores coming from the other cells.

Very well, Lochlánn thought. He stepped out, closed his door. He hoped he would be back before his absence was discovered, since the time had not yet come for him to toss the monastic life aside. He hurried down the hall to the big oak door that led out onto the grounds.

The night was cool and quiet, nothing out of the ordinary that Lochlánn could sense. It certainly did not seem as if there was a heathen raid taking place, which made Lochlánn more suspicious still.

He headed off through the monastery, every inch completely familiar, even in the dark. He cut across the trampled earth toward the place where the late Colman mac Breandan's big house backed up against the outer wall. It was no longer Colman's house, of course. It was no longer a house at all. It was now an ad hoc barracks, home to his men-at-arms, the twenty soldiers who had once formed Colman's house guard.

Lochlánn had taken Senach's words to heart, his suggestion that he, Lochlánn, could remain as captain of the guard and they could ride after Louis de Roumois and the heathens he had joined. There was no one who could realistically stop them. The abbot would forbid it, of course, if

Lochlánn asked him, which he did not intend to do. And if he was not willing to obey the abbot's directions voluntarily, there was no one who could make him obey by force of arms. The strongest contingent of men in Glendalough was Colman's house guard, and they were his men now.

So he and Senach had been making plans. They had been amassing supplies, making certain that horses were available, plotting out where they would search out the renegade Frank. The men-at-arms had taken up residence in Colman's house. That residence, the largest in Glendalough, would have gone to Colman's widow, Failend, but she apparently had run off with Louis. So it stood empty, as Colman's more distant relatives haggled over who could claim rights to it. And while they did, Lochlánn's men made it their home.

Lochlánn could see the peak of the roof of Colman's house, a dark point against the night sky. He thought he could hear the bustle of men turning out in a hurry, and that was good. If Trian had been prompt, the men-at-arms should be ready by the time he reached them. The door in the back of Colman's house opened onto an alley ten feet from the outer wall of the monastery. Senach and the others could go right over the wall at that point and there was no chance that anyone in the town would see them do it, no alarm raised.

It seems we've moved things up a day, Lochlánn thought, *if Louis has really come here with the heathens.*

It was not that night, but the following night, that he and Senach had set as the time for the hunt to begin. That was when they and the other men-at-arms would descend on the stables in the dark hours, bringing with them the supplies and weapons and silver they had amassed. They would saddle up the horses they had picked out and lead them, hopefully unnoticed, out of the monastic grounds and into the town. They would leave silver for payment, then mount up and ride, and by the time they and the horses were discovered gone they would be many miles into their hunt for Louis de Roumois.

That was the plan. And like so many plans, it might have all turned into a big dung heap before it was even started.

Lochlánn was nearing the wall that enclosed the monastic grounds when he heard a noise to his left, a clattering sound, but muffled. He turned and froze, facing the church. He listened. There was nothing more. Still, he was all but certain he had heard it: something falling on the church's stone floor. A chalice? A reliquary? Whatever it was, it meant that there were men in the church at an hour when there should not have been. He turned and broke into a jog, closing the distance to the wall and his men hidden behind.

Thorgrim Night Wolf followed behind Louis the Frank and Harald as they led his men to the small door in the side of the church, leaving Vali and Armod behind to keep watch. He had an idea what to expect; he had been in Christ temples before, a dozen or more times. Usually to plunder. The Christ priests liked their silver and gold and they seemed able to gather quite a bit of it, which drew the raiders like moths to a candle.

He stepped through the door and into the vast space inside. He stopped and took it in, awed by what he saw, and that did not happen very often. It was certainly the biggest such temple he had ever seen, the roof soaring fifty feet above the stone floor, the main part of the building the length of three longships. There were clusters of candles here and there throwing pools of light around. The rest was all but lost in the darkness. It made him very uncomfortable.

"There," he said, pointing to the raised area at the eastern end of the church. There were silver chalices and plates and candleholders on the altar and on either side of it. "We'll start there. Move quietly."

"What will we carry the plunder in?" Olaf Thordarson asked.

"We'll need to find something," Thorgrim said, cursing himself for his stupidity, coming to plunder and forgetting to bring something in which to carry what they took.

Harald turned to Louis and spoke a few words. Louis nodded and hurried off. "He knows of something," Harald said.

The Northmen walked further into the wide space, moving slowly, carefully. They knew they had to be silent, that the intention was to raid the church without anyone knowing. But Thorgrim understood that that was not the true reason for their cautious steps. The place frightened them. They did not know what sort of magic might reside here. They did not know how powerful the Christ God was.

This was not new to any of them, this plundering of the Christ men's temples. But most often it was done during the day, a frenzied and violent affair, a fast raid, sometimes met with resistance, and that meant fighting. It was easy to trample fear under the feet of chaos and action.

But this was different. The church was dark and silent and the Northmen were taking care to make little noise, and that just seemed to invite whatever spirits were there to make themselves known. The raiders found it unsettling. Unnerving.

Thorgrim knew they felt that way because he felt that way himself. He realized he was clutching the Hammer of Thor and the silver cross he wore around his neck. He let go of the amulets and cursed himself for a coward and a fool.

From the far end of the church Louis reappeared with bundles of cloth in his arms, and a tangle of cords. He pulled a cloth bundle free and tossed it to Thorgrim and Thorgrim held it up. It was a white robe, the cloth a fine linen, well worth taking in its own right, and it would make a tolerably good sack to bear plunder away. Thorgrim nodded and Louis tossed the others, five robes in all, to the waiting men. He handed them the cords, which Thorgrim recognized as the rope belts the priests wore around their waists.

"There," Thorgrim whispered. He pointed to various places around the interior where he could see silver glinting in the light. "And there. Go. Look in the shadows as well."

They moved off, working in pairs, mostly, Thorgrim guessed, because none of them wished to be alone in this place. He headed up toward the main altar with Harald and Failend. He climbed the few steps to the raised area at the church's far end and paused. He looked up over his head, up to where the upper reaches of the church were lost in the darkness.

It was magnificent, he had to admit. The intricate carvings of stone, the paintings depicting the Christian gods, or perhaps stories from the Christians' beliefs, the statues painted so real they looked as if they might step off their pedestals. The Norsemen had nothing like this. They did not build such monuments to their gods. He wasn't even sure that they could. He wondered if that angered Thor and Odin, if they were jealous of the Christ God.

He wondered who he could ask.

"Father?" Harald interrupted in a whisper. "Should we take this?" He gestured to the silver and gold pieces on the altar, the tall candleholders, gleaming with jewels.

"Yes, yes," Thorgrim said. Harald was not so much asking as bringing Thorgrim's mind back to the task at hand. He shook out his robe and laid it on the floor. "Get this lot," he said. "I'll get the things back there."

He pushed past Harald, past the altar to the back of the church. Candlesticks of various heights stood like sentries, and in the middle, inset into the elaborate stone carvings, was a small door, not much more than a foot square, but lovely, made of silver and tricked out with ornamentation of gold and jewels. That door alone would make the raid on Glendalough worth the effort. He wondered what greater riches might be hidden behind it.

He took hold of the door's small handle and tugged and the door swung open. That surprised Thorgrim, as he assumed it would be locked in some manner. More surprising still, the small space behind, carved into the stone wall of the church, contained only a gold plate, and on it a half a loaf of bread.

Thorgrim shook his head. *I cannot imagine what it is that these Christ men believe*, he thought.

He reached in to grab the bread and toss it aside and take the plate, but he felt a hand on his arm. He turned. Failend was there beside him, her small hand resting on his mailed arm. She shook her head slowly, then reached in and picked up the gold plate. She walked back to the altar, which Harald had cleared of the various candlesticks and platters and chalices, and slid the bread off the plate onto the polished surface, seeming to take care never to touch it. Then she tossed the plate on top of the other things that Harald had piled on the linen garment on the floor.

Thorgrim watched her and made no protest. He found himself more mystified still by the Christian beliefs, but that was not really his concern at the moment. As long as the Christians believed that their gods wanted a church filled with silver and gold, that was all he needed to know.

He turned back to the small silver door. He put a hand under it and pushed up, hoping to wrench it from the hinges. It moved, just a bit, but remained securely spiked to the stone wall. He pushed again, then pulled down. It shifted a bit more.

Harald stepped up beside him, and without a word he put his hand next to Thorgrim's on the bottom edge of the door. Together, father and son, they heaved up and felt the hinges buckling under the pressure. They put their hands on the top edge and pushed down and to their surprise the heavy door pulled free of its moorings and fell with a great clatter on the stone floor.

Thorgrim froze and Harald froze, and then slowly they turned and looked toward the front of the church. The rest of the men stood motionless, looking back, frozen in whatever stance they had been in at the moment that the door fell. They looked like the statues of the gods the Christians had set around the church. Thorgrim might have laughed if he was not so concerned that he had just announced their presence to all of Glendalough.

For long seconds they remained motionless, staring into the dark, their ears straining to hear any sign that they had been discovered, that the clattering noise had given them away. But there was nothing, no sound at all. Thorgrim could hear the scurrying of a mouse somewhere off in a corner. He realized he had been holding his breath. He let it out, slowly. He bent down to pick up the door and the others returned to their tasks, moving quicker now than they had been.

Failend was collecting up candlesticks and adding them gently to the pile. *She saves the bread but helps us take the silver and gold?* Thorgrim thought. He wondered if perhaps Failend was mad. But he realized that the other Christ men must also believe the bread had some sort of magical charms, or they would not have stored it in that honored place behind the silver door.

Harald searched the rest of the raised area on which the altar stood and came up with a small, ornate silver box tucked into an alcove. He snatched it up and carried it over to the growing pile of plunder on the floor. Before he could set it down, however, Failend stopped him with a hand on his elbow. She said something, soft, and reached for the box. Harald frowned, held it tighter, glanced over at Thorgrim.

Thorgrim nodded. Harald offered up the box and Failend carried it over to the altar and set it down. She flipped the lid open and reached into the box and extracted a white silk cloth on which rested some object Thorgrim could not identify. She spoke to Harald in a whisper.

"She says this is a thing they call a 'relic,' and it's of no value to us, but much value to the Christians," Harald said. "She says we can take the box, but there's no reason to take the relic."

Thorgrim stepped over to the altar. He pulled the silk aside. Resting on the cloth was what looked to him to be a few bones from a human hand, but very old, dried and brown. He looked over at Failend, saw the pleading in her big, brown eyes. He flipped the silk back over the bones and nodded.

Harald put the small silver chest with the other things. That was all there was to find in that part of the church, and the pile was already big enough that Harald had some difficulty wrapping it up in the linen robe, lashing it closed, and hauling the makeshift sack down to the center of the church.

The others were there with their own sacks, some nearly as full as Harald's, some less so, but all bulging with riches.

"Well done," Thorgrim said.

"Like stealing from a sleeping man," Thorodd Bollason said. "We'll be gone before they even know we were here."

Oh, don't say that, Thorgrim thought. *Don't taunt the gods that way.*

And then, like a messenger sent by Odin himself, Vali came through the side door, moving as fast as the need for quiet would allow.

"Thorgrim," he hissed. "There are men coming. Many men. They're armed. And they're coming this way."

Chapter Ten

A large band of wicked men…had been plundering the territories in the manner of the heathens.
Annals of Ulster

There was no need for Thorgrim to tell the others what to do. They already knew.

The plunder had been wrapped and tied into five white bundles and set on the floor. Now these were hefted up over shoulders and the Norsemen followed Vali out the door and into the night.

"Where?" Thorgrim whispered.

"There," Vali said, pointing toward the front of the church.

"Stay here," Thorgrim said to the others. He and Vali moved fast toward the front end of the great stone building, keeping to the shadows near the wall. They found Armod at the corner, down on one knee, peering at the grounds beyond. He stood and stepped back as Thorgrim approached.

"There, Thorgrim," he whispered. Thorgrim leaned an inch beyond the building's edge. There were men moving across the open ground, more than a dozen for certain. Thorgrim thought at first these might be Cónán's men, who were apparently not too keen on plundering a Christian holy place, but happy enough to stand guard.

But these were not Cónán's men, Thorgrim could see that. They carried shields, which Cónán's men and his own did not. Thorgrim could not tell in the dark if they wore mail, but they seemed to have helmets on their heads, another thing the fast-moving raiders had opted to leave behind.

What was it that alerted them? Thorgrim wondered. *Was it my dropping that cursed door?* If so, they had reacted swiftly. He doubted five minutes had passed since the door had hit the stone floor. He wondered if maybe there were armed men kept at the ready, men Louis did not know about. Or men that Louis did know about, but had failed to mention.

Whoever these men were, they were advancing quickly but cautiously, strung out in a line with a few feet between each of them and making for the front of the church. They knew that the Norse raiders were here, somewhere, and they had come to stop them.

"We don't want this fight," Thorgrim whispered. "Let's go." He led the way back to where the others waited by the door. "Armed men," he told them. "About twenty, coming toward the church."

"Where's that Irishman, Cónán, and his lot?" Armod whispered. "Thought they were supposed to be looking out."

"I don't know," Thorgrim said, though he had been wondering the same thing, and wondering if he and his men had been betrayed. Again. "And I don't care right now. We need to be gone."

He looked around. They could not go back the way they had come, they would run right into the blades of the advancing men-at-arms. So they would have to move off in the other direction, keeping the church between them and the soldiers for as long as they could.

"This way, let's go," Thorgrim said. He headed off at a jog toward the far end of the church, which screened them as they moved away from the advancing men. Behind him, he heard the other men and Failend hurrying along. Five robes full of plunder hung over the men's shoulders and they made a soft jingling sound as they ran, a sound that seemed as loud as a bell announcing their presence.

They kept to the shadows as much as they could until they reached the far end of the church, the edge of their shelter. Beyond that, between them and the wall, was a hundred feet of open, moonlit ground. Thorgrim looked back in the direction they had come. He could see no one, none of the men-at-arms who were hunting for them, which meant they were still on the other side of the church. He wondered if they would play it safe and stay together, or be smart and spread out so they could cover all the grounds.

He pointed toward the wall east of them. "We'll get there as fast as we can, get up and over," he whispered. If the hunters kept to the front of the church, then he and his men would be hidden from view as they crossed the open ground.

He took a step toward the distant wall and felt a hand grab his shoulder. He turned and Failend was there, looking up at him. She spoke in a whisper, the words quick and urgent.

"She asks if you mean to go over the wall there," Harald said.

Thorgrim nodded and Failend spoke again.

"She says that wall runs along a gully, it drops twenty feet straight down on the other side."

In his mind Thorgrim shouted in frustration, but he kept his lips pressed together and considered what next to do. But Failend was speaking again and pointing to her right.

"She says there's a door in the wall, there, and it leads to a garden. There's a wall around the garden, but we can get over that," Harald said.

Thorgrim nodded. They would be in the open as they raced for the door, the church no longer hiding them. But if they ran in any other direction they would just be going further into the monastic grounds, moving directly away from their line of escape.

"Very well," Thorgrim said to the others. "We go for the door to the garden." In the patchy moonlight and the deep shadows Thorgrim could not actually see a door, so Failend would have to lead the way, and Thorgrim could only hope that she was not wrong and not betraying them. He turned to her and nodded his head in the direction she had indicated. She nodded her understanding, glanced back toward the front of the church, then took off running.

Failend was fast, like a rabbit, Thorgrim thought as he followed behind. It took only a dozen paces for him to realize she could easily leave him in her wake if she so chose. Behind him he heard the others also running flat out, the mail and the plunder and the weapons making a soft sound as they moved.

It took seconds to cross the open ground, no more. As they came up with the wall Thorgrim could see the door at last, a small wooden affair, the height of a man, set into the stone and surrounded by vines and leaves that made it seem like part of the shadows in the night.

Failend came to a stop, glanced back over her shoulder, and then lifted the latch. The door was partway open by the time Thorgrim and the others reached her. They slowed their pace, keeping as quiet as they could, quiet enough that they could not be heard from the far side of the church, or so Thorgrim hoped. But he was wrong.

The shout came just as Failend was pushing the door open and stepping through, a loud cry that carried with it notes of warning and surprise. There was a pause, another cry, and then the night was filled with noise as someone called out orders in the Irish language. From the grounds at the front and side of the church men came running with no effort made at caution. There was no longer any need for caution.

"Go! Go!" Thorgrim shouted. He stepped aside, pointed toward the open door, drew Iron-tooth as he turned to watch the men-at-arms advance. They were coming at a run, their approach a disorganized rush, which might have been fatal to them if Thorgrim's men had been in a position to put up much of a fight. But the Northmen were outnumbered, loaded down with plunder, and they had no helmets or shields.

The nearest of the men-at-arms was no more than fifty feet away when the last of Thorgrim's men dashed through the door and Thorgrim turned and followed him through. He pushed the door closed behind him and saw there was no latch on the inside. He cursed. A latch might have bought them the few seconds they would need to get over the garden wall and away.

Thorgrim turned and raced into the garden. It was about one hundred feet on either side, enclosed by a stone wall like the rest of the monastery. Paths cut through the grounds at right angles and were intersected by others that formed concentric circles, with a great granite cross at the center. Between the paths were stands of vegetation, no more than dark shapes in the night, and a few statues that stood like guards scattered throughout the place, robed figures of men and women staring serenely toward their unwelcome visitors.

Failend was shouting something and pointing to a place on the wall at the far side of the garden. Thorgrim nodded and Failend took off at a run once more and the others behind her, and then Thorgrim heard the door behind him swing open.

No easy escape for us, he thought. He spun around in time to meet a sword coming down at his head. He raised Iron-tooth, knocked the sword aside, kicked the assailant hard in the stomach, driving him back into the man behind him. They stumbled, both of them, and Thorgrim turned and dashed after the others.

Failend had reached the wall, with Godi right behind her. Godi threw his bundle over, grabbed up the next and threw that as well. But Thorgrim knew they would not be able to get over the wall, not all of them, before the Irish were on them. And that would not do. Either they all got over the wall, or none of them did.

"Too late!" Thorgrim shouted. He could hear the Irishmen at his heels, no more than fifteen feet behind him. "Turn and fight! Turn and fight!"

As he shouted those words he did exactly that, digging his foot into the ground to stop his forward momentum, spinning around, sword up. He could see the look of surprise on the face of the man behind him, but the soldier still had the presence of mind to raise his shield and deflect the blow from Iron-tooth that was aimed at his neck.

Thorgrim leaned to the side, stuck out his leg as the Irishman kept coming. The man's ankle caught Thorgrim's and he went down, face first, landing with an audible thud. Thorgrim could hear the breath knocked from his chest, but he did not wait to see what he or the man behind him would do. He turned and continued on at a run, charging for the wall, even as his men abandoned their attempt to get over and turned with weapons drawn.

A statue stood just to Thorgrim's left, the size of a real man and standing atop a four-foot pedestal, an imposing figure in granite. Thorgrim took three steps and grabbed the statue with his left hand, using it to check his flight and to swing himself around so he was facing his pursuer, the statue between them.

The Irishman paused, sword and shield ready. He was a young man but had the look of a warrior. It was dark, but from what Thorgrim could see there was no fear on his face, no uncertainty. He leaned left, right, then lunged as Thorgrim appeared around the statue's stone-carved robes.

Thorgrim ducked back, lunged from the other side of the statue, but the soldier was fast and he caught the sword with his shield. The Irishman leapt forward, hoping to reach Thorgrim with the point of his weapon, but Thorgrim continued to sidestep around the statue, moving right as the man-at-arms moved left in their weird circling dance.

The Irishman lunged again and Thorgrim twisted out of the way. He twisted back and took a big, ugly swipe at the man, one meant to make him leap in the opposite direction, which obligingly he did. Thorgrim spun around and lunged, backhand, from the other side of the statue, catching the Irishman in the shoulder just as he thought he was ducking clear. Thorgrim felt the tip of Iron-tooth pierce mail and he heard the Irishman shout, more in surprise than pain, and leap back. He was wounded, but not terribly. There was fight in him still.

As the man stumbled away from Thorgrim's blade, Thorgrim half turned and looked around the garden. There were ten individual fights spread out over the enclosed area, his own men each taking on two or more of the enemy, using the statues and the garden beds as cover. He could see blades blinking in the moonlight, could hear the grunt of men putting all their bodily strength into sword strikes and wielding their shields in defense.

Failend had joined in the fray. She was at Godi's side and the two of them were fending off the attack of two of the men-at-arms. It was almost comical, the massive Godi and the diminutive Failend, but she was quick and able to keep out of the way of the Irish swords, able to distract the men-at-arms. She did not have proficiency enough to be an immediate threat to her attackers, but neither could they ignore her. She certainly was capable of driving her seax into an undefended neck or thigh.

This would not last long, and Thorgrim knew it. There was no way for him or his men to get over the wall without being hacked down in the process, and no way they could fight for long against these odds. Already the man Thorgrim had been fighting was coming back at him, his wound not severe enough to put him down. Another was coming to his aid.

Then the night was split by a wild scream, a banshee shriek. Terrible. Thorgrim felt the hair stand up on his neck. The wail came from the monastery grounds, not the garden. It seemed to freeze everyone where they stood, and Thorgrim thought, *This is either Cónán come to help us or the Valkyrie come to take us away.*

In either case, he knew the fighting would be over soon.

Chapter Eleven

He hath need of his wits who wanders wide,
aught simple will serve at home
Hávamál

Cónán was around nine years old when his parents died. They died writhing on their pallets, clutching their stomachs and moaning. Three of his seven siblings went that way as well, all within a week. No one knew what exactly had killed them and few really cared.

Cónán cared. He feared there was some evil spirit that had come for the family. But he also had greater, more immediate concerns. Such as how he might survive.

That worry gained greater urgency a week later when the local rí túaithe sent his men to drive Cónán and his remaining brother and two sisters from their home. It was just a miserable wattle and thatch hut on the three acres of swampy, rush-covered land the family farmed. But with the parents dead there would be no more farming, and thus no more paying rent, and so the remnants of the family had to go.

The children stuck together for a while, but one incident after another split them off until Cónán was alone. It was then that he fell in with a clutch of outlaws, men and women who forged their living in any way they could. The life was hard, ugly, generally short. But it was not a solitary life. Being part of the outlaw band meant being part of something. Not a family, but close.

And, hard as it was, it was not the miserable existence that his parents and grandparents and ancestors on back beyond memory had lived, toiling without respite, laboring to enrich the rí túaithe in exchange for no more than the opportunity to survive, if only for a while.

Cónán was powerless, a boy among men, and treated with the casual brutality that was the lot of any child in such circumstance. But he was suited for the outlaw life, the way a shark is suited to the sea. He grew strong and agile and he could endure extraordinary punishment. That, of course, was true of anyone who survived as a bandit for more than a few months. But he was also smart, which was a trait much less common.

He moved easily between various outlaw bands, even joined with a crew of Norsemen for a while and learned their ways. He came to know nearly all the itinerant criminals in that part of Ireland, and came to know the countryside well, which was as important to survival as cunning and skill with weapons.

And the local rí túaithe and their house guards knew him—and wanted him dead. But he always remained just beyond their reach.

The outlaw bands organized themselves like wolf packs. Outsiders were treated with suspicion. Proving one's self was a long and generally bloody affair. Chiefs led their men through strength first, and cleverness second, and if they showed weakness they were torn apart. All this Cónán came to understand. He learned how to position himself in the pack. As a result, he was in just the right place to goad his former chief into a stupid fight with the Northman, and then step in and take command even as the dumb ox's blood was still running out on the sand.

Cónán was leader now. And he liked it. But leading a band of outlaws had its own problems, one of which was about to become wickedly clear.

He stood in the shadows in the narrow space between two of the small wattle and daub buildings that served as both workshop and home and made up most of the monastic town of Glendalough. His feet were half sunk in some viscous ooze that might have been mud. He was motionless, absolutely motionless. He could hear the tiny sounds of the night, but nothing else. Nothing was moving save the rats rooting around in their hidden places.

His men were secreted and spread out fifty feet in either direction. In the off chance that some townsman was out at that hour, a gang of twenty-five men milling about would cause immediate alarm, even if their weapons and mail were hidden. So he placed his men in alleys and in the shadows of houses and hidden behind fences. They were ready to move at a word, and until then they would remain out of sight.

He had left two men at the wall to keep an eye on what was going on within the monastic grounds and to sing out if the Northmen were discovered and needed help. Otherwise they would all stay put until Thorgrim and his men returned with the plunder.

Cónán, however, kept moving, stepping silently through the alleys and the muddy, beaten yards, speaking softly to his men. He listened for any disturbance, any little sign of trouble. Nothing. The night was still. Thorgrim and his heathen crew, he hoped, were silently and unobtrusively stripping the church of anything of value.

He stepped out from between the houses and toward the wall that surrounded the monastery. He could just make out the looming bulk of the church a couple hundred feet away. He rested his hands on the top of the wall, which came up to just below his chin, and looked over it. Nothing moved that he could see. He had been to Glendalough a dozen times, half of those in the dark hours of night. Things looked no different now than they had then.

He turned and walked along the wall, making his way to the place where he had left two of his men, Fothaid and Cerball, to keep watch on the grounds. Those two were as reliable as any in the outlaw band, which was not saying much. That was why Cónán felt the need to keep his eye on all of them.

He ran his hand along the rough stone wall as he walked, his eyes sweeping the dark, his ears keen. He expected some soft challenge from Fothaid or Cerball as he approached, some indication of their vigilance, a sign that they were at least alert enough to notice anyone who might come up behind them and slit their throats. But he heard nothing.

Another fifty feet and he was all but certain he had reached the spot where he had left them with strict instructions to keep their eyes trained over the wall. But there was no one there. Cónán looked at the ground, but it was too dark to see if there were any footprints that might indicate where they had gone.

He looked up, turned in a half circle, and began to question whether he was in the right place when he heard a sound behind him, a small noise, but not a rodent noise. He turned fast, crouched, and his hand came up from his side with his dagger held lightly in his fingers.

Two men. He could see them, just dim outlines, coming through the shadows in the fenced-off yard behind a house ten yards away. He moved quickly to his left, pressed up against a stack of peat, and knew he would be invisible in the dark. He waited. The two came closer, moving as if they had no worries at all. As they stepped into the dull moonlight Cónán could see the faces of Fothaid and Cerball. They were smiling. Pleased with themselves. Cerball held a sack filled with something. Something heavy.

Cónán remained motionless as they passed, then stepped up behind them, making no sound. His left hand lashed out and clapped over Fothaid's mouth and he jerked the man back as he pressed the dagger against his throat. He saw Cerball turn, eyes wide, but he had sense enough to not make a sound.

"You stupid bastard, I ought to gut you like a fish, right here," Cónán hissed in Fothaid's ear. "I told you to stay put and keep watch." Fothaid said nothing, the needle point threatening to pierce his throat. Cerball's mouth opened and closed, which, ironically, made him appear very fish-like.

"There's nothing to see, there, over the wall," Cerball protested, finding his voice. "And those damned heathens don't need watching. But that over there, that's a blacksmith's shop. And you should see what we found in there!" He held up the sack for Cónán's inspection, a dumb and happy smile on his face.

Cónán let Fothaid go. The man stumbled away, beyond the reach of Cónán's dagger, and put a hand to his throat as if checking to see if it was unscathed. "I don't give a damn what junk you found in that filthy smith's shop," Cónán said, as loud as he dared. "By God, if…"

He got no further with his threat. Someone was shouting from somewhere beyond the wall, the words in Irish, and clear as the water of the Avonmore.

"There! There! At them!"

Cónán looked over the wall and felt his stomach twist. Men-at-arms. While he had been dealing with Fothaid and Cerball the warriors had crossed the grounds to the church, and now they had discovered Thorgrim and his band and they were going after them. Which meant that Cónán and his men, who had agreed to keep watch, had failed completely.

Cónán lifted the dagger, pointed it at Fothaid and then Cerball. "You'll regret this, I'll make sure of it," he said. "Now go and get the others before I kill you here and now."

The two men nodded and ran off in either direction, keeping well clear of Cónán in case he faltered in his restraint.

Stupid, stupid bastards! Cónán thought. He had no great love for Thorgrim and his band, but he could not stand to appear wanting in the eyes of another warrior, or have another think he had failed to keep his word for whatever reason.

Besides, Thorgrim and his heathens must have finished looting the church by now, which meant they had the plunder. If they were taken or killed, all this effort would be for naught.

The need for secrecy was passed, so Cónán climbed up on the wall and stood. He could hear yelling and men running, the clatter of weapons off in the dark. He could see nothing. Whatever was happening was hidden from his view by the church.

Behind him he could hear the sounds of his own men running to join him. They, too, had realized there was no need for quiet. He heard them calling out and trampling fences and knocking obstacles out of the way as they ran.

"Come on! With me!" Cónán shouted. He leapt from the wall, came down on the soft ground beyond, and heard the sound of his two dozen men following behind. He stood and ran off, toward the sound of fighting men. He could hear the clash of swords now, the thump of blades on shields, the shouts of warriors in combat. It was a sound he knew, but not well. This sort of fighting was the province of men-at-arms and raiders from the north, not outlaws. Not men used to striking fast and then disappearing.

The shouts and the clatter of weapons came louder as he raced over the open ground, the dark, hulking church to his left, the wall that enclosed the monastery running in a curved line one hundred feet to his right. He came around the side of the church expecting to see two dozen men locked in battle, but there was only the open ground. He could hear the fighting as loud as if it were right in front of him, but he could see nothing, and he felt a sudden fear wash over him. It was like an army of spirits were doing battle, engaged in a fight that was not for the eyes of mortal men.

"Jesus, Mary and Joseph," Cónán whispered as he slowed to a stop and the men behind him did the same. And then he realized he was being a fool, that there was some other explanation for this. He ran his eye along the wall and stopped at a dark patch of vines and brush. The sounds seemed to come from there, and as he stared he realized it was not only vines, but that the vines framed a door in the wall, and the fighting was taking place on the other side of the door.

He felt a rush of thoughts and they all collided in a great tangle: embarrassment at his senseless fear of spirits, rage at Fothaid and Cerball, and at himself, for letting this happen, suspicion that Thorgrim had been trying to sneak out another way and leave them behind.

He pushed all that aside and drew his sword. The weapon felt a bit awkward, unfamiliar. He had fought with nearly every sort of thing that could kill a man, from a club to a bow and arrow, but the sword was one of the least familiar to him. But he was getting used to it. And he liked it.

"This way, this way!" he shouted, raising the sword and breaking into a run again, his eyes fixed on the door in the wall. He let out a scream, one that he saved for these moments, an unearthly cry he had practiced over and over, out of earshot of the others. He had perfected it to the point where he knew it would turn a man's bowels liquid with the hearing.

He could see through the door now, could see there was some sort of garden beyond and more walls. Ten feet away, and he could see men in the garden, weapons drawn, fighting. He could see shields and he knew those were not Thorgrim's men, they were trained men-at-arms. And he knew that his own men, unaccustomed to such fighting, would not be able to stand up to them in single combat.

Surprise, Cónán thought. *Surprise them and overwhelm them.* That was the reason for the scream: to frighten, to confuse, to put the fear of Satan and his minions in the hearts of the men they were about to attack.

Cónán burst through the door and into the garden, taking in the situation as he ran, never faltering in his forward drive. Men with shields—they numbered far more than Thorgrim's band. Northmen fighting for their lives. Statues. A wall holding them all in.

He shrieked again and ran at the nearest man and had a glimpse of Thorgrim Night Wolf half hidden by a statue. Cónán lowered his shoulder and barreled into the man-at-arm's shield. Cónán was not a big man, not nearly as big as the man with whom he collided, but he was moving fast and he was braced for the impact, and the other man was not. Cónán hit him and grunted and the other man grunted louder as he was knocked clean off his feet, flying back, shield airborne. Cónán stepped on his chest as he charged on, slashed at the man with his sword, felt the blade hit, but did not think he had done him any hurt. No matter.

Surprise…overwhelm them…

There was another man-at-arms, two more, fighting with the big Northman. And Failend. Failend was there too, the Irish girl whose presence, indeed whose very existence, Cónán could hardly understand. No peasant, judging by her speech. Running away with the Frank. No reason for her to come on this raid, and yet she had.

She and the big man were fending off the men-at-arms, and they looked like a bear and a cat fighting side by side. Cónán shouted and one of the men-at-arms turned and the big Northman lashed out with his fist. He hit the man right where his neck joined his shoulders. The force of the blow sent him reeling forward and Cónán had to leap clear to avoid getting tangled with him as he fell.

Cónán spun around. The rest of his men were in the garden now, spreading out, going after the men-at-arms, swords swinging wildly, every lesson that they had been taught over the last week completely discarded as they slashed and hacked. They would all have been dead inside five minutes if the men-at-arms had not been knocked on their heels by the shock of the sudden attack.

But Cónán's plans, such that they were—surprise, overwhelm the enemy—were working as well as he had hoped. And none of Thorgrim's men were down, killed or wounded, as far as he could see.

We might actually get away with this, he thought. *Despite Cerball's and Fothaid's stupidity, we might get away.*

The men-at-arms, whoever they were, were clustering at the far end of the garden. It was the natural reaction to a surprise attack such as this: gather forces, seek safety in combined strength. Like a herd of deer set on by wolves. And the Northmen and Cónán's men were doing the same, running and stumbling and limping toward the wall at the garden's far end.

Cónán turned to Thorgrim. "This is our chance. Only chance we get," he said. "Over the wall with all of us, and let's be gone."

Thorgrim nodded. Sweat was running down his face and threads of his long, dark hair were plastered to his skin. "All of you, over the wall!" he shouted, "Up and over, quick!"

Cónán turned to his men and shouted the same, and thirty-five men and the odd Irishwoman put hands on the wall, hoisted themselves up, and dropped to the other side. To Cónán's surprise there was one man already there, one who had gone over the wall before any order had been given: Louis the Frank.

Cónán heard cries of outrage from the men-at-arms at the far end of the garden, on the other side of the wall, but he did not hear them rushing to follow and renew their attack, and that did not surprise him. They had had fighting enough for one night, he guessed.

Thorgrim was there, at his side. He pointed to five sacks on the ground, the cloth so white they seemed to glow in the moonlight. Thorgrim's men were lifting them and hoisting them over their backs. "From the church," he said. "A good haul."

Cónán nodded. "Now we just have to get clear of here," he said.

Thorgrim nodded. "I'm sure you can get us back safe to our ship," he said. "Any man so smart he can suddenly speak the Norse tongue when this morning he couldn't should have no problem with that."

Cónán smiled. He had meant to keep that secret a while longer, but in the chaos of the fight he had forgotten. His second mistake of the night.

"I can't wait to see what surprise you come up with next," Thorgrim said.

"Neither can I," Cónán said. He turned and headed off toward the high ground that surrounded the monastic town of Glendalough.

Chapter Twelve

Less good than they say for the sons of men
is the drinking oft of ale:
for the more they drink, the less can they think
and keep a watch o'er their wits.
Hávamál

Raven Eye was sinking.

She was Ottar's own ship, biggest of the fleet at Vík-ló, and she had water coming in somewhere just aft of the mast step. Her bow was run up on the mud, and when Aghen came down to his shipyard two days after Valgerd's brutal death, he could see she was noticeably down by the stern.

One of Ottar's men had told Aghen the names of the ships, including those that Aghen himself had built and Ottar had renamed. Now, for a long while he just stood there, hating *Raven Eye,* hating them all.

Let the cursed thing sink, Aghen thought. *Let it become a sacrifice to Njord. Let Jörmungandr devour it.*

It was early, the sun just breaking the horizon, and most of the longphort was still sleeping off the night's drunk. Finally, grudgingly, Aghen approached the vessel. He walked slowly, still not certain he was at all interested in her fate. He stepped into the mud and looked over the sheer strake toward the stern. The water was over the deck boards, some of which were floating. *Raven Eye* rocked with each incoming swell, the motion making little waves that swept back and forth over her deck and broke against her rowing benches aft.

Aghen sighed. He did not care about the fate of Ottar's vessel, but neither could he simply let a ship sink there on the riverbank. He did not think the gods would look on him favorably if he did. He was quite certain that Ottar would not.

Still, he felt no hurry about it. And he doubted there were any of Ottar's men who were sober enough or had heads clear enough to get the ship hauled out on rollers so he could begin the work of fixing her. He did not even know if Ottar wished him to mend the leak, or if he had his own shipwright among his men. He did not know if Ottar would allow him to keep his tools.

Aghen sat on the stack of white oak and ate his breakfast, which he had brought down to the river with him, wrapped in a piece of cloth. He chewed on dried fish and bread and looked to the north, at the sea glittering to the bright horizon and the mountains surrounding Vík-ló. The sun climbed higher and the long shadows drew themselves in.

At last he sighed again and stood. *Raven Eye* was down by another strake aft and he knew he had better make someone aware of it. He wiped his mouth with his sleeve and turned and headed up the plank road to the big hall that had once been home to Thorgrim Night Wolf.

Mar was up and about, pumping his bellows to get his coal glowing orange, hot enough to make iron soft for working. Normally, Aghen would have expected a wave, a friendly smile, some ribbing about something or other. But not this morning. Mar did not look up, did not acknowledge the existence of anything beyond his forge. Even from the road Aghen could see the scowl on his face.

Aghen knew that the blacksmith, his friend, was furious. He was furious that the wealth he had accumulated through a decade or more of pounding iron had been taken from him with a single command from the new lord. Mar felt like a trapped animal, set upon, ready to fight, yet with no meaningful way to get at his tormentors. Aghen knew he felt that way because he felt that way himself. Even after all his grand thoughts about dying soon, but not dying badly, he had no idea of what he would do. What he *could* do.

At least Ottar had not taken his tools. Aghen had not offered them up, of course, and Ottar had not called for them again, not after his initial demand. Aghen guessed he had changed his mind or, more likely, lost sight of what he had said in a blinding fog of mead, wine, and ale. Aghen did not feel much compelled to remind him.

He continued on up the plank road, his shadow stretched out on his right-hand side. Shadows were not too common in Ireland. The bright sun that dried the wood and made it easier to work, and made the work easier to see, that warmed old bones and made joints less stiff, would have normally given Aghen a sense of optimism at the start of the day. But he was not optimistic now. He could hardly recall the feeling.

A great blackened circle on the ground still marked the place where Valgerd had died, and Aghen was pretty sure Ottar would never have it cleared away. It served too well as a silent warning. He might refresh it, add more charred wood and flesh to the pile, but he would not have it cleared away.

Aghen moved past the cluster of longhouses and shops where those people who had lived in Vík-ló before Ottar, before even Thorgrim, made their homes, and approached the big halls by the gate. As he did, the longphort began to look more like the aftermath of a battle, and Aghen was put in mind of the hours following the great fight with Grimarr and the Irishman, Lorcan.

Then, as now, there were men strewn about the trampled dirt outside the hall and lying across the plank road. After the fighting, those on the ground had been mostly dead. In truth, some of these men might be dead as well, killed brawling or dead of too much drink. Aghen had seen both, often enough. But most of Ottar's men, Aghen knew, would rise the way Mar's Irish wife said her God did, and unlike the Christ God, they would set in to drinking and fighting again.

He reached the door of the hall and found it was partway open. He looked through, into the dim-lit interior. He could see more bodies tossed around in various odd positions. Ottar, he guessed, must be somewhere among them.

Aghen pushed the door and it swung open an inch more and then stopped. He pushed harder, felt it move reluctantly. He heard a groan and a muted curse from the other side and realized someone had passed out against the door, so he shoved harder until the man cursed again and the door was open enough for Aghen to squeeze his thin frame though.

Ottar was on the raised sleeping platform that lined the far side of the hall, a great heap of flesh and cloth and yellow hair splayed out on the furs spread out there. The place was a cacophony of snores, but still Ottar's made an impressive base note that could be heard above all others.

Aghen crossed the big room. It smelled of smoke and stale drink, roast meat, vomit and piss. Aghen pressed his lips together. He stopped at Ottar's side. He considered shaking him, but he did not think Ottar would take kindly to that, and, more to the point, he couldn't stand touching the man.

"Ottar," he said in a voice just above a whisper. "Ottar," he said again louder.

Ottar stirred but showed no sign of waking. "Ottar!" Aghen said, nearly yelling, but Ottar just groaned and rolled his massive head.

Aghen reached out with his foot and nudged Ottar's shoulder and shouted again. He nudged harder and Ottar stirred and Aghen put his foot down before Ottar's eyes opened and he saw what the shipwright had done.

"Ravens tear your liver out," Ottar muttered as he struggled to open his eyes and prop himself up on his elbows. When he accomplished that, he looked up at Aghen and tried to focus. When he seemed to have some sense of what was happening, he said, "What is it, you whore's son bastard?"

"Your ship," Aghen said. "*Raven Eye*. It's taking on water. Well down by the stern already."

For a long moment Ottar just looked at him, and Aghen could see the focus leaving his eyes. And then he groaned and fell back once again and he did not move.

Well, I told him, Aghen thought. *I've done my part.* He left the hall and walked back to the shipyard, certain that Ottar had not understood his words, and that by end of day *Raven Eye* would be resting on the bottom, half in the water, half out.

But he was wrong on both counts. A few hours later, fifty of Ottar's men, led by Ottar himself, came staggering down the plank road, their pain obvious, and stopped on the trampled grass where the ships were built. They blinked in the sun and wiped tears away and looked at *Raven Eye,* now considerably lower in the water. Ottar began to curse and he kept on cursing for some minutes, and Aghen got the notion that this was not the first time the longship had taken on water.

Finally a dozen men climbed aboard the ship and found scoops and buckets and began tossing water out of her hull, while others roused out ropes and moved rollers under the bow. The ship was nearly free of water by the time the rollers were in place, and with Ottar still cursing, the men hauled away and the longship came slowly out of the river and up onto the land, like some great sea creature heaving itself up on a rock to warm in the sun.

Aghen, despite himself, supervised the placing of chocks and supports and saw the ship secured on the rollers when she was finally hauled out on dry land. He looked under the hull. Water was running out from the place where she had been leaking. It told him a great deal about the problem, and experience told him how it should be fixed.

And then he remembered that he did not want to fix her at all. He wanted her to sink.

"Hey there, shipwright," Ottar said, stepping up behind him, his voice a growl of implied threat. He might have been talking to a servant or a thrall. "You'll fix that." It was not a question.

Aghen straightened, turned, and looked at Ottar. His mind toyed with various responses, but he said nothing. He frowned, held Ottar's eyes.

"I said you'll fix that," Ottar said again. "You'll fix it so it don't leak, unlike the other fools who've worked on it. For your own sake you will. I have not forgotten that you disobeyed me, that you didn't bring your tools to me as I told you. You've seen what disobedience gets you with me. So, you have your tools still. I suggest you make use of them."

Ottar Bloodax did not wait for a reply, since it was clear there was only one reply he would accept. Instead, he turned and walked away and his men followed behind. They left Aghen Ormsson standing by the dripping *Raven Eye*, wrestling with the question of whether or not he should obey Ottar's orders.

He wanted very much to tell Ottar to piss off. He wanted to refuse to work on *Raven Eye*. But, to his profound disgust, he knew he would not. He knew he would make the ship whole again.

And he did. It was not fear of Ottar that served as his chief motivation. Fear did not really motivate him at all, save for the fear of having his tools taken away. It was the ship and the challenge that the leak presented. Ottar Bloodax might be a filthy beast, but *Raven Eye* was not so bad a ship. A bit boxier and high-sided than Aghen preferred, but not a bad ship overall, and one worthy of his attention.

So, the following day, Aghen climbed aboard the now dry vessel and lifted the deck boards and peered down into the bilge until he found the place where the horsehair caulking was spitting out from the planks. There the wood had been fractured in some long-forgotten grounding, where some dull-brained ox playing at being a shipwright had made a clumsy attempt at repair.

Aghen sat for a long while and stared at the injured strakes and saw in his mind the steps he would perform to make it whole again. This, to him, was the real work. Making it all happen in his mind. Once he had done that, then he had only to let his skilled and experienced hands and arms carry out the tasks.

"Aghen? Aghen the shipwright?" The voice came from behind and it made Aghen jump, so lost was he in his thoughts. He turned, scowling. There was a young man standing there, leaning on the sheer strake. He was not far beyond twenty years, Aghen guessed, a profusion of black hair on his head, thick neck, big of arm. Not the smartest-looking fellow Aghen had seen.

"Yes?"

"My name is Oddi. I have some skills working with wood. Ottar sent me to lend a hand with the work."

Aghen frowned. Ottar had not sent this fellow to help, he had sent him to spy, of that Aghen was certain. But Aghen was planning no mischief, so a spy was not a worry for him. What's more, this Oddi looked strong, so if he could be put to work carrying lumber and doing the more mindless tasks with ax and adz, that would make things easier on Aghen.

"All right," Aghen said. "I'll welcome your help." He pointed to a pile of timber. "That is the white oak, there. Find me a board ten feet in length, at least, with a good grain, and set it on the horses."

Oddi nodded and showed not the least hesitation as he hopped down off the roller on which he was standing and ambled over to the stack of wood. Aghen guessed that Oddi was not among Ottar's most prized and trusted men, which was why he had been sent on this task, far removed from the others. And it was possible that Oddi did actually possess some skill as a woodworker.

The next few days proved that to be the case. Oddi was no craftsman. He was more at the level of an experienced apprentice. But he knew the use of ax and adz and saw and drill, and his help went beyond just carrying the heaviest of loads, which, to Aghen's satisfaction, he was also able to do.

More surprisingly, Oddi proved to be a tolerable companion, not overly talkative, but not one who maintained a grudging silence, either. He seemed to enjoy hard work and his mood was generally good, which made for a nice change from the bitter, angry feelings that had engulfed Aghen and Mar and all the others at Vík-ló since Ottar had made himself lord here.

What's more, Oddi never sang the praises of Ottar Bloodax, as a real, devoted follower might be expected to do. He never once regaled Aghen with tales of the man's brave deeds, his wisdom or generosity. That was something Aghen would have found intolerable. But it never happened. Ottar was never even mentioned.

As the days passed, Aghen decided that Oddi was either the worst spy ever, with apparently little interest in finding out what Aghen was up to, or he was the very best, collecting his information while playing at being friendly, slow-twitted, and somewhat bovine in nature. Aghen suspected it was the former. And that led him to realize that Oddi might be able to tell him the tale he burned to hear: that of the last days of Thorgrim Night Wolf.

They were sitting on benches and eating their midday meal when Aghen decided to broach the subject. "So, Oddi," he began. "You were there, weren't you? At the fighting at Glendalough?"

Oddi nodded. He was chewing.

"I had many friends there," Aghen said. "None of them came back. I've never heard what happened."

Oddi swallowed. "Shameful," he said. "By the gods, it was shameful."

"What was shameful?" Aghen said. This did not sound promising. "The way the men from Vík-ló behaved?"

Oddi shook his head. "No, they fought like men. Their lord, that Thorgrim Night Wolf? He seemed a good man. Fought with courage. And the rest of them. And then we just abandoned them."

"How?" Aghen asked. "How do you mean?" Getting information from Oddi was like using an ax to get a thin strake from a thick oak plank: it had to be got at chip by laborious chip.

"We'd been handled pretty rough by those Irish. They fought harder than any of us thought they would, to tell you the truth. So, we had a plan for the last battle. Thorgrim and his men went to one side of the field. Ottar and the rest of us to the other. This was at night, you see. Plan was, at dawn we would all attack. But then, in the dark, Ottar orders us all back to the ships. Leaves Thorgrim and the others there for the Irish to kill."

Aghen was silent as he considered this new and most surprising information.

"Shameful," Oddi offered again.

"But you served Ottar," Aghen said. "You didn't think what he was doing was right?"

"Right? Of course not. None of us did. Well, that's not true. Ottar has his men, the men close to him; they'll do whatever Ottar says and be glad of it. But most of us haven't been with Ottar so very long, and we weren't happy about it. That Thorgrim, he seemed a decent man, and he fought with us, and he fought well. And Ottar just left him and his men to die."

Once more Aghen remained silent as he thought about those words. There was a lot to consider here, a lot of simple things that Oddi had said that carried with them much deeper implications. But there was one, foremost, that Aghen had to pursue.

"So, Ottar made you abandon Thorgrim and his men," he said. "This was before the fighting the next day."

Oddi nodded. "It was in the dark. We snuck off like thieves in the dark."

"So you didn't actually see Thorgrim killed? You didn't see him die?"

Now it was Oddi's turn to consider Aghen's words. "No," he said at last. "We didn't see him at the end. But like I said, those Irish fought like bears, and once we were gone they were many times the number of Thorgrim's men. I don't know how he could have lived."

Because you don't know Thorgrim Night Wolf, Aghen thought.

"I'll tell you someone who's not sure Thorgrim's dead," Oddi went on, "and that's Ottar. He goes on and on about how he killed Thorgrim, but you can tell he's not so sure. He hates Thorgrim, because Thorgrim humiliated him. A few times. And to be honest, I think Ottar's scared of him. Not sure why, but that's how it seems."

Aghen said nothing. He just stared off toward the empty horizon of the sea. He felt as if suddenly everything had been turned on its head.

They finished the day's work and packed the tools away and made their good nights. Oddi lumbered off to wherever he went at the day's end. Aghen, however, remained at the shipyard, the place where he did his best thinking. He paced along the riverbank and sat on the lumber piles as the sun set and darkness washed over the longphort and, finally, a quarter moon rose above the horizon and cast a feeble light on the scene.

Aghen's mind was reeling. So much information, so many new questions. He did not know what to make of it. How he should act on what Oddi had told him, or if he should act at all. The hours slipped past as Aghen turned these thoughts over and over like flotsam in the surf.

The moon had climbed quite a bit higher, bright enough to make shadows on the ground, when Aghen realized he was not alone by the river's edge. There was something a ways off but moving closer. He could sense it more than hear it. It might have been a person, but he did not think so. It seemed to be something else.

He looked around, turned left and right, peered into the dark. He could see nothing, and he was about to dismiss the feeling as an old man's imagination when he heard a sound, low and grating, like something heavy being dragged over stone. A growl.

He swung around in the direction of the sound and now he could make out a dark shape moving low to the ground, moving with deliberate care. A hunter on the prowl.

Aghen took a step back and stood absolutely still. The shape continued to advance toward him, silent, save for the low and menacing sound it made. Aghen took another step back and with a sudden burst of power the thing leapt. Aghen gasped, twisted, held his arms up, ready for the impact of the body, the sharp agony of teeth or claws in his flesh. But he heard the thing hit the ground, only a few feet away. He could smell its feral scent, hear its snarling.

He opened his eyes. It was a wolf. Crouched, ready to leap again, the growl building in its throat until the sound seemed like a physical thing. Aghen could see the wicked teeth in the moonlight, the gleam of its brutal eyes. The wolf looked up at him, looked right into his eyes. They stood there, motionless, both tensed like drawn bows, both ready to move. Aghen felt the fear welling up inside. He had a vision of his throat ripped clean out by this beast; it could do it before Aghen had time to take a single step. He clenched his teeth, waiting for it.

The growling built in the wolf's throat, louder and louder, until Aghen thought they surely must be able to hear it at the far end of the longphort. He curled his fists, wondered if he could fight off the attack when it came. And then the wolf turned and with two powerful leaps he was gone, swallowed up by the dark, his flight making no sound at all.

For a long time Aghen remained where he was, motionless, teeth and fists clenched, his eyes fixed on the place where the wolf had disappeared into the night. His mind was washed clean of any thought. He just stared.

Then, slowly, his mind came back to the shipyard, the longphort. A word formed in his head, a single word, and it seemed to block out any other thought.

Kveldulf, he thought. *Night wolf.*

Chapter Thirteen

I love not the gloomy waters
Which flow past my dwelling
The Annals of Ulster

Lochlánn looked left and right, his breathing labored, his mind reeling, the ring of weapons striking weapons loud in his ears. He felt his stomach turn over. *Trap*, he thought. *I took my men right into a damned trap…*

The Northmen had lured them into this garden, a tight, walled-in space like a fishing weir. Lochlánn had gone in after them, leading his men against what he thought was an outnumbered and fleeing enemy. They were besting the fin gall, or so it seemed. And then the other half of the heathen band had rushed in behind, and Lochlánn's men were caught between them.

The idea that he had been played for a fool, that he had led his men to their deaths, was the most hideous of realizations for Lochlánn mac Ainmire. Much worse than the possibility of his own death, which did not even occur to him. Brother Lochlánn, well aware of his scant years and his lack of experience, was, of all things, most terrified of being found wanting in his new life as a soldier.

"Men of Glendalough, to me, to me!" he called in as big a voice as he could find. "To me!"

The fight in the garden had quickly turned to a dozen individual duels. That was fine as long as he and his men were overwhelming the heathens, but now they weren't. The second wave of Northmen had come howling through the door. Their battle cries sounded Irish, but they carried swords and wore mail and so Lochlánn knew they were not Irish. Only Irish men-at-arms who served a wealthy lord had those things, and such men did not join with heathens.

"To me!" Lochlánn called again, and Senach added his voice, echoing Lochlánn's orders. One by one the men-at-arms broke off the fighting and backed away and soon all of them who could still move were standing at the wall directly across the garden from the heathen raiders.

"Make a wall! Shield wall!" Lochlánn called next and the men came together quickly, shields overlapping, swords held ready. If they could make a shieldwall, Lochlánn thought, and stand firm, backs to the garden wall, then they might put up enough of a fight to make the heathens give up their attack.

He never had the chance to find out. No sooner had they formed their defense than the heathens hoisted themselves up onto the far garden wall and dropped to the ground on the other side. They were nearly twice the number of Lochlánn's men, but they seemed to have no fight left in them.

I guess it wasn't a trap, Lochlánn thought, and he felt the relief hit him like a blast of hot air from an oven.

It was quiet, very quiet, like a garden was supposed to be when it wasn't filled with dozens of men trying to kill one another. Lochlánn could hear the blood pounding in his ears and his own breathing, which was very loud.

"After them?" It was Senach who spoke, and he spoke in a whisper, which seemed appropriate for some reason.

"No, wait…" Lochlánn said. His relief notwithstanding, he still thought this might be a trap of some sort, and he was not going to have his men fling themselves over the wall and onto the upraised swords of the enemy.

"Follow me," he said. He moved across the garden, his pace just short of a jog. He stopped five feet from the wall where the heathens had gone over and listened. Nothing. He stepped up to the wall, put his hands on the top and pulled himself up. There was nothing to see on the other side, nothing but the dim outline of a few houses and the hills off to the east. The heathens were gone.

Lochlánn dropped back down into the garden where his men stood with lowered shields and the points of their swords resting on the ground. That great surge of energy that came with battle was draining off. Lochlánn could feel it in himself, could see it on the faces and postures of his men. But it was his duty as captain to keep them going, despite their waning sense of purpose.

"We can still run them down," he said. "They're on foot, I would think. We have horses." He gestured to a portion of the men standing to his left. "You lot, see to the wounded. Take any back to Colman's house. Then gather up the weapons, shields, all those things we set aside. We go tonight. Right now. The rest of us will get the horses and meet you at the house, and then we ride."

He stopped. No one moved.

"Go, now," Lochlánn said, suddenly afraid they would not obey, not sure what he would do if that happened. But it didn't happen. They all moved at once, and they moved with resolve. Their sense of urgency might have gone, but they still obeyed when Lochlánn spoke.

Lochlánn brought ten men with him, which he figured was all he would need. This was the moment for which they had spent the last week or more preparing, the moment when they would ride out in search of the heathens. They had thought they would leave at their own time, not one that the heathens forced upon them, but such would not be the case.

They skirted the church, came around the far end. There were figures moving toward them, just discernable in the moonlight, a dozen or so and walking fast. Seeing them, realizing who they were, Lochlánn understood that he and his men might not be leaving at all.

"Who's that? Who's there?" Lochlánn heard the rough, irascible voice of Brother Gilla Patraic, the oldest of the monks, whose charge included keeping the brothers in line so that the abbot would not be bothered by their petty squabbles.

The two groups closed on one another, the men-at-arms and the monks. As far as Brother Gilla Patraic knew, these armed men could be the heathens, come to kill them all. But he seemed not to care. Brother Gilla Patraic was the sort who would try to defeat the Northmen with a tongue lashing, and might well do so.

"Brother," Lochlánn said as they drew close enough to see one another. Some of the monks were carrying staffs and others pitch forks. One had a scythe. Lochlánn tried not to laugh.

"Brother Gilla Patraic," Lochlánn began again, "the heathens have been here, we—"

"We heard some goings-on," Gilla Patraic interrupted, then looked Lochlánn up and down, as if just seeing him. "Brother Lochlánn, what is this? Why are you wearing these…things? I did not give my blessing for this. I—"

It was Lochlánn's turn to interrupt. "The heathens have sacked the church and now they're getting away with their plunder. I said we should not let the men-at-arms break up the dúnad until we knew the heathens were gone. Now"—he gestured to the armed men behind him—"these men and I will ride after them and…"

"You'll ride after them?" Brother Gilla Patraic stammered, as if Lochlánn had suggested they would take wing and fly in pursuit. "You'll do no such thing! You are only a novitiate, and under discipline. How can you think to dress like a man-at-arms without my leave? Is this the work of that renegade, Brother Louis?"

Brother Louis… Lochlánn had all but forgot about him in the madness. He had not seen him in the garden, and yet Trian had said it was Louis who had sent the boy with the warning. He wondered if he should tell Brother Gilla Patraic any of this. But he did not get the chance.

"Brother! Brother!" It was Brother Echach, running from the direction of the church. "They've taken everything, Brother Gilla Patraic," he huffed, slurring the name into a single word as he came to a stop. His face looked paler than usual in the moonlight. He was sweating.

"The heathens!" Brother Echach gasped. "They've taken everything! The altar service, the candlesticks. They ripped the door off the tabernacle!"

Brother Gilla Patraic's face was a mask of fury. He made the sign of the cross. "The host?" he asked. "Did they desecrate the host?"

Brother Echach frowned. "No, actually," he said, confusion evident. "It seems not. The host was on the altar and seemed untouched. Same with the relic of St. Kevin. The reliquary was gone, but the relics themselves were on the altar."

Louis… Lochlánn thought. That was the only explanation. Louis had stopped the heathens from the worst of the desecration.

"See here, Brother Gilla Patraic," Lochlánn said, forcing himself to sound calm and reasonable when all he wanted to do was push past this old man and be on his way. "As Brother Echach said, the heathens have got away with everything. Everything of value in the church. What you heard was us trying to stop them, but they got away. Now I mean to ride after them. Take back the riches of God's house."

Brother Gilla Patraic frowned. Lochlánn could see that he was wrestling between his desire to get back the property of the church and his unwillingness to give this upstart novitiate free rein. And Lochlánn had a pretty good idea which way the old monk would go.

"Very well, off with you," Brother Gilla Patraic said. "But you be back by nightfall tomorrow, do you understand? If you haven't done slaughter among the heathens by then, then you'll never run them to ground."

"Yes, Brother. Nightfall tomorrow, I'll be back by then," Lochlánn said. At some later time he would have to make a confession of that egregious lie.

He pushed past Brother Gilla Patraic and the other monks with their makeshift weapons and led his men to the stables. They found a lantern, and by its feeble light led the horses out of the stalls and saddled and bridled them. They walked the horses out into the night, which was no longer still. The revelation of the heathen raid had brought chaos to the monastery, bordering on panic. Lochlánn could hear men shouting, doors opening, feet running.

Lochlánn smiled. The danger to Glendalough was passed, the heathens long gone. The attack had been more burglary than raid. He could not recall having ever heard of Northmen doing such a thing. But now he could ride out with the blessings of Brother Gilla Patraic, and not slink away as he had planned, as if he, too, were a thief.

He and his men mounted and rode off, leading the other horses behind them. They passed through the gate in the *vallum*, the low wall that marked the boundary of the monastery's sanctuary, through the gate in the higher, outer wall, and on to the home of the late *Colman mac Breandan. The rest of the men were outside already, with shields, spears, bundles of food and bedding, all the matériel they had amassed for their expedition, piled against the wattle fence that surrounded the house.*

Brother Gilla Patraic might wonder why we need all this for a single day's hunt, Lochlánn mused. They had prepared for a much longer expedition than that. But, in truth, if they met with good fortune, they might well be back by the following evening. Lochlánn felt a tremor of disappointment at that thought, though he did not consider it likely.

The riders dismounted and the men set about loading the food, weapons and gear on the horses while Lochlánn conferred with Senach.

"None in the garden were badly wounded," Senach said. "Those men that were down, they took blows to the head, mostly. They're all right. A few gashes. We bound them up. But all will ride with us tonight."

"Good," Lochlánn said, his feigned nonchalance masking the great relief he felt. As a leader of warriors he knew he must both see to his men's welfare and yet not be shy about sending them to be hurt or killed, if need be. That latter part was a problem. He hoped such indifference would come with age, because he did not see it coming any other way.

They watched for a moment as the others finished their preparations, then Senach turned to Lochlánn again. "How do you mean to find them?" he asked, keeping his voice low. "Not much of a moon tonight..."

"I've thought this through," Lochlánn said, which he had, though he had first decided to hunt the heathens down, and then considered whether or not he could actually do it. "They're strangers to this countryside. They'll have to stay to the road. They won't be able to travel under cover in the dark, not loaded down and armed as they are. Even if Louis is helping them, he does not know this country well. We'll find them on the road."

Senach nodded. He seemed impressed with Lochlánn's certainty. Lochlánn wished he could be as impressed himself.

They mounted and made their way out of town. The road made a dark band across the ground, rising and falling with the rolling land, easy enough to follow in the weak moonlight. They headed east, the last pinpricks of light from Glendalough soon lost from sight. They rode in silence, with just the jingling of the horses' tack and the rhythmic thump of swords and shield and the sound of hooves on soft earth to break the silence.

They found no one.

By the time the first gray suggestions of dawn were creeping into the eastern sky, they had covered six miles or so of road beyond Glendalough and had come across no heathens, not even a sign of heathens. The way was deserted, and Lochlánn had to conclude that he had been wrong.

What mistake he had made he still could not guess. He was sure he was right that strangers like the fin gall would not have been able to move through the trails and sundry paths that ran through the woods. Only hunters and bandits who knew that country could hope to do that. He was sure they had gone east. The heathens who raided the church were the heathens with whom Louis had joined, he knew that for certain, and they would be planning to escape aboard their longship.

What am I missing? Lochlánn wondered. *Where did I guess wrong?*

It did not help his status as captain to make such a mistake, but neither did it help to keep his men in the saddle when they were exhausted and it was clear the heathens would not be found. He called for a halt, let the men sleep in the grass by the side of the road while he himself kept watch. He saw no threat greater than a fox that darted past the sleeping men.

The sun was a few hours up when Lochlánn roused the others and told them to have their breakfast. That done, he picked four men who knew that country best and ordered them to follow the paths that ran along the river and see if they could find any sign of the heathens. He and the rest mounted their horses once more and continued along the road as it ran east and then southeast. On their left hand they caught glimpses of the Avonmore River when the trees along the banks thinned enough to offer a view.

They had stopped and were eating their midday meal when one of the men Lochlánn had sent to scout, a fleet young man named Corcc, came jogging up from the river a quarter mile away.

"We didn't find the heathens," he reported after Lochlánn had allowed him to catch his breath. "But we found where they were."

Corcc led the rest of them back the way he had come, down across the field and into the woods, then over a ford in the river where the water came up nearly to their stirrups. On the far side they plunged into the woods once more, and a mile later came out on a sandbar at a bend in the river, a half acre or more of sand, all but hidden from view in any direction.

Lochlánn climbed down off his horse and walked slowly across the dry ground, which made a soft crunching sound underfoot. It was clear that people had been here, quite a few, that they had been here for a while and had left very recently. A wide, blackened pit showed where a substantial fire had been burning. The center was filled with bits of charred wood, the remains of at least a week's worth of fires, and a thin wisp of smoke still rose from the blackened debris. Beef bones lay scattered around. In various places the sand was disturbed in such a way that suggested tents had been pitched and men bedded down there.

Near the edge of the river Lochlánn found a few lengths of wood, not firewood, but wood that had been worked, smooth boards a few feet in length. He picked one up and examined it. It was fresh cut at both ends, and in the middle a section had been none too delicately hacked out. Lochlánn knew almost nothing about ships and shipbuilding, but he guessed this was one of the boards from the Northmen's ship, one that had been cut through to sink it and now had been replaced.

He tossed the board aside and looked downstream. The heathens had made it back to the river with their plunder and headed off, with the current to carry them to safety.

What was the bastard's name? he thought. Trian had told him, and now he tried to recall. One of those odd heathen names.

Thorgrim. Thorgrim Night Wolf. That was it.

And now he and the rest had disappeared down river. *How long ago?* Not long. That morning, perhaps. Lochlánn doubted they could navigate the river in the dark, so they would have had to wait for the sun to rise.

Can we still catch them? Lochlánn wondered. *How fast can their damned ship go in the river?* He did not know the answer and he doubted that any of the others did, either. Not that he intended to ask. Asking would make him appear unsure.

He tossed the plank aside and walked back to where the rest of the men were waiting. "The heathens have taken to their ship, as you can see," he said. "They can't have left more than a few hours ago, since they can't find their way down river in the dark." He waited for someone to challenge that assumption, but no one did, so he continued. "They have but a few hours head start, by my guess."

He saw heads nodding. "So, we go after them?" Senach asked, a hopeful note in his voice.

"Yes, we go after them," Lochlánn said.

And what do we do when we find them? he wondered. But he knew already.

"We go after them," Lochlánn continued. "We'll find them and then we'll set a trap and we'll kill them all. Stamp them out. Like it should have been done the first time around."

It was the thing to do. It was what Louis de Roumois would have done. That, in Lochlánn's mind, was what made it a good idea, but he knew better than to make that point out loud.

Chapter Fourteen

Let them take pains,
These men of note,
To protect themselves
From Snorri's plots
The Saga of the People of Laxardal

Aghen the shipwright stood to one side and watched Oddi's ax take small bites out of the oak strake he was fashioning. The chips flew like spume from a wave breaking on the rocks.

"Careful, careful there," Aghen warned. "You go too fast and you'll make a bad cut and then you've ruined the whole thing. All that work, and it's just kindling."

"If I go too slow you'll call me a lazy whore's son," Oddi said, never pausing in his ax strokes. There was no malice in his words. The opposite, really. He and Aghen had come to like one another, and their banter was more in the nature of friendly ribbing.

"You *are* a lazy whore's son," Aghen said.

He was quite certain that Oddi was reporting back to Ottar, not because Oddi had any love for Ottar but because he had been ordered to do so. Oddi must be telling the new lord of Vík-ló that the shipwright was being cooperative. In good spirits, even. Aghen had had no word from Ottar, no threats from him or any of the lick-ass men around him. That had to mean Ottar was pleased with the work being done to *Raven Eye*, and the only way he could know that would be if Oddi was telling him.

All of that was good news to Aghen Ormsson. Because it opened up a line of attack that Ottar could not see.

"How is our Lord Ottar these days?" Aghen asked as he applied a whetstone to one of his chisels. "He seems to leave us in peace to do our work."

Oddi shrugged as he wielded his ax. "Ottar is Ottar. Drunk. Mean. He doesn't leave his hall much."

Aghen made a grunting sound. "You said he's afraid still of Thorgrim Night Wolf?"

"I don't know," Oddi said. "That's my guess. I've heard him say the name. Saw him fly into a rage once when one of his hirdmen mentioned him. He claims Thorgrim's dead; he says he made sure of that. He says it like he believes it. But not like he believes it absolutely."

Aghen made another grunting sound and worked in silence for a few minutes. "I saw a wolf the other night," he said at last, speaking the words like an afterthought.

Oddi stopped working and turned toward him. "A wolf?"

Aghen nodded. "Just down by the river. I swear by the gods I thought it would have my throat, but it only snarled at me and then ran off."

Oddi's eyes were wide, his mouth hanging partway open, but Aghen turned back to his chisel and whetstone.

"Just a lone wolf?" Oddi asked. "Do you see such things around here, much?"

"Never have before," Aghen admitted. "I was as surprised as I could be, let me tell you. And I'm not ashamed to say I nearly pissed my trousers at the sight of it."

They were silent again, the only sound the soft swish of Aghen's blade running over the rough stone. Oddi turned back to his work, but before he could make another cut, Aghen spoke again.

"Do you know why Thorgrim is called Kveldulf? Night Wolf?"

Oddi turned toward him, his eyes still wide. He shook his head.

"Some say Thorgrim is a shape-shifter. That when the sun goes down his mood turns foul and he takes on the shape of a wolf." Aghen knew Oddi was staring at him, but he ignored the young man. At last, Oddi managed to find words.

"Do you believe this? Have you…have you seen it?"

"I've seen the foul mood come over Thorgrim. As the sun was going down. He's generally a decent fellow. Not one to talk a lot, but that's a welcome thing. Sometimes at night, though, he grows angry and there's no getting near him. He'll generally go off by himself. Those who have known him the longest, like his son, Harald, they say it was worse in his younger days."

"But you've…never…"

"With these shape-shifters, it's the spirit that leaves the body. If Thorgrim's spirit takes the form of a wolf, I've never seen it. No one has, that I know of. But there are stories. Many stories." Aghen let that hang in the air for a moment before adding, "Ottar is not wrong to be afraid of Thorgrim Night Wolf. Even if he thinks Thorgrim dead."

Oddi nodded dumbly. Finally he turned back to his work.

You make sure to tell Ottar all that I just told you, Aghen thought, and he was confident that Oddi would do just that, because Oddi did not have insight enough to understand what was better kept to himself.

They worked in silence for another half an hour and then Aghen put his chisel down. "Well, Oddi, I suppose you're not likely to ruin too much if I leave you alone for a spell," he said. "I must go speak with Mar; I have work for him."

"Mar has work enough," Oddi said. "Ottar has sent him all the spears to be sharpened and told him he must make up arrowheads by the hundreds. For that, he offers to allow Mar to live, no more. No silver."

"Then Mar probably needs some cheering," Aghen said.

He left Oddi to his work and headed up the plank road. He found Mar as Oddi had suggested he would, standing at his anvil and hammering arrowheads from the soft, orange iron he pulled from his forge. He was motionless, save for his arms that seemed to work independent of his body, like limbs on a big oak tree, swaying in the breeze.

"Mar!" Aghen said, coming through the gate. The blacksmith looked up. He did not smile. He stopped his hammering and let his tools hang at his side.

"How goes it with you, friend?" Aghen asked. Mar, not the most talkative in the best of times, made no reply, and that was answer enough.

"See here, I need something from you," Aghen said, stepping closer and speaking low. Mar frowned deeper, but he seemed to perk up at the conspiratorial quality of this.

"Yes?" Mar asked.

"I've had a thought for a new sort of fastener. For securing strakes to one another," Aghen explained. "And I need you to make them. They must be about as long as the end of my finger," he continued, holding his finger up to show Mar. "They must be triangular in shape and notched at the bottom of two sides. And as sharp as you can make them. It's good oak they have to be driven through."

Mar squinted. "This is a way to fasten strakes?" he asked.

"Yes. It's something I've thought of. Might not work, but if it does it will be a great improvement on how we do it now. Can you make them?"

Mar waved a hand at the arrowheads and the bundles of spears stacked up against the wall of his house. "That bastard Ottar sends me this work. He gives me no silver for it, just makes some vague promise he'll pay. And even if he does, it won't be more than a part of what he stole from me already."

"He stole from all of us," Aghen reminded him.

"Yes, but now he steals my labor. And my iron. Arrowheads, spearheads, knives, he has me going all day with these demands. Sharpening swords. There's something going on, he's planning something. Going to attack some sorry bastard. And it's on me to see they have the weapons for it."

The blacksmith was feeling very sorry for himself and Aghen hoped he could ease the man's mind a bit. "And Ottar may yet be made to pay for his crimes," he said. "I saw a wolf the other night."

Mar frowned deeper still at this odd change of course. "A wolf?"

"A wolf. Right down by the river. I thought it would kill me, for sure, but it just growled and ran off."

"What of it?" Mar asked.

"Well, from what I understand, no one here saw Thorgrim Kveldulf killed. Ottar and his men, they left Thorgrim and the rest to be killed by the Irish. But they didn't see it happen."

Mar's eyes widened as Aghen's meaning dawned on him. "Are you saying…do you think…"

Aghen shrugged his shoulders. "I don't know. I'm only saying what I saw," he said. "But please, Mar, make me up my fasteners as fast as you can. If they work out I'll call them Mar's nails and you will be famous as Odin."

He left the blacksmith there and returned to the shipyard, but soon the sun began to drop in the west and he gave Oddi leave to stop work for the day. Once his new assistant had disappeared over the small hill that bordered the yard, Aghen pulled a piece of oak from the pile, a board an inch thick, six inches wide and five feet long. He laid it on a bench and went at it with his saw, cutting it in half, and then clamped one half in place and began to work it with a draw knife and chisel.

He worked until the sun was gone behind the mountains and it was too dark to see. He thought about lighting a fire to work by but decided against it, as a fire in the shipyard might bring someone to investigate. Instead, he hid his work under a stack of scraps and dragged himself back to his small home, his body weary as death, his mind racing like a spooked horse.

He rose before dawn the next day and was back at it as soon as there was light enough. He knew Oddi would not arrive terribly early because he never did, and Aghen hid the work away well before the young man appeared. The two of them spent the day working on *Raven Eye* at something less than a hurried pace. That afternoon Aghen told Oddi he was pleased with his work and wished to show his appreciation by letting him off early. Oddi was too grateful to be suspicious, nor was he suspicious by nature, so it did not occur to him that Aghen just wanted him gone.

Once Oddi had disappeared Aghen again retrieved the oak pieces from their hiding place and chiseled and hammered and drilled until it was too dark to see. He hid them again and headed up the plank road and soon he was knocking on Mar's door. It was opened by Ita, Mar's Irish wife, who welcomed him in.

"People have been talking about your wolf, Aghen," she said, making the sign of the cross as she did. "They don't know what it means. What do you think?"

Aghen shook his head. "I don't know that it means anything," he said. "It was a wolf. An animal. They're no strangers to this country." Aghen, too, had heard people talking about the wolf. A few people had asked him directly, some of the old residents of Vík-ló and even some of Ottar's men. Word was moving through the longphort.

Mar hefted himself up from the bench on which he sat, a small cloth bag in his hand. "Here are your nails, your fancy new nails," he said, handing the bag over. Aghen opened it and lifted out one of the iron points. Triangular, an inch or so long, sharp as a knife.

"That's very well done," Aghen said. "Mar's nails. You'll be famous in every shipyard in the world."

Mar grunted. "My heart's desire," he said.

It took Aghen another day to finish, working with a hammer and chisel on the sleeping bench in his home by the light of the hearth. He worked the oak, and he worked his own resolve as well, keeping it sharp like the chisel, forcing himself to recall Valgerd's death in every brutal detail whenever he felt doubt creeping in. But that was not very often.

The following afternoon, after their day's work, Aghen dismissed Oddi, as he always did. He went back to his home and had his night-meal, which he always did. Then he made his way up to Ottar's hall, which he had not done since the morning he brought the news of *Raven Eye*'s sinking.

Aghen was not at all surprised by what he found there. Vík-ló was not a big place, and the singing, shouting, laughing and fighting that happened nightly could be heard in all corners of the longphort. Aghen was not surprised to find men, drunk and violent men, staggering in and out of the twin halls. A big fire was burning in the pit in which they had killed Valgerd, its tall flames throwing a weird, rippling light around the place, dancing off the walls of Ottar's hall. It reminded Aghen so much of the night Valgerd had been killed he could practically hear the man shrieking.

Aghen waited in the shadows and no one paid him any attention. He marked the faces of the men who came staggering out of the hall. There was no one in particular he had in mind. Nearly any of these bastards would do.

Then he saw his man, the perfect choice. He did not know his name and did not care. But he recognized him as one of those who had shot arrows into Valgerd as he stood bound to the stake. Aghen remembered the man's face and the particular delight he seemed to take in his task.

The man staggered over to the shadows beyond the fire, turned his back to the flames. Aghen could see his arms move as he fumbled with the tie on his trousers. Aghen stepped out of the shadows and over toward where the man stood. He undid his own trousers and the two of them relieved themselves in that dark place.

From the corner of his eye, Aghen saw the man look over at him, then down again, apparently uninterested in who was joining him at the makeshift latrine. He cursed as he clumsily retied the cord on his trousers and was about to go when Aghen stopped him.

"You're one of Ottar's men, aren't you? One of his trusted men?"

The man stopped and looked at Aghen with unchecked suspicion. "I am. I'm one of Ottar's hirdmen. I was with him when he sailed from Hedeby."

"Good. Then you're a man I can trust as well," Aghen said, taking a step closer.

"Trust? With what?" the hirdman said.

"Here's the thing," Aghen said, his voice dropping to a conspiratorial level. "You know the baker? Kalf?"

"Yes."

"Well, I happen to know he's cheating Ottar. When Ottar said we should all put our silver together, Kalf didn't give up all his. He gave up some, but not all. The rest he buried down by the river, near the shipyard. That's how I know."

"You think I should tell Ottar?" the man said.

"No, no!" Aghen said quickly. "That's why I wanted to talk to you. I like Kalf, but I don't like to see him cheating Ottar and the rest of us. If Ottar knows, he'll kill Kalf for it."

The man nodded. "That he would. Like he did the other."

"Exactly," Aghen said. "I don't want that. But I know where Kalf buried the hoard. I thought, if we were to dig it up, you could give it to Ottar and no one would be the wiser."

They stood in silence as Ottar's man worked out the implications of this information. It was clear enough that the man was drunk, stupid and greedy, exactly the traits Aghen was looking for.

"And you know where this silver is buried?" the man asked.

"Yes. Down at the river. Near where the wall of the longphort touches the water. Like I said."

Ten minutes later they came to the place Aghen had described, the lure of this easy stash too much for Ottar's hirdman to resist. The night was dark, but the man had thought to bring a torch, and the guttering flame threw a circle of light bright enough for their needs.

"Here," Aghen said, pointing to a patch of fresh-turned earth two perches distant from the earthen wall that enclosed the longphort.

Ottar's man looked at the dirt, looked at Aghen. "Well, dig it up," he said.

"Let me fetch a shovel from the shipyard," Aghen said. He came back a few minutes later with a shovel and began scooping out the loose dirt. He dug down two feet before the blade made an audible thump against something more solid.

"Is that a chest? Get it out of there!" Ottar's man hissed, even as Aghen was kneeling beside the hole to do just that thing. Aghen reached down and his fingers found a small wooden chest. He pulled it free of the dirt and set it down on the ground and stood.

"Shall I open it?" Aghen asked.

"No, no, get away from it, let me look," Ottar's man said, his eyes fixed on the chest. "Here, hold this," he added, thrusting the torch at Aghen. Aghen took it and held it up as the man dropped to his knees and lifted the lid. He squinted down into the box. He looked up at Aghen.

"Rocks? It's filled with rocks…"

Those were the man's parting words. In one fluid motion Aghen tossed the torch aside, brought the shovel back over his shoulder and swung it with the effortless precision he had developed through hundreds of hours of swinging ship's mauls. The flat of the shovel hit the man on the side of the head and sent him sprawling out on the ground. He did not move. Unconscious or dead, Aghen did not know and did not care. Either would work.

Aghen grabbed up the torch and shoved it in the hole, extinguishing the flames. The weak moonlight would be all he needed. He took the chest and carried it down to the river and dumped the rocks into the water. He set it on the ground and went out into the tall grass to find the new-made tool he had hidden there.

It was an instrument of his own design, the work of his hands and, unwittingly, Mar's. Two long handles fastened together with an iron rivet a third of the way along their length, like an oversized pair of scissors or wooden blacksmith's tongs. The ends of these tongs, however, were carved into elongated triangles, the flat sides opposing one another so it would open and close like a bird's beak. And along the edge of each triangle, securely mounted, were Mar's dagger-sharp nails.

Aghen lifted it from the grass and trotted back to where Ottar's man lay motionless. He took up the shovel and filled in the hole and dragged the man over the turned earth to hide it. He wondered if the shovel blow had killed him, but when he rolled him on his back the man made a soft moaning noise. Aghen was not sure how he felt about that.

He looked down at the man. A week or more of planning, and now the moment had come. The moment he dreaded, the one part of his plan that gave him pause.

And then he remembered the look on the man's face, the twisted smile of delight as he put an arrow in Valgerd's thigh and laughed as Valgerd shrieked with pain.

"Off to Hel with you," Aghen whispered. He pulled the handles of his tool apart and the jaws at the other end opened wide. He plunged it down and felt the row of sharp iron teeth tear into the man's neck, watched as his eyes and his mouth flew open. But before his victim could make a sound, Aghen pushed the handles together and the jaws clamped shut and the teeth tore into the man's neck. His legs kicked and his arms flapped and Aghen wrenched the tool sideways and up, ripping the man's throat out with a gush of blood.

He stepped back and looked at the man in the dim light. He was motionless, the blood dark against his white skin. Aghen could hear his own breathing, fast and shallow. He drew in a deep lungful of air, held it, exhaled, let his breath settle back to normal.

There, he thought. *It's done. Now, let everyone know that the Night Wolf is back, and he's running wild in Vík-ló.*

Chapter Fifteen

[W]ork a ship for its gliding, a shield for its shelter,
a sword for its striking, a maid for her kiss.
Hávamál

The trees on either bank of the river seemed to slip past at a surprising rate. The ship rocked a bit in the current; the oars creaked with their slow rhythm. Failend took it all in. She felt staggered by the wonder of it all.

I am aboard a heathen Northmen's ship, she thought. *I am wearing mail and a sword. I have just helped plunder the church at Glendalough.* She smiled slightly and shook her head. It really was too much to comprehend, like trying to make sense of a dream that had no bonds to the real world.

She sat on the low foredeck facing aft, the place that seemed to be most out of the way of the men working the ship. The other women were there with her, the wives—or whatever they were—of the bandits under Cónán's command. But those women, being Irish, understood that Failend was not one of them, that her place in society was far, far above theirs. Her manner of speaking alone told them that. And so they did not presume to approach her, and she had little intercourse with them.

Instead she sat on the edge of the foredeck, the small chest of silver and gold and jewels beside her, and beside that, Louis de Roumois. They had said little to one another since getting underway. In truth, they had said little since the raid on Glendalough. There had not been much opportunity to talk since then, and Louis was so angry with her that he did not know what to say. She could tell that from the looks he gave her and the few clipped words he spoke.

When they did talk, Failend knew it would not be pleasant. She was not looking forward to it.

But the present circumstances were pleasant enough. More than enough. It was a summer day and warm and not raining. She was floating down the river on this strange ship. She was floating through this strange dream world into which she had plunged.

For some time now her life had not felt entirely real to her. Not since her late husband, Colman mac Breandan, and her lover, Louis de Roumois, had both been called on to defend Glendalough from the heathens. Not since she had contrived to take part in the fighting and had killed the man who, on her husband's orders, had tried to kill her and Louis. Not since she had later killed her husband and she and Louis had been caught by the heathens as they tried to escape to the coast and then had been made to help in the raid on Glendalough.

She looked over the side, watching the shore slip past, the clear water roiling over the stones on the riverbed. She was not sure she had ever moved so fast. Perhaps galloping on horseback. But that was a wild, jarring and short-lived experience. Now, as she was swept along, there seemed to be no motion at all. And yet she was moving so quickly.

Her eyes moved inboard and aft. There were only six men rowing, three on each side. The current, she guessed, was doing the bulk of the work, and the men at the oars were mostly just keeping the ship pointed in the right direction.

They were Northmen rowing, of course. The Irish were strangers to ships and such, and so they had little work to do now that the vessel was underway. They sat on the various chests that Failend guessed would serve as rowing benches if the other oars were being used. They ate and drank and talked in low voices. Some slept.

The Irish gathered in small groups and the Northmen gathered in their own small groups. They were separated by their languages and their very different cultures, but there was still a companionable quality to the whole scene. These men were not that different, Irish bandits and Norse raiders. Together they had just pulled off a bold move against Glendalough. They had relied on one another, had fought side by side. They had made one another considerably wealthier.

Cónán stood on the afterdeck with Harald and the strange one, Starri, the one she had been expected to heal. He was doing better, much better. He was walking about and his color was good and he seemed to have regained most of his strength. The Irishwoman, Cara, had worked a near miracle, though if Starri and Harald and the others wished to believe that she, Failend, had had anything to do with that, she would not disabuse them of the notion. It did her no harm to be thought a valuable person to have around.

Thorgrim was steering the ship. His eyes were everywhere, sweeping the banks, occasionally looking behind them, but mostly looking ahead, downstream.

He must see me when he looks forward, she thought. She wondered if his eyes lingered on her at all, what he was thinking if they did. She wondered what he made of her. He was a hard one to know. Even if she could speak his language, she guessed he would be hard to know.

Thorgrim was about the same age as her late husband, she thought, maybe a bit younger, and that was all the similarity they enjoyed. Colman had been running to fat and was of no great height, and what hair he had left was a mousy gray. Thorgrim, while not overly tall, was taller than Colman, and there was a hardness about him that Colman had lost long before. Thorgrim's hair was dark and long and tied behind his head with a leather thong. His beard, like his hair, was also thick and dark, and both were shot through with gray.

He did not seem like a cruel man or a wanton killer. Certainly Failend's worst fears about what would happen to her in the Northman's hands had not come to pass. Nothing like. Still, there was something dangerous about Thorgrim. In some ways he seemed exactly her image of what a Northman would be. In others he seemed nothing like it at all.

Kveldulf, she thought, toying in her mind with the strange Norse word. *Night Wolf. That's what they call him. What a strange name to call someone.*

"You helped them."

Louis de Roumois spoke for the first time since they had put out into the river, and Failend jumped in surprise. She felt a flush of embarrassment, as if he had caught her in the act of thinking about Thorgrim Night Wolf.

"What?" She let her eyes linger on Thorgrim for a second more before turning to Louis.

"You helped them," Louis said. He was speaking softly but putting as much emphasis as he could into the words. "At Glendalough, you helped them. You helped to plunder the church. You showed them where the garden was. Why would you do that?"

Failend's embarrassment shifted into anger. "You helped them as well. You showed them the door on the side of the church."

"I had no choice and you know it, with Thorgrim holding our hoard of silver. Without that we have no means of escaping Ireland."

Failend's eyebrows came together and her lips turned down as if they were moving of their own accord. She was not sure how the silver had become *their* silver, as opposed to *her* silver, or when it was established that *they* meant to escape Ireland.

"Besides," Louis continued, "I was only pretending to help them. I knew the boy, Trian, would be sleeping in the sacristy. I sent him to warn Lochlánn of the raid. That's why the men-at-arms arrived when they did."

Failend's eyebrows bunched closer still. *You betrayed us?* she thought, and she was about to say as much when she recalled that she was not supposed to be on the side of the Northmen and the bandits.

On the other hand, what Louis had done did not seem right to her. It was all very complicated. Then she thought of another line of attack.

"I can't believe you did that," Failend hissed. "The whole idea of us going on that raid, the whole reason we were to help the heathens, was so they could plunder the church without having any of our people killed! We wanted to avoid a fight, don't you recall? You might have gotten Lochlánn killed, doing what you did."

"Or I might have helped him kill all the heathens," Louis hissed back. "That's what we were supposed to be doing all along. Killing heathens. Don't *you* recall?"

They sat in silence for a long moment.

This is easy for him, Failend thought. *He's certain he's right, as usual. Never mind that Lochlánn and the rest want to hang him for murder. And me, too. He never doubts he's doing the right thing.*

But she did, which was so surprising to her. She should have been as morally certain as Louis de Roumois that the only correct thing to do was to fight the heathens at every turn.

Yet she was not so sure.

Kveldulf, she thought. *An odd language.* She was picking up bits and pieces of it, the odd word here or there.

"You helped train them," Failend said, breaking the silence. "Before we went to Glendalough, you helped train the bandits."

"That was before I knew we would be plundering our own people," Louis said.

"They're not your people," Failend said. "Your people are in Frankia. Your brother is in Frankia, and he wants to murder you. The people at Glendalough are Irish, and they want to hang you. Do you see the difference?"

Louis looked into Failend's eyes and was quiet for a long moment. Failend returned the stare.

"See here," Louis said at last, his tone more reconciling. He put a hand on her arm and she noticed how delicate his fingers appeared. Not like Thorgrim's. She had noticed that Thorgrim's fingers looked strong, but battered, like something well built that had seen a lot of hard use.

"Yes?" Failend said.

"Thorgrim was true to his word. About the silver. He gave it back to us. Now, if he lets us go, we can do as we planned. As we talked about. Find a ship to Frankia. Where I do have some friends."

"'If he lets us go?'" Failend said. "Are we his prisoners?"

"Well, I…" Louis began and then stopped as Failend's meaning sunk in.

After the long march back from Glendalough they had climbed aboard the ship with the others as the vessel was shoved into the river and swept away downstream. They had not even asked, before doing so, for the return of their silver or if they might go free. Thorgrim, however, had never given any indication that he still considered them prisoners.

"I guess I don't know if we're free to go or not," Louis admitted. "We'll have to stop for the night. When we do, we'll speak with Thorgrim. If he gives us leave to go we'll continue on. To the coast. Like we were doing."

"We're going to the coast now," Failend pointed out.

"What?"

"We're going to the coast now. Aboard this ship. We're heading downstream toward the coast. And going safer and faster than we would be if we were on foot."

"You're right," Louis said. "So, we stay aboard the ship? Let the heathens take us to the coast, and then we bid them *adieu*?"

"Yes," Failend said. "Then we leave them."

And go to Frankia. Because that was what they had planned. What they had decided upon. What she wanted. As far as she could tell.

Chapter Sixteen

O god of the sword-spell,
You're unwise to withhold your wealth
From me; you've deceived
The sword-point's reddener.
The Saga of Gunnlaug Serpent-Tongue

Sixty feet aft, Thorgrim Night Wolf gave a small push on the tiller and watched as *Sea Hammer*'s bow moved slightly toward the south bank of the river. The men at the oars were pulling with a slow and steady rhythm, just enough to move the ship a bit faster than the current, so the rudder would have some bite in the water and he could keep the ship from spinning like a leaf.

Starri Deathless was talking.

His health was much improved. Both he and Harald claimed it was the magic of the Irishwoman in the mail shirt, Failend, though as far as Thorgrim could see, the other one, Cara, had done most of the healing. Not that it mattered much. Starri was on the mend, and that was the important thing.

"The gods were not happy, Night Wolf," Starri was saying. "I don't know what you did to offend them so. Who knows why the gods do what they do? Maybe they were not pleased that you joined with the Irishman, Kevin. He really used you, you know. Played you for a fool."

"Yes," Thorgrim agreed. Starri had spent the last few weeks lying on his back, unable to do much more than shift his head and moan. Thorgrim was starting to miss those days.

"Can I ask who this Kevin is? This Irishman?" Cónán asked, the first thing he had said in some time. Cónán was not one to talk a lot, a trait Thorgrim appreciated. The Irishman's surprising grasp of the Norse language, he had explained to Thorgrim, was the result of time spent in the company of fin gall raiders a few years back. That explanation had come like a confession. It seemed Cónán expected him to be angry at the deception, but he was not. He would have done the same thing.

"Kevin's an Irish lord of some sort," Thorgrim explained. "We traded with him when we had Vík-ló. Kevin… what was his name, Harald?"

"Kevin mac Lugaed," Harald supplied. He was the only one among the Northmen who could pronounce Kevin's name, and so the only one who could remember it.

"Ah!" Cónán said, smiling with recognition. "Kevin mac Lugaed. Sure, he's a crafty one."

"You know him?" Thorgrim asked.

"Know of him. After Lorcan was killed fighting you lot, Kevin managed to make himself rí túaithe of Cill Mhantáin. By that I mean he's a king of the lands to the north of here. Like what you heathens would call a jarl. Makes his home at a ringfort at Ráth Naoi. Which Lorcan was also kind enough to leave for him."

Thorgrim nodded. He knew some of that history, though in more general terms. "Well, Kevin came to us when we were at Vík-ló and wanted to trade," he explained. "He dealt fairly with us, I won't lie about that. Then he suggested we join together on this raid on Glendalough. And then he betrayed us. And now he'll die for it."

Cónán smiled. "You have it all worked out, then?"

"I know how this will end. I haven't figured out how we'll get there, yet."

The day wore on, and the Avonmore continued to sweep them along toward Meeting of the Waters. The men at the oars were switched out, the women made the midday meal and served it on wooden plates, with cups and horns of ale, and the countryside moved steadily past *Sea Hammer*'s long, low sides.

As the sun began to drop, Thorgrim kept an eye out for a decent spot to beach the ship for the night. When at last a wide, sandy length of shoreline came into view he pushed the tiller over and ran the bow up onto the soft ground. As usual, Harald was first overboard with a rope to make the ship fast.

It was some hours after that, the sun down, a fire burning on the narrow beach and the men well into the mead and ale, that Thorgrim found Cónán seated with his men.

Thorgrim sat down beside him. "How do you know of this Kevin whatever-he's-called?" he asked. "The one who betrayed us?"

"Oh, I make it my business to know what's going on in the country hereabouts," Cónán said. "It's how I stay alive. Keep my men and women alive. Make us rich."

Thorgrim smiled. "You don't seem very rich," he said.

"I'm richer now," Cónán said. "And you wait. I'll be richer still."

They were quiet for a few minutes, drinking and looking into the dancing flames. "'Richer still,'" Thorgrim said at last. "I might be able to help you with that."

"Really?" Cónán said. "You don't seem very rich, either."

"Oh, but I am," Thorgrim said. "I have wealth at Vík-ló like you've never seen. It was taken from me, but I mean to take it back. Kevin has silver, too. Gold. I mean to take that as well."

"You're more interested in revenge than silver, I can see that."

Thorgrim grunted. "I'm interested in both."

"Revenge can be expensive," Cónán said.

"If it costs me my life, that will not be too high a price," Thorgrim said. "I don't know much about your Christ God, but my gods would not be pleased if I were to let such betrayal go unanswered. Even if the gods didn't care, I couldn't endure it. I wouldn't be much of a man if I could. So, yes, I will have my revenge and I'll pay whatever price I must."

He pulled his gaze from the fire and looked at Cónán and added, "But there'll also be plunder. Quite a bit."

Cónán considered that. "So you want us to stay with you? Help you plunder Ráth Naoi?"

"If that's where Kevin is found, then yes."

Cónán nodded. "I hadn't considered that," he said, which Thorgrim was quite sure was not true. Cónán struck him as the sort who was always considering every possibility that came his way. "Let me see what the others think."

The next morning Thorgrim ordered all the plunder from the church at Glendalough piled onto *Sea Hammer*'s deck and he divided it up among the men, Northmen and Irish. It was what he had agreed to do, and it also served as an enticement to Cónán and the other bandits, a suggestion of what might be waiting for them at Kevin's stronghold.

The takings were weighed out into even piles. Those things that were too big to be part of any one man's share, such as candlesticks and plates, were hacked apart so that the smaller bits could be distributed. The mood was buoyant, smiles all around, save for two of Cónán's men who, by way of punishment for some crime, were getting nothing, and Louis the Frank, who seemed disgusted by the whole affair.

Thorgrim offered a share to him and to the woman, Failend, because it was only right that he did. They both declined. Failend, at least, was polite about it.

"What I wish to know," Louis said, "is what's to become of Failend and me? Are we your prisoners still?"

"Prisoners?" Thorgrim said, with Harald translating. "No. You kept your word, you helped us. I've given you back your hoard. You may go whenever you wish."

"And if we wish to stay with you until you reach the sea? To take passage with you?"

Thorgrim shrugged. "You're welcome to stay. If there's fighting, your sword will be welcome as well." Louis had not done much fighting at Glendalough, Thorgrim had noticed, but then they had agreed he did not have to. Failend, however, seemed unable to stay out of the fray. They might both be helpful yet.

The camp on shore was broken down, *Sea Hammer* loaded and shoved back out into the river, the men settled at the half-dozen oars needed to keep the ship in the middle of the stream. The air was warm and it was still dry, but the sky had clouded over and Thorgrim could smell the rain coming. That was no matter. If anything, he was happy for it. Things had been going their way, everything working out as well as it could, and it made him nervous. If rain was the worst the gods would throw at him, then he would be grateful for it.

They passed familiar landmarks as they pulled downstream. Thorgrim and his men had passed that way only once, on their way upriver to Glendalough, but still Thorgrim recognized many of the points along the way: a beach where they had spent the night, another where they had buried two wounded men who had died. Thorgrim had a good memory for landmarks, and even if he had not, those places were etched in his mind like runes on a stone at a crossroads.

They came around a bend in the river. A straight run for a quarter mile lay in front of them, and at the end a ripple of water that marked where the bottom shallowed out. Harald stepped up beside him and for some time they stood in silence and looked at the riverbanks and the roiling water beyond the bow.

"This was where they ambushed us, isn't it?" Harald said. He spoke softly, for no real reason, but Thorgrim understood why. There were spirits here. This was a place where many men had died. They were not to be disturbed.

"Yes, it is," Thorgrim said, also speaking low. "Those woods, there, that's where they were hiding." It had not happened so long ago, and Thorgrim could see it all clearly. Ottar had been in the process of hauling his deep ships up over the shallows. The Irish had been waiting in the woods, hidden, bows strung, arrows ready.

It occurred to Thorgrim that Louis the Frank might have been with them. *Was the ambush his doing?* Thorgrim wondered.

And then another thought came to him. "Harald, get our men under arms. Shields, swords. Spears. Have them get their mail on."

Harald looked at him. "Do you think…again?"

"I don't know," Thorgrim said. "Just a feeling. But I've been expecting an attack all along. Better we should be ready."

Harald nodded and hurried forward, spreading the word in a low voice. The Irish were confused by this order, surprised. It took them a minute to understand what they were being told to do, and why. But the Northmen understood and they leapt to prepare. They had all been there the last time, and like Thorgrim, they remembered.

The river carried them on, sweeping them down toward the shallow water as Thorgrim leaned on the tiller and kept the long, low ship as much in the center of the stream as he could. The last time they had come this way, Ottar's ships had not been able to make it over the shallows without her men off-loading much of the gear and stores. Thorgrim's ships, less heavily laden, had made it with only the crew going over the side. Now *Sea Hammer* was lighter still, with half the number of men on board and considerably fewer supplies.

Thorgrim hoped very much they would not go aground. He hoped there would not be archers waiting in the woods. If they did hang up on the bottom, and if there were men-at-arms with bows, then the voyage would end right here, just as it nearly had before.

The woods seemed to close in on either side. Thorgrim's eyes moved from the water to the tree line and back. He could see in his mind the struggle in those woods, Ottar's men cut down as they tried to get up the steep banks, oars and barrels and dead men floating in the stream. He felt himself tense, felt his hands grip the tiller tighter than they needed to.

"Stand ready!" he called forward, a pointless command and he knew it, but he felt the need to say something. The men were ready, the Northmen with shields and spears and swords in hand, their eyes, like Thorgrim's probing the dark woods. Starri was stripped to the waist, a battle ax in each hand. Starri Deathless. He was back.

The Irish were ready too, armed and clad like the Northmen, but their faces showed more confusion than wariness. To them, this stretch of river was not the killing place that it was to Thorgrim's men.

Then *Sea Hammer* was in the rough, shallow stretch of river. Thorgrim could feel the vibration in the tiller as the unsettled water under the keel nudged and jostled the hull in a hundred little ways.

"Pull! Harder!" he shouted to the oarsmen and they leaned back hard, pulling with powerful strokes, bringing the oars forward faster now to drive the ship ahead. There were only four men rowing now. Thorgrim had ordered the aftermost two, Godi and Ulf, to take up arms. He needed his men ready to fight, but he also needed men at the oars to keep *Sea Hammer* on course, and the Irish were too unfamiliar with the work of rowing to take a place there. This was the best he could do.

He leaned over the side and looked down. He could see the browns and blacks and whites of the stones on the river bottom, distorted through the churning water. They seemed very close. He looked up again. The place where the Irish had struck was past them now, though they were still in the stretch of shallow water that had hung them up before. Thorgrim cocked his head to listen. He could hear nothing, could see nothing save for a quarter mile of river and bank that seemed as deserted as the parts though which they had already traveled.

Then suddenly Thorgrim heard a thumping noise forward, felt a jarring sensation running down the length of the ship as the keel struck bottom. His hands clenched tighter still on the tiller and he gritted his teeth. He felt the wooden shaft jump in his hand, saw his men looking fore and aft. But the ship did not slow, did not stop, just touched the river bottom and rode over.

And then they were past the shallows and Thorgrim could feel the motion of the ship change as her hull slipped into deeper water and the river once more grew wider. He could see his men visibly relax. He took his hand from the tiller and shook it to work the kinks free.

They continued on down river. Thorgrim looked over the side. The bottom was barely visible. That meant the water was too deep for a man to walk or a horse to ride. He looked up. The banks were too far for a spear or an arrow to be used to any effect.

"All right, you men," Thorgrim called forward. "You can stand easy for now." Helmets were removed, swords slipped back into scabbards, spears laid aside. Up in the bow, Louis the Frank and Failend had been poised with weapons drawn, Louis looking out to larboard, Failend to starboard.

Failend carried the seax Thorgrim had given her, a weapon well-proportioned for her size. Now she sheathed it again, but she did not sit. Rather, she remained standing, eyes looking out toward the riverbank.

I wonder what she's thinking, Thorgrim mused. She was an odd one. He often wondered what could be going on in her head. Women were a mystery to him, as they were to most men, and Irish women doubly so.

Starri came aft, stood beside him. He did not look happy. "Your instincts are growing dull, Night Wolf," he said. "Ornolf would have said you're getting soft."

"I'm sure he would," Thorgrim said. "He would probably be right. But don't despair of getting into a fight. I have no doubt you will. And soon."

"Oh, yes," Starri said. "I know I can count on you for that."

They stood in silence as *Sea Hammer*'s speed slowed in the widening river and the men at the oars returned to their more leisurely stroke. The woods on the riverbanks tapered off, giving them a long view of the countryside, the rolling hills in their deep summer green, the mountains rising off in the distance. Thorgrim could see down river for a good mile or so, to where the woods closed in again and the river bent off toward the south.

"Where are we bound, Thorgrim?" Starri asked, as if it had only just occurred to him to wonder what was to become of them all. Starri had less interest in his own fate than any man Thorgrim had ever known. The only question that was any real concern to Starri was whether or not there would be fighting, and if not, what could be done to change that.

"We go to visit Kevin," Thorgrim said. "Cónán says there's a river, joins this one, runs to within a mile or so of this place Kevin occupies. Whatever they call it."

"Cónán knows this country," Starri observed.

"He's been an outlaw here a dozen years or so," Thorgrim said. "And he's managed to keep alive. Yes, he knows this country well, and the people in it."

They were quiet as *Sea Hammer* came up with the bend in the river and Thorgrim pulled the tiller toward him to help the ship sweep around. Once again the woods gathered at the riverbanks and their long view of the country was lost.

"Shallows here," Starri observed. Starri, of course, did not recall much of the river, they having transited this part after he had received his grievous wound.

"Yes," Thorgrim said. "A little deeper than those last. They should give us no trouble."

"I hope not," Starri said. "I wouldn't care to be stuck here on the bottom of the river while Kevin waits for us to give him his lesson."

"I wouldn't worry," Thorgrim said. "There'll be fighting enough, soon."

And just as he said that, as if his very words had summoned them, the riders came bursting out of the trees. They carried shields on their arms, spears leveled. Their horses plunged into the river, water cresting around them like bow waves before so many longships, as they charged toward *Sea Hammer* and the stunned and unready men aboard her.

Chapter Seventeen

I reckon two blows revenged
the hot blood won for the raven.
Such deeds are told in stories
related by wise men.
The Saga of Ref the Sly

Starri was the first man moving, leaping off the afterdeck and charging forward, even before Thorgrim was able to shout a word of warning. He moved like a rabbit, twisting and dodging anything in his way as he bolted forward, pulling the two battle axes from his belt as he did. Only someone who knew him as well as Thorgrim did could see that he still had not regained all the power he once possessed.

"To arms!" Thorgrim shouted. "They're on us, to arms!" Most of the men aboard *Sea Hammer* had been looking inboard, or aft, and they had not seen the riders in those first seconds when they burst from the tree line. Now, fore and aft, men leapt to their feet, turning, looking outboard, mouths wide with surprise.

"To arms, you stupid bastards!" Thorgrim shouted. He was trapped where he was, hands on the tiller. If he let go, the ship would likely spin out of control, perhaps run up on the bank. He could feel the weight of Iron-tooth on his belt, but he could not spare a hand for it.

It took the Northmen and the Irish aboard *Sea Hammer* a second or two, no more, to see the danger and react, but it was still a delay that would cost them. The riders had halved the distance to the ship in that time, and they were just a couple rods away when the men began to snatch up shields and swords.

"Spears!" Thorgrim shouted. "Take up spears!" The riders were carrying pole arms, and with them they could kill the men confined to the ship and still keep beyond the reach of the Northmen's swords and axes.

The men at the oars were looking over their shoulders and Thorodd Bollason, forward oar, larboard side, was abandoning his when Thorgrim shouted again. "Stay at the oars! Keep pulling! Keep pulling!" The riders had the advantage of surprise and maneuverability, but they would be powerless if the Northmen could get the ship into deeper water.

Harald was standing by the mast, his sword, Oak Cleaver, in his hand. He had no shield or helmet and was making no effort to get them. Rather he was calling to his fellows. "Godi! Ulf! Vali! Amidships, protect the men at the oars! Amidships!"

Good boy, smart boy, Thorgrim thought. Harald understood, as he did, that they had to keep the ship moving, had to keep driving down river. If the riders knew their business, they would go for the men at the oars.

Cónán was in motion too, shouting at his men in their native Irish, pushing the women to the center of the ship, as far as they could get from the fighting, which would not be far, not beyond the reach of the oncoming spears. The bandits were snatching up weapons and shields, stumbling over one another as they did. This was not what they were accustomed to. Few had ever seen a ship before, let alone had to fight aboard one.

Then the riders were on them, the leading man coming at the larboard bow, spear leveled. One of Cónán's men was there and he was still trying to settle the shield on his arm when the tip of the rider's spear caught him in the chest. The force of the blow knocked him backwards, his arms flailing, the sword flying from his grip as he went down in a spray of blood.

Thorgrim, watching from sixty feet aft, hoped the rider would at least lose his spear in the encounter, but the man gave a practiced twist of the weapon and pulled it clear as he rode on past. He leveled it again, charging down the ship's side, the point driving at Thorodd Bollason's back as the Norseman leaned into the oar.

Before Thorgrim could shout a warning, Harald leapt to the ship's side, swinging Oak Cleaver as he did. He brought the blade down on the horizontal shaft of the spear and knocked it out of line. He pulled Oak Cleaver back and slashed at the rider, but the man had reined his horse hard over, away from the ship's side, clear of Harald's sword and the long oar in Thorodd's grip.

The riders had split up and were coming on from either direction, a dozen or so riding at the larboard side, a dozen to starboard. Starri Deathless was at the bow, all the way forward, having pushed Louis out of the way. He could get no closer to the enemy; there was nothing he could do but wait until the riders closed with him.

That would not be long. The rider coming at the starboard bow was now only a dozen yards away, his horse driving through the chest-high water, the river foaming around its legs. The rider had a shield on his arm, his spear leveled at Starri's chest, as horse and ship quickly converged.

What a waste, Thorgrim thought. All that effort they had put into patching Starri up, and if his reflexes were in the least bit slowed he would be wriggling like a fish at the end of that spear.

Ship and rider met. The spear arced in toward Starri with practiced grace, and Starri knocked it effortlessly aside with his battle ax. He put his foot on the sheer strake and launched himself through the air, right at the man on the horse. Thorgrim had time enough to catch a glimpse of the shocked look on the man's face. It was all the reaction he was able to muster before Starri slammed into him and the two of them disappeared over the far side of the animal and splashed down into the water.

"Starri!" Thorgrim shouted, pointlessly. "You stupid bastard!" He had never felt so impotent, tied to the tiller with his men fighting and dying around him. And now Starri had gone over the side. Even if the lunatic was not killed in the fighting he would surely be left astern.

The riders were all around the ship now, plunging in toward it, reining away, following along and thrusting with their long spears as the Irish and Norse tried to fend them off. Four men at the oars and they pulled for all they were worth, looking desperately around as they did.

Godi came charging through the crowd. He had tossed his sword aside and now held an oar in his massive hands, twenty feet of hard, tapered wood, which he swung in a great arc at the horsemen. It was a feat that would have been impossible for any man of smaller size or lesser strength, but in Godi's hands the oar was an effective weapon. Thorgrim saw it miss one of the riders by inches but strike the man next to him, hitting him right at the shoulder and knocking him clean off his horse and into the river.

Thorgrim looked off to the starboard side. The riderless horse from which Starri had pulled the man-at-arms was shying away from the ship, but there was no sign of Starri or the man he was fighting. Thorgrim looked down at the water but could see only the rippling surface. He looked astern wondering if they had already passed Starri by.

And then, not fifteen feet away, Starri burst from the water like a gangly, pale god of the deep, his long hair and beard streaming, the two axes raised above him. He spun around and reached out a long, spider-like arm and drove his ax into *Sea Hammer*'s sheer strake, three feet from where Thorgrim was standing, drove it so hard Thorgrim could feel the vibration of the impact through his shoes. Hand still gripping the handle of the ax, Starri swung his feet up as the ship surged past, flinging his other arm over the edge of the ship and twisting himself aboard.

He landed on his feet, pulling the first ax free as he did. His eyes met Thorgrim's. He was smiling. There was no sign of the Irish horseman who had gone into the water with him.

Without a word Starri turned and raced forward again. Thorgrim wanted to tell him to stay on the ship, that he would not get away with that a second time, but Starri was beyond hearing so Thorgrim turned back to the fight. The horsemen were charging in and out, probing with their spears. Two of Cónán's men were down and Godi and Armod were wounded, blood smeared on hands and faces, but still fighting as if nothing had happened.

"By Thor and Odin!" Thorgrim shouted in frustration. He could not let go of the tiller and he could not call anyone aft to take it from him.

Godi swung his oar at one of the riders who was coming down the starboard side, but the man took the blade of the oar on his shield and, braced for it, managed to deflect the blow. A man named Refkel was on the forward-most oar. The rider lunged forward and caught Refkel's shoulder, driving the point into the Northman's back, and the force of the blow drove the weapon clean through. Thorgrim saw the spear tip, black and covered in blood, tear through the front of Refkel's mail shirt. Refkel shrieked and twisted sideways as the horseman continued on, still holding the spear shaft, levering Refkel around until he was past and the point ripped out again.

Refkel was done, lying writhing on the deck, his oar hanging free. Armod, at the row port just aft of him, leaned forward for another stroke and fouled Refkel's abandoned oar. He cursed, struggling to free it, as *Sea Hammer* began to slew around.

The rider who had driven his spear into Refkel now jumped his horse neatly over the fouled oars and pulled its head around, charging back at *Sea Hammer*'s side. The point of his spear was leveled at Armod now, who had turned to see what was happening behind him, and did not even see the rider coming.

"Ah! Bastard!" Thorgrim shouted. There was no steering now with the starboard oars gone, and Thorgrim could not stand to remain out of the fight for a moment more. He let go of the oak tiller and raced forward, drawing Iron-tooth as he ran. He thought of Starri, moving with the grace the gods had given him, or Harald, able to perform great athletic feats thanks to youth and strength, and he knew he could no longer match either of them.

But he didn't have to. He had only to reach the vulnerable Armod before the horseman did. He put his foot on the first sea chest aft and stepped up, leaping forward to the next and the next. The rest of the men were fighting forward—his path was clear.

He was on the fourth chest when the point of the rider's spear came in over the sheer strake. Thorgrim leapt forward, sweeping the blade of his sword down as he did. He heard the steel ring against the iron point as it connected, saw the spear point knocked away, the momentum of the rider driving it into the deck where it stuck fast.

Thorgrim recovered his balance, turned and swept Iron-tooth at the rider, who was well within the arc of the blade. The rider brought his shield up quick and took the lethal blow on the flat wooden surface.

Their eyes met, Thorgrim and the Irishman. He was young, Harald's age, or maybe a bit older. Thorgrim recognized the man's face. *In the garden? The ambush coming up river?* But then he was gone, abandoning the spear as *Sea Hammer* swept past.

Armod was on his feet. He pulled the weapon free and spun it point outboard as the Irishman drew his sword and wheeled his horse around to make another charge.

The longship was in the grip of the current now, turning in the stream, the tiller unmanned, starboard oars fouled, the useless larboard oars abandoned as the rowers let go of the handles and took up weapons instead.

The horsemen were surrounding the ship. The Northmen and the Irish were massed fore and aft, larboard and starboard, fighting them off. Some of *Sea Hammer*'s men had spears with which to reach out at the attackers, but most held swords or battle axes, not nearly as effective against an enemy that could keep beyond arm's reach.

Starri was still on board, Thorgrim was happy to see. He had abandoned his beloved axes and found a spear. He was racing side to side, screaming his wild berserker cry, leaping up onto the sheer strake, balancing there for a second or two as he made wild thrusts at the riders, then pushing himself off and landing back on board. It was an astounding display of courage, balance, coordination, and pure madness.

Sea Hammer was sideways now, sweeping down river. The ship like a shield wall, a solid and unbroken line pushing all before it, and the riders downstream of the ship were trying to get clear. They could see what would happen—their tiring horses would soon be unable to keep out of the vessel's way. *Sea Hammer*, drifting out of control, would run them down.

They peeled off from the fight, charging off at an angle, trying to get clear of the longship. Thorgrim saw a horse stumble, the rider jerking on the reins, but he was too late. The man looked up as *Sea Hammer*'s stern swung around and slammed into him broadside. Horse and rider went down and the ship swept over them as it continued unchecked downstream. Thorgrim glanced over the other side as they passed, but there was no sign of either the man-at-arms or his mount.

But he was the only horseman who failed to get clear. The rest had all come around to the starboard side now and were pressing the fight home. Thorgrim's men were lining the rail, shields in hand, swords, axes and spears flailing at the attackers. It was the oddest fight Thorgrim had ever seen: a shieldwall along a ship's side fighting mounted men-at-arms.

He pushed past Godi and one of the Irishmen and took his place, Iron-tooth held high, waiting for the next horseman to come at them, waiting for *Sea Hammer* to slip into water too deep for the horses to follow.

Two of the mounted men charged the ship's side, leading with their spear points. Thorgrim batted the spears away, lashed out at the riders, but they were beyond the reach of his outstretched sword. On either side the shoreline continued to sweep past. Then suddenly *Sea Hammer* shuddered, then heeled to larboard as the keel hung up on the bottom and the current pushed the ship over.

"We're aground!" Harald shouted.

One of the mounted men-at-arms—the leader, the one who had tried to kill Armod—shouted something, raised his sword, and the rest turned and rode upstream, twenty yards. They stopped and turned again, facing *Sea Hammer*, making a line abreast. Their shields went up, their spears came down to form a row of iron points.

"Stand ready, here they come!" Thorgrim shouted and Cónán shouted something as well, something in Irish, words to the same effect, Thorgrim guessed. The line of horsemen started forward, the current now helping them build their momentum.

"Shield wall!" Thorgrim shouted. "Harald, tell the Irishmen 'shieldwall'!" Harald shouted the words, his voice cutting through the din of yelling men, but Thorgrim had little hope it would do any good. To the Northmen, forming a shield wall was as natural as getting out of bed, but the Irish were not trained that way. The horsemen's spears would break right through their defense and do great slaughter.

And then Thorgrim had an idea.

"Everyone, larboard side! Come on! Go!" he shouted, waving Iron-tooth and pointing to the downstream side of the ship, the side farthest from the charging Irish warriors. He saw men look over, confusion on their faces, but then Godi moved and Ulf moved and soon they were all rushing across the ship, over to the larboard side, the low side. Thorgrim heard the bilges scraping the bottom as the ship rolled further with the weight of all those men and women and the water piling up to starboard.

He turned. The riders had not slowed in their charge, but now they were breaking right and left, sweeping around the bow and stern to get at the men, crowded and disorganized on the other side. They were shouting, and though Thorgrim could not understand the words, he could hear a victorious note to their voices. The hated fin gall ship was hard aground and the enemy trapped aboard. There was nowhere for them to go, save to their deaths.

Odin, all father, Njord, lord of the water, please make this work, Thorgrim prayed as the first of the horsemen came sweeping around the bow.

"Now, back to the starboard side! Everyone, go! Go!" Again he pointed with Iron-tooth and this time he led the way, charging up the steeply slanting deck toward the upriver side. "Get a leg over the side, get a leg over the sheer strake!" he shouted as the men once again crowded against the upstream side. He threw a leg over the sheer strake himself, to demonstrate his meaning, and the other Northmen, at least, understood now what he had in mind and they followed suit.

"Cónán!" Thorgrim shouted. "Get your men over the edge, like this!"

Cónán nodded, clearly bewildered, but with sense enough to follow orders without questioning them. He shouted to his men in their native tongue and they, too, crowded up to the larboard side, and as they did, Thorgrim felt *Sea Hammer* come up on a more even keel. He felt her shudder under his feet and, to his profound relief, he felt her move.

The mounted warriors were all downstream now, having swept around to the far side of the ship only to find their enemy had once again run to the other side. They were shouting and wheeling their mounts around when *Sea Hammer* gave another, more pronounced lurch and her keel came free of the river bottom.

Even Thorgrim Night Wolf, to whom the Irish language sounded like so much meaningless animal noise, could not miss the change from victory to alarm in the shouts of the mounted men. Once again the big ship was sweeping down on them, driving them along as they tried desperately to get clear.

Those closest to the bow and stern were able to pull their mounts around and charge off for the riverbanks. Those amidships turned and raced down river, but Thorgrim could see the water getting higher and higher on the horses flanks as they left the shallows behind. He could see men looking over their shoulders as they sheered off toward the shore and kicked their mounts to move faster.

Sea Hammer bumped again and then Thorgrim could feel she was floating free. She began to spin in the current, turning to larboard this time, turning so her bow was heading downstream.

"Man the oars!" Thorgrim shouted. "Get some men on the oars!"

Harald and Vali, farther aft, turned and leapt for the looms of two of the oars that were dragging in the water, and the other two oars were manned as well. To the Northmen the work of rowing was as ingrained as walking, and without a word they fell into the rhythm and *Sea Hammer* gathered way again. Thorgrim looked aft. Godi had taken up the tiller and was turning the bow further downstream.

The mounted warriors were astern of them now, sitting atop their horses and watching the ship moving away. There was nothing else they could do. *Sea Hammer* had passed over the shallows and was now once more in water too deep for a horse to go, save to swim. The Irish could not carry on the fight if they wanted to, and Thorgrim did not think they wanted to.

Cónán stepped up beside him. "I don't know what you did, but it worked, and we may thank God for that."

"You may thank my gods," Thorgrim said. "I don't think your God would side with us in that fight."

"I guess you're right," Cónán said. They were quiet for a moment as they watched the horsemen receding into the distance.

"Do you know who they were?" Thorgrim asked, nodding toward the mounted men.

"I don't," Cónán said. "Not for certain. But I believe they're the men we fought at Glendalough."

"Glendalough? Really?" Thorgrim said, and Cónán nodded.

"The shields," Cónán said. "I recognized some of their shields."

"They followed us all this way?" Thorgrim asked. "Waited until now to spring their trap?"

"It would seem so," Cónán said. "Crafty bastard, that one leading them."

"He is that," Thorgrim said. "And persistent."

"He is persistent," Cónán agreed. "Which means we've likely not seen the last of him. And we'll likely not be as lucky the next time. Or maybe your gods will not be so kind."

At that Thorgrim could do nothing but nod his agreement.

Chapter Eighteen

Long is the round to a false friend leading,
e'en if he dwell on the way:
but though far off fared, to a faithful friend
straight are the roads and short.
Hávamál

There was some brouhaha going on by the earthworks that surrounded Vík-ló, down near where the wall met up with the river. A crowd of men had gathered. There was shouting. People were racing off in various directions, others hurrying to the spot.

Aghen Ormsson watched it from his shipyard, a couple hundred feet away, glancing up from his work every now and then to see what was going on. He showed no interest beyond that. He had a pretty good idea of what had caused the commotion.

He was looking through his tool chest for an auger bit when he saw the bulky form of Mar the blacksmith coming up over the rise and heading in his direction. The man seemed not to be in much of a hurry, but then he never did. He was more the whale—slow, ponderous, powerful—than the shark.

Aghen found his bit, slipped it into the handle, and looked up as Mar approached.

"Lord Mar," Aghen said and Mar gave a weak smile at the jest. He nodded his head toward the crowd of men by the wall.

"Big goings-on," Mar said. "Have you heard?"

"I've been watching them scurrying around. Haven't heard what it's all about."

"No?" Mar asked. "Not curious at all?"

"New lords here in Vík-ló, and I think curiosity is not always healthy."

Mar smiled at that. "No, it's not." He looked around. "Where's your boy? Your spy?"

"I don't know," Aghen said. "He's not one to be here bright and early, but he's not usually this late."

Mar nodded. He glanced over at the men by the wall and back at Aghen. "You really don't know what's going on over there?"

Aghen shook his head. "No. I get the idea they might have found someone dead. But it seems like a lot of fuss for something like that. Do you know? Being Ottar's dear friend, and all?"

"They did find someone dead," Mar said. "And I think they'll be asking you about it."

Aghen felt a flash of panic, but he held his face firm. "Me? Why would they ask me about it?"

His mind tore through the events of the night before, trying to recall something that might have given him away. Did someone see him at Ottar's hall, speaking with the man who now lay dead? He was pretty sure that no one had. Was one of the iron teeth Mar had made for him found in the man's neck? No, before hiding his special instrument he had checked that they were all still there.

"They'll talk with you," Mar said, "because the man's throat was torn out. By a wolf, it seems."

"A wolf?" Aghen asked, sounding suitably surprised.

"You're surprised?" Mar asked. "Didn't you say you saw a wolf?"

"Yes, I did. I said that."

"And you *did* see a wolf? You honestly saw a wolf in the longphort?"

"Yes," Aghen said, and this time there was no lack of conviction in his voice because this time he was telling the truth. "By all the gods I swear I saw a wolf. Here. Not twenty feet from here."

Mar nodded. "I don't doubt you. I don't think anyone doubted you. No one I've spoken to, anyway. What Ottar and his lot think, I don't know."

"A wolf…" Aghen said, as much to himself as to Mar. He scratched at his long, gray beard and then shook his head in disbelief. "Was he…torn up, at all? Eaten?"

"No," Mar said. "Not from what I hear, though despite what you say I'm not exactly in Ottar's inner circle. All I heard was his throat was ripped out and the bite looks much like the bite of a wolf. That was it. There were no other marks on the man."

Aghen shook his head again. "Well, it was damned strange, I can tell you, seeing that wolf. Why the beast didn't rip *my* throat out I can't imagine."

"I can't either," Marr said, and there was something in his voice that Aghen did not like. "Anyway, that's why I thought Ottar's men would want to talk to you. Because you saw the wolf."

"No, no one has spoken to me yet," Aghen said. "Ottar and his men, they don't speak to me much at all, and I'm happy about it."

"Sure," Marr said. "They don't speak much to me, either. 'Sharpen these swords, make arrow heads, we'll pay you if we feel like it'—that's about all the talk I get from them."

They were silent for a minute. "Even Grimarr was a better lord than this Ottar," Aghen said, his voice dropping.

He thought about telling Mar what he was doing, how he had staged the wolf attack. Having an ally, someone to talk to, would be a great relief. But even as he considered it, he knew that he could not confess his crime. There were two reasons. One was that doing so would put Mar's life in as much risk as his own. The other was that he really did not know what he was doing. Mar would ask him why he had done the deed, what he hoped to achieve, and he had no answer for that.

"I was wondering," Mar said, breaking into Aghen's thoughts, "about those nails. Did they work out as you hoped?"

"Oh, you know, I haven't even had the chance to try them," Aghen said. "I have them up at my house. I haven't had the chance to put my idea to the test."

"Really?" Mar said. "You seemed in such a hurry to get them." Now Aghen was certain the man was probing. Mar, he guessed, had a sense that something was going on, but had no idea what it might be. Aghen was not much worried that he would figure it out, or if he did, that he would tell anyone. Mar could be as dense and inflexible as the iron bars he pounded.

"Ha!" Aghen said. "You know how that goes! You think you'll have time to do a thing, and you're eager to get at it, and then a hundred other things come along to get in your way."

At that Mar nodded knowingly. He was about to speak again when, to Aghen's relief, Oddi appeared on the plank road, hurrying toward them. Aghen nodded in his direction and Mar turned to see who was coming.

"Your watchdog," Mar said.

"Oddi's not so bad," Aghen replied. "I've learned more from him than he or Ottar has from me." Aghen's voice dropped again. "Oddi's no great friend of Ottar, and it seems many of the others aren't either. Ottar has his household guard, and the others who're close to him, but a lot of these men joined him not long ago, before they knew what he was, and they don't have much love for him. Ottar thinks they are more loyal than they are."

Oddi was nearly within earshot so Aghen stopped talking and he and Mar turned to watch the young man approach. What Aghen had taken to be a cap of some sort on his head he could now see was a bandage. A red spot on the cloth marked the location of the wound underneath, just above Oddi's right eye.

Before Aghen could ask about it, however, Oddi started in. "Have you heard about what's happening there?" he asked, jerking a thumb toward the men by the wall. Mar began to reply, but Aghen cut him off.

"We've heard some things. Rumors. What do you hear?"

"Well, Thorlaug Gyduson was killed," Oddi began, words tumbling out. "Killed last night and it seems killed by a wolf! Probably your wolf, Aghen."

"Really?" Aghen said. "And who's Thorlaug Gyduson? Or, who was Thorlaug Gyduson?"

"He's one of Ottar's household guard, one of those closest to him," Oddi explained. "I don't think Ottar would have much cared if it was someone else."

Aghen and Mar made grunting sounds of acknowledgement. The three of them turned and looked toward the knot of men by the wall. Someone had brought a large piece of cloth and four men were lifting it by the corners. In the sling of the cloth was, they imagined, the unfortunate Thorlaug Gyduson.

"Ottar was not happy about this?" Aghen asked.

Oddi shook his head, his eyes growing wider with the recollection. "No. He was near insane. Ranting like a lunatic. I've never seen him like that. I haven't been with him long, you know, but I've still seen some pretty lunatic behavior with him. But nothing like that.

Interesting, Aghen thought. *Did he love this Thorlaug Gyduson so much?*

"What happened to your head?" Mar asked, nodding toward the bandage and the patch of blood. "That have anything to do with Ottar and his madness?"

Oddi flushed a bit with embarrassment. "Yes, it does," he admitted. He said no more, apparently hoping the subject would be dropped, but he was not that lucky.

"Well?" Mar demanded. "What happened?"

"Ah, well," Oddi began. "I was at Ottar's hall. I am there sometimes, you know…."

I know, Aghen thought. *And I can just imagine why Ottar wants you there.*

"And of course, all the talk was about Thorlaug Gyduson and how he was killed and your wolf, Aghen, and all. And then I remembered what you told me, about the old lord here, Thorgrim Night Wolf."

"What of him?" Mar asked.

"Well, Aghen told me…and I suppose it was well known…he told me that this Thorgrim…was thought to be a shape-shifter. That he could turn into a wolf."

"Bah!" Mar said. "Stories to scare children." He did not sound so sure of that, however.

"So, I told Ottar that," Oddi continued, ignoring the blacksmith. "I told him what you said, about Thorgrim. He listened, and he made me say it again. He was real quiet and I repeated the story. And then when I was done he went absolutely mad. You'd have thought I poked him with a red hot iron. He jumped up, turned a table over, started screaming. He threw a cup at me, hit me here." He pointed to the bloody spot on his forehead.

"Then what did he do?" Aghen asked.

"I don't know. I didn't stay around to see. I was out of there like a rabbit."

"Smart," Mar said.

"Did you mention my name?" Aghen asked and Oddi's flustered embarrassment grew considerably more pronounced.

"Ah, yes, I think I did. I had to tell him who told me, so he would know it was not just some fool babbling away. I didn't think he'd carry on like that. I'm sorry."

Aghen waved it away. "It's no matter," he said. "I'll deal with Ottar, if it comes to that." His words sounded much more certain than he actually felt.

"So," Oddi said, with a tone that suggested he would be grateful for a change of subject. "What labors do you have for me today?"

They were quiet for a moment as the cluster of men carried the cloth with Thorlaug Gyduson's body inside up to the plank road and disappeared over the rise. Aghen turned to Oddi.

"Too much excitement today, and I'm afraid your already weak mind has been made weaker still by Ottar's cup. I think we'll take the day off. We've earned it."

Oddi nodded, clearly pleased with this decision. He bid his good day and Mar did as well, and soon Aghen found himself alone, surrounded by his tools and his wood and the ships and the sea, all the things he loved, and none of those that he despised.

And that was good. His mind was in a whirl. So many things to consider, so many trails to look down to try and see where they might lead.

The next morning Oddi was back and the day settled into its normal routine. They sharpened tools, worked on *Raven Eye* and the other vessels, talked of what was going on beyond the shipyard. Ottar, Oddi reported, had not left the hall since Thorlaug's death. He had sent men out to patrol the longphort and stationed those he trusted most on the top of the wall with torches, keeping a look-out through the night hours.

Aghen nodded. He had seen them. And though he did not mention it to Oddi, he, too, had been patrolling the longphort in the night.

As the days passed, the state of alarm that had tightened around Vík-ló began to ease. Fewer armed men walked the grounds at night. There were not as many torches lining the top of the wall. The sound of shouting and singing could once again be heard from the twin halls, loud and raucous, if not quite so pervasive as it had been.

Aghen the shipwright tried to make sense of it all.

He had been moving by instinct. He had no plan. He had no notion as to how Ottar would react to the violent death of his man. The idea for the wooden wolf jaws had come to Aghen and he had acted on it. He was not sure why.

I saw the wolf, he reminded himself. The wolf had appeared to him and then run off. It had not harmed him. And the wolf had come to him for a reason.

Either the gods sent it, or… He could not even make himself form the thought, though he knew what thought was there. *Or it was Thorgrim himself, come to goad me into action.*

Ottar's reaction had been far beyond what he had imagined it would be. Another mystery. Though Ottar had never seemed much concerned with any man's life, Aghen knew he would be angry if one of his trusted men was killed. Maybe even a little frightened. But Thorlaug's death had sent him into a wild rage, and according to Oddi he had only left his hall twice since then, and that only briefly.

There were things happening here, and Aghen knew that most of it he did not understand. It was, however, becoming clearer what he needed to do.

If this makes Ottar wild with rage, then it's a good thing, he concluded. Anything that knocked Ottar back on his heels was good.

There is opportunity here, Aghen thought. *If Ottar's in a panic, he might make some grave mistake.* Aghen had no idea what sort of mistake that might be, but he guessed that when he saw it, he would recognize it. And with any luck be able to take some advantage from it.

So, four nights after the brutal death of Thorlaug Gyduson, Aghen Ormsson found himself walking slowly along the earthworks that ringed Vík-ló. He kept to the shadows. He was not hiding, not really. Not so much that he would seem suspicious if noticed, but he was certainly making an effort to not be seen.

He studied the faces of the men he could see in the torchlight. He recognized most, but he did not know their names. Like Thorlaug Gyduson, a man whose name he did not learn until long after he had sent him to Hel's realm. These men were something new that had appeared at Vík-ló, like weeds sprung up in a familiar garden and soon overrunning it.

Aghen was making his second tour of the earthworks when he saw the man he wanted. Tall and thin, with a hook nose, Aghen recognized him right off, though he had not seen him since he had watched the bastard gleefully shoot an arrow into Valgerd's right shoulder. The man was apparently someone of authority, as he was standing on the top of the wall and issuing orders to the others, his arms sweeping left and right.

Stepping back into the shadows of a longhouse, Aghen watched and he waited. He waited as the man finished his instructions and paced back and forth along the wall for a bit, looking out over the palisades into the dark countryside beyond. He waited as the man spoke some last words Aghen could not hear, and then found the ladder and climbed the ten feet down to the ground.

Still Aghen waited. He looked in every direction, searching for anyone who might witness this transaction, but there was no one around. He waited as the man walked toward the plank road, passing ten feet from where Aghen stood, not seeing him there.

This is your idea of vigilance? Aghen thought. He stepped from the shadow and called to the man's retreating back.

"You, there."

The man visibly jumped and spun around, and he pulled his sword as he did. Aghen stepped closer, hands up in a placating gesture. The man cocked his head as he peered at Aghen in the dim light.

"You're the shipwright," he said. "The one who saw the wolf."

"Yes," Aghen said. "That's why I need to talk with you."

The man took a step closer, but he did not relax. "What about?"

"The wolf," Aghen said. "The one that killed Thorlaug. I think I know something of it. I found something that might explain it all. Something Ottar would be happy to know."

Ten minutes later they were down by the river, well beyond the shipyard, where Aghen had promised to show the man something that would be of great amazement. Aghen explained that he dared not bring it to Ottar himself, that only one of Ottar's most trusted men should do that. But if Ottar offered some reward for it, which no doubt he would, Aghen expected a share.

The man agreed. But he did not relax in his wariness and he did not return his sword to its scabbard as Aghen led the way.

"Here it is," Aghen said, stopping in the knee-high grass. "I found it just today." He leaned over and retrieved his mechanical wolf jaws and held them up.

Ottar's man squinted in the weak moonlight. "What is it?" he asked.

"It's some tool," Aghen said. "And I think whoever killed Thorlaug Gyduson used it to rip his throat away, to make it seem as if a wolf had done it."

The man stepped closer, running his eyes over the long wooden shafts and the rows of iron teeth. He slipped his sword back into the scabbard and reached out with both hands. "Let me see that," he demanded.

Aghen handed it over. Ottar's man grabbed the handles and worked the jaws open and closed. "By all the gods…" he muttered.

"There's this, too," Aghen said. The man looked up as Aghen lifted a length of oak from the grass, three feet long and two inches around. His expression was just changing from confusion to fear as Aghen whirled the staff around, a powerful, accurate blow that made remorseless connection with the side of the man's head.

Chapter Nineteen

Whenever I bring it to mind
It inflames the limits of my heart,
Cold flags over temples of the buried
The Annals of Ulster

Lochlánn felt the horse pushing back against the rush of the water, and he knew he should lead his men out of the river, but he couldn't, not just then. He sat in the saddle, motionless, watching the heathen ship slipping away downstream.

Just moments before, the air had been filled with shouting and screams, the clash of weapons, the frantic cry of horses. And now it was quiet, the ship moving noiselessly, the weapons still. The only sound was the water—water pushing against the horses' legs, and the splashing of the men who had dismounted and now thrashed around looking for their comrades.

"Airt's gone," Lochlánn heard one of them announce. He did not turn to look.

"Gone?" he heard Senach reply. "Dead?"

"I guess," said the first. "He's gone. Can't find him. I guess the current took him away."

Airt's gone, Lochlánn thought. He could picture that wild Northman launching himself off the side of the ship and taking Airt down into the water with him. What had become of them, Lochlánn did not see. He had had time only for a second's glance. He remembered hoping that Airt would kill the man. Apparently he had not.

My God, my God, what have I done?

He heard another saying, "Come along, Fintain, you can sit a horse. Let me help you up." He heard them splashing through the water, the restless whinny of the horse as they held it steady for the wounded man.

Fintain lives, anyway, Lochlánn thought. *How many have we lost?* He did not want to know. He wanted to ride away, leave all this behind, all this for which he was now responsible. He wanted to, but he knew he never would.

Instead he pulled his eyes from the ship, which was moving toward a bend in the river and would soon be lost from sight in any event, and wheeled his horse around. Most of the men who had ridden with him were still in their saddles, he was pleased to see. Most had spears in hand and shields on arms and were watching the heathens' ship disappearing down river, as he had been doing.

He looked over their faces. He expected to see fury there, or disgust, or some sign that they were done with this whole venture. But he saw none of that. He saw only what he took to be a patient resolve, the faces of soldiers who were waiting for orders, and who would follow them when they came.

Senach gave his horse a nudge with his heels and rode over to Lochlánn's side. "Airt's killed, and Cerball. Didn't find either of them. Fintain and Colcu are wounded, but they'll be fine. That's it. Not too bad for a bloody fight like that."

"Not too bad," Lochlánn agreed, which was not at all how he felt about the whole affair.

It had been his idea, of course. Standing on the sandbar where the heathens had made their camp, he had resolved to go after them and hit them hard. He had thought at first to set the trap in the same spot where Louis de Roumois had set it before, when they had done so much hurt to the heathens coming up river. But it occurred to him that the heathens might expect that.

What's more, Louis's trap had relied on archers, which they did not have, and on the heathens having to tow their ships over the shallows, which might not be the case this time. A new plan was needed, so they rode hard to get ahead of the heathens' ship and explored the banks of the river until Lochlánn found the spot he thought most suited.

It was not as ideal a spot, but Lochlánn guessed that the heathens would not be expecting an attack there. And judging from the frantic scramble he had witnessed aboard the ship when he and his riders had first come from the trees, he reckoned he was right.

"Did you see him?" Senach asked.

Lochlánn nodded. "I saw her, too," he said. Louis de Roumois and Failend. Neither Lochlánn nor Senach was certain they had been with the heathens at Glendalough. Senach thought he'd seen Failend in the middle of the fighting. The boy, Trian, had said Louis sent him with the warning. But still it was not clear if the two of them had joined with the heathens or not. Until now.

"They were up in the front of the ship," Senach said, "and they were fighting side by side with the heathens." Lochlánn nodded. He had seen that as well.

At least, he had seen Failend fighting. There was no question in his mind. He had seen her swipe at the riders with her short sword, had seen her take up a spear and fend off the attackers. He had seen Louis as well, sword in hand, but he could not say he had actually seen the man engage in combat.

Of course, he had seen none of it clearly. It was not like he had been sitting back watching the whole thing as if it were some pageant on a stage. He had been in the middle of the fight, had been fully engaged, and anything he had seen had been only in quick glimpses and fleeting impressions.

You only think Louis stayed out of the fight because you want to think that… Lochlánn scoffed at himself. *You saw what you were hoping to see.* But still he was not so sure.

Fintain was settled on his horse, but it took a minute for him to get his feet in the stirrups and look as if he would not fall off. Senach turned his horse so he was facing Lochlánn and he did the one thing Lochlánn would not have expected. He smiled.

"That was a damned good fight," he said. "I've been in some bloody scrapes, but that one we'll be talking about when we're old men by the fire. Horsemen against a ship!" He shook his head.

Lochlánn was not sure what to make of that. He had been chastising himself, mentally flagellating himself for having led these men into such a place of death. And here Senach was delighting in it.

He tapped his horse's flanks and took the animal closer, so he and Senach could talk without being heard. The rest of the men were in a line ten feet up river. Most had secured their shields on straps over their backs and were slumping in their saddles, feeling the great wave of exhaustion that comes on the heels of a battle's surge.

"Senach, are the men angry about this? What are they thinking?" Lochlánn asked. These were his men now, but he was not one of them, and he was very aware of that fact. And he was grateful to have Senach by his side, because Senach was indeed one of them and had their measure.

"Angry?" Senach sounded surprised by the question. "No, they're pleased. These are fighting men. They're always happiest when they're fighting and have a captain who's not afraid to fight."

"Really?" Lochlánn said. "Won't they want to return to Glendalough now?"

Senach shook his head. "They saw Louis, there on the ship. They want him. They want to see justice for Aileran. And they want their revenge on the heathens, for all the evil they've done. And don't forget…all the plunder from the church at Glendalough is on that ship, along with anything else the heathens have stolen."

Now it was Lochlánn's turn to smile. *Of course*, he thought. *The plunder from Glendalough.*

It was not honor or vengeance alone that drove these men. There was a fortune aboard the ship. Even if most of it would have to go back to the church, there would certainly be enough that some would find its way into their purses. And of course, only the church's wealth had to go back to the church. Anything else aboard would be considered proper spoils.

"So, we should…?" Lochlánn asked.

"We should get out of this damned river and go after the heathens once more," Senach said.

And that was what they did. Lochlánn spurred his horse on and with a wave of his arm led the men back toward the bank, then up and onto the grassy field that ran off to the north. They found the road again, the road that roughly followed the course of the river, and headed off at an easy pace. They could no longer see the heathen vessel, but they knew where it was. That was the good thing about tracking a ship in a river—there was only one path it could follow.

They rode on as evening approached and the first drops of rain began to fall. They found a small farm enclosed by a dubious ringfort and asked if they could spend the night, though the request was really more of a demand phrased as a question. With eighteen armed, weary, and impatient horsemen behind him, Lochlánn was not surprised that the farmer readily acquiesced.

Before they put the horses up, Lochlánn called for two volunteers to ride down to the river and scout out where the heathens had stopped for the night. When all eighteen of the men volunteered, Lochlánn picked the two youngest and least weary looking and sent them on their way. They were not gone long. Supper was still being prepared over the smoky fire in the hearth when they returned and reported the heathen vessel run up on the opposite shore not two miles away.

The men ate, they drank, they found places on the dirt floor to sleep. The house was cramped and filthy and smelled of stale sweat and years of bad cooking, but the men, listening to the rain drumming down on the thatch, were grateful for it. Lochlánn gave the farmer silver, more than the food and drink and hospitality were worth, and that secured the man's enthusiastic and continued cooperation.

He and Senach sat on the raised platform that lined one of the walls. They drank a nasty brew the farmer called ale and spoke as softly as they could and still make themselves heard over the men's bovine snoring.

"Here's the thing of it," Lochlánn said. "It seemed the heathens had twice our numbers, at least. We have the horses, we have the men-at-arms, we're on our native land. But in the end we can't beat them if they outnumber us so."

Senach nodded. He drank, made a face, looked down into his cup, then drank again. "But what do we do? Sure, we can't go back to Glendalough and ask more men. Brother Gilla Patraic expected us back two days ago. He won't be happy, and you can bet he's spoken to the abbot. They're not likely to let us find more men-at-arms. I'd rather fight a hundred heathens than get a tongue lashing from either of those old men."

Lochlánn nodded. He had been at the receiving end of Brother Gilla Patraic and the abbot's rage plenty of times.

"Very well…" Lochlánn said. He took a drink and stared into the fire and let his mind toy with the various possibilities. And then a thought came to him.

"You recall, on the last day we were fighting the heathens, back at Glendalough," he said, "there was one of the rí túaithe showed up on the field. Kevin mac Lugaed, of Cill Mhantáin. You recall?"

Senach nodded. "He makes his home at Ráth Naoi," he said. "That's but two days' ride from here."

"Exactly," Lochlánn said. "He has men; he's already shown he has an interest in fighting the heathens."

"You must go to him, see if he'll give you men-at-arms," Senach said. "Me and the rest, we'll stay and keep watch on the heathens. I'll send word where they've gone."

Lochlánn shook his head. "My place is with the men. You should go."

"Kevin mac Lugaed won't listen to me, a man of my station," Senach argued. "If there's any chance to convince him, it will have to be you."

And Lochlánn knew he was right. Despite the fact that he, Lochlánn, was nothing beyond a renegade novitiate leading a gang of men-at-arms on an illicit wild goose chase, he still stood the best chance of convincing Kevin mac Lugaed to help. Lochlánn was not low born, and his speech and his manner and the quality of his mail and sword spoke to that fact.

As to the illegitimacy of their mission, Lochlánn did not feel it was necessary that Kevin be made aware of that.

The next morning, even before the sun was up, with the rain still falling hard, Lochlánn mac Ainmire and three of his men mounted up and rode out of the little ringfort. One of the three men was Fintain, whose wound proved none too threatening, which was good, because Fintain knew the country of Cill Mhantáin and the way to Ráth Naoi well.

"I wish you luck, Captain, talking with Kevin mac Lugaed," Fintain said as they rode, the gray sky growing lighter with the rising sun.

"Why do you say that?" Lochlánn asked.

"Well, he's not known as an open, generous spirit," Fintain said. "Tightfisted, that one. And crafty. No one's quite sure how he ended up as rí túaithe, but there he is."

They spoke more, on and off, over what turned out to be two days of miserable travel in near constant rain. Fintain told him all he knew about Kevin mac Lugaed, which was by his own admission little and mostly hearsay. But that scant information did suggest that Kevin might not be as open to giving aid as Lochlánn had hoped.

It was late afternoon on their second day when they arrived at the ringfort at Ráth Naoi, a more expansive and altogether more impressive fort than the one from which they had left. The earthworks described a circle a hundred yards across, and even from a distance they could see the high-peaked thatched roofs of the houses within.

Lording it over all of them was the building Lochlánn took to be Kevin's hall. It was a substantial structure, a third again as tall as the next tallest building. Smoke billowed from an opening in the roof, and that suggested warmth and relief from the rain and it made Lochlánn very eager to be there.

They were no longer alone on the road. A few miles short of Ráth Naoi they had run into patrols sent out by Kevin mac Lugaed, a precaution he apparently maintained at all times, weather notwithstanding. The rain and the cold made the patrol a bit short-tempered, and they were none too gracious in their demand to know Lochlánn's business. But Lochlánn had said only that he was from Glendalough and needed to speak with Kevin, all of which was true, and Lochlánn's association with the wealthy and important monastery was enough to secure the patrol's cooperation.

Kevin's men led the way, and the big gates were swung open for them and they rode through, Lochlánn and his men following behind. They were escorted to the hall, made to hand over their weapons, and then let in through the heavy oak door that creaked on iron hinges.

The hall was everything Lochlánn had hoped: lofty and wide with a massive fire burning in the hearth that gave the place a cheery look, particularly in contrast with the gloom of the rainy late afternoon from which they had stepped. He could feel the warmth as he came through the door, and did not wait for an invitation to walk closer to the flames.

Kevin mac Lugaed was there to greet him. Lochlánn had met him before, at the dúnad, a small man with a beard trimmed short and cut neatly into a point. His clothing suggested wealth, though not as much as did the heavy gold chain around his neck. He was smaller than Lochlánn remembered, several inches below Lochlánn's own height. Thin and slightly nervous-looking. He reminded Lochlánn of a squirrel.

"I am Kevin. Kevin mac Lugaed," he said, stepping forward and offering a hand, which Lochlánn grasped and shook. "I am rí túaithe here in Cill Mhantáin."

"Yes, lord," Lochlánn said. "And I am Lochlánn mac Ainmire, most recently of Glendalough. We met briefly at the dúnad. I don't imagine you would remember me."

"Of course I do, of course," Kevin said, and Lochlánn could not tell if that was the truth or not. "But look, you're soaked through and hungry, no doubt. You and your men, come up to the fire. Dry out a bit and we'll have food and drink and then you'll tell me why you've come."

If Kevin was tight-fisted, it was not evident in his hospitality, which was not wanting in the least. Lochlánn and his men were seated at benches by the fire. Lochlánn could actually see steam rising off his clothing. The heat was nearly painful, but he relished it. They were fed and given ale and were almost dry and in danger of falling asleep when Kevin said, "Now, pray, tell me why you've come, what I can do for you."

Lochlánn sat straighter and stretched his back. "I've come mostly because I recall the noble part you and your men played at the fighting near Glendalough," he said, and Kevin tilted his head in thanks for the compliment. "As you know, there was a great slaughter done among the heathens. But some got away. What's more…and you will hardly believe this…they had the impudence to return to Glendalough like the thieves they are and plunder the church in the night."

"They plundered the church?" Kevin said. "Animals."

"Animals, indeed. My men and I, at the abbot's behest, we followed them and we fought them and did them a deal of hurt. But we are only eighteen or so men, half the heathens' number. I'm here to ask you for more soldiers. Give me the use of thirty men-at-arms, I beg you, and I will be able to stamp out this vermin."

"Hmmm," Kevin said in a very serious tone. "Thirty men, you say? That's quite a lot, given how few men I have. I don't know as I dare weaken my forces so."

Judging by the number of armed men Lochlánn had seen just since his arrival there, thirty did not seem like many at all, but he resisted making that point. Rather, he said, "But, Lord Kevin, sure you're safe here. There are no enemies about, except those I'm proposing to crush. And I would need the men only for a short while."

"Don't presume to tell me how safe I am," Kevin said, and for the first time his gracious demeanor slipped a bit, revealing something less kind underneath. "There are any number of men around here who would like to take my place and are just looking for the moment to strike. Irishmen and heathens."

Lochlánn thought about the patrol that had met them on the road, the numerous armed men standing out in the rain and ringing Kevin's hall, the men on the walls and the heavy gates. What enemies Kevin might have

Lochlánn did not know, but it was clear Kevin was wary of them, and very cautious.

"But tell me," Kevin said, his voice was once again smooth and conciliatory, "you say the heathens plundered the church. But surely they're not staying in the neighborhood? Are they not trying to escape?"

"Well, yes," Lochlánn said. He could see where this was headed.

"Then they are no threat, if they are trying to escape. A shame if they do, but I would not care to see my men killed just so the wealthy abbot of Glendalough doesn't lose a few communion plates."

"We think they're trying to escape, but we don't know," Lochlánn said. "They're crafty. Led by one they call Thorgrim Night Wolf, and he seems a clever one indeed."

Kevin looked up quickly, his expression quite altered, enough that it took Lochlánn by surprise. Just a moment before his host had seemed disinterested in the whole affair. Now, suddenly, he seemed very interested indeed.

"You know Thorgrim Night Wolf?" Lochlánn asked.

"No, I don't know him," Kevin said, nearly snapping the words, but then once again regaining his equilibrium. "I know of him. He styled himself lord of that longphort the heathens have established on my coast. The one they call Vík-ló. I make it my business to know what goes on in this country, so I knew he had a part in the raid on Glendalough. But I heard he had been killed."

"I have it on good authority it was Thorgrim Night Wolf who just plundered the church," Lochlánn said, sensing a possible opening here. "He and his men are the ones we fought. They may have been trying to escape, but if so, they seemed in no great hurry. I got the idea they meant to remain in this neighborhood a bit. Even if not, we don't want them to get back to that Vík-ló, where they can do more mischief."

Kevin shook his head. He was looking into the fire now, as if trying to read something in the flames. "No, Thorgrim won't try to return to Vík-ló," he said, and he seemed to be speaking as much to himself as to Lochlánn. "Ottar is lord at Vík-ló now. He's a real beast, but I thought I only had to contend with him alone. Not him and Thorgrim Night Wolf. I thought Thorgrim was dead."

He looked up at Lochlánn and Lochlánn shook his head. "No," he said, "Thorgrim's out there."

"Very well," Kevin said. "We…we can't have him threatening Glendalough, that sacred place. You'll have the men you want. The men you need to crush Thorgrim Night Wolf and his band, once and for all."

Chapter Twenty

Flann son of Mael Sechnaill led an army both of foreigners and Irish into the North.

The Annals of Ulster

The rain was coming down hard, filling *Sea Hammer*'s bilges fast enough that ten minutes out of every hour were needed for bailing. It would have been much worse at sea, of course, with rain, spray, and green water coming over the sides. But they were on a river, tied to the bank, all but motionless, and it was only the relentless downpour that threatened to swamp them.

Thorgrim Night Wolf stood in the open, in the stern, despite the rain. He looked across the wide Avonmore River toward the northern side, where another river joined it. This tributary, however, hardly deserved the title of river. It was a glorified stream, really, a few inches of water, fifteen feet wide, tumbling over stones and gravel before it merged with the Avonmore through a cut in the grassy bank.

Cónán stood beside him, the two men alone on the afterdeck. The rest had retreated under the sail spread to form a great tent over the middle section of the ship. It was cramped under that shelter, with Thorgrim's men and Cónán's men and women clustered there, but there was still space enough for all of them to get out of the deluge.

"You call that a river?" Thorgrim asked.

"It's a river," Cónán said. "You asked was there a river and I said yes, and there it is. Runs to within a mile of that Kevin mac Lugaed's ringfort."

Thorgrim shook his head. "I meant a river that we could float the ship on," he said.

"Well, you didn't say that, did you?" Cónán said. "You just asked about a river. I don't pretend I know the first damned thing about your damned ships."

"We couldn't float a log on that stream," Thorgrim said. "Which means we're on foot from here."

Cónán's Irish bandits, he guessed, would be even more put out by this news than his own men would. He was sure that they had come to very much appreciate travel by ship. No trudging through the mud, no carrying supplies and weapons, no sleeping on the ground. The river would bear them along and they could sit under the tent made by the sail and move faster than they might otherwise, and with no more effort needed than it took to sit by a hearth. For Cónán's people it was a newfound luxury, and there wasn't much to dislike.

"We're on foot, for sure," Cónán agreed. "But to where, I don't know."

"Kevin's ringfort. Like you said."

"Ah!" Cónán said. "That's where you're going. But whether or not me and my people are with you, that we have yet to decide."

Thorgrim pulled his eyes from the stream that Cónán had called a river and looked at the Irishman. What the man said was true. So fixated had he been on sacking Kevin's hall and having his revenge on the man, he had forgotten that he and Cónán had come to no agreement.

"All right," Thorgrim said. "You want to be coy about this…what do you want?"

"I want to get out of this rain and sit down and talk like civilized men," Cónán said.

Thorgrim smiled. Neither of them were what most would call "civilized men," but he had to agree that getting out of the rain would be preferable. He led the way under the sail tent. The men seated on the sea chests aft made room for him and Cónán, crowding forward to give the two leaders more room and as much privacy as could be offered in that cramped space.

Once out of the rain, Thorgrim shed his cloak. The day was wet, but it was not cold, and that was a relief. Cara, the healer woman, brought cups of ale for him and Cónán.

"I've spoken with my men," Cónán said, "and they're willing to join with you on this raid."

Thorgrim nodded, but thought, *Half of that statement is a pile of dung.* He had no idea what Cónán said to his men, since he spoke to them in Irish, but he doubted that Cónán ever asked for their opinions. It seemed more likely that Cónán simply told them what to do. But no matter. Cónán's men appeared happy enough with that arrangement, and if Cónán wished to make it seem as if his men had a say in affairs, then that was fine.

"I'm glad to know you and your men will fight with me," Thorgrim said, "but I'm guessing there's more to it than that."

"There is," Cónán said. "This Kevin mac Lugaed, he took power after Lorcan was killed, like I told you. He made a lot of enemies doing that. His hold on the *túatha* is not so strong."

Thorgrim held up his hands. "'Túatha?' I don't know that word."

"Ireland is made up of many…kingdoms, you might call them. They are the túatha. The men who rule them are the rí túaithe. Like Kevin."

"I see," Thorgrim said. It all seemed terribly complicated, though he had to admit that the situation in his native Norway was not any better, just more familiar to him.

"Kevin doesn't feel too secure with his hold on the territory," Cónán continued. "So he's surrounded himself with men-at-arms. He pays them well, and that means he's well protected."

He pays them with the silver I gave him to provide food and ale and mead for Vík-ló, Thorgrim thought, but he kept that to himself. Rather, he said, "You're saying it will not be so easy to defeat him."

"I'm saying if we try with just the men we have here, we might as well cut our own throats. It'll be just as effective."

Thorgrim's first impulse was to assure Cónán that he did not care. He was going to kill Kevin mac Lugaed whether it meant his own death or not. In fact, the only part of it that gave him pause was knowing that if he died killing Kevin he would not have the chance to kill Ottar as well. He had been played for a fool by both of them, the greatest humiliation he had suffered since reaching manhood, and he would never let it happen again.

Still, he was willing to listen to what Cónán had to say. He knew better than to think he could forever avoid all entanglements. But he was more wary now, and unwilling to yield even a bit of control.

"What is it you have in mind?" he asked the Irishman

"There's another band, like us, me and my men, and they're not far from here," Cónán said. "About thirty men. Still a lot less than what Kevin has, but they're tough bastards and it'll make things more even. I think they'd join us."

Thorgrim looked at Cónán without responding as he turned this over in his head. *What game are you playing here?* he wondered. *What is it you stand to gain?* The Irish already outnumbered his Northmen by more than two to one, so he did not think Cónán was looking for that sort of advantage.

Cónán, he imagined, was genuinely interested in sacking Kevin's hall—it would be a profitable venture if it could be done—and, as with Glendalough, he doubted Cónán's men would have the nerve to try without the Norse raiders taking the lead.

But still Thorgrim suspected there was more to it than that.

That's all right, he concluded. Whatever Cónán was up to, it had to do with Irish affairs, not those of the Northmen. As far as Thorgrim was concerned, these Irish bastards were free to kill one another at will, as long as they did no harm to his men and did not interfere with the retribution he meant to bring to his enemies.

"These others will join us…why?" Thorgrim asked. "The promise of plunder? Your good looks, your charming speech?"

"All those things, yes," Cónán said. "Mostly the promise of plunder. Real plunder, not the rubbish they're used to stealing. But we might do better if we give them a taste of it, you know. A hint of what might be theirs for the taking."

"What do you suggest?"

"The Frank, Louis," Cónán said. "He's got a silver hoard. The way I see it, that's yours, your plunder, by rights. He's your prisoner. Let me hand some of that around, and you'll have some very cooperative men on your side."

Thorgrim looked forward. Louis was sitting by himself, as he was wont. It used to be that Failend was invariably with him, not so much anymore. As often as not she was sitting with the other Northmen. She had picked up a word or two of their language, he had noticed.

"No," Thorgrim said. "He's not my prisoner. I gave him his freedom. And returned his hoard. I won't go back on that." In truth, he had the impression that the hoard was as much Failend's as Louis's, and he would not rob Failend of her silver. She had already proved helpful, and probably would again.

"Very well," Cónán said in a tone that suggested Thorgrim was making a mistake. "I can see if they'll come with us for a promise alone."

"No, you need not do that," Thorgrim said. He stood and opened the sea chest on which he had been sitting, his own sea chest. He fished out a leather purse and handed it to Cónán.

"That's my share from Glendalough. Use that. Tell these men there's more where that came from."

Cónán took the purse with some reluctance. "This is your full share," he said.

"It doesn't matter, not at all," Thorgrim said. "I told you, I have more, much more, back at Vík-ló, which I mean to take back. Or die in the attempt. Either way, that purse means nothing to me."

Cónán nodded.

"But here's what does matter to me," Thorgrim said. "I mean to kill Kevin, and I mean to kill Ottar at Vík-ló. I care about nothing else, save for the lives of my men. You make sure that these men you're speaking of understand that. I don't care what reason they have for joining us. I don't care what game you might be playing, either. There'll be plunder to be had, and they're welcome to it. But anyone who is with me will do as I say, or I'll kill them as well. Just so you understand."

"You are a sweet one with the words," Cónán said. He smiled and stood. "Lucky for us I'm the one who'll do the talking. And between my words and your silver I think we'll have men enough to kill Kevin mac Lugaed, and Ottar, and send them off to hell where they belong."

It was an hour later that Cónán, well-fed and with a belly full of ale, a dry cloak over his head and Thorgrim's purse full of silver hanging from his belt, hopped off *Sea Hammer*'s bow and onto the soft mud where she had been run aground. He climbed up the bank and then disappeared into the woods lining the river.

It felt odd to be on his own, to not have the men and women for whom he was responsible there with him, hindering his mobility so that he could move no faster than the slowest among them. It was like lifting a mail shirt off after having worn it for some time, a surprising lightness, a forgotten freedom of motion.

How long since I was last on my own? he mused as he pushed his way through the undergrowth. In his younger days he would sometimes spend weeks by himself, living off the countryside, purposely avoiding his fellow Irishmen. There were some who would enslave him, some who would rob him, some who would hang him for a thief. There were few who would do him any kindness, and fewer still who would do so unless there was some benefit to themselves. Such was the way of the world, as Cónán had learned early on, and so he avoided others. You don't join the wolf pack until you can run with the strongest of them.

He came to the edge of the woods and paused there, sweeping his eyes over the open country beyond. Wide fields of startling green, some patches of wood, smoke rising up from some place off in the distance. A ringfort or a campfire in a stand of trees, maybe. With the rain falling as it was, he did not expect to see anyone abroad, and he did not.

He was acting out of long habit. Pausing, watching, assessing. It was not entirely necessary, and he knew it. If they had all been with him, the women, the younger ones, the wounded ones, then he certainly would have taken this precaution. But he was on his own. One man alone would not attract much notice, particularly one such as Cónán, who looked like any of the pathetic *ócaire*, the lowliest of the freemen in Ireland's complex hierarchy.

Nor would Cónán have been much concerned if there had been others about. He knew he could escape from most anyone who might want to do him harm, and kill those from whom he could not escape. He looked like a helpless tenant farmer because he wished to look that way, but in truth he was anything but that.

He stepped out from the trees and headed across the open ground, moving away from the river and the Northmen's ship.

Thorgrim Night Wolf, he thought. *There's quite a fellow.*

He had taken the man's measure when they first met, when Thorgrim had done him the kindness of killing the outlaws' former leader and saving him the trouble. Hard man. Uncompromising. Though maybe a little more sentimental than even he himself realized. That nonsense about Louis the Frank's silver was proof enough of that. Still, Cónán had the feeling he was a man who could be trusted, and not a man to be crossed.

For three hours Cónán continued moving south and west. He moved fast, walking at times, jogging at others, relishing the ability to push hard like he used to. The rain was unrelenting and he was soaked through, but he hardly noticed that anymore after half a lifetime spent mostly out of doors. He saw riders once, off in the distance, and a small huddle of people trudging along a road, but no one paid him any attention.

He slowed his pace as he neared his destination, mostly because he did not actually know where his destination was. He was looking for an outlaw band much like his own. He knew he was in their territory, but that territory encompassed many miles and they could be anywhere within those bounds.

Their túatha… he thought and he smiled at the thought. *We are the lords of the fields and the woods, whether those in the great halls know it or not…*

He saw smoke in the distance and guessed that as likely as not it marked the location of those for whom he was looking. He moved off in that direction, more alert now, keeping himself more hidden than he had been. He doubted that there would be anyone keeping watch that far from the camp, but he always liked to remain vigilant, because men who remained vigilant remained alive.

He covered another half mile before he could see the stand of trees from which the smoke was rising. There was nothing but open ground between him and the wooded area, no cover, but he did manage to find a small hill behind which he could conceal himself and survey the woods before making his approach. He crouched behind the hill, made his way carefully to the crest and looked over.

There you are, you bastards, he thought.

The cows gave it away. He was not sure what he was seeing at first. Movement in the trees, a flash of white. He let his eyes settle on the wood line, and finally it became clear what he was looking at, half hidden in the shadows. Cows.

Most of the wealth in Ireland was measured in cattle. Lesser lords paid overlords in cattle. Neighbors lashed out at neighbors by staging cattle raids. And outlaws stole cattle from anyone who had it. But only outlaws secreted their cattle in stands of trees.

You've been busy, he thought. He knew these men. He had been with them once, some time back, before moving on to greater opportunities. The separation had not been entirely cordial. That, he knew, would mean that something less than a warm reception awaited him.

He untied the purse that Thorgrim had given him, spilled half the silver, gold, and jewels into the palm of his hand, then hid them in a secret pocket sewn into his tunic. *If Thorgrim's feeling generous*, he thought, *there's no reason why these bastards should get it all.*

He stood and headed off toward the woods in the distance. He walked, he did not run, ambling along with a practiced lack of concern. He could see men now, moving through the trees, watching him approach. They were trying to keep hidden and probably thought they had succeeded, but to Cónán they were as obvious as if their hair were on fire.

Stupid, clumsy fools, he thought. He could have entered the woods unseen, come up behind them, and the first sound they heard would have been his knife cutting their throats. But that would not serve his purpose.

Your lucky day, he thought.

He reached the woods and pushed his way onto a worn trail, into the welcome shelter of the trees. The rain was still loud overhead, but few drops managed to reach him, which was a relief. He flipped his hood off his head and walked farther in.

He had not covered ten feet before the men were on him, three men, young, a bit scared. One carried a spear, another a cudgel, the third a short sword in lamentable condition.

"Hold up!" the spear-man said, and Cónán stopped, his hands slightly raised. The spearman stepped closer, squinted at Cónán's face.

"Cónán!" he said, with more than a hint of mocking triumph, as if he had somehow brought this capture about through his own quick wits. "Look who's here. It's Cónán, come back!"

The others stepped closer, grinning. Cónán made a quick move in their direction, arms shooting out, a lunging half step toward them. They leapt back, gasping, weapons coming up. Cónán shouted "Boo!" and laughed.

The others did not laugh with him. "Still reckon yourself funny, do you?" the spearman asked. His name was Fergus, Cónán recalled. He recognized the others but knew he would never remember their names. Nor did it matter.

"Yes, I do, Fergus," Cónán said. "But it's Blathmac I've come to entertain, not you."

"Oh, you'll entertain Blathmac, have no doubt of it," Fergus said, clearly still smarting from the embarrassment of having been startled. "We'll go see him now. But first we see that you don't play anymore tricks." He reached over and carefully pulled Cónán's cloak back. There was a short club in his belt and a long knife encased in a leather sheath.

"Ha!" Fergus said. "We'll take those, thank you." He handed his spear to one of the others and pulled the weapons from Cónán's belt. Cónán made no objection. The weapons were sacrificial. Having found those, Cónán guessed they would not look any further, would not find the seax lashed to his back, hidden by the cape. And he was right.

"The purse as well," the one with the cudgel said. "Get the purse." Fergus reached for it, but Cónán grabbed his wrist and held his arm motionless.

"Not the purse," Cónán said. "That's business for me and Blathmac."

Fergus struggled against Cónán's grip, but not blatantly, not so it was obvious to the others. They stood that way for only a few seconds. That was all it took for Fergus to realize he would not budge Cónán's arm, so he gave it up and pulled his hand away. "Fine," he said, "we'll let Blathmac deal with you."

They led Cónán further into the woods, down a worn path that suggested this hiding place had seen long use. *Interesting*, Cónán thought. He wondered why Blathmac was staying put, if he was losing his nerve, afraid of leaving his hiding place. If his men were growing restless because of it.

They came at last to a clearing that Cónán remembered, though it had been a few years since he had been here. Thirty or so men were gathered around a smattering of campfires. Women were cooking over the flames or tending to other chores.

All heads looked up as they stepped into the open place and Fergus said in a loud voice, "Look who we caught sneaking around." Cónán looked from face to face. Many he recognized, some were new to him. He saw a woman with whom he had once been intimate and he smiled at her, but she frowned and looked away. He heard his name muttered as he passed.

Then they were in front of Blathmac. He was shorter than Cónán, and a little beefier, with a massive beard that only seemed to emphasize his lack of stature. He always made Cónán think of a *luchrupán*, one of the little people of old legends. He was standing with arms folded now, waiting for Fergus and the others to present the prisoner to him.

Fergus grabbed Cónán's arm and jerked him to a stop five feet in front of where Blathmac stood waiting. For a moment they were all silent, Cónán and Blathmac holding one another's eyes.

Finally Fergus broke the silence. "We found him…" he began, but Blathmac cut him off.

"Cónán," he said. "It's been some time."

"It has," Cónán said.

"When you're in front of me now," Blathmac said, putting emphasis on each word, "you kneel."

Silence again. Blathmac waited for Cónán to reply. Cónán glanced at Fergus, who stood to one side of him, and then the men who stood on the other. He wondered if they would try to make him kneel. He wondered if he should break their arms if they did.

"See here, Blathmac," Cónán said, turning back to the chieftain, and speaking in a tone that made it clear he would not be kneeling anytime soon. "What happened between us is over. Gone. History, old as Noah and the flood. Now I come to you to offer you a chance. A great chance. For real plunder. Even greater than the silly herd of cows you have hidden in the trees."

"You've come with an offer for me?" Blathmac said. "As if I would ever believe anything that came out of your lying mouth?"

"Don't believe me. Believe this." Cónán pulled the purse from his belt and shook it so it made an enticing jingling sound. "I bring this as a gift to you, and just a taste of what more might come your way." He tossed the purse to Blathmac, tossed it easy so Blathmac could catch it without dropping it. Now was not the time to embarrass the man.

Blathmac caught the purse and tugged it open with a feigned disinterest he had not really mastered. He looked into the purse and Cónán could not miss the widening eyes, the little jerk of his head in surprise, the obvious effort Blathmac needed to contain his enthusiasm.

"I accept this gift," Blathmac said, drawing the purse closed and tucking it into his belt. "Though it hardly equals what you owe me. Now, I give you leave to speak."

Give me leave to speak, Cónán thought. *Like he's the damned* rí ruirech, *the damned high king.* I *give* you *leave to live. For now.*

But he kept that to himself. Instead, he took a step forward, and in a low voice said, "We must talk, because I am onto something here that could make us all rich as lords."

Twenty-One

The unwise man is awake all night,
and ponders everything over;
when morning comes he is weary in mind,
and all is a burden as ever.
Hávamál

The chaos of the evening was over, and the dark hours of night had settled on Vík-ló when they pounded on Aghen's door. He was not surprised. Nor was he afraid.

Aghen had not been asleep. He doubted anyone in all of Vík-ló had been asleep. Patrols of armed, torch-bearing men were flocking through the streets and along the wall and down by the river. They had been shouting to one another all night, warnings that proved to be false alarms, admonitions to check here or there. Every once in a while the voice of Ottar Bloodax came howling through the dark, loud, demanding, sounding the way a bull might sound if a bull could issue frantic and barely comprehensible orders.

After the first man, Thorlaug Gyduson, had been found dead by the wall, his throat torn out by a wolf, the longphort was thrown into an uproar. That night, and for the next few nights, Ottar's men lined the earthen wall and paraded through the streets, looking out for the renegade beast. It seemed to Aghen an excess of excitement.

It was a strange thing, to be sure, having a man killed by a wolf right there in the longphort, but such a thing was not impossible. Even for those who did not know how it had happened, which was everyone save for Aghen, it should not have caused so much consternation. But that, apparently, was not how Ottar felt, and Ottar's rage spread like a drop of blood on white linen until all of Vík-ló felt it.

It did not last very long. A few nights after Thorlaug's death, and with no further signs of the creature, the men of Vík-ló began to relax. The walls were not manned so heavily, the patrols not so ubiquitous. Ottar, according to Oddi, was less frantic than he had been.

And then Thorstein Kodransson was found dead, the second victim of the wolf.

Like Thorlaug, Thorstein was part of Ottar's household guard. Thorstein, however, had been with Ottar longer, had sailed from Norway with him, apparently had known him since childhood.

According to Oddi, Ottar had gone mad on hearing the news, flinging anything that came to hand across the hall, smashing furniture, ordering his men to man the walls, patrol the grounds, to find and kill the wolf, or see that it had no chance of getting into the longphort again.

The banks of the river were searched, the walls lined with men. Every inch of the earthworks were scoured for some gap, some imperfection where a wolf might get in and out unseen. Nothing was found, nor was there any sign of the wolf—none at all—save for the dead man, his face white, his eyes staring blankly up toward the sky, his body resting on a great circle of blood like a carpet on which he had fallen.

"All those men, and they found no sign at all of the wolf?" Aghen asked Oddi the next day, pausing in his work on a new mast step for one of Ottar's other ships. "No prints, no scat?"

"Nothing," Oddi said. Oddi was not working in the shipyard that day. Like all of Ottar's men, he had been put to work searching for the wolf or walking the earthworks or circling Ottar's hall with weapons ready. Oddi's duties had taken him down by the river, and he used that chance to stop and have a word with Aghen.

"Interesting..." Aghen let the word hang in the air.

"What?" Oddi said. "Interesting? How is it interesting?"

"Well," Aghen said, feigning reluctance to speak. "A proper wolf usually leaves signs, doesn't it? Footprints, like I said. They kill to make a meal. They don't just kill and run off. And yet, this beast..." Again he let the words hang in the air.

"You think maybe...this isn't a proper wolf? It's something else?" Oddi said. What he really wished to ask, Aghen could see, was *Do you think this is Thorgrim Kveldulf, come back in the shape of a wolf?* But he could not bring himself to ask it directly, and Aghen pretended that he did not understand.

"I don't know. It's odd, is all," Aghen said. He wondered if Oddi would report these insinuations to Ottar, or if he had learned his lesson from the last beating. Aghen was not sure. Oddi was not a particularly quick learner.

With the second killing, Vík-ló was once again in a frenzy, then once again the panic that washed over the longphort receded. Vigilance began to wane, and word spread that the constant presence of torches and men on the lookout were keeping the wolf at bay, probably encouraging it to hunt elsewhere. No one suggested that this wolf might be driven by something other than hunger. Folks thought the wolf was gone because they wanted the wolf to be gone.

And then it killed again. The dead man, predictably, was another of Ottar's household guard. He was also one of the men who had helped kill Valgerd, but if anyone made that connection, Aghen never heard about it.

The degree of panic and general terror that followed that killing was more than Aghen could have imagined. Even during the daylight, virtually no one but Ottar's armed men ventured out into the streets, despite the fact that all the killings had happened during the darkest hours of night. The one exception was Aghen, who continued with what others considered remarkable fearlessness to do his work down by the river.

Ottar raged and cursed and swore that not one more man would die by the teeth of the cursed beast. He ordered his men to keep watch over every inch of the longphort, to maintain the highest vigilance, night or day, while he himself remained shuttered up in his hall.

And then a few days later, two more men were found dead behind the baker's house, their throats ripped out just as the others had been.

Those two would be the wolf's final victims, at least for a while, though Aghen alone knew that. The third man had been tricky enough to lure away. All of Ottar's warriors had been admonished to never venture anywhere alone. That one had only been willing to come see the shocking thing Aghen had claimed to discover after Aghen pointed out that he would not be alone, that the two of them would be together. Aghen had hinted at a great stash of silver, and the man's greed eclipsed any skepticism or suspicion.

Aghen had to wonder, in that fraction of a second when the man saw the club swinging at his head, when he opened his mouth to scream, too late, if he understood everything, and realized the truth about the wolf, and what a fool he had been. He wondered if that was the man's last thought before being whisked off to the afterlife. He hoped so.

The old shipwright felt pretty certain he would not find another so foolish, and he was right. The last two men to die by the jaws of the wolf had died together because they were not so stupid as to go alone with Aghen. Thinking this might happen, Aghen had buried a small chest that actually contained silver, a small hoard he had secreted at the shipyard and failed to turn over to Ottar. The sight of the riches had distracted the men enough that Aghen could put them both down before they could react.

Those two had been discovered the day before, and the frenzy in Vík-ló had not subsided in the least. Aghen wondered if any of Ottar's men were allowed any rest at all, or if the Lord of Vík-ló was keeping them on constant patrol. That seemed to be the case, given the number of men thronging the streets. Ottar, after all, had less than three hundred warriors under his command. Vík-ló was not Dubh-linn, but it was big enough, certainly more than Ottar's men could easily cover.

Rumors were as ubiquitous as torches and spears in the streets. The latest was that Ottar believed the beast was hiding somewhere in the longphort, and so every effort was directed toward locating its hiding place. All of Vík-ló had been searched and nothing found. The only places left to look were inside the buildings. Aghen guessed that the men pounding at his door were coming to search his house.

"Come!" Aghen called, but the door was already swinging open. Aghen was stretched out under a wool blanket on the raised platform at the back end of the single-room home. He sat up and shielded his eyes from the glare of the torches in the hands of the men who pushed their way through the door.

"Aghen Ormsson?"

It was Ketil Hrafnsson, who, with the death of the others, seemed to have been raised to the position of head of Ottar's house guard.

You have much to thank me for, Ketil Hrafnsson, Aghen thought.

"Yes, yes," Aghen said, swinging his legs off the platform. "Have you come to search the house? For wolves?"

"No, we've come for you, Aghen. Ottar would speak with you."

At that Aghen looked up at the man. The flame of the torch cast an odd, flickering light around the interior of the house and made Ketil's already menacing face look more frightening still. Ketil's men had spread out around the room and were searching in the corners and under the platform, but whether they were looking for the wolf or something else, Aghen did not know. He hoped they were looking for the wolf.

"Ottar would speak with me, at this hour?" Aghen protested. "What would he have to say to me?"

"That's Ottar's business. Now get dressed and come along."

Aghen stood and stretched. He reached for his tunic and hoped this display masked the cold fear that was taking hold of him. This was not good, not good at all. Had Mar told someone about the nails? Had they found the wooden jaws? Oddi could not have talked because Oddi knew nothing. Or did he? Was he only pretending to be as dim as he seemed?

He tugged his tunic in place and settled his linen cap on his head and followed Ketil out into the night. The scene that greeted him was what he had imagined it would be, but still it was a shock. The top of the earthen wall was lined with torches along its entire length, a great arc of torches half a mile long, as if some grand festival were taking place. Clusters of men moved along the top of the wall and through the streets, no fewer than five for six warriors in each group, with half of them bearing torches, the other half with spears. Dancing points of light from the torch-ends were scattered like fireflies in a summer field all across the longphort, from the river's edge right up to the twin halls by the gate.

Ketil led the way to the plank road with Aghen behind and the rest following him. Ketil made no effort to speak, but Aghen, his mind whirling, could not keep quiet.

"It's a terrible thing, for sure, all these men being killed, but is this the thing to do?" he wondered out loud. "Sure it would make more sense for everyone to just bar himself in his house until the wolf has gone?"

At first it seemed that Ketil would not make reply, but finally he said, "Ottar does not want to hide. He wants this thing dead."

Ottar doesn't want anyone else to hide, Aghen thought, *but as for him, he hasn't left his hall in a fortnight.*

Aghen, like a real wolf, was acting on instinct. He had no idea why he was doing what he was doing, what he hoped to achieve. He had thought only to knock Ottar off balance and see what would come of it.

Perhaps I'll find that out tonight, he thought, and a new wave of fear came over him. Images of Valgerd screaming out his life at the stake came unbidden to his mind.

If the earthworks looked as if they were part of some festival, Ottar's hall appeared to be a high temple to Odin, with the god himself in residence. The building was ringed by torch-bearers and spear-bearers, nearly a solid line around the entire perimeter. The light from the torches bounced off the daub walls, making a thousand shadows along the rough surface and creating a circle of light that spread twenty feet from the foot of the building.

They approached the door and the guards there stood aside. Ketil knocked loudly and called, "It's Ketil, Lord Ottar! I have the shipwright!"

There was a muffled response and Ketil opened the door and stepped in and Aghen followed behind.

The hall, like the area around the building, was crowded with men, all armed, many wearing mail. They were not eating and drinking as men in halls were wont to do, nor were they conducting business of any kind. They were, as far as Aghen could tell, standing guard.

No wolf could attack here, Aghen thought, *it couldn't find the room.*

But it was not so much the crowd that surprised him as the light. There were torches lining the wall and a great fire burning in the hearth. The entire space was filled with light. Aghen had never seen a room so well illuminated after the sun had set. The night was warm and the fires and the closed up room and the crowd of men made for a smoky, fetid atmosphere.

Ottar was the only man moving. A space had been cleared in front of the high chair that sat on the raised platform by the wall and Ottar was pacing back and forth. He did not pause or look up when Ketil and Aghen entered and the door was shut and barred behind them.

Aghen watched Ottar walking back and forth, his eyes on the packed dirt floor below his feet. The man looked bad, there was no other way to describe it. His face was drawn, which made the terrible scar stand out more pronounced, and there were dark circles under his eyes. His hair was in a wild profusion, his beard unkempt with bits of food still stuck in the uncombed tangle. His tunic was stained.

Aghen frowned. *This is odd, indeed,* he thought. A man like Ottar was no stranger to death. He was not shy about bringing death to others, in fact he seemed to enjoy it. There was no chance he could have lived the life he had without seeing men he cared about die along the way. Had the lives of his household guard meant this much?

Or was it the wolf that put this fear in him? A wolf was a frightening thing, sure, but not this frightening.

He glanced over to the right and was startled to see Oddi standing there, looking back at him. Oddi was dressed in leather armor and had a sword hanging from his belt, but he did not appear to be part of Ottar's guard. Which led Aghen to guess he was there for another reason. To tell tales, perhaps.

The sight of Oddi roused more than one emotion: anger, fear, disgust. Aghen looked Oddi in the face, searching for the smug sense of triumph he expected to see there, looking for the expression that said, *Who's the fool now, old man?*

But it was not there. Oddi did not look smug; he looked guilty. And ashamed. He held Aghen's eyes for only a second, then looked away.

"The shipwright…" Ottar said.

Aghen looked up. Ottar had stopped pacing and now stood just a few feet away. Diminished as Ottar seemed, the man still towered over him.

"Ketil said you would speak to me…Lord Ottar," Aghen said.

Ottar made no reply, just stared at Aghen as Aghen's discomfort grew. Then, just as Aghen was thinking he had better break the silence, Ottar did.

"You saw the wolf," Ottar said. "You are the only one who has seen the wolf and lived. You seem to know a great deal about it."

Aghen shook his head. "I saw it. I know nothing about it."

Ottar's arm shot across his chest. He grabbed the hilt of his sword and pulled the weapon free and Aghen flinched despite himself. But Ottar did not impale him or strike him down, as he expected. Instead, he held his sword straight out and said in a loud voice, a demanding voice, "Lay your hand on my sword and swear an oath, by Odin, that you saw the wolf! Swear it!"

Aghen held Ottar's eyes and laid a hand on the warm steel. "I swear by Odin that I saw a wolf in Vík-ló," he said.

They were silent, Ottar and Aghen, staring into one another's eyes. "Swear you saw the wolf that killed my men," Ottar growled, but Aghen pulled his hand away.

"I will not swear that, because I don't know that it's the truth," Aghen said. "It probably is. Wolves are not so common here. Certainly not lone wolves. But I don't know."

They were silent again. Aghen wondered how deep Ottar's madness ran, if he would still respond to reason, or order him tied to the stake for that answer. But then Ottar grunted and sheathed his sword once more.

"You say you know nothing about this wolf, and maybe you don't, but you seem to have many thoughts on the subject," Ottar said, now sounding more in control of himself. "You seem to think this might not be an ordinary wolf."

Aghen did not bother asking how Ottar came to know his thoughts. He glanced over at Oddi, who was looking at him, his face an expression of misery. Oddi, Aghen decided, had not realized that telling tales to Ottar might go badly for them both.

"I'm a shipwright," Aghen replied. "I know about wood and tools. I know nothing of wolves."

"You knew Thorgrim Night Wolf," Ottar said, the words sounding more like an accusation than a statement.

"I did. You did, too."

Ottar seemed to consider Aghen for a moment, seemed to take his measure, as if trying to decide how he should react to that impudence. Aghen did not expect him to react well. But when he spoke again he still sounded like a man in control, though one struggling to maintain it.

"This wolf, whatever it is, is not in the longphort," Ottar said, his voice low, as if he were growling. "We have searched every inch. So it must be in the country beyond. So here is what will happen. You will go out into the country with fifty of my men. You'll find this thing and you and my men will kill it. You will bring it back here. Do you understand?"

Aghen did understand. All too well. He was silent for a moment and then he said, "And if I don't find it?"

"You remember the other one, the stupid bastard who tried to hide his silver from me when first I took command of Vík-ló?"

"Valgerd, yes," Aghen said.

"Valgerd," Ottar said. "Well, if you return without this wolf, you will beg for as easy a death as he had." He turned and began pacing again. The meeting was over. Aghen's job was clear, the price of failure clearer still.

Twenty-Two

I fed the wolf with corpses
Killed them all myself.
Egil's Saga

The rain, thankfully, had tapered off to a mist before Cónán returned from his recruiting mission. That was a good thing, because Thorgrim knew that none of the men under his command would be very enthusiastic about leaving the comforts of the ship and the easy travel it represented to trudge across open country. Doing so in the pouring rain would be less inviting still.

He did not delude himself into thinking they would be without rain for the entire march. He had been more than two years in Ireland and he knew that any break from the downpour was temporary. But still, it would be better for all their spirits to set off when it was dry. Or dry by Irish standards, anyway.

But rain or no, they would be leaving. Whether Cónán was able to bring more men to the fight or not, they would be leaving. Even if Cónán and his bandits abandoned the attempt as hopeless, Thorgrim meant to march across country and find Kevin and kill him, and then return to Vík-ló and do the same to Ottar.

He would not be alone, not entirely. Harald would go with him, and Starri and Godi and the others as well, he imagined. He would give them a choice and would not shame them if they chose not to go, but he imagined they would welcome the chance for glory and riches, or a good death with weapon in hand.

How he would kill Kevin and kill Ottar and get Vík-ló back he did not know. He supposed it would depend on whether he had seventy men under his command or ten or three. But he would think of something. He did not doubt that.

While they waited for Cónán to return, they shifted *Sea Hammer* a quarter mile downstream, to a place that Harald had found where the riverbank had eroded away, leaving a cut in the shoreline and trees overhanging the water. They ran the ship up close to the land and made it fast with four stout lines. Then all hands were set to work cutting branches from trees inland from the river and piling them over the ship to hide it from any but the most careful scrutiny.

That done, the Norsemen took blankets and sacks and packed up whatever they wished to bring with them. The Irish did not have to prepare for the march, because they always kept themselves ready to move. Then Harald and Thorgrim led the way ashore, using battle axes to hack a makeshift path through the undergrowth.

"Those Irish, they're not so happy about this," Harald said as they stood shoulder to shoulder, swinging their weapons as if they were in a desperate fight with the bracken.

"No?" Thorgrim asked.

"No," Harald said. "I was among them just now, when they were making ready to go. Packing food and such. I don't think they knew we'd be leaving the ship so soon. I think they like the ship."

"I would guess they do," Thorgrim said.

"One said this was the first time they'd had anything like shelter for a month."

"A man could get tired of that," Thorgrim said. "A woman probably even more tired of it. But Cónán's their leader now, and if there's one thing you can count on, it's that he has some kind of plan."

They continued to push their way through the trees and the scrubby brush, looking for the edge of the wood. Once they were clear of the trees, Thorgrim meant to work his way back to where *Sea Hammer* had been tied to the bank when Cónán left. After Cónán and the others met up with them, they would find a place to ford the river and head off toward this ringfort where Kevin would be found.

"What about Louis the Frank?" Thorgrim asked. "Is he coming with us? And Failend?" Thorgrim, intent on getting underway, had failed to check if those two had parted company with them.

"They're coming," Harald said. "Failend actually seemed excited about it. I've never met a woman like that."

Thorgrim cut a sapling away with a blow from the ax. "She's an odd one, for certain," he said. He had met a few women like her over the years and the miles, women who preferred sword and shield to hearth and loom. But not many, and none who were Irish.

"And Louis?" Thorgrim asked.

"He's with us," Harald said. "I don't know why. He says he won't fight Irishmen and I said that was all right. It is all right, isn't it?"

"Fine," Thorgrim said. Louis's presence would at least make it seem as if there was one man more, and there was less chance of him getting up to some mischief if he was with them. "But why does he want to come?"

"I don't know," Harald said. "I think maybe he doesn't want to leave Failend."

Thorgrim raised a hand to cut Harald off. Harald stopped and behind them they heard the others pushing through the undergrowth stop as well. Thorgrim could see the trees thinning ahead. They had come to the edge of the woods.

Moving cautiously, Thorgrim advanced to the tree line and looked out over the open country beyond. There was no living thing, animal or man, that he could see. He stepped out of the shelter of the woods and the rest followed him into the open; then Thorgrim let one of Cónán's men, who knew that country well, take the lead. The Irishman headed off at an easy pace with Thorgrim and Harald following and the rest stretched out in a line behind them.

They were as odd a group as one might find trudging across the countryside: an Irish bandit at the head of the column, followed by ten Norse warriors, an Irish woman in mail, a seax on her hip, a Frankish warrior, then a dozen more bandits, then a handful of women, and then another dozen of the Irish outlaws forming the rearguard.

Thorgrim looked back over his shoulder. He shook his head. *How by all the gods do I find myself in this situation?* he wondered. It was not the first time in his life he had wondered that. Not even close.

They continued on until the late afternoon, sometimes walking by the river, sometimes skirting the woods that bordered the watercourse. Thorgrim was feeling the first hints of exhaustion when Cónán's man announced that they had reached the spot where *Sea Hammer* had been tied the day before. Whether that was true or not Thorgrim did not know, because the river was blocked from view by a wide band of trees, but he took the man's word for it and passed word that camp should be set up here.

In surprisingly short order campfires were lit and meat set to roasting and ale handed around. Thorgrim took a cup from one of the Irish women and nodded his thanks and thought, *There's much to be said for this idea of bringing women along when one is going a'viking.*

He looked over at Failend, who was sitting and drinking ale with the Norsemen. She was making no effort to help the other women in their cooking and making camp, and she did not look like she intended to, or as if she had done much of that sort of thing in the past. The other Irishwomen seemed in no way put out by this, and from what little Thorgrim had seen of their interactions they seemed to show Failend great deference.

I wonder if she's royalty of some sort, or wealthy. She certainly did not have the worn, haggard quality he saw in many of the poor Irish women, including those who accompanied Cónán and his men. He had seen her hands, and they were not the hands of a woman who had scrubbed clothing and tended a fire all her life.

He shook his head. *She's an odd one*, he thought. *But at least she'll likely prove to be a good hand in a fight.* In truth she already had.

Thorgrim posted guards, arrayed in a great arc far away from the camp, so they would not be taken by surprise during the night. He sent them in twos, a Northmen and an Irishman in each pair. His men and Cónán's had already fought side by side, but anything that helped reinforce that sense of brotherhood would only make them all the more formidable in a fight.

Once everything was arranged to his satisfaction, Thorgrim lay down near one of the fires and pulled a blanket over himself, covering his head to keep the light mist that was still falling off his face. He slept deeply, the sleep of an exhausted man, and the sun was above the horizon, illuminating the wolf-gray sky when he finally woke.

Breakfast was oat porridge and cold beef. Thorgrim was well into it when Vali appeared in camp, breathless from having run from his station to the south where he had been keeping lookout through the second half of the night.

"Men coming," he said to Thorgrim as he sucked in breath. "Coming from the south. About thirty or so."

"How far off?"

"A mile or so. They don't seem to be trying to hide or sneak up or any such thing."

"Very well," Thorgrim said. This was most likely Cónán and the men he had gone to find, but if it was not, it would not do to be caught with leggings down. He ordered the men to arms and then he and Harald and Godi took up shields and swords and followed Vali back to the place from which he had come.

They crouched behind a tall patch of rushes and watched the strangers approach. They were closer now. Thirty men, as Vali had said, spread out and walking toward them in a manner that did not suggest they were looking for a fight. Some of the strangers carried shields, but they were slung on the men's backs, not carried on arms. No weapons were evident, save for a few spears resting on shoulders.

For another five minutes Thorgrim and his men watched from their hidden place. Then the Irishman who had been on watch with Vali spoke.

"He says it's Cónán; he's certain," Harald translated.

Thorgrim nodded. He had just come to that same conclusion. He recognized Cónán's easy gait, like a big cat, and he thought he could see the shock of rust-red hair and the green tunic from that distance. He stood and stepped from behind the rushes and the others followed. He could see the surprise of their appearance ripple through the approaching men, some hesitating, some swinging spears down to the ready. But Cónán never broke stride and soon the others were with him again.

Thorgrim waited for Cónán to reach him, and he clasped the Irishman's hand once he did. He was pleased to see Cónán again, and that surprised him, because generally he had to know a man well before he cared in the least about him. The men who had come with Cónán hung back and looked warily on. Thorgrim turned to them, ran his eyes along their disorderly line.

They appeared much the way Cónán and his band had when they first approached *Sea Hammer* across the sandbar: ragged and poorly armed, with a hungry look, an undisciplined look. Their hair was long, their beards unkempt. They wore tunics and leines and various bits of cloth in sundry configurations. Their weapons, up close, were even less impressive than they had been from a distance. Clubs, farmers' axes, a smattering of sorry-looking blades, a few spears.

"These are the men to help us beat Kevin and his warriors?" Thorgrim asked, giving the doubt in his voice free rein.

"Ah, don't be taken in by their fair looks," Cónán said. "They're some hard bastards, these, used to a fight and eager to take down a whore's son like Kevin mac Lugaed." He took Thorgrim's arm and led him over toward one of the newcomers who was standing apart from the others, a small, stout man, a man whose beard was the most obviously impressive thing about him.

"Thorgrim, this is Blathmac, who commands this lot," he said, gesturing toward the stout man. He turned to Blathmac and spoke in Irish, gesturing toward Thorgrim.

"Cónán says that you are the famous warrior Thorgrim Night Wolf," said Harald, standing at Thorgrim's side and leaning close, "and he says I am your son, and he takes care to tell this fellow I speak the Irish tongue."

At that Thorgrim smiled, just a bit. *You're a tricky one, Cónán, you son of a whore*, he thought, but with no malice. He liked Cónán. And he trusted him. To a certain degree. Which was not much.

He looked at Blathmac and found that Blathmac was looking him up and down, appraising him. Thorgrim extended his hand and Blathmac hesitated, just a heartbeat, before reaching out and grasping it. As they shook, Blathmac spoke to Cónán and Thorgrim was all but certain he saw Cónán wince.

"This Blathmac says you don't look like such a famous warrior," Harald said, "and he tells Cónán that there had better be more men than just this."

Thorgrim finished shaking Blathmac's hand and released it. As a rule he tried not to judge any man on their first meeting. He had been wrong in the past. But Blathmac he had disliked with the very first glance, and nothing so far had altered that assessment.

Cónán was talking again, talking to Blathmac. "He's telling Blathmac that there are more men, fin gall and his own men, waiting near the river," Harald said. "He says…"

Harald got no further. Blathmac grunted and pushed past Cónán, past Thorgrim and Harald and Godi, and marched off on his own toward the river, his men following behind. Cónán stepped after him, but Thorgrim grabbed his arm and jerked him back. Cónán was clearly not pleased with such treatment, but Thorgrim did not care.

"Who is this miserable little shit?" Thorgrim asked. "Who does he think he is? And who does he think I am?"

Cónán glared at him, but then his expression softened. He held his hands up, palms toward Thorgrim, as if in surrender. "He *is* a miserable little shit," Cónán agreed. "But I've told him who's in command here. He'll listen to you. He's too greedy not to."

For a long moment Thorgrim just held Cónán's eyes, and Cónán returned the stare without flinching. Then Thorgrim spoke.

"I made it clear. I am going to kill Kevin and I'm going to kill Ottar, and if the gods will favor me I'll take back what's mine. I don't care about anything else. Or anyone. Not you, not your men, and certainly not this little whore's son you've brought to me. I'll kill any man who stands in my way. I'll kill you if I must."

"Yes," Cónán said. "You said you would. Many times. And you're welcome to try whenever you wish. But if you look close you'll see we're still fighting with you, not against you. And until that changes let me suggest you keep your sword in its scabbard."

Thorgrim remembered a time when he was a boy and found himself hanging from a rope over the water. The rope hung from a cliff edge above the bitter cold fiord on which he lived. He couldn't recall now how he had come to be in that position, clinging to the rope, trying to pull himself up. The strength had gone out of his arms and he was slipping down, inch by inch, and he knew that it was only a matter of time before he plunged into the icy sea.

That memory just leapt into his mind, standing there in that field in Ireland. He could still recall the sensation of his grasp finally giving out, of the rope whipping from his hands, of the cold rush of wind as he fell, the shocking pain of the ocean water wrapping itself around him. He had managed to kick his way to the shore, drag himself out onto the gravel beach, heaving for breath and shivering so hard he could barely move.

He felt that way now. The rope burning though his fingers, his hold on circumstances slipping, slipping. This was how it had happened before, when he had first agreed to take part in the raid on Glendalough, yielding control inch by inch, first to Kevin and then Ottar, until his grip gave out and he fell.

But he was not a boy any longer. And he was not a fool. His grip was strong and he would not let it slip ever again. Cónán could make his plans and Blathmac could think what he wished. Thorgrim Night Wolf would pull himself up the rope until he was on top once more.

He nodded at Cónán. He rested his hand on Iron-tooth's hilt and headed off through the thigh-high grass toward his men waiting by the trees.

Chapter Twenty-Three

Make the tyrant flee his lands,
Frey and Njord; may Thor
The land-god be angered at this foe,
The defiler of his holy place.
Egil's Saga

Aghen had forty men under his command, though it was not entirely clear whether or not he was in charge.

Ottar had picked the men for the wolf hunt. He had not asked for volunteers, which was understandable judging by the lack of enthusiasm Aghen was seeing among those who had been chosen. Ottar had also named one of his household guard to take charge of the reluctant forty, a tall brute of a man named Einar Skulason. Einar might have been loyal to Ottar, but he did not strike Aghen as one of the inner circle, one of those closest to the new Lord of Vík-ló. Of course, in the wake of the mysterious wolf attacks there were not so many of those left.

Einar had charge of the men, but he made it clear he expected Aghen to devise the means by which they would trap and kill the wolf. "This is your business," Einar said flatly after Aghen had posed the question of which direction they should go. "I know nothing of this. Ottar said it was on you to find this thing. You find it, me and my men will see about killing it."

Why do you think I know anything about this? Aghen thought, but he resisted saying it out loud. He seemed to now be considered the expert on wolves simply because he had seen one in Vík-ló and it had not killed him. It actually had not killed anyone, but that was not a point that Aghen could make.

It was not clear whether Einar thought Aghen had some sort of preternatural knowledge of the wolf, as Ottar seemed to believe. What was clear was that Einar did not intend to take responsibility for any potential failure. If they actually succeeded in killing a wolf, Aghen guessed the man would be more willing to own up to his part in the effort, but unless that happened, failure would be Aghen's concern.

They were gathered in the open space by Ottar's hall. The men were in armor, some wearing mail, most wearing leather. They carried swords and spears, the latter considered the most effective weapon against an enemy they wished to hold at bay. A horse stood patiently in the traces of a wagon. The wagon was piled with food and ale and shields and tents.

It was anyone's guess how long they would be gone. No one cared to return without a dead wolf to show Ottar. Aghen might have been the only one whose life had actually been threatened, but no one thought Ottar would be very forgiving of anyone if they failed.

"Very well," Aghen said, giving his voice a decisive tone and surveying the distant mountains as if this were something he did all the time. "We'll need bait, of course. I think the haunch of a pig. Fresh killed. We'll drag it behind the cart, make a trail with the blood and the scent."

"Drag a haunch?" Einar said, and Aghen was sure he was about to argue that doing that would only attract the man-killer to them, but Einar caught himself before the words came out. "All right," he said and turned to one of the others and issued the orders. Fifteen minutes later a fresh-killed sow was hefted into the back of the wagon and there were no valid excuses left for their remaining in the longphort.

Einar waved his arm at the men at the gate. They lifted the bar and swung the big wooden doors open, and the hunting party reluctantly moved out toward the open country and the mountains in the distance.

"We'll head off this way," Aghen said, pointing in a generally northwest direction. He spoke the words with certainty, as if he had chosen that course after much consideration, but in truth he was making it all up. He had no reason to go that way, had no clue as to how they would find and kill the wolf, had no idea what he would say to Ottar when he returned empty-handed.

There was a road of sorts running off in the direction Aghen had indicated, one reason perhaps he was drawn to that direction. It was not so much a road as a wide, worn track, but it had seen enough traffic over the past winter, with the Irishman Kevin sending wagonloads of supplies to Vík-ló and returning to his home with silver in his purse, that it was rutted and well-defined. They set out on the road, moving no faster than the horse was willing to pull the cart.

Half a mile from the gates of Vík-ló, Aghen called a halt. "Let's get the pig haunch dragging astern the wagon," he said. With expert strokes of his knife, one of Ottar's men separated one of the rear legs from the dead animal and made it fast to a length of rope tied to the back of the cart. Soon they were moving again, the pig's leg bumping and jarring behind, leaving an ever-diminishing streak of blood on the grass and earth.

Aghen, leading the small band, turned to see how the others were fairing. He almost laughed at the sight of the men, walking with spears poised, looking intently in every direction as if they expected to be set upon by a hundred wolves that might spring bodily from the earth.

They walked for a few hours, zigzagging back and forth, crossing and recrossing the road but generally following it northwest. Aghen was not sure how far he wished to get from Vík-ló, or how far from the dubious protection of the longphort the men would be willing to go. If no wolf was found, he realized, it would be far better for him to not return to Vík-ló at all, and he toyed with that idea as he walked.

Around midday they stopped for a meal, the men sitting gratefully on the ground, their former vigilance all but abandoned. The horse was released from the traces and turned happily to the grass beneath its feet.

Oddi, who was one of the men sent on the hunting party, sat by Aghen, a strip of dried beef and an oat cake in hand. "This is a lot of walking for an old man like you," he said, smiling as he spoke. "How are you fairing?"

"Fine, fine," Aghen said. "I'll ride back in the wagon after the wolf has killed you all." As soon as he spoke he could see this joke did not sit well with Oddi, and he was about to assure him that such a thing would not happen, when Einar joined them. He did not sit, but rather squatted on his heels, coming down to Aghen's level but making it clear he would not remain.

"You have a reason for going in the direction we're going?" he asked. There was suspicion and accusation in his tone.

Aghen shrugged. "Just a feeling. It's all I have."

Einar looked up the road as if hoping to see something in the distance. "From what I've been told by those who were at Vík-ló over the winter, this road leads to the ringfort of that Irishman, Kevin."

"Yes," Aghen said. He, too, had been in Vík-ló over the winter, which Einar knew but apparently dismissed. "We're still some miles from that place, however. Or so I think. I've never been this way. Is that a problem?"

"We don't want to go near Kevin's stronghold," Einar said. "Ottar would not allow it."

Aghen made no reply at first as a host of thoughts crowded into his head. He wanted to ask why Ottar would care. He wanted to insist they keep on in that direction so that he could blame their failure to find the wolf on Einar's refusal. But before he could speak, Einar stood and walked off.

Aghen turned to Oddi. "Why doesn't Einar want us to get near Kevin's ringfort?"

It took Oddi a moment to chew and swallow a mouthful of the unforgiving beef and cake before he could speak. "I don't know for certain," he said. "But we joined up with this Kevin when we were going to Glendalough."

Aghen nodded. "I recall when he came to Vík-ló and talked Thorgrim Night Wolf into joining him."

Oddi nodded. "I guess he talked Ottar into joining him, too. Because we did meet up with him and his men. By the river. Where the two rivers meet. Of course I only hear rumors, but as I understand it, Kevin was supposed to fight with us, but then he switched sides. I don't know about that, but I know for a fact he and his Irishmen were not fighting on our side. They just disappeared. Some said they saw him fighting against us, but I don't know for certain."

"Hmm," Aghen said as Oddi braved another bite of food. He considered this new information. Ottar had betrayed Thorgrim, and so had Kevin. No wonder Thorgrim and his men had been wiped out.

"So Ottar has reason to hate this Kevin?" Aghen asked. "To want revenge, maybe?"

Oddi nodded vigorously as he swallowed. "Oh, yes, Ottar is crazy for vengeance against Kevin. He used to talk of it all the time. In fact, he was making ready to lead a raid on Kevin's ringfort when this whole wolf business happened. And then he went crazy about that."

Aghen did not respond, his mind too choked with thoughts. Oddi seemed not to notice as he tore into his food with the appetite of a young man who had walked many miles since breakfast.

Kevin betrayed both Thorgrim and Ottar, Aghen thought. *What does all this mean? How can I make use of this?* He had no idea. He turned back to Oddi.

"What you say, that's very interesting," Aghen said.

"What?" Oddi asked.

"About Thorgrim Night Wolf wanting to get revenge on Kevin as well as Ottar."

"Did I say that?" Oddi asked, genuinely confused.

"Not exactly," Aghen said. "But it stands to reason. If Kevin betrayed Ottar, he betrayed Thorgrim as well. Of course Thorgrim Night Wolf would want revenge as much as Ottar."

"But I don't know that Thorgrim is still alive," Oddi protested. "All I ever said was that I didn't see him get killed."

"True," Aghen said. "But Thorgrim Night Wolf's a hard man to kill. He's not like other men. That might explain a lot of the strange things that are happening."

At that Oddi's eyes went a little wider, but he did not ask questions and Aghen did not elaborate. He had been watching Oddi. Oddi was a talkative fellow, often conversing with the other men. And it would do Aghen no harm to have them all believe they were dealing with more than just a wolf made of flesh, bone and blood.

They were moving again soon after, continuing their odd meandering march across the countryside, the increasingly unappetizing pig haunch dragging behind the cart. Their track was tending more to the west now, Einar making it clear they would go no farther in the direction of Kevin's stronghold.

"Very well," Aghen said when Einar finally insisted on a change of course. "If we don't find this wolf because you won't go where I think we should, let it be on your head." But Einar did not seem in the least intimidated by that threat.

They stopped and made camp with an hour or so of daylight remaining. Aghen had no idea how far they had come from Vík-ló. Four or five miles, he guessed, though they had walked twice that distance at least, weaving back and forth as they had.

Once again Einar came over to talk as Aghen was eating. Once again he squatted down, unwilling to sit with the shipwright—a friend of Thorgrim Night Wolf and disliked by Ottar Bloodax—any longer than he had to.

"Now what?" Einar asked.

"Well," Aghen said, "every time the wolf has appeared, it's been at night. We dragged the haunch to get the beast on our trail. With any luck it's followed us. Now we set the bait out, somewhere out in the dark, and we position men around it. Hidden. With spears. If the wolf shows up, they kill it."

"Out in the dark?" Einar asked.

"Yes, out in the dark. The beast won't come near the fire. Don't be a fool."

Einar frowned and looked around the camp. Aghen could well imagine what things he was wrestling with. None of these men would be very eager to go hunker down in the dark and wait for the wolf to arrive. Einar, as their leader, should take it on himself to join them, but he was probably not too eager for that, either.

"Very well," Einar said at last. He stood and walked off, calling to the men as he did.

Aghen remained seated where he was and enjoyed watching the little drama play out. The men spoke in low voices, but even though he could not hear the words, Aghen had a good idea of what was being said. Einar pointed toward a place about a hundred yards from the camp. He pointed to a handful of men. He saw the men's faces turn angry, saw heads shaking. He saw, in fact, much more resistance than he thought he would, even considering how undesirable the duty was that the men were being ordered to perform.

Not one of them, Aghen was sure, would have hesitated for an instant to take their place in a shieldwall and plunge into combat against a vastly superior enemy. Yet the thought of sitting in the dark waiting for a wolf, or worse, the spirit of a wolf, to come out of the night made their courage falter.

But not for long. Soon their fear of Ottar, made manifest by Einar, overcame their reluctance and the first watch moved out and took up their places.

Oddi came lumbering over and sat down beside Aghen. "Looks like I get the second watch tonight," he said. He did not sound happy.

"The men," Aghen said, "they argued more with Einar than I would have thought they would."

"They don't like him very much," Oddi said.

"No? But he's Ottar's man," Aghen said. "Aren't they loyal to Ottar?"

"Not much," Oddi said. "No more than me. And that's not much."

"I thought Ottar would have sent his most trusted men on this hunt," Aghen said and Oddi smiled at that.

"No," he said. "The opposite. I don't think Ottar expects anyone to come back from this alive. So of course he didn't send the men who've been with him a long time. He sent the ones who joined just before Glendalough, the ones who aren't as loyal to him as the rest. Like me."

Interesting… Aghen thought.

"So…Ottar really thinks this wolf will kill us all? One wolf?" Aghen asked.

Oddi shrugged. "Ottar doesn't talk much to me. But I've been watching him, when I can. There's something about this whole wolf business. He doesn't act like someone would act if there was just a wolf running around. It seems like there's something else, some reason he's more afraid of the whole thing than you would expect someone to be. Ottar's a real son of a bitch, no question, but he's not a coward. Yet this seems to have really scared him."

Interesting… Aghen stared out into the gathering dark for a bit, then turned to Oddi to ask another question, but the man was already on his side, mouth hanging open as sleep approached, and Aghen did not have the heart to disturb him.

Instead he looked off toward the mountains and let the disjointed thoughts swirl around in his head. He was a shipbuilder, and his mind worked like a shipbuilder's mind. He liked things to move in an orderly progression, one task, then the next task, until the whole was complete. He liked to know what would come next; he preferred to do the job at hand with an eye toward what would follow. He liked to have his world ordered in that way.

But his situation, this business with the wolf, there was nothing orderly about it. The appearance of the beast by the river was a mystery he had never solved. The part he had played, the killing of Ottar's men, making it seem as if their deaths had been wolf attacks, he had done with no plan in mind, with no thought as to what would come next, what he might achieve.

Now this. Kevin, Thorgrim. Einar, whom the men hated. What could he make of all this? He had no idea. It was as if he was looking at a pile of seasoned wood, a well-stocked tool chest, coils of rope, everything he needed to build something great, right there in front of him. But he did not know what to build.

And then he realized something else, realized it with startling clarity: he was certain that Thorgrim Night Wolf was alive.

He had never really thought about it in anything but the vaguest way. But now he realized that ever since the moment Oddi had told him that he had not seen Thorgrim killed, Aghen had believed that Thorgrim still lived. Everything he had done he had done because of that belief.

That was the reason Aghen had wanted to knock Ottar off balance with the wolf attacks, to give Thorgrim a greater chance at the vengeance Aghen knew he would seek. But now he realized that Thorgrim was probably just as eager to get revenge on Kevin. Maybe even more so, since Kevin had been the one to start all this business about Glendalough and then had turned on him.

Thorgrim Night Wolf is alive, Aghen thought, *and whether he's coming for Ottar or coming for Kevin, he's coming this way.*

Chapter Twenty-Four

A better burden can no man bear
on the way than his mother wit
Hávamál

The horsemen were lined up on the crest of a hill a little more than half a mile distant. Thorgrim Night Wolf, kneeling behind an outcropping of rock, the damp seeping through his leggings, tried counting them as best he could.

Twenty-six, twenty-seven…is that one horse or two? It seemed to him that his eyesight was not as keen as it once had been.

Cónán, kneeling beside him, was the first to speak. "I can't count them all," he said in a low voice, which, at that distance, was not entirely necessary. "Forty or more, that's certain."

The others who were with Thorgrim and Cónán behind the rock—Harald, Godi, and Cónán's man, Fothaid—nodded in agreement. Thorgrim abandoned his effort. Cónán's estimate was close enough. It didn't matter how many there were. There were a lot of the bastards, that was all he needed to know.

"These are the men from the river?" Thorgrim asked.

"It seems it," Cónán said. "Hard to say for certain from this distance, but I'd wager my life they are." He paused to consider those words. "No, not my life," he said. "But I'd wager Blathmac's life."

"You must not be so sure," Thorgrim said. "I don't think you put any more value on Blathmac's life than I do."

"All right, then, I'd wager all my plunder from Glendalough."

"Well, that's something," Thorgrim said. They looked back at the mounted warriors. Thorgrim had to agree that some of the riders at least appeared to be the same men who had attacked them aboard *Sea Hammer*.

"There're a lot more men on that hill than there were at the river," Thorgrim observed.

Cónán nodded. "Their numbers do seem to be growing," he said. The enemy they were looking at now was at least twice the size of the force they had engaged earlier.

Thorgrim, of course, also had nearly twice the number of men under his command than he had had at the river, but he found little comfort in that fact. It had been two days since Blathmac and his band of men and women had joined with Thorgrim and Cónán. For two days they had dragged this unwieldy force overland, following the shallow river that Cónán said would lead to a place he called Ráth Naoi, the ringfort that was Kevin mac Lugaed's stronghold.

Despite Cónán's continued assurance to the contrary, Thorgrim did not consider Blathmac's men as some great addition to their company. The Northmen, his own men, were trained, experienced, tested and loyal, but they were few. Cónán's men seemed to have some degree of order and discipline, more than one might expect from Irish outlaws. At Thorgrim's insistence they had trained every day with sword, ax, and shield. In a stand-up fight they would do an enemy some genuine harm, but they were not what Thorgrim or any Northman, or any Irish man-at-arms for that matter, would consider proper fighting men.

Blathmac's men were worse, far worse. They were as tattered and ugly a rabble as Thorgrim had ever seen, half-starved mongrels who looked as if they were more accustomed to a good whipping than a good meal. Their weapons, such as they were, were sorry things, and the men seemed to hardly know the use of them. The only real spirit that Thorgrim had seen among them, the only thing for which Blathmac's men had shown any enthusiasm was the chance to eat and drink.

"Sure, they're a poor, dirty lot," Cónán said when Thorgrim first expressed his disgust with the newcomers. "But in a fight they'll be right with us, you'll see. Good fighting men."

"They'll stand in a shieldwall?" Thorgrim asked. "They'll stand fast with mounted warriors coming down on them?"

"Well, no, they won't do that," Cónán admitted. "But they'll have other uses, you'll see."

"Once the fighting's begun we can use their corpses to build a rampart," Thorgrim suggested.

"There you go, now you're thinking," Cónán said.

"I don't know if Blathmac will live long enough to be part of that wall," Thorgrim said. "I'm not sure he'll live to see another sunrise."

Blathmac alone seemed not to notice how miserable and useless his men were, what a pack of feral dogs he was leading. He seemed to think he commanded an elite unit of royal foot soldiers, chosen men, trained and outfitted to be the finest in the land, and he their lord and master.

From the start, Blathmac set about making himself intolerable, ordered the women in camp, both his and Cónán's, to attend to him, keeping himself apart like the nobleman he seemed to think himself to be, insisting on telling Thorgrim what they might achieve and how.

Thorgrim could endure arrogance from men whose achievements warranted arrogance—he saw enough of that among the Northmen—but such an attitude from a cur like Blathmac made him desperate to wring the man's neck, if he could find it through his beard. Thorgrim could not recall any man he had wanted to kill as much as Blathmac whom he had not simply challenged to a *hólmganga*, a formal duel, and killed. But somehow Cónán had managed thus far to dissuade him.

"Have you ever seen a child playing at man-at-arms?" Cónán asked. "Going about ordering adults here and there for fun?"

"Yes," Thorgrim said. His own boys had loved playing that way.

"Well, that's Blathmac, do you see? Think of him like that. And like any child, we'll see he gets a whipping when the time is right."

Thorgrim only grunted in reply, but for the time being, with greater things on his mind, he was willing to take Cónán's suggestion in that matter. He did not want to drive Blathmac's men away. His talk of using their corpses to build a wall was mostly a joke, but not entirely. In a fight, those sorry men could at least serve as fodder for the mounted spearmen, armed and flung in the riders' path to slow them down so the real warriors could do their work.

And now it seemed as if that time had come. The riders on the far hill were in a loose line, most sitting in their saddles and letting their mounts graze. A few, the leaders, Thorgrim imagined, were gathered in a small group, no doubt discussing their next move. They were not aware of the five men watching them from behind the rock, or the rest of Thorgrim's *ad hoc* army a mile back, down by the riverbank.

The column of Northmen and outlaws was well hidden just then, but generally there was nothing stealthy about it. All told they were about fifty-five men and a dozen women and they tended to spread out over quite a stretch of country as they marched. They carried bundles of food and small casks of ale and a boar that someone had killed slung from poles resting on the men's shoulders. They stopped frequently to rest, or at least more frequently than Thorgrim would have liked.

Blathmac could not resist shouting orders and chastisements at his men and at anyone else who fell under his eye. Save for the Northmen. He had sense enough not to yell at the Northmen. They would not have understood the words, and the tone would have put his life in serious jeopardy.

Thorgrim and Cónán both knew the dangers of having their people spread out that way, particularly in open country with mounted warriors hunting for them. Trying to keep them together was pointless, so they had sent scouts out well ahead and off in several directions, the younger, fleeter, smarter men who would make certain they did not blunder into a trap or get taken by surprise by a sudden charge at their flanks.

Fothaid had come running back to camp an hour earlier with a report of horsemen in the distance. He had led the others to the hiding place behind the rock.

"I don't think they know we're here," Cónán said, nodding toward the mounted men. "I don't mean just us. They don't know about the others back at the river. They don't look as if they're getting ready for any sort of attack."

"I agree," Thorgrim said. "But they're between us and Kevin's ringfort, so unless they move soon, go further west, we'll have to fight our way through them." He stood, still crouching out of sight from the riders on the hill. "Let's get back to the others. We have a battle to make ready for."

Twenty minutes later they were back with the rest. Blathmac's men had lit into the dried meat and ale as soon as Thorgrim and the others had gone off, and they were still at it when they returned. Just the sight of them, dirty and stupid-looking, wide-eyed, their clothes in rags, desperately gnawing at beef bones, made Thorgrim despair of defeating the mounted warriors they were facing. He had been unsure of their chances when he thought there were just twenty riders arrayed against them. Now he was looking at forty or fifty horsemen at least.

"I don't know what use we'll make of Blathmac's dogs," Thorgrim said to Cónán as the two surveyed the fighting men at their disposal. "They'd be useless in a shieldwall, and we don't have shields enough for them in any case."

"They would be useless," Cónán agreed. He turned to Thorgrim. "See here…you Northmen, you have your way of fighting. Shieldwalls and all that. It's not how we fight. I don't mean Irishmen, Irish men-at-arms. They do all that shield and sword nonsense. But those who live by their wits, like me and my men, even Blathmac's men, we have our ways. It's how we keep alive. We have to fight these bastards on the horses. Let's fight them my way."

Thorgrim frowned. "What are you thinking?" he asked.

"I'm thinking we use our brains, and not just our strength of arm," Cónán said. "This might be a new thing for you Norsemen, but hear me out."

They spoke. Thorgrim called Harald and Godi to him, and, reluctantly, Blathmac, who added little but seemed at least willing to take part, no doubt because the plan that Cónán laid out put him in little personal danger.

"We'll need four or five men to go out after the riders, no more," Cónán said. "A few quick, clever men can do worlds more than dozens of dull ones."

The others nodded. "I'll go," Cónán continued. "How about you, Thorgrim?" he asked. He was grinning, enjoying this. "We'll have to move fast. Can you keep up, old man?"

Thorgrim had no idea if he could keep up or not, but he had no choice now but to agree, and Cónán, he was sure, knew it. "I'm with you," he said. "I'll try to not make you look a fool in front of your men."

"Good," Cónán said. "And we'll take your boy, Harald; he's smart and strong. Fothaid's a good man if someone's keeping an eye on him, and fast as the wind. I'll bring him along. And let's take your man. The crazy one."

"Starri?"

"Yes, Starri. He's made for this sort of thing, I can tell."

Thorgrim hesitated. He was not certain that Starri was recovered enough for this. Then he remembered Starri flinging himself off the edge of *Sea Hammer* and taking the Irish horseman down with him, and he told himself to stop acting as if he were Starri's mother. Or his grandmother.

"Starri, come here, come with us," he called and he was rewarded with a look of delight on Starri's face as he ambled over, the delight that comes with anticipating something very good.

They took another ten minutes to finish preparations, then Cónán said, "Let's go." He took off at an easy jog, following the still visible path through the tall grass that they had made on their way back from reconnoitering the horsemen, Thorgrim and the others following behind.

They were less encumbered than usual, which did not make Thorgrim feel particularly comfortable. They had left their shields, helmets and mail shirts behind, because Cónán meant for them to move fast, which they could not do while weighted down with those things. Even their swords had been left behind, Iron-tooth and Oak Cleaver given over to Godi for safe keeping.

Still, they were not without weapons. Thorgrim wore a seax on his belt, as did most of the others. Cónán and Fothaid carried bows and quivers of arrows. Starri had two battle axes tucked into his belt.

They covered the ground swiftly and were nearing the place where they had last seen the horsemen when Cónán slowed, held up a hand, and dropped to one knee behind the crest of a small hillock. Behind him, the others did the same, Thorgrim dropping by Cónán's side.

The riders were in front of them now, not more than a hundred yards away, sweeping forward at an easy pace. They were spread out in a line abreast and they covered a wide swath of ground as they rode.

"They still don't know where our people are," Thorgrim said. "They're hunting, but they don't know where they are."

"Well, they found us," Cónán said. "Actually, we found them, which is all the better. Come on."

He nodded his head toward a scrubby strip of trees and brush running along a creek a few hundred yards to their left. The far end of the line of horsemen would pass close by that place if they continued on the heading they were on.

Cónán stood and hurried off toward the tangle of trees and bushes, Thorgrim on his heels and the others behind. They were running now, because they had to reach the brush before the riders crested the hillock and saw them. Thorgrim was not heaving for breath; he was not even breathing hard, but he knew that he would be soon. He wondered if the pride that had forced him to join Cónán on this venture would turn and bite him in the ass as he tried to keep up with men near half his age, or, in Harald's case, less than half.

They reached the brush just as Thorgrim was starting to hear the rasping sound of his breath. They went crashing into the undergrowth and stopped. Thorgrim sucked air as inconspicuously as he could. He glanced over at Cónán and Cónán grinned back at him.

They all took a moment to recover, and then Cónán pointed farther into the trees and said something to Fothaid in Irish. Fothaid nodded and hurried off. Cónán pointed in the other direction. "Starri, there."

"What do I do?" Starri asked.

"Create madness," Cónán said, still grinning. "I know it's something you can do. Wait for me to get their attention; then Thorgrim and Harald will have a turn. Then you. You'll know what to do when it's time."

Starri nodded and headed off. Thorgrim was looking at Cónán, considering the man. *He understands*, Thorgrim thought. *He understands Starri and his ways. That Irish bastard might be half berserker himself.*

"And us?" Harald asked.

"You wait here with me," Cónán said. "I'll start the dance and run off. They won't know you're here, and when you hit them, it will turn them end over end."

Harald nodded. Thorgrim was going to ask for more clarification when he realized that asking would do no good. Cónán didn't know what was going to happen. He had no real plan. He was counting on his own ability to spread chaos, to improvise as things fell apart.

The mounted warriors were in view now, not more than fifty yards away and still moving in a line abreast. The rider nearest them would pass not more than a dozen yards from where the three men crouched hidden in the brush.

Thorgrim remained absolutely motionless, his mouth half open to let the breath come noiselessly in and out. He could hear the shrill call of some bird in the woods behind him. He could smell the familiar scent of horses as the riders came closer.

Silently Cónán pulled an arrow from his quiver and nocked it on the string of his bow. They could hear the soft thumping of the horses' hooves as the riders approached. Through the foliage Thorgrim's eyes followed the mounted warriors, watched as they drew even with their hiding place and then passed it by.

The nearest rider was twenty feet beyond them when Cónán stood at last, barely making a sound in the undergrowth as he did, drawing the bowstring as he rose. He made a small adjustment to his aim and let the arrow fly, dropping to his knees again as the string made its telltale twanging sound.

In that instant the quiet afternoon was torn apart. Thorgrim saw the rider arch back, the arrow jutting from the shoulder of his mail shirt, and heard him shout in surprise and agony. Instinctively the man reached a hand back for whatever had embedded itself in him. He jerked the reins. The horse whinnied loud and reared. The rider to his left shouted and wheeled and the neat line of horsemen broke apart as one after another they turned to see what was happening.

Cónán was on his feet again, another arrow on his string. He stepped forward, this time in full view of the horsemen as he loosed off another shaft, sending the arrow straight and true into the rider at the first victim's side. The arrow struck the man in his stomach and he roared in pain and pulled his horse to one side. But he, too, was dressed in mail and it was not clear how deep the wound would be.

But that did not matter so very much. Killing men was not important just then. That would come later.

The line of horsemen had turned now and they were charging at the stand of trees, converging on the place where Cónán stood, screaming and laughing like a lunatic. With the nearest rider not twenty yards away, Cónán burst out of the trees and raced away, running like a rabbit flushed from a bush as the horsemen put the spurs to their beasts and charged after him.

"Come on!" Thorgrim said to Harald, the need for stealth long passed. He raced out of the brush and into the open, Harald at his side. So intent were the Irish riders on Cónán that none of them noticed the two Norsemen. Thorgrim saw a log lying half-hidden in the grass, saw one of the horsemen charging up from the left, and he could see the timing would be perfect.

His foot landed on top of the log and he leapt off just as the rider came up beside him. The man on the horse never saw him coming until Thorgrim grabbed him around the neck and jerked him back as his horse raced on beneath him. The man hit the ground with Thorgrim on top of him. But the Irishman was no pathetic farmer; he was a warrior and he was swinging a leather-clad fist at Thorgrim even before they landed.

Thorgrim jerked his head back and the man's hand grazed his chin. Thorgrim punched the man square in the face, a quick, sharp jab that snapped his head back and sent blood flowing from his nose. Then Thorgrim leapt to his feet. He had no time to do more than what he had done. He snatched up the spear that the rider had dropped and swung it around, point first, as another horseman came charging down on him.

He glanced off to his right. Harald had also taken a rider down and was delivering a wicked backhand blow to the side of his head.

Thorgrim turned back to the horse and rider coming at him, spear leveled, his mount's hooves pounding the dirt. Thorgrim stood his ground, let him come on, ten feet, five feet. The tip of the Irishman's weapon was aiming for Thorgrim's chest when Thorgrim brought the wooden shaft of his spear down on that of the rider, driving it into the dirt, then lifted his own spear up again as the horsemen charged onto the point.

Thorgrim felt the dagger-sharp tip break the links on the man's mail shirt, but the rider pulled his horse over hard and knocked the iron point aside with his hand. Thorgrim drew the shaft back and swung it in an arc, slamming the long wooden pole into the man's head, knocking him sideways in the saddle.

"Harald, let's go!" Thorgrim shouted. They were done, for the moment. Harald nodded and followed Thorgrim as he raced back for the protection of the hedge. The line of mounted warriors had broken down into a swirling and chaotic riot of horses charging in every direction, men shouting orders or warnings, Thorgrim guessed, or yelling in pure surprise.

He looked to his left as he ran, toward the place where the riders had chased after Cónán. Another man staggered in the saddle, an arrow stuck in his mail shirt. Cónán or Fothaid finding their mark. And for the Irish, the biggest surprise was yet to come.

Thorgrim reached his arms up and pushed the bracken aside as he ran into the undergrowth, Harald right behind him, the sound of pounding hooves close by. He felt something bounce off his arm and a spear flew past and drove itself into the vegetation a few steps ahead, a desperate throw by the rider on their heels, an attempt to drive a spear point into the Northman's back before he disappeared from sight. Thorgrim grabbed the spear shaft and jerked it from the ground. He could make use of that weapon.

Ten feet into the brush and the trees, Thorgrim and Harald stopped and turned together. Thorgrim was heaving for breath and he was pleased to see that Harald was not doing much better. Harald opened his mouth to speak when an unearthly shriek cut through the cacophony of pounding feet and shouting men in the open ground beyond them.

It was a scream calculated to bring terror, and even Thorgrim and Harald might have been unnerved by the sound if they did not recognize it:

Starri, giving full vent to his berserker madness. To them, it was not a frightening sound, it was a welcome sound. It meant Starri Deathless was back.

They inched closer to the tree line where they could see through the cover of leaves. Starri had come bursting from the brush thirty yards away, screaming as he ran, his battle axes clenched in his hands. The nearest horseman whirled around as he heard him, turning just in time to see Starri leaping clean off the ground and sweeping one of the axes sideways as he came airborne in a move that only Starri Deathless could hope to perform.

Thorgrim shook his head. His own epic leap at the horseman had been only a poor imitation of Starri's.

The rider had his arm up, but it did no good. Starri's ax knocked it aside and tore through the mail that covered the man's chest. The rider went sideways in a spray of blood and his horse bolted as Starri came down on his feet like a cat. There was a streak of blood across his face and he was grinning wide as he crouched, ready to spring again.

Five lengths away another rider turned and spurred his horse toward this new threat. He raised his spear and hurled it, straight and true, but Starri dodged it easily. Starri straightened, waiting, axes in his hands. The horseman pulled his sword and raced down on him, weapon raised. He came up with Starri, and Starri leapt at him, but the rider was ready for him and swerved hard, slashing at Starri as he did. Thorgrim heard steel clanging on steel as sword and ax connected, and then Starri was down in the grass and the mounted warrior was charging past.

In a flash Starri was up again, still smiling, still screaming and keening. He wanted to draw the attention of the riders and he had. Men who seconds before had been wheeling their mounts, looking for their elusive enemy, now came charging down at him, half a dozen riders coming on at once.

"I don't think Cónán meant for Starri to stand and fight," Harald said. "I think he was supposed to go back in the woods like we did."

"Yes, he was," Thorgrim said, and he cursed himself for letting Starri get into the fight this way, unaided, expecting him to show restraint in such a brawl. Starri didn't need help fighting, but he needed help breaking it off.

The riders converged on Starri at nearly the same instant and for a second he was lost from sight. Then Thorgrim saw him as he rolled under one of the horses, coming to his feet on the other side, swinging one of his axes backhand. He caught the surprised rider in the arm with the wicked trailing edge of the blade and jerked him from the saddle.

The rider was down, his foot still caught in the stirrup, as the horse spooked and bolted, driving through the other riders, dragging the flailing man with it. But the Irish warriors knew their business and they dodged the frightened animal and spurred toward Starri, some holding spears, some with swords drawn, five mounted men against one madman with a pair of axes.

"Starri! To the woods!" Thorgrim shouted and even as the words left his mouth he knew it was pointless. With his mind in that battle fever, Starri was unlikely to hear orders, and more unlikely still to obey.

Starri drew an ax back and smacked one of the horses hard with the flat of the blade, right on the side of its head. The horse reared, lashed out with its hooves, but Starri leapt sideways, jumping clear as another rider slashed at him with his sword.

Seeing the sword coming, Starri met it with an upraised ax. The sharp blade struck the wooden handle of Starri's weapon and stuck fast. Starri pulled his arm back, jerking the man on the horse off balance, and slashed at him with the second ax. It was an awkward blow, and though the hit landed square on the man's chest, Thorgrim doubted it did much hurt.

All of that had taken half a minute, no more, but it was enough to attract the attention of the other mounted men. Thorgrim saw arms and swords pointing toward the melee with Starri at its center. Starri was the only enemy still visible on the open ground, and so the men-at-arms were turning their attention in his direction.

"Forty against one, that might be too much even for Starri Deathless," Thorgrim said. He thought about calling out once more for Starri to retreat back into the woods, but he knew it would do no good. Starri was having too much fun.

"Come on, Harald," Thorgrim said, resigned to the only course open to them. "Let's go get this lunatic before the Irish do."

Chapter Twenty-Five

Flying spears bit,
the peace was rent;
wolves took heart
at the taut elm bow.
Egil's Saga

They came out of the trees yelling, just as Starri had done, though neither Thorgrim nor Harald were able to produce the same unearthly sort of noise that Starri could make. But it was good enough. They wanted to distract the riders cantering toward Starri, and in that they succeeded.

Thorgrim's eyes moved from Starri to the riders surrounding him to the other men-at-arms charging at them. There was no time to amuse themselves the way Starri was doing. They had to get free and get to cover. There was still much to do.

"Harald!" Thorgrim shouted. "Get Starri and get him into the trees!"

Harald nodded and rushed past Thorgrim, off to where Starri was whirling and somersaulting and leaping like some dancer performing at a great jarl's feast. Thorgrim ran to his right, further into the open, still shouting to get the attention of the riders who were closing with them. He saw two men pull their reins over, changing direction, heading for him now rather than Starri. They rode side by side with ten feet separating them, and Thorgrim could see they meant to pass on either side of him and stick him like a boar as they did.

Thorgrim did not move, the spear he had recovered from the woods held loose in his hands. He was not thinking now; he was acting on instinct, the wolf's mind driving him. Everything seemed to happen slower; every action he took seemed to come from some place far deeper and more ancient than conscious thought.

The riders were twenty feet away, their horses at a full gallop, their spears pointed right at his gut, when Thorgrim leapt to his left, too late for the riders to adjust. He came down on one knee, jammed the butt of his spear shaft against his foot, and angled the iron tip up at the rider bearing down on him.

He was too low for the spear tip to reach the man on the horse's back, but the horse, on that heading, would impale itself on the point. The rider was trying awkwardly to shift his own spear from his left hand to his right when he saw what Thorgrim was doing. He shouted, pulled the reins hard over, and kicked the horse in the flank, twisting the animal out of the way.

Thorgrim saw the tip of his spear pierce the horse's dark brown hide, a bright flash of blood appeared, and the horse, reacting to the pull of the reins and the stab of the spear point, jerked hard to his left, careening into the second rider who had closed the gap in hopes of getting at Thorgrim as well.

Heads tossing, hooves thrashing, the two horses slammed into one another as the men tried to stay in their saddles, but Thorgrim had no more time for them. He stood and turned and raced toward Harald and Starri who were fighting side by side now, almost back to back, as the horsemen pranced and whirled around them, looking for an opening. Six mounted warriors, coming at the two men with spears thrusting and horses kicking and snapping. Harald and Starri could not last long in the face of such an assault. Maybe not long enough for Thorgrim to reach them.

Right ahead of him Thorgrim saw one of the men-at-arms raise his spear, arm cocked to throw. He was not more than fifteen feet from Harald and it seemed impossible he could miss, or fail to deliver a wound that was anything less than fatal.

Thorgrim raised his own spear as he ran, brought his arm back, then skidded to a stop as he let the spear go, letting the momentum in his arm give the weapon that last little shot of power. The spear struck the man in the small of his back and there was no question as to its piercing his mail and driving full into his guts. He shrieked, arched his back, dropped the spear he was preparing to throw.

This was all the distraction Thorgrim needed. The other riders looked over at the sound as they realized they were again being attacked by an enemy they had not seen coming.

"The woods! To the woods!" Thorgrim shouted, waving as he ran. He reached behind and drew the seax and drove the point into the rump of the horse as he passed, sending the animal bolting away, careening into the others massed for the kill.

Even Starri did not need convincing now. They turned and ran and Thorgrim heard their footfalls on the grass behind him as the trees and brush loomed in front. A spear came sailing past, but Thorgrim ignored it. Voices shouted in Irish at their backs, but he knew better than to turn and look.

Fifteen feet, ten feet, and then they were once again into the brush and they kept going until they were surrounded by scrubby trees that hid them entirely from view. The trees were their refuge, their protection. Not because they kept the Irish men-at-arms at bay but because they kept the Irish from knowing how many they were facing.

If the mounted warriors had known their enemy consisted of only five men, they would have come down from their horses, plunged into the woods, and sooner or later killed them all. But they did not know that, because the sudden attack and retreat had thrown them into confusion and denied them the chance to assess the force that opposed them. And so they would have to be more cautious.

For a full three minutes Thorgrim, Harald, and Starri stood doubled over, gasping, listening to the shouts of the Irish warriors from somewhere beyond the foliage. Finally Thorgrim straightened, his breathing nearly back to normal. He was going to ask if the others were all right, but he could see they were. Starri, grinning as he was, actually looked better than Thorgrim had seen him look in some time, despite the wild hair and the blood that streaked his face and bare chest and the ugly remnants of the wound in his shoulder, swollen and red.

Thorgrim jerked his head in the direction that led further into the trees and headed off, pushing the bracken aside, twisting through the saplings. He heard the other two following him, heard Harald curse softly as a branch whipped him in the face.

They were no more than thirty or forty feet into the trees when they stepped out of the woods again and onto the bank of the small creek that Cónán had assured them would be there. Thorgrim looked upstream. The water tumbled and fell over the rocks, running inches deep on its path through the trees. Far off he could see the mountains rising up over the foliage. Closer, a hundred yards away, he could see Cónán and Fothaid step from the trees as well.

Thorgrim headed off again, walking half in the water, half on the narrow bank, sometimes stepping into the stream as the trees crowded the watercourse, Harald and Starri behind him. They met up with the Irishmen at a place where the water raced over a wide, flat, smooth rock. Like Starri, Cónán was grinning.

"Well, that got them in an uproar," he said. "Just listen to them!"

They fell silent, listening. The breeze was rustling in the trees and the water making its soft sound over the streambed, but behind it all they could hear the horsemen shouting, could hear the pounding of hooves as horses rode hard, the warriors moving around the stand of trees.

"So, now they think they have us surrounded here, trapped in these woods," Cónán said.

"But they do, don't they?" Harald asked.

"No," Cónán said. He paused. "Well, yes. They do. But we only have to outrun them."

"They're on horseback," Thorgrim said.

"We have to run fast," Cónán said. "But see here, they still don't know how many we are, and after the fright we just gave them, they won't be in any hurry to come in here after us. Certainly not on foot."

"They can ride down the stream bed, if they know it's open enough for them," Thorgrim said. "Come after us that way."

"I'm sure they know that," Cónán said. "Some of these men, they probably know this country near as good as I do. I'm counting on it."

"So now what do we do?" Thorgrim asked.

"Confuse them some more. Scare them some more," Cónán said. "You Northmen, you sit around on your ships all the day, eating and drinking ale. I don't expect you to be able to run like an Irishman can. So the three of you, you go down to the downstream end of this stand of wood. Just hide yourselves in the trees. If any riders come by, you stay put, stay hidden, understand?"

Thorgrim and Harald nodded. Cónán looked at Starri.

"Stay hidden. Don't attack them. Understand?"

Starri frowned, then nodded. Thorgrim turned in the direction that Cónán had indicated and then the three of them headed off at a jog, splashing through the cold water, the day still punctuated by the call of the horsemen as they sorted themselves out in the wake of that wild and utterly unexpected assault.

It took only a few moments to reach the far end of the trees and tuck themselves in among the foliage, standing perfectly still, invisible to anyone looking in from the open place made by the stream. And it was not more than a minute after that when the first of the horsemen appeared in view, right in front of them and fifteen feet away.

He rode slowly past, another man coming behind him, and then another. They moved with great caution, and Thorgrim could see their heads swiveling, their eyes peering into the dark woods, and he could well imagine how vulnerable they must feel. An enemy of unknown size, of proven courage and versatility, hiding in the trees, unseen, ready like a pack of wolves to pounce.

But tempting as it was to fall on the riders, Thorgrim remained still and let them pass. Even Starri, who was twitching and jerking his limbs in that odd pre-battle way of his, did not move from the place where he stood.

Ten horsemen. Thorgrim counted them as they moved past. Ten mounted warriors, and then there were only the trees and the tumbling water once again.

Thorgrim took a careful step toward the edge of the foliage, moving to a place where he could see upstream. The riders who had passed them were still keeping to the water, and more riders were coming from the other direction, moving in the same slow, tentative way. There seemed to be ten in that second column as well. Twenty riders moving along the streambed, another twenty circling the woods. Riders to flush the tormenters out and riders to cut them down as they ran.

The Irishmen at the head of each mounted column met about fifty yards from where Thorgrim stood. He heard them speak in low voices. One pointed a gloved hand upstream, and then suddenly he jerked as if someone had yanked a leash around his neck. He slumped sideways, an arrow in his chest, and then the man to whom he was speaking was knocked right off his horse, coming down on his back in the stream, flailing, kicking and shouting, clawing at the arrow in his neck.

Once again the quiet scene burst into chaos as the riders whirled in place, trying to find where this new attack was coming from. Another man slumped sideways, and Thorgrim saw a horse twisting as its rider grasped for an arrow jutting from his upper arm.

Cónán and Fothaid were shooting as fast as they could, and that seemed very fast indeed. Thorgrim guessed they were moving through the woods, downstream, toward where he and Harald and Starri stood waiting. An arrow bounced off a mail shirt, the rider shouting in surprise and pointing at the trees and spurring his horse on, one of the Irish bandits apparently in sight.

"Get ready, I think this is where we start running," Thorgrim said, and no sooner had the words left him then he heard someone crashing through the trees and bracken. A second later Cónán and Fothaid came racing through the brush, making no attempt at stealth now.

"Here we go, here we go!" Cónán shouted as he ran, his eyes wide and wild-looking, a crazy grin on his face. He was enjoying himself, genuinely finding pleasure in this. Thorgrim was impressed, and a bit envious. He himself felt like a sea-worn ship, battered about, tired and waterlogged. It had been some time since he had felt such unabashed exhilaration.

Cónán and Fothaid raced past and Thorgrim followed behind and Starri and Harald after him. They leapt over rotting logs and pushed tall ferns and thin oaks and maples aside as they ran. Cónán was a wonder to see, dodging here and there, side to side, under branches, around trees. Thorgrim could do nothing but stay in his wake and try to follow.

Even Fothaid could not keep up with Cónán, and by the time they had covered fifty feet he was three steps behind. Starri, however, had caught up with the Irishman and was running at his side, matching him step for step, dodge for dodge. Starri could not help but turn such a run for his very life into a competition of speed and agility. It was just who he was.

They burst from the trees and into the open country, never breaking stride. There were no horsemen near; the closest were sixty or seventy yards off and looking in an entirely different direction. If this was by Cónán's design or a happy coincidence, Thorgrim did not know, and he told himself to ask Cónán later if they happened to still be alive.

There was a shout from the left, and another off to the right.

They've seen us now, Thorgrim thought. He could hear more shouting and the pounding of hooves, growing louder and more rapid as the horses built speed and thundered toward them.

We have to run fast.

Thorgrim remembered Cónán's words. Stupid Irish bastard, was this really his idea, to simply outrun the horsemen? Cónán had never been very specific about this part of his plan. Now, as Thorgrim's breath came harder and he began to feel a burning in his chest and he realized he was falling behind the other four as they raced across the open ground, he wished he had asked more questions.

They were going uphill, climbing one of the innumerable hillocks that rolled like waves across the countryside. Thorgrim's legs were beginning to tire and he was starting to consider just turning and fighting. How many of these Irish whores' sons could he kill with his seax before they sent him off to the corpse hall?

Cónán was up over the crest of the hillock and lost from sight, and then Starri, Fothaid and Harald. Thorgrim pushed up the last few feet and reached the top. He expected to see the ground roll off downhill on the other side, but it did not. Instead it just ended with a sharp six-foot drop to the ground where the back side of the hillock had eroded away into a small dirt cliff.

Thorgrim felt his feet come down on air and he fell, hit the ground, and sprawled out on the grass. He felt hands grabbing him and pulling him and he looked around to see the other four pressed against the bank of dirt, hidden under the overhanging sod above them where the earth had been chewed away.

Thorgrim half stood and scrambled toward them, dropping in a spot between Harald and Cónán, back to the earthen wall, mouth hanging open as he gasped for breath. He could hear the riders getting closer, could feel the little vibrations in the ground from the pounding of the horses' hooves.

The horsemen swept past from the right and the left, coming into view as they raced around the partial hill, which hid Thorgrim and his men, from one direction at least. They pounded off toward the small river which Thorgrim's people had been following. The horsemen, Thorgrim guessed, must have thought the five of them were further ahead, maybe hidden behind one of the other hills. That was why they were still riding even though their quarry was no longer in sight.

At last Thorgrim's breathing settled enough that he trusted himself to speak. "Did you know this was here?" he asked Cónán, gesturing toward the dirt bank against which they were concealed. "Or are you just very lucky?"

"I'm very lucky," Cónán said, "but I also knew this was here." He turned and looked out over the countryside, toward the riders racing off in the distance. "There's fifteen of them," he said. "So there's at least another twenty or thirty still back at the woods who'll catch up with them. And pretty soon they'll figure out that they're not chasing us any longer."

Thorgrim nodded. "So we run again? Very fast?"

Cónán smiled. "No, we can't outrun horses for long. Not even you."

"So what do we do?" Thorgrim asked.

"Now we get some horses of our own."

Chapter Twenty-Six

The foreigners inflicted a battle-rout on Flann son of Mael Sechnaill…
The Annals of Ulster

Lochlánn had seen enough of fighting to know how quickly it could all fall apart, but still he was amazed that his plans had collapsed around him so fast and so completely.

He whirled his horse in a circle, confusion and chaos on every hand. It could not have been thirty or forty minutes since he had led his line of horsemen forward, but it seemed like a week, so completely had his world been turned upside down.

Until that moment it all seemed to be going as he had prayed it would. Once Kevin mac Lugaed had agreed to give him the additional men, Lochlánn had thought he was on the road to an easy victory. He could see now he was wrong.

The head of Kevin's household guard was a man named Niall. Kevin had insisted he go with Lochlánn and the rest, no doubt to make certain that whatever Lochlánn did, it was in Kevin's best interest. And that was fine with Lochlánn, because his interest and Kevin's interest were the same—kill Thorgrim Night Wolf and his men, capture Louis de Roumois and hang him. The hanging could come after a trial or before, either way. It did not matter to Lochlánn.

Lochlánn had even received further proof that God was blessing his mission. Senach and the rest of the men from Glendalough had joined them ten miles from Kevin's ringfort with the surprising news that the heathens had left their ship and were approaching overland. Lochlánn had envisioned a punishing ride along the banks of the Avonmore, trying to overtake the heathens' ship before it reached the sea. But now, far from having to chase them, the heathens were walking right into their arms, with, apparently, a covey of Irish outlaws in tow.

This news also meant that Kevin had been right to fear the return of Thorgrim Night Wolf. In that stretch of country there was not much of any value between the River Avonmore and Kevin's ringfort at Ráth Naoi. If

Thorgrim was coming this way, he was probably coming for Kevin mac Lugaed.

Lochlánn and Niall worked out their plans. There was little disagreement.

"They must be down by the river," Lochlánn said, pointing to the south. The horsemen had stopped at the top of a small hill that gave them a view of the countryside beyond. "I say we advance in a line, right down to the water. We'll certainly sweep them up if we do that. Once we're driving them like deer it should be no great hardship to ride them down, kill the lot of them."

Niall agreed. They gave the men leave to have a meal, then mounted up again and moved across the hilly ground, Lochlánn and Niall near the center of that long line of horsemen. Lochlánn had been about to suggest to Niall that they pick up their pace, close faster with the heathens, when the shouting had started on their right flank, right by the stand of trees that bordered a small creek there.

He and Niall had wheeled their horses at the sound, but it was not at all clear what was going on. The riders by the woods were turning out of line as if their horses had spooked. Lochlánn was still trying to decide if he should leave his place and go see what was happening when a man came out of the trees, shouting, bow in hand, and Lochlánn realized they were under attack.

"After him! After him!" Lochlánn shouted, digging his spurs in, pushing his horse to a gallop as the man ran out into the open and sprinted away ahead of the line. He was an Irishman, Lochlánn was all but certain. He had the red hair of a Norseman, true, but the clothing was Irish.

Quick son of a bitch, Lochlánn thought, as the Irishman bounded away and the mounted warriors continued in pursuit.

Why show himself? Lochlánn wondered next. If the man was hidden safely in the trees, why come out in the open where the horsemen could ride him down?

An ugly feeling was forming in Lochlánn's gut, a sense that something was wrong, and so he was not too surprised when he heard more shouting behind him, from the place where the bowman had come from the woods. He pulled the reins over, turned his horse toward this new sound. More men had come out of the woods, and they already had two of his riders down on the ground.

How many are they? Lochlánn wondered. Were the woods crowded with heathen killers, or was it only a handful? That was the crucial question, and he had no way to answer it. He raced off toward this new fight while Niall continued to lead his riders after the Irish bowman.

This is bad, Lochlánn thought. He could feel his control over the situation slipping, chaos taking hold. There were men riding in every direction, with no purpose and no leader directing them. Men-at-arms were all but useless if they did not act together as a unit. Louis de Roumois had taught him that.

"You men! You men! Form on me! To me!" Lochlánn shouted, but if anyone heard him, they did not obey. The Irish bowman had disappeared into the trees and so had the other two men who had surprised his riders. Time for Lochlánn to get things back under control, to gather his men-at-arms and think about how they would flush these bastards out of the trees and kill them.

Then the air was split by a terrible shriek. Lochlánn felt the hairs on his neck stand up. He twisted in the saddle. Further off to his right another man had come racing out of the woods, bare-chested, a battle ax in each hand.

"Bastard!" Lochlánn shouted. This one he recognized. He could still recall him leaping from the side of the heathen's ship and taking Airt down to his death. Once again he spurred his horse to a run, lowered his spear. This one he would personally stick like a boar.

But he had some distance to cover before he did, and already more of his men were converging on the wild Northman. It was a frantic melee with horses turning and prancing, riders trying to find an opening to strike at the heathen, and the heathen moving like an eel, fast and slippery.

Lochlánn was still thirty yards away when the other two came running out of the woods, and now, being closer, he recognized them as well, the broad one with the yellow hair and the one with the dark beard. He recognized them from the fight in the garden at Glendalough and from the fight on the river. The bearded one had been steering the ship, he recalled.

Are you Thorgrim Night Wolf? Lochlánn wondered. But he did not have time to wonder long, as the two were rushing to the aid of the shirtless heathen with the axes. Lochlánn turned his horse a bit, charging at the newcomers, ignoring the wild man who was already surrounded.

There was more shouting to his left now, and Lochlánn, despite himself, turned to look. Once again his men were charging around in frantic circles. He remembered the bowman running into the trees there, wondered if he was once again putting arrows into his men. Or if there were others who had not revealed themselves.

"Ah, damn you!" Lochlánn shouted in frustration. These sons of whores had played him and his men for fools, had thrown them into confusion, made them react just as they wished and then taken advantage of each twist and turn. It had to stop.

He whirled his horse around again, once more facing the mad, shirtless one, turning just in time to see him and the two others disappear back into the trees.

"To me! You men, to me!" he shouted, putting his every bit of strength into his voice, and this time his words cut through the panic and confusion. One by one the riders pulled their horses' heads around and trotted over to where Lochlánn waited, well out of range of the bowmen in the trees.

"Where's Niall?" he asked. "Does Niall still live?"

"Here he comes, yonder," one of the horsemen said, and a moment later Niall rode up. His face was red with exertion and an arm was hanging at his side, a bright stream of blood running down the links of mail.

"You're wounded," Lochlánn said, nodding toward Niall's arm. Niall made a dismissive gesture.

"Arrow," he said. "Not too deep. Mail did its work."

Lochlánn nodded. "All right, these bastards have led us on a fine dance so far," he said. "Now it will stop. They've gone to ground in the woods, and they have no way out, save through us. If we can flush them out, we can ride them down and kill them."

He made a gesture with his hand that took in a dozen of Kevin's men. "You lot, ride around the far side of this stand of trees. Make certain those heathen swine don't escape that way. Listen well for my orders." The men Lochlánn had indicated wheeled their mounts and rode off, kicking their horses to a gallop, aware of the importance of not letting their tormentors escape out the far side of the woods.

"How many are they, do you think?" Senach asked.

"I don't know," Lochlánn said. "A dozen? Not much more than that. We outnumber them for certain." He grew angrier as he spoke, thinking of how that handful of men had done his warriors such hurt.

Don't get angry, you'll lose every time... He could still hear Louis de Roumois's voice in his head.

"There were sixty at least that we saw marching along the river," Senach said. "Men and women. If there's but a dozen in the trees, that means the rest are still out there." He nodded toward the country south of them.

"That's right," Lochlánn said. "And these bastards in the trees will want to get back to them. We have men around the far side of the woods. We'll keep more on this side. There's a creek that runs right through this stand of trees. Ten men ride up the stream, ten down from the other side. We'll fight them on foot or horseback, whichever makes sense. We'll try to flush them out into the open and ride them down."

The rest of the men nodded agreement. Lochlánn ordered them off in different directions: ten men to the downstream end of the trees that ran for about two hundred yards along the water course, and ten to the upstream end. He positioned the twenty men he had left with him in a long line that stretched the whole length of the woods. When the heathens came running out into the open, the men patrolling the edge of the trees would be called on to ride the swine down and kill them. And Lochlánn intended to be one of those.

That done, there was nothing left but to wait and see what would come barreling out of the trees.

The wait was not so very long. For ten minutes the afternoon was quiet, the only sounds the breeze in the branches, the running water, the occasional bird call. It seemed very odd after the violence and chaos of the past half hour. And then it ended with the sound of shouting from the stream bed, lost behind the screen of trees, the thud of horses' hooves as the animals were spurred to a gallop, the crash of men running through the woods.

"Here they come, here they come!" Lochlánn shouted. He could hear bodies tearing through the brush and he had to guess it was the heathens they were hunting. He peered into the trees, hoping to see them, to gauge where they might emerge, but he could see nothing but the leaves and the undergrowth.

He cocked his head, straining to hear, to make sense of the sounds. His men were riding down the stream bed, he was sure of that. He could hear shouting in his native Irish and the sound of the horses, and he imagined they were pursuing the fleeing enemy as best they could, given the difficult ground.

And then, to his right, he saw men come bursting out of the woods, moving at a full run, with the crazy, shirtless heathen and the Irish bowman in the lead. Lochlánn was a full hundred yards away, but still he was the closest of all the mounted warriors to them.

"There! There! After them!" he shouted as he put the spurs to his horse and leaned forward and whipped the reins. He saw the other horsemen wheel and kick their mounts to a gallop as well. He felt his horse's speed building under him, a good animal, smart, fast, not at all skittish. The quarry were running like rabbits across the open country and Lochlánn's eyes were fixed on their backs as he rode them down.

That's it? he thought. *Five, just five?*

It did not seem possible that five men alone had done so much hurt to his warriors, and he wondered if this was yet some other trick. But even if it was, it did not matter because he knew these five were the men who had surprised his riders and killed and wounded a number of them, and now they would die under his spear and his sword. They were running across open country and he was on horseback and it was only a matter of time. A few minutes, no more.

With that thought he readjusted his grip on the shaft of his spear. He was half standing in the stirrups, taking the motion of the running horse in his bent legs. He held his spear up at shoulder height and he could already see in his mind what he would do: ride up alongside the fleeing men, drive the spear into the back of the first one he reached, then draw his sword, slash at the next, feel the razor edge cut through his arrogant heathen flesh.

The five men raced over the crest of a small hill and were lost from sight. Lochlánn did not follow, because his shortest path to intercept them took him around the hill. He charged across the open ground, flew past the grassy rise, the country opening up before him, but he still could not see the men he was chasing.

Behind that far hill, Lochlánn thought. It was the only place they could be, though it did not seem there had been time enough for them to reach it. But it was rolling country, and he knew his prey would go in and out of view as they ran through the dips and over the high spots.

He raced on, the next hill rising in front of him, and he was certain the men he was chasing were very close now. He might well run right into them as he came over this rise. He held his spear a bit tighter, raised it a few inches to give more strength to that first cathartic thrust.

As he came up over the hill, the ground rolled away before him to another stand of trees a half mile distant, down where the shallow river ran to Ráth Naoi. And the men he was chasing were nowhere to be seen.

"What in all hell?" Lochlánn shouted out loud. There was no place between him and the river where the men might be concealed, and they most certainly had not had time enough to reach the river. They had just disappeared.

And then he heard shouting from behind, a mad shriek like he had heard earlier, voices shouting in Irish, and he felt the bottom of his stomach drop away. He pulled the reins to check his horse's forward momentum, no easy thing with the animal running flat out. In a flurry of thrashing mane and straining legs the horse came to a stop and Lochlánn whirled it around and once again drove his spurs into its flanks to get back to a gallop, heading back the way he had come.

Up over the hill again, and now, one hundred yards back, Lochlánn could see that the first hill he had ridden around was hollowed out on the backside and the five had been hiding there, but they were hiding no longer. They had run out into the open, shouting and waving, as more of his horsemen had come around the hill. Then, as Lochlánn's men had wheeled in surprise, the heathens had set upon them.

Lochlánn pushed his tiring mount as hard as the animal could run, but he was still some distance away, unable to do anything but watch. He saw the crazy, shirtless Northman drag one of his men from the saddle, chop down with his battle ax, then leap on the now riderless horse. He saw another of his men go down. He saw one of the horses rear in fright, sending its rider toppling to the ground, and then the Irish bowman was on the animal's back.

Lochlánn was fifty yards short of reaching them when the big, yellow-haired Norseman swung himself up into a saddle, and then all five of them were up and kicking their horses to a gallop. Lochlánn realized his fingers ached from gripping so hard on his spear and he threw the encumbrance away. His clenched his teeth, whipped his horse with his reins.

Again…bastards…they did it again… He could not recall having felt fury like this, not for a long, long time.

He looked over his shoulder. The other riders, those still alive and still mounted, had also seen what was happening and they, too, were giving chase. Lochlánn felt just the slightest bit of hope. They were still thirty against five, and the heathens and Irish outlaws could not be as skilled riders as were his own men. Their luck and fine tricks could not last forever.

The five hunted men had been running in one direction, but now they were riding off another way, heading more south than they had been going, trying to flee as directly away from their pursuers as they could. Audacious as these bastards might be, even they had to know there was a limit to what they might get away with.

Lochlánn could see more and more of his men taking up the chase, riding hard in the wake of Thorgrim Night Wolf and the others, falling in behind the quarry. It was a fox hunt now, the prey flushed from the woods, running in open country, outnumbered, and they could not run forever.

In the distance Lochlánn could see the shallow river that Thorgrim's band had been following in their approach to Kevin's ringfort, the watercourse dotted with an occasional stand of trees. He thought they would likely head for the trees, try to lose themselves in the woods as they had before, but instead they seemed to be racing for an open field of high grass that ran down to the water.

He was thirty yards or so behind the fleeing men and overtaking them, his horse fast, his skill as a rider greater than any Northman's. He wondered if he would reach them before they reached the river. He had only to get a sword-length away, make the whore's sons turn and fight, and then the rest of his men would be up with them and it would be over.

The rest of the heathens… Lochlánn thought. *I wonder where the rest of the heathens are?* Senach had told him there were near sixty of them, men and women.

He felt that now familiar and unhappy sensation in his gut. *What are you up to?* he thought. Every time so far he was sure the Northmen had made a mistake, the mistake had been his. But the five were alone and he was right behind them and he did not see what trick they might pull.

He reached his hand across his belly and drew his sword from the scabbard, took comfort in the feel of the familiar grip in his hand. He raised the weapon so the point rose above his head like a banner. It would rally his men and give him more momentum when he brought that first blow down on the men he was rapidly overtaking.

Then ahead of the five fugitives and off to the right Lochlánn saw movement, saw someone rise from the tall grass, saw him burst from cover like a startled pheasant and come running toward him, shouting and waving one arm, clutching a cloth sack with the other.

Trap! Lochlánn thought. They had ridden into a trap and now it was closing. He looked up at the five he was chasing and saw they were reining their horses over, some to the right, some to the left, their actions sudden and confused. They seemed as surprised as Lochlánn.

Lochlánn pulled back on his reins, trying to stop his horse as quick as he could. He did not know what was happening, but something in his head was shouting a warning. He looked back at the figure who had emerged from the grass, still yelling, still running directly at him. A familiar figure, very familiar.

Louis de Rumois…

Louis was running his way, shouting, and now Lochlánn could hear the Irish words in the Frankish accent. "Lochlánn! It's a trap! Go back, go back!" Louis shouted, and suddenly there were forty men rising up from the grass, fifty feet beyond where Louis had emerged. They were holding swords and spears and some had shields. Thorgrim and his small band had been leading Lochlánn and his men right into their midst.

Louis was closer now, still running, waving, shouting. "Wait for me! Wait!" he called and Lochlánn, who was about to turn and charge off, paused. The other men in the tall grass were starting to run as well, coming for Louis and for Lochlánn. The five men on the stolen horses had managed to get their mounts stopped and were turning back the way they had come.

Ten feet from where Lochlánn sat on his prancing horse, unsure of what to do, Louis reached out a beckoning hand. His face was a mask of desperation. He stumbled toward Lochlánn, beseeching, as the Northmen and the Irish bandits closed in behind him.

Lochlánn stretched out his arm. He grabbed Louis's hand and pulled and Louis leapt off the ground, pivoting on the grip he had on Lochlánn's hand and landing on the back of Lochlánn's horse. Lochlánn put the spurs to the animal, pulled the reins over hard, and the horse bolted away, gaining speed, leaving the shouting heathens behind as it ran.

Ahead, Lochlánn could see that the rest of his men, those who had taken up the chase, were now stopped in their tracks. They watched as Lochlánn changed direction and raced away from this new threat, and then, almost as one, they did the same.

Louis had one hand on Lochlánn's belt, and presumably held the sack in the other. Lochlánn could hear his breathing, loud in his ear. He thought of the bowman, the Irish outlaw who had hidden in the woods and done such lethal damage to his men.

If he shoots, he'll hit Louis and I'll be spared, Lochlánn thought. *And that will be two problems solved.*

Chapter Twenty-Seven

I'd the option just now
Of able judges;
Now the one thing left
Is the wolf's tail.
The Saga of the Confederates

Ottar Bloodax stood six feet five inches tall and weighed over twenty stone. At the age of eleven he had taken his first drink of ale, and hardly a day had passed since then that he had not consumed ale or mead or both. As a result, it took quite a lot for him to get drunk. But still, through perseverance, he managed.

It seemed to him that over the past few weeks, and just when he felt in most need of alcohol's soothing influence, it had become harder still. He had come awake that morning—or it might have been midday, he was not sure—with his head pounding and his eyes watering and his hands shaking. The hall was lost in a twilight gloom, the windows shuttered tight, but the grey light that crept in around the imperfectly fitted slats told him it was not nighttime.

He did not trust himself to walk, so he crawled to the platform against the back wall where an oversized cup of mead sat waiting, pulled himself up onto the raised section, lifted the cup and began pouring the contents down his throat. He managed to swallow at least two thirds of it, the rest pouring down his beard and tunic and over the furs that were scattered on the platform. He threw the cup aside and closed his eyes and waited for the drink to work its magic.

None of his men were in the hall. A dozen of them would be encircling the building, keeping the wolf at bay, or they should be, at least. Once Ottar had poured enough mead down his throat to give him sufficient courage, he would stand and look out the door, and if he found there were not enough guards stationed around the hall then someone would die on the stake.

Who? he wondered. *Who's left?* His mind was swimming. In his head he was staggering blindly. *Ketil Hrafnsson,* he thought. *That's right, incompetent whore's son, he's the one left in charge now…*

The only ones in the hall besides Ottar were half a dozen slaves, all of whom were cowering behind the wattle wall that sectioned off the back of the hall from the front room. They may have been hiding, but they were also paying attention because they knew the price they would pay if they did not. And no sooner had Ottar's empty cup hit the dirt floor than one of the servants was picking it up, refilling it with mead, and handing it warily back to Ottar, who took it without acknowledging in any way the frightened man's existence.

Night Wolf, Night Wolf, Night Wolf…

Ottar poured the fresh cup of mead into his mouth and felt the first hints of the drink's effect, and with it he felt the panic start to subside.

Night Wolf…

Of all the men he could have met, here was one with the name of Night Wolf. A man who had earned that name because it was supposed that he…

Ottar could not bear to think about it. He had hated Thorgrim on first sight, had hated him more when he learned of the nickname Night Wolf.

"Ah, bastard!" Ottar shouted and flung the cup again, this time with enough force to shatter it against the table, which was overturned and broken.

The raid on Glendalough had been an undeniable failure, but still Ottar had managed to take some pleasure in the outcome. They had sailed off with all but one of Thorgrim's fleet of ships. They had left Thorgrim and his men to be killed by the Irish. And best of all, they had taken Vík-ló for themselves. Vík-ló and the considerable hoard of plunder that Thorgrim and his men had accumulated.

The timing was fortunate, to say the least. Ottar had suffered one failure after another, sacking monasteries that turned out to have nothing worth taking, having his ship all but sink under him. His frustration had become so great, and his leadership so precarious, that he had been driven mad by the worthlessness of the village they had taken at the river mouth. In his madness he had killed every Irishman, woman, or child there on whom he could get his hands or blade.

He knew that others wanted to challenge his position as leader of the men, and it was only a matter of time before someone found the courage to actually do it. And then the day would come that Ottar met a man who could defeat him. It might be years, and many men might die at his hands until then, but the day would come.

Or maybe that day had come already; maybe he had already met that man. Thorgrim Night Wolf was not in the least intimidated by him, and that made Ottar furious, and just a bit unsettled. But the gods had favored Ottar, as they always did. In one stroke he had gone from the edge of the abyss to being Lord of Vík-ló, with the longphort and all its wealth now his and his men's to share out.

"Son…of…a…whore…" Ottar stammered. He was trying to summon the resolve to rise and find his slave and beat him to death for his negligence when the frightened man came dashing out from behind the wall with another full cup of mead. Ottar snatched it and took an awkward swipe at the servant, but the man ducked and was gone in an instant and Ottar did not have the energy to pursue him.

Night Wolf…

It was the only flaw in all his good luck, the only imperfection in his success. But it was a huge imperfection, like a gaping hole in the bottom of an otherwise perfect longship. He had not seen Thorgrim die. He had left Thorgrim in such a way that it seemed impossible that he could live. But he had not actually seen the man die, and so he could not be certain that he was, at that moment, half frozen in the bitter realm of Hel.

It had not seemed like so great a problem at first. Any worries had been tamped down by the wealth found at Vík-ló, the respect he had gained among his men, both those who had been with him some time and those more newly joined.

But then came the business with the shipwright seeing the wolf. And then the dead men.

Ottar threw the cup away and struggled to his feet. He had not wandered more than twenty paces from the door of his hall since the first man had been found with his throat ripped out. He knew that his men were starting to talk about it. Soon they would do more than talk.

There was a knock on the door and Ottar gasped in surprise and jerked his head in that direction, then cursed himself for a weak fool. "Come!" he shouted and the door opened, Ketil Hrafnsson standing at the threshold, framed by a grey, midday sky. He stepped in quick, closed the door behind him. Ketil knew, as did all Ottar's men, that the door was not to remain open long.

"What?" Ottar demanded. His eyes were tearing up and he was having trouble focusing. He looked around for his slave and another cup of mead.

"I was down by the shipyard, down where the shipwright, Aghen, works," Ketil began.

"Aghen?" Ottar said. "Is he back? What news?" He felt a sudden flash of hope. Was the wolf dead and hanging from a pole just outside his door?

"No, lord, Aghen has not come back," Ketil said, with just the hint of a patronizing tone in his voice. Ottar was about to slap him down, verbally, at least, but the man spoke again before he could summon a response.

"I was down at the shipyard, like I said," Ketil continued. "Looking for some planks. For a new table. We talked about that."

"Yes, yes," Ottar said.

"As I was going through the stacks of wood there I saw where something had been buried. I dug it up and found this." Ketil lifted his arm and Ottar noticed for the first time that he held something at his side, a tool of some sort, it seemed, but nothing Ottar recognized. Ketil held it out and Ottar took it in both hands, squinting at it in the dull light, trying to make sense of what he was seeing.

There were two handles, joined at a pivot, like the tongs a blacksmith might use, but they were made of wood. The ends opposite the handles were shaped into two triangular sections of wood with rows of short arrowheads or knife points or some such all fixed along the edges.

Ottar frowned. He wanted to ask Ketil what it was, but he did not want to appear ignorant. He held the handles and pulled them apart and the triangles at the other end gaped open. He pushed the handles together and the triangles closed, the arrowheads coming together. Like jaws.

Like a wolf's jaws.

Ottar froze. He felt his breath grow shallow. He stared at the thing in his hand. *Aghen…* he thought. *At the shipyard…* Aghen who had seen the wolf, who knew all about Thorgrim and his shape-shifting.

With a curse Ottar pushed past Ketil, threw the door open, and stepped out into the muted light of the late afternoon where he could get a better look at this thing in his hands. He held it up and worked the jaws. Open, closed, open. The long handles would allow a man to clamp the jaws down with considerable force. The wicked teeth would be more than sharp enough to rip the throat out of a man's neck. The business end was shaped in such a way as to perfectly mimic the bite of a wolf.

He held the jaws up closer to his face. They had been washed, but imperfectly. He could see streaks of blood clearly enough, even bits of dried flesh clinging to the teeth.

"Son of a bitch!" Ottar roared with the sort of power and authority that had once been his norm, but which had been missing the past week and more. He flung the wooden wolf jaws aside.

He had been played for a fool, and he felt the fury and humiliation that came with that realization. And he felt relief as well, like the sun breaking through the clouds. Because there was no wolf, and Thorgrim Night Wolf was a man, no more, and if he was not dead already he soon would be.

But he would not be the first to die. That honor was reserved for the shipwright, Aghen. And his death would not be as merciful as that of the cheater, Valgerd.

"Ketil!" Ottar roared, and Ketil, who had been standing just outside the door to the hall, came over in three quick steps. "Send riders out to find that bastard dead man Aghen and…" Then he stopped.

No, he thought. *The gods are speaking to me here.* It could not be mere chance that he had smashed the table in a blind, drunk rage and then sent Ketil to find planks to replace it. And that instead Ketil had found Aghen's instrument of lies. The gods did not want Ottar to avenge himself on Aghen alone; they wanted vengeance against them all. That was why they had freed him from his self-imposed prison.

"Riders, lord?" Ketil prompted.

"No riders," Ottar said. "Men. I want men, under arms. We are going to go out and find that bastard Aghen and show him and everyone what happens when men play tricks. And then we will go to where that Kevin mac Lugaed lives and we'll teach him the same. And if Thorgrim Night Pup still lives, then I know the gods will send him to me so that I can kill him, too. Like I should have done."

"Yes, lord," Ketil said, then turned and hurried off. Ketil was not the smartest or the most loyal; those men had died—at Aghen's hand, apparently—but Ketil knew better than to do anything but obey, and obey immediately.

"We'll hunt them down and we'll kill them all," Ottar said out loud, but to no one in particular. It felt good to say it. It felt good to be back in command.

Chapter Twenty-Eight

I am an outlaw to most men;
only arrow-storms await me.
Gisli Sursson's Saga

At first there was nothing that Louis de Roumois could do, nothing he could think about, save for not falling off the horse. Lochlánn was riding hard, a full gallop, the animal bouncing and jolting over the uneven ground as they raced away from the ambush.

Louis was seated behind the saddle, straddling the horse's haunches with no stirrups for his feet, gripping Lochlánn's belt with one hand and the sack that held the small silver casket with the other. He knew that if he fell he would probably die. Not from the fall itself—he had tumbled off horses more times than he could remember—but at the hands of the heathens and Irish who were no doubt chasing them. The ones he had betrayed just moments before.

He craned his head around as far as he was able, but he could see nothing of the pursuers. The horse took an odd step and Louis felt himself slip and he used his thighs and his grip on Lochlánn's belt to reposition himself. A lesser rider, someone not as athletic as Louis, would have been in the grass long before that. But Louis, strong, well accustomed to horses and with a keen sense of self-preservation, managed to hang on.

Ahead of Lochlánn and on either side of him the other men-at-arms reined their mounts over and raced back in the direction they had come, back toward where they had been before Thorgrim Night Wolf and the Irishman, Cónán, had so cleverly led them into that trap.

Louis had a grudging appreciation for what they had done. When the five had headed off toward where Lochlánn's mounted warriors were making ready to attack, and the other Norse and Irishmen under Godi's command had found their place in the tall grass, Louis imagined that this would be an end to his problems. He did not see how Thorgrim, Cónán, and the others would not all be ridden down and killed. He certainly had not imagined they would come riding back, unscathed, on stolen horses, leading Lochlánn and his men into an ambush.

He felt Lochlánn lean back a bit as he brought his horse from a gallop to a jog. Louis twisted around and looked back over his shoulder. The heathens and the Irish were three hundred yards behind and seemed to show no interest in pursuing the mounted men-at-arms.

Pushed your luck far enough, Thorgrim Night Wolf? Louis thought with some small satisfaction, but it did not change the fact that Thorgrim and Cónán had played Lochlánn and his men for fools.

Louis had counted on Lochlánn's defeating Thorgrim. When he failed to do so, it meant Louis had to make a number of hard decisions fast, make them right there while he crouched in the tall grass with the others, pretending that he, too, was taking part in the ambush. And the first of those was deciding which side he was on.

He did not particularly like the Irish, did not feel he had been treated all that well by them. It was possible they were still looking to put him on trial for the killing of Colman's man Aileran, and maybe even for killing Colman as well.

The Northmen, however, he loathed bitterly. Nearly half his life had been spent fighting the heathens in his native Roumois as they tried to plunder that county in the same way they plundered Ireland. Of the two, he would choose the Christian Irish over the heathens. If it came to it, he would choose Satan and his minions over the heathens.

What's more, he liked Lochlánn very much. He had taught Lochlánn nearly all he knew about warfare, had fought side by side with him. He felt like an older brother to the young Irishman.

But warning Lochlánn of the trap and running off to join the mounted Irish men-at-arms meant abandoning Failend to the Northmen. A week before, that would have been unthinkable. He would have died protecting Failend from Thorgrim and his band. But quite a bit had changed since then.

Failend, it seemed, no longer needed protecting from the heathens. None of the Northmen had shown any inclination toward molesting her, which Louis found surprising. But more to the point, Failend had apparently decided to join with them. Despite all her protests about going to Glendalough to keep any Irish from being killed, Louis could see the truth. Failend was going heathen herself.

So that left only the question of whether he should take the casket of silver which he had been carrying for safekeeping. Failend had killed her husband to obtain it, Louis was quite sure, and that made her claim to the hoard a bit more tenuous in his mind. That silver was his only chance of getting back to Frankia, but if Failend kept it, and she stayed with the heathens, then it would no doubt end up in the Northmen's hands.

That, for Louis, was the final argument, and if it was all a load of self-serving manure, he didn't care and he did not examine it further. He leapt to his feet and ran waving and yelling toward Lochlánn as Lochlánn led his men into the trap. He saved them all, saved them from humiliation and death. And, he had to admit, he felt pretty good about it.

Lochlánn slowed the horse to a walk and the other riders, about thirty in all, closed in around them and matched Lochlánn's pace. They rode on toward the stand of trees to which Thorgrim and Cónán had lured them earlier, and more riders came from around the far end and joined the retreating band. Louis waited for Lochlánn to say something, a thank you, a greeting, anything. But they rode in silence.

He's got a lot to think about, Louis thought as he readjusted his seat on the horse's back.

They came at last to the crest of a low hill and stopped. "Dismount," Lochlánn called, and the weary men around them slipped off their mounts. Louis swung his leg over the horse's rump and dropped easily to the ground, and then Lochlánn followed him. He tossed his horse's reins over the saddle and turned to look at Louis for the first time.

"Lochlánn," Louis said. "Not the best circumstances but I'm glad—"

The blow was so unexpected that Louis barely had time to realize it was coming before Lochlánn's gloved hand connected with the side of his head. He felt the unwelcome but all too familiar sensation of impact. His head snapped around and he was falling before he was quite aware of what was happening, and by the time he knew for certain, he was in the grass.

He landed facedown, and by instinct and training rolled over fast, face-up, to see if another blow was coming. Lochlánn was standing over him, red-faced, a deep scowl on his lips, hands bunched into fists. Louis felt the pain in the side of his head in the wake of the blow, the surprise, the swimming sensation, the humiliation of having been struck. But all of it was overshadowed by the brilliant rage that swept over him.

He rolled to his right, rolled away from Lochlánn and up onto his feet in one deft move, drawing his sword as he rose, coming to rest in an en guarde stance. But Lochlánn was not taken by surprise, and by the time Louis was on his feet, his blade was out as well. Louis took a step toward him but was drawn up short by the sound of a dozen other swords clearing their scabbards.

"You bastard!" Louis said, his voice low as he struggled for control. "I saved your sorry hide, you and the rest of these miserable creatures! All your heads would be on the heathens' pikes if not for me!"

"Yes, you're a great friend to us," Lochlánn said. "Like you were at Glendalough, and back at the river."

"I warned you at Glendalough," Louis said. "I sent the boy to warn you that the heathens were there. At the river I was a prisoner on board the ship. I had no choice but to be there, but I did not fight against you." That was partially true, anyway. He may not have been a prisoner, but he had not lifted a weapon against Lochlánn and his men, and that was the point that mattered.

Lochlánn lowered his sword, just a few inches, but it was enough to tell Louis that the young man was no longer so certain of Louis's guilt. "You killed Aileran. You told me you did. You must answer for that."

I didn't kill Aileran, Louis thought. *Failend killed him, despite what I told you before.* He almost said it out loud. It was the truth. But he realized how craven and mendacious it would sound, so instead he said, "All those things I'll answer for later. Right now we have greater concerns."

"Such as?" Lochlánn asked, and Louis almost laughed out loud.

"Such as the heathens who are coming this way. The heathens who just killed so many of your men. Whom I just saved you from."

"I don't need your help to fight the heathens," Lochlánn said, but there was such a lack of conviction in his voice that Louis did not even bother to argue the point.

"They'll be advancing soon," Louis said. "They move slow. They have women, and a lot of supplies. Not the heathens, but the Irish bandits who are with them. If we get up the river we can stage an ambush like they tried to do to you. Something they'll never see coming."

Lochlánn nodded slowly as he considered this. And then another thought occurred to him, Louis could see it on his face. "Where's Failend?" he asked, and the suspicion was back in his voice.

"She's with the heathens," Louis said. "I didn't abandon her, if that's what you're thinking. She's joined with them. I don't know what demon has got hold of her, but she's thrown in with them. She killed her husband, I'm all but sure. So she probably is not too keen to go back to Glendalough."

Louis's words had the ring of truth because they were the truth and he could see Lochlánn believed him. Then Senach stepped forward. Senach, who had been one of Aileran's men before joining with Lochlánn.

"This one's a serpent," he said, nodding toward Louis. "Talks as sweet as the serpent in the garden. There's a fine big oak yonder, and I have a length of rope in my bag, and I don't see any reason why we shouldn't do what's right this very moment."

"No," Lochlánn said, with a note of command that made Louis both proud and relieved. "We won't do that. That's what the law is for."

"The law?" Senach said. "Damn the law, he killed Aileran. He said so." Louis heard the others muttering their agreement. He wondered if Lochlánn had authority enough over these men to keep them from hanging him in the next few minutes.

Then another of the men-at-arms stepped up, an older man whom Louis did not recognize, and he realized for the first time that Lochlánn had far more men with him than he had thought he did.

Where did these others come from? he wondered. And then the new man spoke.

"See here," he said. "I don't know what in all damnation's going on here and I don't care, either. Who is this bastard?" he asked, nodding toward Louis.

"His name's Louis de Roumois," Lochlánn said. "He was…" And Louis was sure he was about to say he was a novitiate at the monastery at Glendalough, but before the words left him he realized how absurd that would sound. "He was a man-at-arms. In Frankia. Very experienced in fighting heathens." The words came out grudgingly.

The new man nodded. "Well, whoever he is, he has a point. The heathens by the river, coming for Ráth Naoi, they're our chief concern."

"And who are you?" Louis asked.

"I'm Niall. I'm head of these men," he said, gesturing toward the horsemen standing a little ways away. "Kevin mac Lugaed's household guard. Kevin sent us to join Lochlánn's men to fight the heathens, not to worry about any argument they have with you." As he said that he gave Lochlánn and Senach a withering look.

"Very well," Senach said. "Bind this bastard up so he don't run away again and we'll deal with him later."

Louis could see the hesitation on Lochlánn's face, but once again it was Niall who spoke. "We need this one with us," he said. "He's been among the heathens we're fighting. Heathens and Irishmen. He knows what they can do. You say he's a trained warrior. He'll be of use."

"He's a traitor and a murderer," Senach spit.

Niall turned to Lochlánn. "What say you? Do you trust him?"

Louis watched the play of emotions on Lochlánn's face, the anger, the uncertainty, the search for what he truly believed. Finally, hesitatingly, Lochlánn said, "Yes. I trust him."

Senach made an expulsive sound of disgust and turned and stomped off, but Lochlánn and Niall ignored him.

"Very well," Niall said, turning back to Louis. "I saved you from a hanging, it seems. Tell me about these whores' sons who are heading toward Ráth Naoi."

"I will," Louis said. "And then I'll tell you how to beat them. Because I want them dead every bit as much as you."

Chapter Twenty-Nine

A household like this man's household
There is not under valour-provoking heaven.
The Annals of Ulster

Kevin mac Lugaed's chief ambition had always been to rise to the level of rí túaithe, and now he had. He was Lord of Cill Mhantáin and master of the fine ringfort at Ráth Naoi. He had more than one hundred men-at-arms in his service. He was wealthier than he would have ever thought possible. And yet he seemed to derive very little pleasure from all of that. Very little indeed.

His current unhappiness was through no fault of his own, he was at least sure of that. His plans had been laid to waste by the priest. Father Finnian. If not for that bastard, then he would be safe and content within the walls of his ringfort, and not the pacing, caged, frightened animal into which he had devolved.

He was pacing at that very moment, back and forth across the packed dirt floor of his hall. Pacing and thinking and muttering to himself.

It had all been organized so beautifully, so carefully. Thorgrim Night Wolf and Ottar Bloodax, convinced that they could make an easy raid on Glendalough, Kevin mac Lugaed to supply men to help sweep aside what little force opposed them.

But there was no little force defending Glendalough; there was a significant force. Kevin knew that and he kept it from the Northmen. He had meant for the defenders of Glendalough to kill Thorgrim and kill Ottar and all their heathen hoard and to be significantly weakened in the process. Then he would sweep in and sack the monastery himself.

And even if he did not have the chance to loot the monastic city, he would have Vík-ló, the longphort the heathens had built in his territory, and all the wealth he knew to be hidden there. And Ottar Bloodax, who was becoming a bigger and bigger threat to that part of Ireland, would be dead as well. No matter what happened, Kevin mac Lugaed would be the better for it.

Except he wasn't. The damned priest had made him join the defense of Glendalough. Ottar had managed to escape, Ottar the vicious madman, the damned lunatic. He had taken Vík-ló for himself and now he was a bigger threat than Thorgrim ever was. Thorgrim at least could be reasoned with, a rarity among the Northmen, but Ottar was as reasonable as a mad dog, and no more predictable.

Kevin had thought Thorgrim, at least, had been killed, but here came word that, far from dead, Thorgrim was advancing on Ráth Naoi with some unknown number of men.

"He'll want his revenge." Kevin stopped pacing and spoke out loud, though there was no one within earshot. "He's coming for me, and he'll want revenge."

He began pacing again. The thought that Thorgrim would come looking for vengeance was actually no great insight, and saying it out loud did not help clarify the situation in Kevin's mind. He stopped pacing again.

"Eoin!" he shouted and immediately Eoin appeared from the back of the hall, hurrying over. Like all of Kevin's household, Eoin was hovering around, keeping out of sight but ready to spring to his lord's side when summoned.

They fear me, Kevin realized and the thought surprised him. Kevin was under no delusions that he was anything but a craven, plotting, avaricious coward, not the sort who would generally frighten others, but here it was. In any other circumstance he might have been flattered and pleased to have other men react to him that way, but at the moment his mind was too full.

"Lord?" Eoin said, coming to a hesitant stop ten feet away. Normally Kevin would have turned to Niall for advice, but Niall was off with the other one, Lochlánn, hopefully putting a sword through Thorgrim Night Wolf's guts at that very moment. But in Niall's absence, Eoin would do. Might do better, in truth. Eoin had lived with the heathens and spoke their tongue and would better understand how they were likely to react.

"I had this thought, Eoin," Kevin said, though it had just come into his head and was more a disorganized swirl of impressions than a genuine thought. He paused as he organized these ideas into something resembling a plan.

"As you are aware, Ottar has taken Vík-ló," Kevin continued. "I don't like having any of these heathen bastards, Thorgrim or any of them, in possession of that place. But I would rather it be Thorgrim than Ottar. I wonder if we might find Thorgrim, if he is coming this way, and talk him into joining us in a fight to drive Ottar from Vík-ló?"

"Hmmm," Eoin said, with a grave look, like he was giving this genuine consideration, though Kevin could tell he was not. Because it was a pathetic, ridiculous, groping idea. Kevin realized that as soon as he spoke.

Thorgrim would know perfectly well that Kevin had betrayed him. He would not make any deals.

He'll come here, Kevin thought. *He'll overrun my guards; he'll cut my head off and put it on a stake...* He had this image of four of the heathens holding him down on the floor of the hall and Thorgrim Night Wolf, a none-too-sharp knife in his hand, slowly cutting away at his neck as he screamed and bled, screamed and bled.

"My lord?" Eoin said, and now his expression was one of concern.

"What?" Kevin asked. Had he said something out loud? Made some noise? He could not recall, so overwhelmed had he been by that horrible image.

"I was going to say, Lord Kevin, that your idea of joining with Thorgrim Night Wolf is excellent, excellent, but to be perfectly honest I have my doubts..."

Kevin was about to stop him there, but before he could, the door to the hall opened, letting a blast of cool, damp, fresh air into the closed and fetid space. One of the guards posted around the hall's perimeter was standing there.

"Lord?" the guard said. "It's Cathail, come back."

This news gave Kevin a jolt of fear. Cathail was another of the few men he trusted. He had been sent to keep watch over Vík-ló and to report any move that Ottar might make. Thus far Ottar had stayed put, and Cathail had sent the occasional messenger back with word that nothing was stirring in the longphort. But now he had come in person, and his arrival might herald bad things indeed.

"Send him in," Kevin said, and a moment later Cathail stepped into the hall and bowed. His tunic and leather armor were mud-splattered and his face was red, like he had been riding hard.

"What is it?" Kevin snapped.

"Well, lord," Cathail began. "There was a group of armed men, come out of Vík-ló. About forty. On foot. And a cart with them. They left the longphort by land, headed across country."

Kevin felt his stomach sink. Ottar was making a move of some sort. "When was this?" Kevin demanded.

"Ah," Cathail said. "It was about four days ago, lord."

"Four days ago!" Kevin shouted. "And I am only hearing about it now, you incompetent bastard?"

"Well, lord," Cathail stammered, his tone defensive. "The thing of it is, they are wandering all over the countryside, lord. I had no idea of where they were going or what they were about. To be honest, they didn't seem to know, either."

Kevin frowned. "So, where are they now?"

"About five miles from here, lord, by the river. Like I said, there's but forty of them, and they're coming this way. Sort of. In truth they're wandering around like the Jews in the desert."

For a long moment there was an uncomfortable silence as Kevin considered that. "Forty men, you say? On foot? Even lacking the men we sent with that Lochlánn we should be able to crush them easy enough."

His mind was working now. He could hurt Ottar with no great risk to himself or his men. Thirty of his men were off with Lochlánn. If he sent sixty off to crush Ottar's band he would still have warriors to guard the ringfort. But not that many. Did he dare weaken himself thus?

"Ah, lord, there's another thing," Cathail said, still speaking in his sheepish way. "Just this morning, more men came out of Vík-ló. Quite a few more, actually."

"How many?" Kevin asked, now once again worried. His level of fear was going up and down like a boat in a heavy swell.

"It was near hundred and fifty, as far as we could tell," Cathail said.

Kevin worried he might vomit. *Near one hundred and fifty?* he thought, the words like a shrieking in his head. *And already he has forty in the field?* He straightened and forced some composure into his voice.

"And where are these one hundred and fifty heading? Are they wandering about, like the others?"

"No, lord," Cathail said. "They sent riders out, and I'm guessing it was to find the first lot of men. But the rest, they're just staying to the road. The road…to here, actually."

Kevin nodded and walked as steadily as he was able over to the big chair that served as a sort of throne. He sat in it, holding his face in an expression he hoped looked like intense concentration and not an effort to avoid having his knees buckle under him.

He had seen what Ottar had done to prisoners, men who had done no more than join in battle against him. He could well imagine what the lunatic Northman would do to one like himself, who had betrayed him. It would make having his head cut off by Thorgrim with a dull knife look like a mercy. He needed some time to let his panic subside so he could think again.

Luckily, the first order that needed giving was obvious and required no thought or reflection. "Cathail," Kevin said, and he was pleased by the strength in his voice. "Niall is to the west of here with thirty of my men. Ride out and find him and tell him I desire he return with the men immediately. And tell the other one, Lochlánn, that if he does not want to see his men slaughtered by the heathen he had best come along as well."

The sun was nearly behind the hills and the wolf hunting party was just setting up camp for the night by the bank of a narrow river when they saw the rider far off. He was to the south and maybe two miles away, a dark spot moving fast over the lush green fields, illuminated by the low-hanging sun to the west.

"Who could this be?" Oddi wondered out loud. He had been the first to spot the rider, and now most of the men had stopped what they were doing to look, as if staring at the newcomer, barely visible in the distance, might reveal his identity and purpose.

"Coming from that direction he must be coming from Vík-ló," Einar said. He looked directly at Aghen, fixed him with an ugly stare. "Probably sent by Ottar to find out why we haven't yet killed this wolf."

The shipwright returned the stare, unflinching. "And I'll tell him," he said. "Like I told you. If the wolf doesn't want to be lured to us, it won't be lured. And we've no other way to find it."

Aghen had indeed told Einar as much. He repeated the caveat each of the numerous times Einar had suggested that Aghen was failing in his task, through either malice or incompetence. But even as he said it he was thinking, *Why do you ask me about this? I'm a shipwright. I know nothing of hunting for wolves…*

But Ottar had decided differently, and so now the man who knew only how to hunt for leaking seams and rotting strakes was hunting for a predator that might or might not exist.

Einar growled an order and the hunting party returned to their work, some setting up tents, some staking out the newly replaced pig haunch far from the camp, some hoisting barrels of meat and ale off the cart. Oddi knelt on the ground and piled charred linen tinder, wood chips and kindling on the spot chosen for the fire ring. Aghen stood beside him, leaning on the long iron poker they used for tending the fire. Oddi clicked a length of flint against his steel striker, raining sparks down on the tinder until it caught.

"My guess is, whatever this fellow has to say, it won't be good," Oddi said softly, nodding toward the distant rider as he applied the nascent flame to the wood chips and blew on them. The wood smoked and the flame faded away. Oddi gave it another practiced breath and the fire burst into life.

"I don't usually agree with Einar," Aghen said, "but I think he's right. This is likely someone sent by Ottar to see what's going on."

"Ottar won't be happy when he hears we haven't killed the wolf," Oddi said. "He's probably not happy now. Some of the others, they don't much care to return to Vík-ló empty-handed. They think Ottar will take it out on all of us."

"I suspect he will," Aghen said.

"So, do you think we'll catch this thing? Bring this wolf back to Vík-ló so Ottar is pleased?"

"No," Aghen said. "We won't." He saw the look on Oddi's face. Disappointment. Worry. A lot of worry. It was the look Aghen had expected to see. What he had hoped to see.

"So..." Oddi said, looking for something positive he might grab onto. "What can we do?"

"We could not go back to Vík-ló," Aghen said.

Any further talk was interrupted by the sound of hoofbeats getting louder, splashing through the shallow river, as the horseman closed the last hundred yards and reined his foaming, sweat-streaked mount to a stop. The rider was a man named Galti who was most certainly a part of Ottar's inner circle. He hopped down from his horse and strode with purpose toward the cluster of men in the camp as Einar hurried over to him.

"Galti, what brings you here?" Einar said, but Galti did not answer him, did not even look at him. His eyes were fixed firmly on Aghen as he approached and stopped just a few feet from the shipwright.

"Aghen Ormsson, your lies have been discovered," he said, his voice low and menacing. "Your lies about the wolf, all of it."

He spoke louder, addressing the other men who were now gathering closer. "There was no wolf," Galti said and he pointed a finger at Aghen. "It was Aghen. He murdered the men you serve. And now Ottar and more than a hundred men are riding out to see justice done, to take vengeance on the Irishman, Kevin. But first, all of you will come back to Ottar's camp and Ottar will see this one gets what he deserves for his crimes. And any who were foolish enough to help him." With those last words his eyes flickered over toward Oddi and then back to Aghen.

Aghen could form only one clear thought through the twisted confusion in his mind. *How does he know? Could someone have found the jaws?* He had buried them by his stack of lumber. He was the only one who ever went there.

He was aware of a low murmur running through the watching men, but he had no sense for what they were saying. He saw the wide-eyed look of fear on Oddi's face. The young man had not missed Galti's glance or the meaning behind it. Everyone there could envision the horrors Ottar would unleash just to determine whether a man was guilty or not.

"You are accusing me..." Aghen began, but Galti cut him off.

"Arrest this man! Bind him up, hands and feet, and break camp. We go back to Ottar now."

No one moved. No one spoke. No one took hold of Aghen.

Einar stepped up. "Arrest this man, now! Get hold of him!" he said in as commanding a tone as he could. Einar might have been Ottar's lickspittle, but he was no fool and he knew what could happen if he did not maintain control of the men.

I'm a dead man, either way, Aghen thought. That was all the insight he could muster, the full extent of his planning, his weighing options, his exploration of possible consequences. The rest was just instinct and a visceral understanding that he had nothing at all to lose.

The point of the iron poker was resting on the ground, his right palm resting on the handle. He spread his fingers, wrapped them around the end of the iron bar, and swept the poker up and back over his shoulder. He grabbed hold with his left hand as well and swung the poker horizontally, the iron shaft making a smooth, perfect arc through the air until it found the side of Galti's head. It connected with an ugly crunching noise and bounced off in a new direction.

Galti was flung sideways, the blow so fast and hard he had no chance to even make a sound that might indicate surprise or concern. He fell to the turf with a soft thumping noise, like a sack of grain dropped from shoulder height.

No one moved. No one spoke. Eyes shifted from Galti to Aghen and back. Both men remained motionless. For Galti, that condition appeared permanent.

Einar, to his credit, was the first to recover. "You bastard!" he shouted. He grabbed the hilt of his sword and began drawing the weapon. Aghen still held the poker, held it horizontal, but he, like the rest, was too stunned to react.

Then Oddi moved. He half-turned and grabbed the poker and pulled it from Aghen's hand and Aghen let it go. Oddi twisted toward Einar, leading with the poker's slightly blunted point. He rammed the end into Einar's stomach, half a fathom of good iron, pounded into shape by Mar's deftly wielded hammer and trust, with all the strength of a young man who had spent half his lifetime at hard physical labor.

If Einar had not been wearing mail, the poker would likely have impaled him. But he was wearing mail. All the men there were wearing mail or leather armor and they never took it off as long as they thought the wolf might be lurking. The mail saved Einar, and allowed him to live for another fifteen or twenty seconds.

He doubled over with the blow, the air bursting from his chest in a great whooshing sound. Oddi pulled the poker back and lifted it high and brought it down on the back of Einar's bare head. It made the same ugly sound it had made on Galti's skull and Einar went down just as fast and just as noiselessly. He twitched a few times, which was more than Galti had done, and then he was still.

No one spoke. No one moved. Oddi dropped the poker. "Now what?" he asked.

"Well, we don't go back to Vík-ló," Aghen said, and the rest nodded and muttered their agreement. "And we can't just wander around the countryside either," he continued. He turned and looked toward the west, his face illuminated by the setting sun. "Thorgrim Night Wolf is out there. I know it. Not sure how, but I know it. We'll go that way. We'll join with him."

The others nodded. No one offered any objection or any other suggestion. No one had a better plan or, indeed, any plan at all.

Chapter Thirty

[T]wo kings of the Norsemen, laid siege to the fortress and at the end of four months they destroyed and plundered it.
The Annals of Ulster

Thorgrim did not like what he saw, which was nothing.

He and Cónán and Blathmac stood at the top of a small rise, looking out toward the east, along the course of the river they had been following and the open ground to the north of it. There was nothing of interest, good or bad, in sight. A plume of smoke on the horizon that Cónán said was not Ráth Naoi but a smaller ringfort of no great interest. There was a herd of cows off to the northwest, maybe forty of them, about a mile away. But no horsemen, no mounted men-at-arms, nothing but open country, calling to them with the promise of easy marching.

"My men saw a few riders yesterday," Cónán said. "Scouts from Ráth Naoi, part of the men we nearly lured into our trap. None today. They've gone back to the ringfort. No desire to tangle with us again on open ground."

Thorgrim made a grunting noise, which conveyed neither agreement nor the opposite.

"They're gone. Nothing to fear," Cónán said, reassuring and just a bit condescending. Thorgrim could hear the tone in the Irishman's voice. He did not think he would be able to ignore it much longer.

It was just the day before that he and Cónán and the others had enjoyed their manic game of wild goose chase with the mounted men-at-arms, a game that might have ended in a great slaughter of the horsemen if Louis the Frank had not betrayed them. After the horsemen had fled, Thorgrim and his party continued on toward Ráth Naoi, but their column was slow-moving. They had camped and taken up the march again that morning. All day they had moved east in their plodding way, with a screen of scouts out ahead looking for signs of the enemy.

They had found none. Now they were once more stopped for the night, and the leaders of the three factions that made up this strange army were considering the next day's move.

"Ráth Naoi is that way," Cónán said, pointing off to the northeast, "five or six miles. We have to leave the river and move across country."

"Yes," Thorgrim said, "but not until we know we're not walking into a trap."

Blathmac spoke. Cónán replied.

"What does he say?" Thorgrim asked.

"He wants to know what we're talking about."

Cónán turned to Blathmac and spoke to him in their shared tongue. Thorgrim could not understand the words, but he could understand the tone. If Cónán was acting a bit condescending to him, he was being outright contemptuous of Blathmac, or so it seemed. Judging from Blathmac's expression, Thorgrim guessed he was right.

Blathmac spit some words back at Cónán. Cónán turned to Thorgrim. "He agrees with everything I say," Cónán said.

"So it seems," Thorgrim said. The three men looked out over the open ground again.

"First light, we move on Ráth Naoi," Cónán said. "No reason to delay. They know we're here, they'll only get more prepared every minute we give them."

What Cónán said made sense. Thorgrim knew it. But he also knew there was something wrong. He could feel it in his gut.

"We'll see," Thorgrim said, and he said it in a way that made it clear he was done with talking. He turned and headed back toward the camp and let the others follow behind.

Ten minutes later he was back among the people, his handful of Northmen and the Irish bandits. The cooking fires were burning, the women were bustling around, filling pots hanging over the flames, cutting meat from stolen cows and sundry scavenged greens to toss into the boiling water. The men were scattered around the area, segregated into their groups, drinking ale, talking softly.

This is getting to be like home, Thorgrim thought, looking around, taking in the familiar smells and sounds. This had been their world nearly every night since Cónán had led his band out onto the sand spit on the River Avonmore.

Thorgrim shook his head. *How odd, how very odd this is.*

He ate, he drank, and he talked with Godi and Harald and Starri about what they would do next. But he did not have much to say on that account because he did not know.

"The way looks clear," he said as he drained the last of the ale in his cup. It was bitter and stale and generally unpleasant. He could not help but think of the ale they had made themselves in Vík-ló. It was not like this.

"Cónán wants to leave the river, make a push for the ringfort tomorrow," Thorgrim continued. "He thinks if we move fast we can overwhelm them. A ringfort's no real kind of defense, as you know. More to show a man's importance than to hold off an attack."

The others nodded. "So, what will we do?" Harald asked.

"I don't know," Thorgrim said, which was the truth. He did not know. There was nothing more he could say.

The sun went down and Thorgrim and Cónán talked about the sentries that would be posted and how far out from the camp they would venture. Neither man intended to be caught by surprise. Once both were satisfied, Cónán headed off to bed down with his men and Thorgrim wandered out into the night, moving silently far out from the camp, listening, watching, trying to get a sense for what was going on out in the dark.

He had wolf dreams sometimes. Dreams where he seemed to see things through wolf's eyes and sometimes in those dreams he could discover things that were out there, and what he saw in the dreams was generally the truth. Some men, he knew, thought these were something more than dreams, but Thorgrim was not sure.

Whether they were dreams or not, they could be helpful. They brought visions that would let him know what to do next, or what not to do. But as he grew older he found the dreams came less often. In some ways this was good. The dreams were generally preceded by a mood so foul that no one dared approach him, no one could speak to him, and he could not tolerate the presence of others.

Except Starri Deathless. Starri was the only man he had ever known who could stay with him when the black mood descended, the only one on whom he would not turn. It was one of the reasons he liked Starri and tolerated his madness when others generally shunned berserkers. He figured Starri had some magic about him.

I wish I could see what was going on out there, he thought, looking out into the dark, out toward the countryside now hidden by the night.

But he knew what he was really wishing for. He was wishing the wolf dreams might come and let him see what was out in the blackness. He had never wished for the wolf dreams before. Thorgrim did not like the black mood. He did not like the thought of what might happen when the wolf dreams came on. Still, sometimes they were helpful.

But he could not summon them. He was getting older and the wolf dreams were a thing of his youth, he could see that. He turned and made his way wearily back to camp.

He was lying on a bearskin, mail on the ground beside him, Iron-tooth resting on top of the mail. The night was warm and dry, a gift from the gods, and Thorgrim had no blanket over him. The camp was quiet, the fires dying to embers, heaps of snoring men scattered over the ground.

He closed his eyes and, despite the worries pinching at him like swarming crabs, he felt sleep washing over him, warm and seductive. He was almost off to the dream world when he heard a voice, soft and close.

"Thorgrim?"

He opened his eyes, confused. It was a familiar voice but not familiar like Harald's or Starri's voices were familiar. Failend was crouching beside him, her small frame barely illuminated by the dying fires. She was dressed in her leine, her brat around her shoulders. She held her mail shirt and seax draped over her arm.

"Failend," he said, still halfway between sleep and waking.

"Louis's gone," she said. Thorgrim was not sure if it was a question or a statement. In the short time she had been with them, Failend had picked up a surprising amount of the Norsemen's language. She could generally make herself understood. But she was far from fluent.

"Yes, he's gone," Thorgrim said, figuring that was true regardless of what Failend meant. *And if he comes back I'll kill him*, he added, though he kept the words to himself.

Failend nodded and looked away for a moment, as if trying to make sense of that. She looked back at Thorgrim. "I'm sorry," she said.

Thorgrim frowned slightly, shook his head, not sure of her meaning.

"Sorry he…betrayed you," she said.

Thorgrim's frown turned to a partial smile. He reached out, put his hand on her knee. "Not your doing," he said. He was quiet for a moment, and then asked, "Why didn't you go with him?"

Now Failend was quiet for a moment. Then she shrugged. She looked around. "I like heathens," she said and smiled and Thorgrim smiled as well. She pointed to the ground in front of her. "I sleep here?"

That took Thorgrim a bit by surprise. Failend was still something of an enigma to him; when he thought about her, which admittedly was not too often, he was not sure what to make of her. He was not sure what she had on her mind now, but he nodded his agreement and shuffled back on the bear skin to make room.

Failend smiled and nodded her thanks. She laid her mail and sword carefully on the ground, then lay down beside Thorgrim, close but not too close, a foot at least separating them. She smiled at him. "Good night," she said, then turned over, her back to him, and did not move again.

Thorgrim looked at her dark hair, her small shoulders, her shapely form through the thin fabric of her leine. *Maybe with Louis gone she's afraid to sleep among the others,* he thought. That was reasonable, though none of the Northmen had ever given her cause to worry, and the Irish seemed to treat her like some sort of princess.

She's an odd one, Thorgrim thought, and it was the last conscious thought he had before he, too, drifted off to sleep.

He woke before dawn, as he'd been doing since the Irish had joined them, to the sound of the women getting the fires going again, the women who seemed to have a preternatural means of waking when they wanted, long before any of the snoring men. Failend was pretty much where she had been the night before, maybe a few inches closer, her back still toward him. His hand was resting on her waist. He had no memory of placing it there. He gently lifted it and drew it back. Failend made some soft, sleeping sound but did not stir.

Carefully, Thorgrim rolled away from her, stood and lifted Iron-tooth and his mail, which made a soft noise like a footfall on gravel, and then was still. He moved away from the sleeping girl and toward where the women were stoking the cooking fires. Cara was there and she handed him a bowl of water and he washed his hands and rubbed the cold water on his face, a reviving act. He ran his dripping fingers back through his long hair. He had not combed it in some time and he felt the effects of that negligence now.

"Thorgrim." He turned to see Cónán ambling over to him, stretching his arms as he walked. "I've ordered my men to have their breakfast. First light we leave the river, advance across country to Ráth Naoi. Leave the women here until it's safe."

"Are you asking me," Thorgrim said, "or telling me?" He sincerely hoped Cónán did not think he was giving orders, because that would not end well.

"Not telling you," Cónán said. "I thought we agreed that this was what we'd do."

Save those tricks of the tongue for Blathmac, Thorgrim thought. He shook his head. "No. I don't believe the riders have all gone back to…Kevin's hall, whatever you call it. We can't allow ourselves to be played for fools."

"There's a time for caution," Cónán said, "and a time to be bold. Now is the time to be bold."

"Don't think you can teach me such things," Thorgrim said, his voice more of snarl than he had intended, but Cónán's words were goading him. "You may be master of the cow pastures around here, but I have crossed oceans and fought men you could not imagine."

Thorgrim could see the muscles in Cónán's jaw working. The Irishman looked away, composing himself before he made a response. They were both proud men and they were both leaders. So far they had been in agreement on what needed to be done, and that was lucky, but it could not last forever.

Cónán turned back to Thorgrim, looked him in the eye. "My men say the way is clear."

"And I say it is not. We cannot go blundering across the open ground."

Thorgrim hoped that Cónán would not ask how he knew that, because in truth he knew nothing. It was a gut feeling. And worse, it was a gut feeling that told him to take the cautious route, a route Thorgrim generally shunned, a route that could lead to whispers of cowardice. But Thorgrim also knew that such feelings were often the sound of the gods whispering to their chosen and were not to be ignored.

"I spoke with some of your men," Cónán said. "Godi, Starri. They agree with me."

Thorgrim felt the rage, red-hot, like iron in a forge. His hand shot out and he grabbed a fistful of Cónán's tunic and pulled the Irishman toward him until they were inches apart. "Don't you talk to my men behind my back. I'll break you in two, you little bastard," he snarled. Cónán's teeth were clenched as he too felt the rage sweep over him. His hand clamped down on Thorgrim's wrist as he tried to wrench the Northman's hand away.

Cónán was strong, very strong. Thorgrim could feel it in his grip and in the force with which he levered his arm. But he was not strong enough to break Thorgrim's hold on his tunic. Not when Thorgrim was driven by the sort of rage he felt at that moment.

"Father?" The voice came sounding through Thorgrim's fury. He looked over. Harald was there, and Godi and several of Cónán's men. They looked worried, and they looked ready to fight, each for their own leader. If he went on like this, Thorgrim realized, they would all kill one another, right there in camp, long before Kevin's riders had a chance at them.

He released Cónán, giving him a little push as he did. "Do as you wish," Thorgrim said and turned and walked away.

Chapter Thirty-One

The heathens were driven from Ireland…and they abandoned a good number of their ships,
and escaped half dead after they had been wounded and broken.
The Annals of Ulster

What Cónán wanted to do was to march his men overland and attack the ringfort at Ráth Naoi. That was clear. No sooner had his altercation with Thorgrim ended than he went back to where his people were gathered and told them in a tone that brooked no debate that that was exactly what they would be doing.

"I don't think his men were too happy about it," Harald told Thorgrim as they ate their breakfast of porridge and dry bread. He had remained close to Cónán's camp so he might overhear their discussion. "He told them about the plunder to be had at the ringfort and that seemed to help a bit, but still they didn't seem too happy."

"I'll bet not," Thorgrim said.

Unless Cónán had another wily trick to play, he was looking at a stand-up fight against Kevin's trained men-at-arms, which would be a slaughter, and nothing less. But Thorgrim understood that pride was driving Cónán now, and he would lead his men to their deaths, and his as well, before he would admit he could not do this without Thorgrim, or that Thorgrim could be right.

Thorgrim might have thought such actions a waste and stupid, if he had not known for certain that he would do the same thing himself.

Breakfast finished, Cónán's men at the far side of the camp stood, and those who had mail pulled it on and those who had leather armor put that on and they strapped on the swords they had been given by Thorgrim, who in turn had plundered them from Ottar's men, and picked up their shields which were still foreign to their arms. Some men stretched and yawned, and Thorgrim knew that was a sign of fear, not weariness.

He sighed, tossed his wooden trencher away and stood. He could see when a ship was heading for the rocks and disaster, and such was happening here. "Let us go and speak with Cónán," he said and led Harald and Godi and Starri across the camp to where the Irish were making ready.

"Bid us fare well," Cónán said as they approached. "Next time you see us we'll be in Kevin's hall, counting the plunder that will be ours alone." He usually said such things in a jesting tone, but that was gone now, and he spit the words at Thorgrim.

"Blathmac?" Thorgrim asked. "Does he go with you?"

"Blathmac's a coward," Cónán said, making it clear he considered anyone a coward who would not join him in this venture. Thorgrim said nothing. He forced himself to not react. Cónán tightened his sword belt around his waist and adjusted the way the sword hung at his side. It was a fine weapon, one that Thorgrim had given him just weeks before.

"So, just you and these men?" Thorgrim asked, indicating the twenty-five or so bandits under Cónán's command. They looked better and more confident than they had when Thorgrim had first seen them on the riverbank, but that was not saying much.

"Yes," Cónán said, also ignoring the implied criticism. "As you've seen, I beat all Kevin's horsemen with fewer. I'll do it again." He looked around at his men, who had finished what little preparations they had to make. "Let's go," he snapped. He pushed past Thorgrim without a word and headed toward the edge of camp, and his men filed in behind him.

Thorgrim said nothing, just watched them as they headed off toward the northeast, toward the countryside that Cónán's scouts assured him was clear of enemy horsemen. If they were right, and if Cónán had some trick that would allow him to take Ráth Naoi with ease, then Thorgrim knew he would look pretty foolish, even cowardly. But he did not think either would prove true.

"What will we do, Father, while they're off?" Harald asked. It was the very question Thorgrim had been considering as he tried to sort through all the things jumbled together in his mind: indecision, worry, doubt. And foreboding. Mostly foreboding.

"Get the men under arms, get them ready to move if we must," he said, and Harald hurried off to obey. A minute later Thorgrim's handful of men were dropping mail shirts over their heads and running whetstones over the edges of their weapons. And while most of his men were donning more protection, Starri was pulling off his tunic and sticking his fingers in the mud underfoot and drawing dark lines on his bare face and chest.

Thorgrim watched as Cónán's men marched off. He did not move until the last of the Irishmen had climbed the small hillock from which he and Cónán had surveyed the countryside the night before. Once they had all disappeared from view, Thorgrim followed behind.

By the time he reached the top of the rise, Cónán's men were in a column two hundred yards ahead and moving quickly away. It was a loose and undisciplined line, but if Cónán was certain there were no enemies near he would not feel the need to get his men into any sort of fighting order until they were closer to Ráth Naoi.

Thorgrim pulled his eyes from the Irish bandits and scanned the countryside around, turning so he could take in the full circle of the horizon. Everything was pretty much as it had been the night before. There were no men to be seen, save for Cónán's. A few hawks circled overhead, and the trees moved a bit in the light breeze. The herd of cows was still there, a bit closer than it had been the night before, the animals milling around in a circle and mindlessly working at the grass. The plume from the distant fire they had seen the night before was gone.

"Nothing," Thorgrim said to himself. "Not one thing to see."

He heard footsteps behind, soft on the grassy turf, and Harald was at his side. "The men are ready, Father," he said, though Thorgrim knew he had not really come to report this. There was no need. They both knew that with these men when an order was given it was as good as completed. In truth, Thorgrim knew, Harald wanted to know what was going on, and he did not blame him.

"Good," Thorgrim said. He nodded toward Cónán's column, quickly growing smaller in the distance. "So far it seems he was right. The way is clear, the horsemen back at Kevin's ringfort."

"Maybe," Harald said. "But there's still miles between them and the plunder." Harald had an unwavering faith in his father's judgment, or so it seemed to Thorgrim. Why, Thorgrim could not imagine. By his own reckoning, half his life had been one pathetic blunder after another. Sometimes he thought Harald was the only decent thing he had to show for his forty and more winters in Midgard.

"We'll get our men moving, keep to the cover of the riverbank," Thorgrim said. "Cónán's women can come or stay, as they wish. Are Blathmac's people moving?"

"Some," Harald said. "Some are still sleeping. Some of them got pretty drunk last night. I don't think they're used to having great quantities of ale available to them."

Thorgrim had to smile at that. "I think you're right. I don't think they're used to having much, beyond a cuff on the ear and a kick in the ass."

They turned to head back to camp when they heard a noise, far off, from the direction of Cónán's men. A single, sharp noise, like a cry of alarm. They turned again, looked back the way they had been looking a second before.

Something was happening, but from the distance of half a mile or so it was not clear what. Cónán's long, straggling line of men was breaking up, men rushing off in various directions. Thorgrim could hear a voice, someone shouting, and he thought it was Cónán, but he could not be certain. The herd of cows was on the move as well, scattering this way and that, just as the Irish were doing. It was an almost comical effect.

"Is it the cows?" Harald asked. "Are they afraid of the cows?"

Absurd as it seemed, that was how it appeared to Thorgrim as well. Then suddenly there were figures among the cows, but higher, like they were on the cow's backs, men climbing up onto the cows.

"What, by all the gods…" Thorgrim said and then the riders came surging forward and he saw they were not on cows; they were on horses, horses that had been secreted in the grazing herd. Half a dozen, a dozen, more, leaping up onto the backs of horses that had gone unseen, charging through the frightened cattle and riding down on the Irishmen who, unsuspecting, had marched to within a hundred yards of them.

"Ah, Cónán, you're not the cleverest fox in the woods, are you?" Thorgrim said as he saw this unfold. He turned to Harald. "Come. We need to get the others, go save these sorry bastards."

They ran down the hill, raced back toward the camp. By the time they reached it Thorgrim's breath was coming in gasps, but Harald had wind enough to shout, "Cónán's men! They're being attacked! Riders were hiding in the cows!"

It was an odd way to put it, but the others sensed Harald's urgency and they did not question him. Instead, they grabbed up shields and axes and spears. All except Starri Deathless. Starri, who had been sitting cross-legged on the ground, sprung to his feet as if being hoisted on a line, his two battle axes in hand, and without a word he took off running.

Thorgrim sucked in air, trying to find breath enough to order Starri to stop and wait for the others. They had to go in as one; it was the most effective way. But by the time he had filled his lungs Starri was gone, halfway to the hillock at a full run and not likely to be brought back with words alone.

He turned to Harald and Godi, jerked his head in the direction that Starri was running. "Go," he said. "You know what to do. I'll see to Blathmac and the other Irishmen."

Harald nodded, turned and raced off, Godi and the rest with him. Among the men he saw Failend, shield in one hand, seax in the other, and he realized he had nearly done a foolish thing. He called, "Failend, wait!"

She stopped, turned to him while the others ran on. He waved her over, pointed to Blathmac and his men. "I have to talk to them. You'll translate?"

She squinted at him, unfamiliar with that word.

"You'll talk? Norse? Irish?" he said and she nodded.

He led the way to where Blathmac stood, fists on his hips, his scowling face all but lost in his beard. Thorgrim looked Blathmac in the eye and said,

"Failend, tell him Cónán's being attacked and he and his men must come and fight. You understand?"

"Yes," Failend said.

"Speak loud so they all can hear," Thorgrim said. She turned to Blathmac and spoke, and though her voice was naturally soft, she managed to make herself heard by all of Blathmac's people. Thorgrim watched the odd play of reactions on Blathmac's face: resentment, fear perhaps, and that strange deference with which the Irish always seemed to regard Failend.

But deference or no, Blathmac folded his arms even before she was finished, and when she was done he shook his head and spoke, biting off the words.

"He says no…won't save Cónán," Failend said.

Thorgrim could hear shouting now, carried on the breeze, faint at that distance, and he knew that men would die for every second they wasted arguing. Blathmac's men, ill-trained as they were, made up half the warriors under Thorgrim's command, and he could not afford to let them loll around in camp when there was fighting to be done.

He took two quick steps forward, so fast Blathmac had no time to react. Thorgrim's hand shot out and he seized the Irishman's great beard. Blathmac's eyes went wide and his hands were coming up when Thorgrim jerked the beard hard, pulling Blathmac's head down as he brought his knee up.

Blathmac's face and Thorgrim's knee met at about belt height, the concussion making a dull thud, like a horse stamping its hoof. Thorgrim let go of Blathmac's beard and Blathmac's head snapped up again, blood streaming from his nose, his mouth open in shock, surprise, and pain. Thorgrim grabbed his arm and spun him around. He planted a foot on Blathmac's rear end and shoved, sending the little man sprawling in the dirt. He turned and pointed at the man he took to be Blathmac's second in command.

"Ask him if he wants to be next," Thorgrim said. Failend translated and then translated his reply, which was not entirely necessary. There was no defiance, only shock on the men's faces as they grabbed up their weapons, and that told Thorgrim all that he needed to know. He turned and ran off for the distant hill, Failend at his side.

Chapter Thirty-Two

In rings I'm not rich, but –
I revel in telling it –
I hoodwinked those heroes,
Hurling dust in their eyes.
The Saga of the Confederates

Thorgrim ran toward the growing sound of battle and he could hear the rest of Blathmac's men following. Up over the rise and the fight was spread out before him, a wild melee covering an acre of ground in the distance. The riders were racing off in every direction, chasing after Cónán's men who were dodging and sprinting like rabbits trying to get away. It was exactly what the horsemen would have hoped for: to have the men on foot panicked and scattered so they could ride them down and kill them, one by one.

And that was what they were doing. Thorgrim saw one of the Irish bandits in a flat-out run, one of the mounted warriors charging up behind. The man, sensing he was being overtaken, turned to fight, turned just in time to take a spear thrust in the chest. Thorgrim saw him go down, disappearing in the thigh-high grass as the rider jerked the spear free and wheeled, looking for his next victim.

His own men were halfway to the fight, running across the open ground, and if the riders had seen them at all, they were ignoring them. And why not? The Northmen did not yet pose any threat, and the further they had to run the more exhausted they would be when they finally got into the fight.

Not all the Northmen were so far from the fighting, however. Starri Deathless was outpacing the others and had nearly closed the distance to the nearest rider. As he ran he let out his berserker shriek, that terrifying howl that Thorgrim knew all too well, the last sound on earth that more than a few fighting men had heard. Thorgrim had to marvel at a man like Starri. Nearly dead three weeks earlier, now he could run that far, that fast, and still have wind enough to shriek at such a volume that Thorgrim could hear him from near two hundred yards away.

I guess Starri's on the mend, he thought, but he knew that the gods infused berserkers with powers normal men did not have or even understand. Starri himself did not understand it.

Thorgrim pushed on, trying to watch the fight even as he ran to join it. He saw one of the riders turn and make for Starri, spear down. He saw a flash of dull metal, Starri's battle axes wheeling and slashing. He saw the rider come down off his horse, half pulled, half falling, and then a second later Starri was up in the saddle, feet in the stirrups, axes in each hand. He kicked the horse and the animal seemed to obey, turning and racing back for the fight.

How does he ride so well? Thorgrim wondered. He had never known Starri to have any great familiarity with horses and had been surprised at the man's ease when they had taken the mounts from the Irish a few days earlier. Starri might have been a skilled rider all his life, Thorgrim realized, or he might have never been on horseback before. With Starri it was hard to tell.

The swifter of Thorgrim's men were getting up with the fighting now, but Thorgrim did not want them racing in one man at a time, because that would make it much easier for the riders to kill them all. He considered shouting out orders, but he didn't think he had the breath to make himself heard, far back as he was. The others had gained a considerable lead on him while he was forced to waste time with Blathmac.

Then he heard Harald's voice shouting just the orders he would have shouted, in just the words and tone he would have used. "Men of Vík-ló! Men of Vík-ló! Form on me! Form a shield wall!"

Good boy, Thorgrim thought. They needed some sort of defense, some way to make a stand. If Cónán and his men could get free of the riders, get into the shieldwall, they might be able to do something.

He turned. Blathmac's men were right at his heels. Many of them, he suspected, could have easily outrun him, but they seemed in no hurry to get into the fight any sooner than they had to. Thorgrim held up his hands and the men stopped and he indicated that they should move up to where Harald was gathering the others. He would put the men with shields in the front, form two lines, see what they could make of that.

His own men were taking up their places in the shieldwall, weapons ready, shields overlapping. About a third of Cónán's men were lost from sight now, dead or wounded or hiding in the grass, Thorgrim could not tell. But those still standing were fighting back. Cónán had his bow, and he stood like a rune stone, firing arrow after arrow, turning and firing, dropping the riders who came charging at him before they could get close enough to him to use sword or spear. But Cónán's supply of arrows was not unlimited.

Thorgrim reached the shieldwall at last. He pushed Blathmac's men left and right, got them positioned as he wanted them. "Advance! Advance!" he shouted and the front rank of Northmen and a handful of Irish stepped off and the second rank followed. They were Irish and did not understand the words, but the meaning was obvious, and they did not want to be left standing there without the shieldwall.

Come on, come on, Thorgrim thought to himself as he watched the horsemen and Cónán's bandits doing their weird, frantic dance though the grass. He needed the riders to see the shield wall and react to it, to give Cónán's men the few seconds reprieve they needed to join with them.

"Shout!" Thorgrim ordered, "Loud as you can, shout!" Godi led off, bellowing like a gored bull in his deep voice. Harald joined him, his voice deep but not as deep as Godi's, and soon they were all yelling as they advanced, the Northmen calling insults the Irish would not understand, the Irish shouting words Thorgrim did not know.

But the effect was what Thorgrim had been looking for. He saw horsemen pull back on reins, wheel their mounts, turn to this new threat. He saw arms pointing, could hear the sounds of instructions flying back and forth as the riders realigned themselves, turning their attention to this new line of attack.

"Stand fast, here they come," Thorgrim shouted as the horsemen turned, one after the other, and came charging down on the shield wall. Thorgrim stood behind the ranks, and in front of him one of Blathmac's men stood gawking stupidly, his spear held vertically in his hand. Thorgrim stepped up and grabbed the spear and lowered the point until it was just above horizontal, thrust out over the shoulders of the men in the front rank, then handed it back to the Irishman with a menacing look. All along the short line the other spearmen followed suit.

Stupid, useless bastards, Thorgrim thought.

And then the riders were on them, pounding toward the shieldwall, but the front rank was made up mostly of Thorgrim's men and they knew their only chance at living was to stand firm. The Irishmen among them were brave enough, but they were strangers to this sort of thing, shieldwalls, fighting on open ground. Yet they followed the Northmen's lead and did not flinch.

Thorgrim prowled behind the second rank, making certain their spears were level and that none of them broke and ran. He held Iron-tooth in his hand and he made it clear that he was more of an immediate threat than the riders coming at them.

Ten feet from the shieldwall, well short of the reach of the iron-tipped spears, the riders broke left and right, shearing off in either direction, their charge ineffective, lacking coordination. They turned and rode back up the field, but Thorgrim knew they would regroup and come again. He had seen all this before.

He looked past his own men, past the riders farther off. Cónán, as he had hoped, had made use of the momentary reprieve. With most of the horsemen occupied with the shieldwall, and the rest chasing a laughing, howling, still-mounted Starri around the fields, Cónán had gathered his men and now they were racing in a wide circle for the dubious safety of the shield wall.

There were not so many of them. Ten maybe, of the twenty-five Cónán had led out of the camp. The mounted men-at-arms had done considerable damage, but they'd not gone unscathed themselves. There were riderless horses wandering through the grass, trained animals who remained calm despite the chaos around them. The cows, however, were not so sanguine. They had moved off a couple hundred feet, and yielding to their herd instincts, had bunched together and now looked warily on.

Thorgrim had a sick feeling deep in his stomach as he watched the horsemen gathering for another charge. This was Glendalough all over again: the desperate stand on open ground, the assault by mounted men-at-arms, slamming into his warriors again and again until the shieldwall broke apart and they were cut down in pieces. Nearly every man Thorgrim had brought with him to Glendalough, the crews of four ships, had been killed that way.

And here he was again.

He looked from north to south. The riders in front, Cónán's men circling around to the right, and all around them, open country, no place to run, no place to make a stand. Then once again his eyes were drawn to the cows.

"Harald!" he shouted, slipping Iron-tooth back into his scabbard. "Come with me, we need horses!"

Harald nodded as if this made all the sense in the world. He sheathed Oak Cleaver and stepped out of the shieldwall, which closed up behind him. Thorgrim looked around again. Every man on the battlefield seemed to be holding his breath as they all waited for the next act to begin. Time to go.

Thorgrim took off running. The nearest horse stood about two hundred feet away, waiting patiently for its rider to return, a rider who was likely dead or dying and would not be coming back. There was a second horse about fifty feet beyond that one. Thorgrim thumped Harald on the shoulder as they ran and pointed to the far horse and Harald nodded.

There was shouting behind, and Thorgrim turned to see some of the mounted men pointing toward them and kicking heels into their horses as they came in pursuit. He pulled his eyes away, looked back at the nearest horse. One hundred feet and the animal still hadn't shied or bolted.

Then Thorgrim was up with it, scooping up the reins and slipping his foot into the stirrup as he swung himself up into the saddle. Harald ran past and seconds later he had the other horse and he too was mounted.

The horsemen were still coming for them, a few hundred feet away, their mounts worked up to a full gallop. But what they could not see, and Thorgrim could, was Starri Deathless coming up behind them.

He was standing in the stirrups, leaning forward against the momentum on the horse. His long hair was streaming behind him and he held an ax in each hand, his arms stretched out above his head. He looked like some kind of mad demon from another world as he came charging up behind, and the Irish warriors did not even realize he was there until he was up with them, howling and bringing both axes down at the same instant.

"Come on!" Thorgrim shouted to Harald. "The cows!" He turned his horse and kicked his heels into the animal's haunches and the horse responded, leaping ahead and building speed, and Harald was right at his side. He rode off in a wide circle, coming around behind the herd, getting the cows between him and the Irish men-at-arms. Like most Northmen, Thorgrim had spent as much of his life farming as he had raiding, more probably. Driving cows was as much a part of him as driving a longship, and he had raised Harald to that life.

The cows knew something was going on. They backed away en masse, big brown eyes watching as the Northmen came riding hard around the backside of the herd. Then Thorgrim pulled his horse's reins over and charged right for the center of the packed cattle and Harald did the same. Thorgrim reached across and drew Iron-tooth and as he charged at the nearest cow, the animal turned to bolt and Thorgrim smacked it hard on the rump with the flat of his blade.

The cow gave a satisfying bellow and leapt forward, colliding with the animal in front of it and making that one leap as well, spreading panic through the rest. Harald, who saw what his father had in mind, charged off to the far end of the herd to keep the animals moving the way they wanted, driving them toward the riders who were massing for another attack. Oak Cleaver was out and Harald was whacking cows and shouting and kicking as he rode.

Panic spread through the herd as one after another of the beasts tried to flee from the mounted madmen behind. They bounced off one another and bellowed and charged forward in terror, their speed building like an avalanche.

They had not gone unnoticed by the Irishmen on horseback. Warriors who were seconds before gathering for another charge at the feeble shieldwall now raced off in every direction, desperate to get out of the way of the manic herd before they and their mounts were trampled underfoot.

As the horsemen raced off, Thorgrim saw Godi holding his sword high and leading the shieldwall forward, following the riders in their retreat while keeping well clear of the frantic herd. But the cows were starting to lose their cohesion as the animals scattered over a wider and wider area, and that made them less effective as a fighting force.

"Try to keep them together!" Thorgrim shouted at Harald, but he could see that was not going to happen. Then suddenly Starri was there, charging through the herd, screaming his war cry, still standing in the stirrups. Any desire the animals had to remain bunched together was gone as they bolted in every direction, frantic to get clear of the mounted berserker.

"Starri! No!" Harald shouted, but it was pointless. Thorgrim just shook his head. Starri, he guessed, was one of the rare Northmen who was a stranger to farming—he would never have the patience to tolerate it—and he probably had only the loosest grasp on what Thorgrim had been trying to do.

Off in the distance, closer to the river, Kevin's Irish men-of-war had stopped and were turning, forming a line, the fight not yet out of them. Thirty men or more, mounted, well-armed and trained, and despite the reprieve Thorgrim had won with the cows, he and his men were still fighting them on foot on open ground. If the Irish horsemen had courage and strength in their arms they could still win the day.

Then the mounted warriors were moving again, but not the way Thorgrim had expected. He was waiting for a coordinated charge at Godi's shieldwall, which was still advancing on them. Instead he saw the Irishmen scattering once again, riding off left and right, disorganized, near panic. He looked to see if Starri was responsible, but Starri had ridden far off to the east, as if his horse had finally had enough of him and bolted.

"Harald, can you see what's happening?" Thorgrim called, but Harald only shook his head. Thorgrim squinted at the distant scene. Now, as the wall of horsemen parted, he could see there was another group of men coming at them, running up from the direction of the river. They were far off, half a mile or so, but from the round shields and the way they were bunched together, like a swine array, Thorgrim was willing to bet they were Northmen.

"Who by Odin's eye is this?" Thorgrim asked and again Harald shook his head.

Whoever they were, they were enough for the Irish men-at-arms. With Godi's line coming from one direction, the cows still charging around, the lunatic Starri somewhere out there and this new attack from the river, they had had enough. Thorgrim heard an order called, saw horses wheeled around, and a second later all the mounted warriors were charging off, riding toward the northeast, off in the direction that Cónán had said Ráth Naoi would be found.

"Let's see who this is," Thorgrim said, and he and Harald got their horses moving, the cows parting like a confused sea before them as they rode. With the Irish riding off, the strangers from the river had slowed their advance and their swine array had devolved into a group of men, about forty, Thorgrim guessed, walking across the open ground. Godi's line had stopped, but they were still in their shield wall, a good precaution until they knew who these others were.

Thorgrim and Harald closed the distance and the men who had come from the river stopped and waited for them to approach. The one who had taken the lead in the swine array stood a few feet in front of the others. He reached up and pulled the helmet off his head, and Thorgrim's first thought was, *By all the gods that looks like Aghen Ormsson, the shipwright...*

Chapter Thirty-Three

My sword was stained with gore,
but the Odin of swords,
sword-swiped me too…
The Saga of Gunnlaug Serpent-Tongue

Ottar Bloodax remained in his tent for as long as he could. He heard the sounds of the camp coming to life, the men rising, stoking up the fires, urinating, getting breakfast. He lay on his pad of furs and listened. He was listening for the staccato hoofbeats of a rider galloping into camp with word of what was happening out in the country beyond. He was listening for the sound of the forty-man hunting party returning. But he heard none of those things.

The sun was well up by the time he forced himself to stand, aware that remaining in his tent much longer might prompt the men to talk. He stretched, felt his muscles protest. His tent was wedge-shaped but big, covering an area ten feet across by fifteen long, six and a half feet from the ground to the apex, just tall enough for him to stand upright.

He grabbed his sword belt and strapped the weapon on, then tossed the flap back and stepped out into the morning. They sky was gray and thick with clouds, but it did not seem as if it would rain anytime soon. The camp was a bustle, the men engaged in the multitude of tasks required to keep an army in the field. They moved with the kind of efficiency he would expect from men well used to this sort of thing. But they did not move with purpose, because they had no purpose. They did not know what they would be doing that day or the next or the next. That was no surprise. Ottar didn't know either.

Ketil came hurrying over as if he had been watching Ottar's tent, waiting for Ottar to emerge, which he probably was.

"Lord Ottar, I had the men get their breakfasts," he said, then paused, hoping Ottar would tell him what his plan was, where the army would be going, what it would be doing. Ottar knew that was what Ketil wanted and he ignored it.

"Well?" Ottar demanded instead.

"Well?" Ketil asked. "You mean…about Galti?"

Of course about Galti! Ottar thought. The stupid turd Ketil knew exactly what he meant. Ottar wanted to thump him on the side of the head.

"He didn't return last night or this morning, lord. No word."

Ottar frowned and looked away, considering this. "Bastards…" he muttered to himself, but it was just a word with no connection to anything that was taking place. Because he did not know what was taking place.

He had sent half a dozen men off in various directions to find Einar and the murdering coward whore's son, Aghen, and bring them back so that he could deal with them as they should be dealt with. They had all returned, having failed to find Einar's hunting party. All save for Galti, one of his most trusted, a man he meant to put in Ketil's place on his return. But he had not returned. And there was no word from him, and no word of Einar and the forty men with him. All gone.

It couldn't be, Ottar thought. *It was all Aghen's doing…I saw the damned tool he made. There was no wolf…is no wolf. Damn him.*

But the fear was back, and while Ottar would have killed any man who suggested he was afraid of a phantom wolf, or of anything for that matter, still, he could no longer deny it to himself. It did not seem possible, any of it, yet forty men had been sent out specifically to hunt this creature down, and now they were gone. And Einar and Galti were gone, too.

Even if all the other traitorous bastards had run off, Einar and Galti would not have done so. Reluctant as they might be to admit failure, they would have come back to camp. They would have told Ottar what was going on.

"Lord, that Irishman, Kevin, his ringfort is only a day's march from here, maybe a little more," Ketil prompted, and this time Ottar did hit him, swinging a massive hand around in a wide arc and, before Ketil had time to react, smacking him open-palmed on the side of the head. Ketil staggered but did not fall because Ottar had not struck him as hard as he could—a warning, not a punishment.

"Don't you tell me such things, you sorry pile of dung!" Ottar roared. Ketil straightened, a hand over his bruised cheek, a sheepish look in his eyes. "I know where the ringfort is and we'll go there when I say we go there!" Ottar shouted.

"Yes, lord." Ketil nodded, backing away. "Is there..."

"Get out of here, you worm," Ottar snarled, the words Ketil seemed to most want to hear. He nodded, gave a sort of bow, then turned and raced off.

The scar on Ottar's face was throbbing, as it always did when he was worked up in that way. He tried to organize his thoughts. He had to craft some plan, even the hint of a plan, but his head was filled with random curses and images of wolves and of Aghen the shipwright and of Thorgrim Night Wolf and he could not make them go away.

It had been so clear before, like a well-trodden path through the woods. Once he had Aghen's wolf jaws in hand, once he realized what had happened, he had seen the way forward. Take his men out in the field. Find Aghen, which should have been no great difficulty since he was with Einar and the rest, bring him back and make his death and the deaths of any of his confederates an example to remember. March on Kevin's ringfort. Take it, plunder it. Do to Kevin what he had done to Aghen.

But now he was not so sure. He told himself over and over that no one animal could have slaughtered a hunting party of forty armed men. He knew that there was no wolf; he had seen how the trick was played. But deep down he was not at all sure about any of it, and now his uncertainty was keeping him and his men, an army near two hundred warriors strong, planted on this piece of land.

Ottar wanted to move, but he could not. He could not act until he found something—anything—that would show him what course he would be best to take. But there was nothing. Only doubt.

From the top of the earthen wall that surrounded his ringfort, Kevin mac Lugaed watched the riders approach, and he did not get a good feeling from what he saw. They were too far off still to count their numbers, but he did not need an exact count. Between his men and Lochlánn's, fifty mounted warriors had ridden out of Ráth Naoi to hunt down Thorgrim and his heathens. The men returning now did not number fifty. Not even close.

Oh, damn them, what have they done? Kevin thought, panic and despair rising up. He reminded himself that he still had more than a hundred men, good men, under his command, and that eased his mind a bit.

Eoin was standing by Kevin's side, but he had sense enough to keep his mouth shut, because Kevin was clearly in no mood to talk. As they watched the band of horsemen approach, it occurred to Kevin that Niall might be among the dead, and that sparked the panic once again. The situation was growing more desperate all the time, and if he had to face it without Niall to make the decisions with regard to fighting he did not know how he would manage.

For another five minutes Kevin and Eoin watched the horsemen draw nearer, and by then Kevin felt like he had to speak or he might explode. "How many are there, do you think?" he said, nodding toward the riders.

Eoin did not answer at first, presumably working up a number. "Thirty-five, lord," he said. "Somewhere around thirty-five."

"Can you see if Niall is among them?"

"Not for certain, lord," Eoin said. "But I see a horse looks like his brown mare, and the rider sits it the way Niall does, so I'm thinking that might well be him." Eoin was younger than Kevin by fifteen years at least, and his eyes were much better, so his words gave Kevin hope.

The men-at-arms were not riding like soldiers who had just won some great victory. They seemed to slump in the saddle, and the plodding pace they maintained spoke of weariness and defeat. Kevin grew more concerned with each yard they covered. At last he turned and looked down at the men on the ground fifteen feet below him. "Open the gates," he called.

Two men lifted the heavy bar that secured the gates, two more pushed the doors open. The riders were close enough that Kevin could make out individuals, and one of those was most certainly Niall and that eased his mind somewhat. Lochlánn was there as well. About thirty-five men, as he had thought. A few were leading riderless horses behind.

As the horsemen closed the last hundred yards, Kevin thought, *I'm standing here waiting like some worried old grandmother.* A show of anxiety was not proper for one of the rí túaithe, and he had shown more than enough of it already. He turned to Eoin.

"Have Niall and that other one, Lochlánn, sent to my hall as soon as they arrive," he said, then climbed down the ladder and hurried across the beaten ground to his big hall in the middle of the ringfort. One of the guards opened the door as Kevin approached and closed it behind, leaving Kevin alone in the spacious room. He looked around, trying to decide what he should be doing when the men came in, what would make him appear the most unconcerned.

Sit? No, he was far too agitated to sit, and it would look entirely too contrived. *Should I be eating a meal?* That was good, but the very thought of food made him sick.

Finally he pulled a map of Ireland from a trunk by the wall and spread it out over the table. His eyes traced over the lines and the Latin script and the elaborate drawings of strange beasts in the sea, but his mind did not even register what he was looking at. He was thinking instead about Thorgrim Night Wolf.

There was something unnerving about the man. Kevin had known a few Northmen over the years. It became more and more difficult to avoid them, as they spread like the plague over Ireland. Most were like Ottar, with all the nuance and subtlety of a wild boar. But Thorgrim was not like that. He made Kevin think of an onion; peel back one layer and there was another beneath it and another and another until you thought you might never get to what was at the heart of the thing. It was profoundly unsettling.

He was still thinking along those lines when the knock came and the guard opened the door and announced, "Niall, Lord Kevin."

Kevin looked up from the map. "Send him in," he said, straightening and stepping around the table as the guard moved aside. Niall came in, mud-splattered, his hair wild, dried blood on his cheek and more on the mail that covered his arm. Weary-looking. Behind him came Lochlánn and a third man Kevin did not know.

"Well?" Kevin said.

"We fought them, lord," Niall said. "More than once. They're slippery bastards, slippery as eels. We ambushed them today, fooled them completely. Or almost. We would have had them, but there were more of the heathens than we thought. They had another forty men down by the river, and they came into the fight at the last minute and that was all we could do. We pulled back, and then Cathail showed up and said you ordered us to return here."

Kevin let this news settle before he asked the next question. "How many men did you lose?"

"Ah, fourteen, lord. And nine horses," Niall replied.

Kevin shifted his gaze to Lochlánn who stood to Niall's side and a step behind him. He looked defiant, as if he was expecting a verbal assault and was ready for it. And he was right to expect that.

"You said with thirty of my men you would stamp out this vermin. Those were your very words, damn you, and now instead you've led half the men I gave you to their deaths!" Kevin spat, but Lochlánn did not flinch.

"Not all the dead men were yours, some were mine. Most were mine," Lochlánn said.

"I appreciate you seeing your own men slaughtered as well," Kevin said. "Thoughtful, indeed."

The third man, the one by Lochlánn's side, stepped forward. "For the love of God, both of you," he said. "Could there be a more pointless waste of time? And even as the heathens get closer by the minute."

Kevin shifted his eyes from Lochlánn to this other man. Young, early twenties, but he had a confidence about him. He spoke Irish, but his accent was foreign.

"And you are?" Kevin asked.

"Louis. Louis de Roumois. I am the second son of *Hincmar, the late count of Roumois. I was…studying in Glendalough."*

"He's the one who came up with the idea for our ambush," Niall offered. "Damn clever. Would have worked."

"I see," Kevin said. He was not impressed, but he imagined that this fellow would be one more sword to defend Ráth Naoi. He needed all the men he could get, and he feared that they would still not be enough. "And so," Kevin continued, turning back to Lochlánn, "do you still believe it was Thorgrim Night Wolf and his men whom you fought? With such little success?"

Before Lochlánn could reply, Louis was speaking again. "It was most certainly Thorgrim Night Wolf. But he has only ten of his heathens with him. The rest of his number are Irish bandits, a covey of them under the command of some whore's son named Cónán, and another gang of thieves, just joined with Thorgrim, led by a man named Blathmac."

Kevin turned back to Louis. "I see," Kevin said again. "And you know this…how?"

"I was Thorgrim's prisoner," Louis said. "He captured me at Glendalough. I escaped when Lochlánn and Niall attacked Thorgrim's men."

"Indeed," Kevin said. "Cónán I know about. A lowly criminal; he's been a plague around here for years. Blathmac I've never heard of. But see here, you say Thorgrim had but ten of his heathens, yet Niall says there were forty more attacked from the river. Drove you off."

Niall frowned and looked at Louis, as did Lochlánn. "Thorgrim had ten heathens with him, and the rest Irish. Who those forty were I do not know, but they were not with Thorgrim two days ago."

"Ah, the damned heathens are dropping from the sky!" Kevin shouted and threw his hands up in frustration. "They spring up like maggots from dead flesh!" He turned around in a full circle as if hoping to find some answer behind him, or to make certain no heathen was stalking him and ready to pounce.

"So now there are forty more with Night Wolf," Kevin continued once he was again facing the three other men in the hall. "And on top of that, Ottar Bloodax has come out of Vík-ló. I have no doubt he and Thorgrim plan to join up to kill us all. So now we don't have ten heathens and a bunch of filthy bandits heading toward us, we have two hundred heathen warriors out for our blood! We might as well cut our throats right now."

"Ottar Bloodax…has come out of Vík-ló?" Niall asked. He alone understood the gravity of this.

"Yes," Kevin said. "With near all his men. More than one hundred and fifty."

"Who is Ottar Bloodax?" Lochlánn asked.

"He's one of the bastards who attacked Glendalough," Kevin said. "Leader of one of the heathen armies. Thorgrim led the other. They're the ones we fought off when they came to sack the monastery. Ottar has since taken the longphort of Vík-ló. He's lord there now. And now it seems he and Thorgrim have made another alliance to come and take Ráth Naoi from me." He tried and failed to keep the despair from his voice.

The four of them were quiet for a moment, considering this. Then it was Louis who spoke, to everyone's surprise.

"No," he said. "No, that's not right. Thorgrim was coming here...*is* coming here...that's true. I was with them for weeks; I know what they're about. He wants to have his revenge on you. But when he's done he means to take revenge on this Ottar as well. Talked about it all the time. It seems Ottar betrayed him."

Louis looked up, met Kevin's eyes. "And you as well," he said. "He thinks you betrayed him. How did you betray him?"

Kevin cleared his throat. This would take some clever words to talk away, but Kevin could use words the way men like Niall or Thorgrim could use swords. "I won't lie to you," he said. "Trading with the heathens is a profitable business. Thorgrim was lord at Vík-ló before Ottar. They needed food, ale, and such. They had silver. We traded with them. I think Thorgrim came to believe that meant I would fight with him as well, even against my own people.

"But when I took my men to Glendalough, we went there to fight against him, him and that Ottar. To defend the monastery. You might recall we arrived just in time to turn things around in the battle, just when they were looking darkest. So that's why he thinks I betrayed him. Because I would not side with heathens against Irishmen."

The others were nodding. Niall knew with certainty that this was a lie, but he could be counted on to keep his mouth shut, if for no other reason than his own complicity in the scheme to sack Glendalough. The other two seemed to accept this explanation.

"This is all well and good," Kevin said, steering the talk away from his dubious alliances with the Northmen and back to their immediate concerns. "But the fact is both Thorgrim and Ottar are descending on this ringfort and we don't have the men to defend it."

And then Louis de Roumois laughed. It was practically the last sound anyone expected to hear in the midst of this grim conversation, but there it was: he laughed, a short, mirthful burst of sound.

"Yes?" Kevin asked.

"Don't you see?" Louis said. "This is perfect. Ottar and Thorgrim want to kill one another. *We* know that Ottar is there, but Thorgrim doesn't. We don't have to fight Thorgrim, we only have to drive him back until he runs into Ottar's men. They'll kill each other and then we only need to stamp out what remains. Thorgrim might have fifty of his heathen warriors, but the rest are a rabble of undisciplined thieves, and you still have more than a hundred trained, mounted men-at-arms. We can certainly push Thorgrim's miserable host back into Ottar's arms."

Kevin frowned, but he liked the sound of this. His greatest fear was a heathen army surrounding his ringfort. The earthen walls and palisades were more to demonstrate the status of the man who occupied the place than to present any serious defense. But now this Louis was proposing they push the heathens as far from Ráth Naoi as they could, and let Ottar Bloodax, the bloodthirsty lunatic, take care of the lot of them.

"Good, good," Kevin said. "I like this plan. I approve of it. Let Thorgrim come. We'll drive him and the swine who follow him right off to be butchered. As swine should be."

Chapter Thirty-Four

He hath need of fire, who now is come,
numbed with cold to the knee
Hávamál

It was indeed Aghen Ormsson, the shipwright, but Thorgrim was not sure at first. The Northmen he led, who had appeared seemingly from nowhere, were numerous, about the size of a ship's crew, and Thorgrim approached them with caution. They had done him and Cónán a great service driving the Irish men-at-arms from the field, but that did not mean they were any friends of his.

He walked his horse across the open ground, Harald at his side, the cows now scattered enough that they were of no concern. "Father," Harald said, "I would swear by the gods that's Aghen, from Vík-ló."

"I thought the same," Thorgrim said. "I would have been sure of it if I could think of any possible reason Aghen should be here."

They were still fifty feet away when the man who appeared to be Aghen raised his arm and called out, "Thorgrim Ulfsson! Lord of Vík-ló!" and the voice was unmistakably that of the curmudgeonly old craftsman.

"Hah!" Thorgrim shouted and he slipped down off his horse and covered the last of the distance on foot. He grabbed Aghen by the shoulders and hugged him and felt Aghen's strong arms hugging him back. Finally he pushed away and looked into the man's smiling face.

"I knew you still lived, Night Wolf," Aghen said. "I knew it." He turned to the young man beside him. "You see, Oddi, I knew it would take more than a dung pile like Ottar to kill this man!"

Thorgrim shook his head. "Kind words, Aghen. But if you and your men hadn't shown up when you did, the Irish might well have done what Ottar did not. I can't imagine how you happen to be here, unless the gods themselves lifted you in the air and set you here."

"Nothing like that, but still a tale you'll enjoy," Aghen said. "But first you must know that Ottar's left Vík-ló. He meant to hunt me down, and when he had me he was going to plunder the hall of that Irishman Kevin who rules hereabouts. Ottar can't be more than a day away. Closer, I would think." Aghen turned and looked to the east, as if they might see Ottar and his warriors coming over the nearest rise.

Thorgrim was eager to hear Aghen's story, but he was more eager still to get his men and Cónán's men together, because he could not be certain that the Irish men-at-arms had given up the fight. He and Cónán and the others gathered the men who could still walk and located the wounded who could not and hoisted them up onto the captured horses. They made their way back to the place where the women had been left in camp, over the ground they had covered that morning in their push to Ráth Naoi.

"Guess you were right about the horsemen," Cónán said when he and Thorgrim met up on the trampled grass of the battlefield. His voice still carried a note of defiance, though it was much diminished.

"Guess I was," Thorgrim replied. It was all that was said about the morning's event. It was all that needed saying.

The day was well on by the time they reached camp. The women had food cooking in the iron pots and bandages and poultices at the ready, and they set about ministering to the weary men.

Blathmac was nowhere to be seen. "Cara tells me he ran off," Cónán said, sitting down beside Thorgrim, a bowl of steaming potage in his hand. "She says you pulled his beard and kicked his ass and that was the end of him."

Thorgrim nodded, swallowed the mouthful he was chewing. "He might have reckoned it would be hard to keep command of his men after that," he said.

"Looks like he didn't care to stay around and find out." Cónán turned his attention to his food, and then a few bites later said, "That's the second time you've saved me the trouble of killing someone who was standing in my way. If I keep near to you I'll be high king of Ireland one of these days."

"Could be," Thorgrim agreed. "You'll take command of Blathmac's men?"

"Already have," Cónán said.

It was nearly full dark by the time a messenger came in, sent by the scouts in the field. They reported that the horsemen had returned to Ráth Naoi. The scouts had followed them nearly to the ringfort itself. And this time Thorgrim knew it was true. He could feel it. The way was clear.

They slept that night with men still out in the dark, watching, but no enemy came. Two of the wounded died before sunrise and in the morning they were buried by the riverbank. The men ate their breakfasts and sharpened their weapons and made temporary repairs to their mail. The women broke camp and lashed tents and cookware to the newly acquired horses, grateful to not have to carry those things. It was late morning when they left the site by the river and headed out overland to the ringfort at Ráth Naoi.

It was not flat country they crossed, but a landscape of steep, rounded hills that rolled along like ocean swells. From the crest of the hills the land could be seen for miles around, and in the narrow valleys between there were only the green fields rising up on either hand, the stands of trees here and there, the occasional pond or brook. It would be easy to forget just how limited one's view was, but Thorgrim and Cónán did not forget, and they made certain that a screen of riders was spread out in every direction, ready to sound the alarm if danger appeared. There would be no surprises.

The column was as slow-moving and frustrating as ever, and even the horses did not add much to their speed. Thorgrim insisted they keep together, and that only made the whole thing more plodding, the speed of the advance reduced to the pace of the slowest in that odd mix of folk.

But for all that, they were now a respectable force. Between Blathmac's men and Cónán's original band there were near fifty of the bandits left. Blathmac's men seemed not at all distressed by their leader's running off, nor did they seem to resent Cónán's taking charge of them. Indeed, their spirits seemed somewhat lifted by that change of circumstance, and by the considerable plunder that Cónán kept telling them would be theirs at Ráth Naoi.

Aghen had forty men with him, experienced warriors, many of whom had raided in the lands to the east, the land of the Angles and the Picts and in Frankia, before joining up with Ottar. Aghen told Thorgrim the story of Ottar's taking Vík-ló, of the grumbling discontent that had arisen among the men who were not as loyal to Ottar as those who had been with him longer, of the chaos he himself had sown by creating terror in the longphort.

"These men," Aghen had said, gesturing toward the forty who had come with him. "They're good men. They're looking for a lord to serve. They know your reputation. They'll swear loyalty to you, if you'll have them."

Thorgrim was indeed willing to have their service, more than willing. And so, with Ottar's former warriors and his own men, he now led around fifty experienced Northmen, and the army that he and Cónán led numbered around one hundred men, no insignificant force.

The afternoon was getting on by the time one of the scouts returned from the direction of the ringfort. He was on horseback and seemed grateful for it, and Thorgrim could imagine that is was a great relief to not have to run over miles of hilly ground for once. He remembered how much the Irish had enjoyed their time on *Sea Hammer.*

"Nothing much to see," the scout reported, Cónán translating his words for Thorgrim. "Some mounted patrols around the ringfort, but they're staying close by. Mostly clear from here to there."

The day was too far advanced and the men too worn out from the march to consider action that day, so they made camp and Thorgrim and Cónán and Harald and Aghen headed out with the scout to guide them to a place where they could see Kevin's stronghold for themselves.

It took them less than half an hour to reach the crest of a hill, beyond which sat Ráth Naoi, about a mile distant. Thorgrim lay on his belly in the cool grass and looked out over the fields toward the rounded earthworks covered in grass so they appeared to be just some odd deformity in the otherwise relatively flat ground that stretched from the hill to the gate. Crowning the earthworks was a palisade, which looked to be seven feet high or so.

"There'll be no sneaking up on that," Thorgrim observed. It was the reason the ringfort was surrounded by open ground, some of it meadow, some pasture, some cultivated fields, for a mile in any direction.

"No," Cónán said. "And they'll light fires around the perimeter as soon as it's dark. They don't want surprises any more than we do."

For a long time the four men were silent, looking out at the ringfort, the mounted patrols moving lazily around the walls, the smoke crawling out of the gable end of the big hall that rose up from the center of the place. Overhead the sun went down behind a solid mass of cloud and the ringfort and the country around it grew less distinct in the gathering dark.

"You know, Cónán," Thorgrim said at last. "The way you led the horsemen on that chase, led them right into a trap, that was clever. Very clever."

"Yes, it was," Cónán agreed.

"And it makes me wonder," Thorgrim continued, "if we couldn't play that trick once again. And bigger still."

Well before the next morning's dawn, hours before the sun showed any sign of rising, the ringfort at Ráth Naoi was a bustle of activity and Lochlánn mac Ainmire wondered if it would even be necessary. They were making ready to meet the enemy: Thorgrim Night Wolf and his Northmen and the bandit, Cónán. But they did not really know where those men were.

Lochlánn had wanted to send scouts out the night before. There had to be some men at Ráth Naoi who would be able to slip out in the dark and see what the enemy was doing without being seen themselves. His man Fintain, who had accompanied him on his first visit to Kevin's hall, would be capable of such a mission. He was smart and quick and knew the country well. But Kevin would not have it.

"I'll not weaken the defenses by even one man," Kevin had protested. He and Lochlánn, Niall and Louis had been seated at the table in the big hall, glasses of wine in front of them, a fire in the hearth. "If the heathens capture your spy they'll drag information out of him. What we're planning, how many we are. I won't risk that."

Lochlánn thought to point out that Fintain was his man, not Kevin's, and he could give him orders as he wished, but he did not want to wander down that road. He turned to Louis.

"No need," Louis said with a wave of his hand. "We know where they are. They're near, a day's march from where we left them after the last fight. They'll be here on the morrow. And then the fun will begin."

Lochlánn pressed his lips together to contain his irritation. Louis had very much ingratiated himself with Kevin, who seemed quite impressed with the Frank's pedigree. As a result, Louis had assumed a position of leadership, undefined but definitely recognized. It made Lochlánn want to mention to Kevin that when this was all over they would likely be hanging Louis by the neck, but he held that back as well.

He did not bother turning to Niall. That would be pointless. Niall would agree to any thought that Kevin had. If Kevin suggested they summon the wee people of the forest to come and fight the heathens, Niall would vigorously back that plan. So Lochlánn had gone to bed with no further knowledge of the enemy and no more than the hope that things would work out come morning.

The sound of servants getting breakfast together had woken him up, and he swung his legs off the raised platform on which he and two dozen others were sleeping in the big hall and set his feet down on the packed dirt of the floor. The fire was little more than embers, but in their light he could see one of Kevin's people adding bits of kindling and blowing them into living flames. He stood and stretched.

The order that all should be ready for battle before sunrise had been given the night before, issued by Kevin himself and with no prompting from Lochlánn, who was happy that he did not have to argue about that, too. With that precaution taken, and the watchmen stationed on the walls, and fires set all around the perimeter of the ringfort to prevent an enemy approaching in the dark, Lochlánn was reasonably certain they would be prepared when Thorgrim appeared. If Thorgrim appeared.

Lochlánn ate a breakfast of oat porridge, pulled on his mail and strapped on his sword and took up his helmet. He stepped from the hall, with its oppressive smells of smoke and cooked food and men, into the clean, cool air of the predawn morning.

The grounds of the ringfort were crowded with horses tethered out. Under normal circumstances a smaller ringfort one hundred yards to the north of the one that encircled Kevin's hall served as an enclosure for the animals. But the horses were too important to the coming action to risk leaving them so vulnerable, and so they spent the night just a few dozen feet from their riders.

Stable boys were weaving in and out of the lines of horses carrying great armfuls of hay, and others were struggling with buckets to fill the various water troughs. Lochlánn found his own mount and inspected it to be certain it was fit for the day's work, and when he saw it was, he left it to the care of the boys and climbed up onto the earthen wall by the ringfort's gate.

The sun was still down, but the sky was growing lighter in the east when he stepped out onto the space where the tall palisade wall was interrupted by the main gate and where he could have an uninterrupted view of at least half the horizon. There was little to see, just the dark outlines of the distant hills against the pale sky. He could hear nothing but the sound of insects and the insistent cry of birds as they, too, began their day. No sign of an enemy, no suggestion of anything but peaceful countryside.

He remained in that place for an hour, waiting patiently as the sun rose behind the cloud cover and spread its light across the open ground that stretched away from Ráth Naoi in every direction. It revealed no enemy, not even a hint of an enemy. Lochlánn climbed down from the wall and made ready to do the thing that warriors did best, the thing that warriors did most. He made ready to wait.

And wait Lochlánn did, Lochlánn and the host of restless men-at-arms within the ringfort's walls. They waited as the sun climbed up overhead, just the suggestion of the sun, really, lost behind the thick overcast. They waited as the servants struggled to feed all the men and horses in that place and Kevin grumbled about the cost of it all and wondered out loud if the enemy was actually coming or if he was just wasting his precious silver boarding all those extra men.

Incredible, Lochlánn thought as he sat at the long table in Kevin's hall with the others and listened to the rí túaithe complaining. *Last night you were ready to shit your leggings you were so scared of Thorgrim Night Wolf, and now listen to you, you parsimonious bastard.* Twenty-four hours' exposure to Kevin mac Lugaed had not improved Lochlánn's impression of the man.

The midday meal was done and those men-at-arms lounging around the ringfort were just beginning to think the enemy would not come at all—Lochlánn could overhear their murmured speculation—when the first warning sounded.

It came from one of the men stationed on the wall, a young man with sharp eyes who called, "There's men on the far hill!"

Lochlánn sat upright, jerked his head in the direction of the watchman's voice. The man on the wall was pointing toward the west, still shouting. Half the men-at-arms leapt to their feet and snatched up weapons as if the enemy were bursting through the gates at that very moment.

Lochlánn hurried to the ladder that ran up to the wall, but he was not alone, and he yielded to the unspoken hierarchy. Kevin was there and they all stepped aside to let him go up, then Niall behind him. Louis de Roumois stepped up next, but Lochlánn stepped in front of him and took his place behind Niall.

Get as puffed up as you wish, Lochlánn thought as he climbed the rungs, *you're still my prisoner, you Frankish son of a bitch.*

It was crowded on the wall, in the narrow space where the palisades did not interrupt the view, but they managed to position themselves where they all could see. There were indeed men on the far hill, tiny figures moving here and there, and the larger shapes of horses, though only a few. There were little spots of color in the gray and dull green day and Lochlánn recognized those as shields. The Northmen were making ready for battle.

"How many are they?" Kevin asked.

"Somewhere around sixty, lord," answered the lookout who had first seen them, "but they're so far, I can't know for certain."

"Sixty?" Kevin asked. "Does that seem about right?" There was a quickness to his speech that suggested fear.

Still worried about the cost of all these men? Lochlánn thought.

"Seems about right," Niall said.

"There were near sixty with Thorgrim when I escaped," Louis said. "The heathens that joined him numbered thirty or so. Take away those we killed and wounded, and some I would guess ran off, and I would say sixty's about right."

"And we have more than one hundred, and all our men are trained and well-equipped and mounted," Kevin said, as if calculating out loud. His voice sounded more buoyant now. "Good, good."

They watched as the men on the far hill formed a loose line and that line began advancing down the slope of the hill, sweeping forward toward the open ground before Ráth Naoi.

"We'd better mount up and meet them before they get too close," Lochlánn said, and the others made noises of agreement. They went down the ladder in the reverse order they had ascended, save for Kevin, who remained on top of the wall.

Not joining us? Lochlánn thought when he saw that Kevin was making no move for the ladder. He had assumed Kevin would lead the men-of-war into the fight. That was the proper role for the rí túaithe, as far as Lochlánn was concerned, but Kevin apparently did not see it that way.

Just as well, Lochlánn thought. *You stay here and watch in safety and stay out of our way.* He crossed the grounds of the ringfort toward where his men were gathered, calling orders as he did, and Niall did the same, yelling for the men-at-arms under his command. Five minutes later they were armed and mounted. The big gates swung open and the hundred and more horsemen came pounding out of the ringfort, spreading out into a line abreast seven hundred feet long and calculated to give pause to the heathens and ragged bandits facing them on foot.

Niall rode at the center of the line with Louis and Lochlánn on either side. They rode hard, the horses galloping over the flat ground. They wanted to put fear into the invaders' hearts and to put some distance between the fighting and the ringfort.

They were a quarter mile from the walls of Ráth Naoi when Niall called for a halt and reined his horse in and the men along the line followed suit. The heathens and Irish bandits had reached the bottom of the hill and were advancing across the open ground, an ideal place for mounted warriors to ride them down and kill them.

"They're making this easy," Niall said. "We'll wait here, see what these sorry bastards have in mind, and then we'll advance and begin the day's slaughter."

"Recall," Louis said, "we don't want to fight them, we want to drive them. We want to drive them right into Ottar's arms."

"I won't be shy about killing any if the chance is there," Lochlánn said dryly. "Perhaps, Louis, you have become such great friends with the heathens you can't bring yourself to do them any hurt."

"Watch what you say to me, boy," Louis said. "I won't stand for your insinuations. Kevin does not want to lose men for no reason, and any captain with a turd's worth of experience knows you don't throw lives away. Let Ottar do our work for us."

"Here, see," Niall said, interrupting the heated exchange, nodding toward the men in the distance. They had stopped about three hundred yards from where the horsemen were formed up and were assembling themselves into a shieldwall of sorts, but not one that was terribly impressive.

"Half of Thorgrim's men are these bandit vermin," Louis said. "They have no training or experience in this sort of fight. I tell you, our biggest problem will be catching them all when they bolt."

"Our biggest problem may be underestimating them," Lochlánn said. "It has bit us in the ass before today."

Louis made a derisive noise, but Niall interrupted him, calling down the line of horsemen in a voice that could be heard from one end to the other. "The twenty men on either flank, you'll ride around the ends of their shieldwall and get behind them. Us in the center, we'll go right at them. Kill them if you can, but what we really want is to get them running off to the east!" All of this had been explained before. Lochlánn understood that Niall just wanted to be certain that it was not ignored in the coming excitement.

Niall looked at Lochlánn and then at Louis. "You ready?" he asked.

"Ready," Lochlánn said. "Damned ready." Louis nodded his head.

"Let's go," Niall said. He put his spurs to his horse and bolted ahead of the line and on either side of him a hundred horsemen did the same. The riders pounded forward, loud and unstoppable. Spears held upright came down to the horizontal. The terrible iron points were leveled at the wavering line of shields ahead and the promise of death came thundering down on the Northmen and the Irish, on Cónán's men and those of Thorgrim Night Wolf.

Chapter Thirty-Five

A skirmish at Loch Cuan between the fair heathens and the dark heathens, in which Albann, king of the dark heathens, fell.

The Annals of Ulster

The midday meal was usually a boisterous and much relished affair in Ottar Bloodax's camp. But this time it was not, and Ottar could not help but notice. The men were quiet for the most part, and when they were not quiet they were muttering, which was worse, much worse. They talked low so only those few around them could hear, not a good sign at all.

Ottar ate in his tent. He wanted no part of that, and he wanted no part of the ugly looks thrown his way. Men were sewing discontent; he knew it. There were half a dozen of them he was ready to butcher, the half dozen most responsible for this plague of sullen anger.

Those six Ottar wanted to tie to stakes and rip out their bowels and burn them alive as they shrieked their last, and he was pleased with himself for having not done so. He took it as proof of his good leadership that he recognized that such a course would not solve the problem. It might, in fact, make it worse.

He knew what he needed to do. He had to decide whether to continue pressing on to Kevin's ringfort or return to Vík-ló. Those were his choices, but he knew they were not really choices at all. He could not return to Vík-ló having accomplished none of the things he had so loudly proclaimed he would do: find and kill the traitor Aghen, plunder Kevin's stronghold and see the Irishman tied to a stake as well. If he went back to the longphort with none of those things done, then the talk would grow much louder, and soon it would be more than talk.

He tossed his wooden bowl aside, the contents splattering against the side of his tent. He felt like the cloth walls were squeezing in on him and he stood with a roar of frustration and threw back the flap and stepped out into the camp.

There were dozens of men close by, some standing, some sitting, some lying down, and they all looked over at Ottar as he emerged. None of them spoke.

How many of you bastards are loyal to me, really loyal? Ottar wondered, casting his squinting eyes around the camp. *Thirty? Forty?*

Of those who had originally sailed with him from Hedeby to the lands to the east, and then around to Ireland, there was only one ship's crew left, about fifty men. They were loyal, sworn to him. The others? He had picked them up here and there. They had been loyal enough when he was winning them silver. The plunder from Vík-ló had sated them, even though Ottar had kept the far greater share for himself and his closest men. But now they were getting restless.

Greedy bastards…never satisfied, Ottar thought. The worst of the lot, those he trusted the least, he had sent off with Aghen and Einar because he did not think, deep down, that they would be coming back, and that proved to be a good decision.

But now it left a question in his mind: what had become of them? Killed by enemies? Every last one of them? Or was the wolf out there, the wolf that was more than just a wolf? Until he knew the answer he could not summon the will to advance further into the hills.

How will I discover what it was? Ottar asked himself. His thoughts were bordering on despair, when he heard a cry from the far edge of the camp, a shout of surprise, a sound that said something extraordinary was happening.

Ottar stood straighter and he frowned in the direction of the noise. His view was blocked by tents and horses on a tether and he could not see what the commotion was about. But he felt a spark of hope, like this might be a gift from the gods, a reward for his bravery and sacrifice over the years. It might be the gift he wanted above all else: an indication of the proper way forward.

A dozen men came from behind the row of tents, heading in Ottar's direction. Two of the men in the center of that crowd were supporting a third who stumbled and slumped and seemed as if he would collapse into the mud if the men holding him up were to let go.

They came up to Ottar and stopped in front of him. Ottar looked hard at the man being supported by the other two. He was in bad shape, his hair wild and matted, blood streaking his face, his mail ripped and gaping open in several places, his torn tunic and torn flesh visible through the rents. He was splattered with mud, and his leggings were in shreds.

Ottar looked at his face. *I've never seen this man before*, he thought, and even as he thought it he realized that was not true. He knew him, though he could not recall who he was. And then suddenly the man's name came to him.

"Jorund," Ottar said. Jorund was one of those who had been sent with Aghen's party, Ottar recalled, and the implications of this washed over him like the sun breaking through clouds. This man, this man would know exactly what had happened out there.

"You whore's sons!" Ottar roared at the others. "Get Jorund something to sit on! Get him some ale. The man's half dead, can't you see that?"

In less than a minute, Jorund was seated on a stool with a cup of ale in his hand and that was all the respite Ottar was willing to grant him. "The lot of you," Ottar roared at those still crowded around, nearly all of the camp by then. "Be gone, give us some room here, the man's not to be gawked at!" The men grumbled, and reluctantly they dispersed.

Ottar sat on a stool of his own, facing Jorund, and leaned in close. "Tell me what happened," he said. He spoke softly. He wanted to hear the tale himself before he let anyone else hear it. It might not be something he wanted generally known, in which case he would have to kill Jorund then and there.

"It was Aghen, Aghen the traitor," Jorund said. He took another long swallow of ale. "He led us all over the countryside, trailing that stinking bloody haunch, pretending he was hunting for the wolf."

"The wolf!" Ottar said. "Did you find it? Find any sign of it?"

Jorund shook his head. "There was no wolf. It was Aghen the whole time. But we didn't know that. Not until Galti showed up and told us all."

"Galti found you? Where is he?"

"Dead. Once he told the truth and tried to seize Aghen, the old man turned on him and killed him. The rest of those traitorous bastards were on Aghen's side. There were some who weren't. Like me. The others went after Einar, too. That's how I got these wounds. Me and some of the others, we fought to save Einar's life, but it was no good. We were too few. They killed Einar and took me prisoner."

Ottar leaned back, frowning and looking into Jorund's face, but the man was too battered and weak to react to Ottar's gaze. Ottar let those things float around in his mind. *Aghen and the rest killed Einar and Galti…I knew they were disloyal cur, the lot of them.* Then another question came to him.

"Why didn't they kill you, too?" Ottar asked, suspicion suddenly inflamed.

"Some wanted to," Jorund said. "But some were my friends, men I'd sailed with. They decided to take me prisoner. Me and two others who had fought for Einar. I escaped in the night. I've been wandering around for two days now, looking for you."

Ottar was silent again. This was all very interesting, but there was only one thing that really mattered, one bit of intelligence that he really cared about.

"There was no wolf, you say?" he asked Jorund. "You never saw any wolf, no wolf attacked you? Killed anyone?"

Jorund shook his head. Ottar felt as if the sun was coming out. "And what of Aghen? And the others? What became of them?"

"That's why I was so desperate to find you, lord. Warn you. Aghen and the others, they went to the ringfort of that Irishman, Kevin. They meant to swear loyalty to him. And they're on their way here, now. Aghen and those men and all of Kevin's men-at-arms. Mounted men, a hundred or more."

There was an edge of panic in Jorund's voice, but there was no panic in Ottar heart, none at all. One hundred mounted men? That worried him not in the least. He welcomed that, cherished the thought of going sword and shield against them. Bring them on, every filthy Irish bastard. He was ready. Because there was no wolf.

He stood, straightened up to his full height, which he had not done for a while. "Ketil, you stupid son of a bitch!" he roared. "Get the men ready for battle! Get your weapons, all of you, you sorry bastards! We have some Irish to kill!"

Even from a hundred yards away Lochlánn could see that the shield wall was wavering. The line of horsemen that he and Niall and Louis led was sweeping forward like the wrath of an angry God, and he could see the Northmen and the Irish in particular were already sensing the horror of what was about to be visited on them.

He looked to his left and right. The riders on the flanks were starting to peel away. They would make wide arcs around the ends of the shield wall, get in behind the men, and that would break them completely. A minute of that and they would all be running and then they would be easy prey for the horsemen.

The mounted warriors could probably kill them all, and do it with ease. This was open country, no place to hide. But the idea was still to drive them to the east, push them into the shields and swords of Ottar Bloodax. Let them fight, heathen on heathen, let them weaken Ottar as well as themselves. Then it would be time for Lochlánn's men-at-arms and Kevin's to kill the ones still standing.

Lochlánn was leaning forward in his saddle, his spear thrust out ahead of him. He sighted down the shaft, past the iron point, picked out the place in the line he would strike, the shield of the man he would kill first. He kicked his heels into his horse's flanks to coax more speed from the animal. And then he saw that all their plans were starting to collapse around them.

He had been counting on the shield wall standing fast at least until the horsemen reached it. Louis and Niall had been counting on the same. But even as Lochlánn looked down his spear, he could see the defense falling apart, men breaking and running in fear, some even flinging shields aside as they ran.

"No, you cowardly bastards!" Lochlánn screamed as he tried to make his horse run faster still. "No, come back here, you whores' sons!"

The line was dissolving like salt in hot water. What just a second before had been a near solid line of men and shields was now just a wild mob racing off for safety, running before the lethal force coming at them.

Niall was at his side now and he looked over and shouted. "They're running east!" he called, and Lochlánn could see he was smiling despite the effort of riding hard with weapon in hand. "They're running east!"

And then Lochlánn understood what he was saying. The heathens and the Irish bandits were running off in exactly the direction they had hoped to drive them, exactly in the direction of Ottar's camp.

Perfect! Lochlánn thought. It would have been a fine thing to kill some of them there on that ground, but that was not their chief goal. Their chief goal was to drive them east, but the stupid shits were going that way on their own.

The heathens were not heading back the way they had come, which was good. That way was uphill, up the sloping fields they had just descended, and Lochlánn guessed that path would not tempt them. It would be slower and more tiring running that way, and the riders would be on them before they reached the top.

Instead, they were fleeing in a more easterly direction, where the land sloped away into a low valley between two hills, a valley perhaps a mile across with a pond and a long stand of trees at its low point.

They'll run like water...Lochlánn thought. *They'll run downhill, like water.*

The fleeing men were racing over the slope of the hill that ran down into the valley and disappearing from sight, one after another. All along the line the horsemen called insults, calling for the cowards to turn and fight. But there was still close to a hundred yards between the riders and those they were riding down, and Lochlánn could barely here the calls himself over the pounding of hooves. He did not think the heathens would be much inclined to fight even if they could hear the taunts of the men-at-arms.

The land began to slope away as Lochlánn and the others reached the edge of the narrow valley, green fields running downhill, a pond at the bottom, dark under the gray sky. On the far side of the water stood a patch of woods a hundred yards wide and stretching for two hundred yards across their path, like a massive green ship floating on a lighter green sea. Beyond the edge of the wood the trees yielded once again to open ground that ran uphill to the valley's eastern side.

Niall slowed his horse to an easy trot and Lochlánn and the others followed suit. They still had miles to go before they succeeded in driving these fleeing men into Ottar's camp and they did not want their horses blown. Neither did they want to go charging into a possible ambush. This enemy could be wily and dangerous; they had already proved as much.

But there was no ambush, no trap waiting for the men-at-arms. The heathens and the Irish were still running, fleeing headlong down the long slope to the pond at the foot of the hill. The same number of men as had been in the shieldwall; no one was lurking in wait, nor was there any place on the open ground for them to lurk.

"Damn them, they'll get in the woods!" Lochlánn said. He could see that the heathens and the Irish were racing for the dubious protection of the trees, and he could see as well that the riders could not stop them before they reached that place.

"We can surround the woods," Louis said. "Flush them like birds."

"No doubt they're hoping we do just that," Lochlánn said. "The last time this happened they did a great slaughter of our men. We won't be lured into that trap again."

Niall nodded in agreement. "I'd guess they're hoping to cut us up the way they did the last time. But we learned that lesson. We can surround the woods, but we don't get any closer than the distance of an arrow shot."

Louis did not agree with such caution, Lochlánn could see that. He probably thought he and Niall were being a couple of old women, but he kept that opinion to himself.

Niall kicked his horse and headed down the slope in the wake of the heathens, and the rest of the line of horsemen followed behind. They walked the horses. There was no point in riding fast now. The swiftest among the enemy had already reached the woods and were disappearing into the stand of trees.

"They can't hide there forever," Niall said.

"No," Lochlánn said. He looked up and over his shoulder, trying to judge how far the sun remained above the horizon. "But they can stay in there until dark, and that might be all they need. Once it's dark they might well manage to sneak away."

"We have men enough to screen that stand of woods," Niall said. "Make a great circle of men all around it. They won't get out."

"We drive them east," Louis said. "Don't forget, we drive them east."

The line of horsemen reached the edge of the pond, the water standing like a moat between them and the woods on the far side. All of the enemy had now gone into the trees, every man of them lost from sight, as if they had been swallowed up by some great sea creature. Niall spurred his horse ahead, then turned so he was facing the others.

"Forty of you will go with Louis around to the far side of the woods," he called, his voice carrying down the line of men, over the snorting, restless horses, the jingle of tack and chain mail.

"Keep spread out, cover the whole tree line," he continued. "Twenty men with me around the southern end, and the rest with Lochlánn on this side. Get no closer than a long arrow shot from the trees. If they come out in any direction but east, we want to drive them back. We want to keep pushing them east."

The horsemen nodded, wheeled their horses around, and trotted off to take up their places. Lochlánn saw his men deployed along the line of trees, a long, thin line of horsemen studying the woods for any sign of movement, but getting no closer than seventy-five yards or so away, a distance at which it was unlikely even a good bowman could hit an individual on horseback.

Once again Lochlánn looked up and to the west. The sun had passed its zenith back when they were still lolling around the ringfort, and now it was on its way to the horizon. Two or three hours were all they had left before it would be too dark to effectively chase their enemies. Try to flush them out and it could be a bloodbath, let them remain in the woods until dark and they might lose them entirely.

"Ah, damn you, you heathen bastards!" Lochlánn said out loud, no longer able to contain his frustration. And no sooner had he said it than the heathens came bursting out of the woods.

They came out of the trees almost directly in front of where Lochlánn was sitting his horse. Twenty, thirty of them, skirting the edge of the pond, swords held high, shields on arms, screaming as they came. Lochlánn recalled the madman who fought shirtless with the two axes in hand and he looked to see if he was among these men, but if he was, Lochlánn could not see him.

"Here they are! Here they are! After them, drive them back!" Lochlánn shouted and he spurred his horse forward. He was frantic to get at them, to ram the point of his spear into one of their bellies or their fleeing backs, but he was not so crazed that he forgot that they wanted to drive them east, always east.

To his left and right Lochlánn saw the horsemen turn and close on him, all racing for a single point: the nearest of the heathens who were charging their way. The Northmen had picked a good spot to sally out, keeping the pond on their left side, which shielded that flank. Still, Lochlánn had to wonder why they had come out at all, and in that direction.

What are they thinking? They were going back the way they had come; it made no sense, and that made Lochlánn immediately suspicious.

"Watch for bowmen, watch for bowmen!" he shouted as he rode. He searched the enemy in his front for archers, but he could see no one with a bow.

More riders were coming around the far ends of the path of woods, Niall's men and Louis's men responding to the sounds of alarm and the cries of the men-at-arms as they raced toward the enemy.

And just as suddenly as the heathens had started this mad run from cover, they stopped, as if realizing how bad an idea it was. The lead man paused in his rush, held up his hand, and the men behind him stumbled to a halt. There were no more than fifty yards between him and Lochlánn now; Lochlánn could see it all with perfect clarity. The whole lot of them, Northmen and Irish bandits, stopped in their tracks and seemed to notice the riders for the first time. Then once again panic swept over them and once again they turned and ran for the woods.

"Stop, you whores' sons, stop!" Lochlánn shouted. Once again these slippery bastards would deny him the chance to come to grips with them. He spurred his horse hard, desperate to get a spear point in one of them at least before they disappeared into the dark tree line.

And then he remembered the rain of arrows that had caused such carnage the last time he thought he had the bastards trapped in the woods. He pulled his horse to a stop, spun the animal around, and the men with him did the same, not questioning, just following his lead.

"Back, back!" Louis shouted and he rode back over the ground he had just covered. He realized that he was hunching his shoulders, bracing for an arrow in the back. But it never came, and soon he was too far from the woods for that to be a concern.

Niall was there, reining his horse to a stop. "What was it?" he asked.

"The heathens," Lochlánn said. "They came out of the woods, looked like they were trying to run off, but west, not the way we wanted. We drove them back before they got far."

Niall nodded. More and more men were coming around the far side of the woods to join them, men who had heard the action but could not see it for the trees and did not know it was over now.

Louis de Roumois came riding up at a gallop, then stopped with a flourish beside them. "They tried to run?" he asked. "Came out of the woods?"

"Yes," Lochlánn said. "There." He nodded to the place from which the enemy had come and where they had disappeared again. "They came out and then they turned and ran back."

"Cowardly bastards," Louis said, and for a moment they were silent, looking at the trees.

"By my guess we're still three miles from where we'll run into Ottar Bloodax's camp," Niall said. "We have to get them moving."

Then from far off, from the far side of that stretch of wood, came a cry, a single voice. It was too far and too muffled by the trees for them to make out the words, but the tone of alarm was unmistakable.

Lochlánn looked around. There were a lot of the horsemen there, men who had ridden to counter this new threat. Nearly all of their riders, in fact. He turned to Louis.

"How many men did you leave on the east side of the woods?" he asked.

Louis shrugged. "A few. The fighting was here," he said, but it was clear from his forced nonchalance that he recognized his mistake.

"Oh, damn them!" Lochlánn shouted and his shout was greeted by another cry from the far side of the woods, and then a second, as the handful of men Louis had left there tried to make their warnings heard. The heathens had lured nearly all the mounted warriors to the west side of the woods, then had crossed to the east and made a run for it, slipping through the trees where the horsemen could not follow.

"Come!" Niall shouted and he turned his mount and put his spurs to it and raced off around the perimeter of the woods. Lochlánn and Louis did the same, and the rest of the men followed, once again moving as fast as they could push their horses to run. If the men-at-arms on the far side of the trees shouted further warnings, none of the riders heard their cries over the pounding hooves and the thump and clatter of their war gear.

The ground flew by underfoot, the trees sweeping past on their right-hand side as they raced to get around the barrier and rejoin the chase. Lochlánn could not help but recall how the Irish bandit sons of bitches seemed able to disappear at will the last time they had played this game. He vowed he would not let them do that again, would not let them out of his sight.

Which of course he already had. And he had no idea if they would be in sight again once he cleared the end of the woods.

They came pounding around the north end of the tree line and beyond that they could see the fields sloping up the far side of the little valley, and on those fields sixty or so men, running as hard as they could run, visibly struggling to get up the slope and once again disappear over the crest of the far hill.

"Come on, push them, push them!" Niall shouted and the horsemen raced off across the field, up the sloping pasture, stretching out into a long line as the faster horses and better riders surged into the lead.

Lochlánn was one of those. His mount, purchased a few years before by his wealthy father, was an excellent animal, and Lochlánn an excellent horseman, and soon he and Niall and a few others had pulled ahead of the pack.

And once again they were just a bit too late. The first of the running men had reached the crest of the hill and were disappearing over the top, even as Lochlánn had halved his distance behind them.

"No matter, no matter, we want to push them," Niall shouted as if he could read Lochlánn's thoughts, feel his mounting frustration.

"Push them!" Lochlánn called in agreement. By his estimate they had a mile or two to go before their quarry ran into Ottar's warriors.

He watched as the last of his enemy struggled to the top of the slope. If the shirtless madman was there, Lochlánn still had not seen him. Nor had he seen that big one, the massive heathen he had noticed in the fight on the river. No worry. It was difficult to see clearly while riding hard.

Then the last of their enemy was lost from sight, up and over the crest of the hill that formed the far side of the valley. Fifty yards and then Lochlánn would be over the crest as well and once again he would have them within a few lengths of his spear point. But he could not ignore the ugly feeling in his gut.

Niall was first over the top and Lochlánn just a half dozen strides behind him. He heard the man's horse whinny in protest as Niall pulled back hard on the reins, forcing the animal to a halting, clumsy stop.

Don't stop, don't stop! Lochlánn thought as he raced up the last few feet of hill, but he also knew that Niall would not have stopped if he had not had a reason to do so, and that reason probably meant something bad was happening.

Up and over the crest and Lochlánn pulled back his own reins to come to a stop at Niall's side. There were men arrayed before them across a couple hundred yards of open ground, and they were not the frightened heathens and Irish bandits they had been chasing. There were a hundred of them at least, bright shields forming a shieldwall, helmets and mail showing dull gray in the muted light of late afternoon. They were not running. They were advancing.

"Ottar," Niall said, matter-of-factly. "Ottar and his warriors."

Lochlánn looked to the left and right, across the fields that stretched away before dipping down into another valley. Thorgrim's men were nowhere to be seen. Once again they had managed to disappear.

"We weren't driving them into Ottar's men," Lochlánn said bitterly. "They were leading us."

He looked over at Niall, and Niall shook his head in disbelief. And then a roar went up from Ottar's ranks and the great line of Northmen surged forward.

Chapter Thirty-Six

There has never tasted death fearlessly,
Nor reached the known dead,
The cultivator's soil has never covered
A more wonderful keeper of tradition.
The Annals of Ulster

As Aghen and Cónán's men formed their ugly shieldwall and the horsemen sallied out of Ráth Naoi, Thorgrim had been watching from the crest of the hill that looked down on the fields below. He had smiled at the sight of it. It was amusing. And if things worked out as they had planned, it would continue to be amusing.

Good, good, he thought, *so far, good.* The riders formed a line just as he and Cónán had guessed they would. The horsemen would think it no great matter to overrun the men on foot and kill them on open ground. And normally they would be right.

Thorgrim turned to Starri, lying beside him in the grass, looking out over the country below. "How many riders, do you think?" he asked. Starri's eyesight was as legendary as his prowess in battle.

Starri took a long moment to count. "About one hundred," he said.

"One hundred," Thorgrim repeated. "Good. There can't be too many left in the ringfort. It seems Kevin wants the fighting to happen out here. Eager to see we don't get too close to his hall."

"What if Kevin's not in his hall?" asked Harald, who was lying on Thorgrim's other side. "What if he's leading the horsemen? What then?"

"He's not," Thorgrim said. Kevin, he was certain, would remain in his hall. Where he thought he was safe.

They heard a shout, then a low rumble building in volume as the line of horsemen suddenly swept forward, charging the shieldwall, ready to crush it under the weight of their attack. Which they would have done, and easily. Those mounted men-at-arms were smart, Thorgrim had no doubt about that. He could see the riders on the flanks intended to sweep around the ends of the shieldwall, come in behind, where they would have slaughtered his men.

But happily they were denied the chance. The riders had not covered half the distance between the ringfort and the shieldwall before the Irish and Northmen broke and ran in apparent panic. They raced for the little valley he and Cónán and Aghen had scouted out the night before. And from the crest of the hill, Thorgrim and those with him—Harald and Godi, Starri Deathless and the other men of *Sea Hammer*—watched as they disappeared from view down the long slope that led to the pond and the stand of trees below.

Failend was there as well. She had insisted on coming and Thorgrim had not argued. He liked her, and he was starting to think she brought luck, even though she was a Christian.

"That was well done," Godi said, and Thorgrim nodded his agreement.

"So far," Thorgrim said. He knew better than to tempt the gods by making a comment about any future success.

There was still a lot that could go wrong, but it was all out of Thorgrim's hands now, that part, at least. They had done all they could to bend things their way.

Aghen's man, Jorund, had selflessly volunteered to return to Ottar's camp and fill Ottar's head with tales of Kevin's army coming for him. Jorund had agreed to being slashed by Iron-tooth in order that the disguise would be more believable. The cuts Thorgrim had made were flesh wounds, no more, but they were deep and he knew well how agonizingly painful they were.

But Jorund had endured them with not even a whimper, an act of bravery which by itself should have warranted the approval of the gods, and their help as well. The bleeding man had stumbled off in the direction of Ottar's camp. Thorgrim hoped that he had met with success, but he would not know until all of this had played out.

Likewise with Cónán. He and Cónán and Aghen had scouted out the valley and planned the moves they would make in the face of the horsemen. Cónán had dismissed all of Thorgrim's concerns, waved off any suggestion that this might be at all difficult.

"They're not fools," Thorgrim had warned. "We did this to them before, they'll be ready for it this time."

"Exactly!" Cónán said. "They'll think they know what we're going to do. So we'll do something else."

Someone who did not know Cónán well might have taken comfort in his overweening confidence. But Thorgrim knew better. He and Cónán had not been together long, but they had seen and done much in that short time. Thorgrim understood that Cónán always projected confidence, regardless of how he really felt.

"Just take care," Thorgrim said, and Cónán only grinned.

Now the first act had played out, and it had gone as they had hoped. The horsemen from Ráth Naoi had chased the men of the shieldwall down into the valley. They should have reached the trees ahead of the riders, but Thorgrim could not see into the valley from the hilltop, and in any event, that was Cónán and Aghen's business now. He had his own affairs to look to. Which, at first, meant waiting.

They waited for hours. They had the day's last meal on the back side of the hill, with the hill's crest shielding them from any watchmen on the ringfort's walls. They kept low so they would not be silhouetted against the horizon. They waited to see if anything more would happen at the ringfort, if more men would emerge, or if the riders would return. But they saw nothing. Just an Irish ringfort slipping peacefully into evening.

The sun went down and soon it was full dark and they could see nothing at all. If the moon was up it was lost behind the clouds, leaving the land as black as it could be. They waited for fires to be lit around the perimeter of the ringfort, but none were. They waited another few hours, but still nothing.

"No fires?" Harald asked.

"Seems not," Thorgrim said. "I guess Kevin's confident that the men-at-arms have his enemies on the run." Which was good.

With the moon and stars lost to sight there was no way to gauge how much time had passed. Quite a lot, it seemed to Thorgrim, and nothing had happened in the ringfort that they could observe. Every once in a while a tiny point of light showed where someone was walking the walls with a torch in hand, and occasionally the glow from a hearth fire was visible. That was it. They saw nothing else, heard nothing at all.

"Let's go," Thorgrim said.

He stood and headed down the slope of the hill, walking in the direction of the ringfort, though he could not see it. He heard the others behind him, soft leather shoes on the sod, the light jingling of buckles against mail as they crossed the pitch-black fields. Thorgrim had worked out an elaborate plan for getting past the watch fires unseen. He still thought it would have worked, but they would not find out that night.

They're making this easy for us, he thought, and that thought made him apprehensive.

The night was so dark that Thorgrim was not entirely certain where the ringfort was, an odd thing to have so large a structure utterly lost to sight. He wondered if they would blunder right into it or walk past it in the dark. Then he saw a glow ahead of him, blooming in the distance like a hint of sunrise. It was not a point of light but a soft illumination, like a fire hidden behind a short wall.

And Thorgrim realized that was exactly what it was. They must have lit a fire on the grounds inside the ringfort. Apparently they wanted to see what was happening within the confines of the stronghold, even if they could not be bothered to illuminate the approaches to the place.

Thorgrim led the others across the open ground, perfectly concealed by the night. They stepped softly and listened close, but there was no sound of alarm, no sound at all that they could hear, save for the occasional watchmen calling back and forth.

"They say 'All's well,'" Harald whispered when they were close enough to make out the watchmen's words. Thorgrim smiled to himself. The men within had no idea.

They were no more than forty feet away from the wall when a watchman appeared, torch in hand. Thorgrim stopped instantly and he heard the others behind him do the same. The watchman was standing on top of the wall where the line of palisades was interrupted by the gate. He seemed to be talking to some others hidden behind the row of sharpened logs sunk into the crest of the earthworks.

The light from the torch fell on the ringfort walls, an earthen mound heaped fifteen feet high. It was tall enough that it might have formed a significant defense, but the walls, being made of piled earth, were rounded, wider at the base than at the top, and thus not too difficult to scale. The palisade added a further hindrance to someone coming over the wall, but not much.

The watchman with the torch turned and stared out into the dark. He seemed to be looking directly at Thorgrim and his men, but Thorgrim knew the man would be blinded by his own torchlight and would never see them, even as close as they were. Still, with the watchmen and the fires there would be no sneaking into Ráth Naoi. But that was all right.

Thorgrim turned to Starri Deathless, who was standing beside him. In the thin light shed by the watchman's distant torch he could see that Starri was doing that odd jerking thing he did with his arms when a fight was imminent. He was making a sort of whimpering noise, as he was straining to hold all this terrible power in, as if he could not hold it long. But that was all right, too. He did not have to.

"Starri," Thorgrim whispered. "Go rid us of those watchmen on the wall."

With that, Starri was gone. Their stealthy approach had been like a damn holding him back, but with Thorgrim's words the damn had burst and the irresistible rush of power that was Starri Deathless came surging forward. He ran at the ringfort, his two axes held out at his sides at arm's length, and he howled as he ran.

The watchman on the wall froze and stared out into the dark, head sweeping left and right.

Stupid bastard, Thorgrim thought. His torch was blinding him and he did not see Starri until Starri reached the edge of the ringfort's walls and kept on going as if they were not even there. He leapt at the wall and his forward momentum carried him one, two, three steps up the steeply sloping earthwork. The watchman had time enough to swing his torch part way around at Starri's head before Starri's ax slammed into him, knocking him back off the wall, the spray of blood visible in the firelight as he fell. Then Starri wheeled and went for the other men on the wall, hidden from Thorgrim's view.

Starri was not the only one getting into the fight. As soon as he had headed for the wall the others did as well, running hard in Starri's wake. Harald, Vali and Armod, the youngest of them, were soon a few paces ahead, with Thorgrim and Godi taking up the rear.

They reached the wall less than a minute after Starri and already they could hear the screams of fear and pain on the other side of the earthworks as Starri cleared the path for them. Harald reached the wall and clambered up the sloping side, not as effortlessly as Starri had done, but close, and Vali and Armod were on his heels. Thorgrim and the handful of men with him stopped at the edge of the earthworks, and just a few seconds later they heard the heavy bar of the gates tossed aside and the creak of one of the big doors swinging open.

Thorgrim stepped up and grabbed the edge of the gate and pulled it until it was wide enough for him to slip through, which he did, the others behind him. From the outside the ringfort had seemed like a large affair, but Thorgrim was still surprised by how much area was encompassed by the round earthen wall.

A couple hundred paces away, a massive bonfire was burning in an open area, casting its light in a great circle around the space. The light of the flames danced off the walls of the big hall behind. Sundry other buildings, dozens of them, were just visible, scattered around the ringfort grounds as if they were trying to keep to the shadows.

All this Thorgrim took in with a single glance around. The fighting by the gate was pandemonium and it needed his attention. There was a dead man on the ground, probably the watchman Starri had struck down, and now Starri was engaged with two others on the wall above them. Harald and Vali and Armod had come down from the wall, and after unbarring the gate, had turned to fight the men-at-arms who had come running up at the sound of the commotion.

From the direction of the hall, Thorgrim could hear more men shouting, feet running, the sound of alarm and panic spreading.

Can't waste time with this, Thorgrim thought. In the flames of the bonfire he could see men running to meet this new threat. A dozen maybe. He hoped there were not too many more than that. He was counting on it.

"Come," he said to Godi and the others and they flung themselves at the five or six with whom Harald, Starri and the others were engaged.

Swords flashed in the orange light and the space near the gate was filled with the sounds of clashing steel and the grunts of men wielding weapons, thrusting, parrying, slashing with wild, desperate strokes.

Two more went down. Dead or wounded, Thorgrim did not know or care as long as they were down, and the other men-at-arms turned and fled, leaving the Northmen alone by the gate. But they would not be alone long. Men were rushing toward them from the direction of the bonfire and the hall behind it.

Thorgrim looked around. The way to the left seemed clear, and that direction would work as well as any.

"This way, let's go," he said. "Harald, make certain Starri is with us!" He pushed past Godi and Olaf Thordarson and raced off, skirting the edge of the earthen wall, looking for the nearest cluster of buildings in which they could lose themselves.

There was shouting all around. Thorgrim could not understand the words, but he had a good sense for the meaning. He could hear it in the voices. Confusion. Uncertainty. A bit of fear. There were enemies within the walls, and the men-at-arms whose job it was to protect the ringfort did not know what was happening. But Thorgrim did, because he was the one making it happen.

They came at last to a place where four or five buildings stood clustered together. They were round and daub-covered with conical thatched roofs. The nearest stood about fifty paces from the outer wall. Each had a yard fenced off with a wattle fence. They could see hints of animals moving around in the yards, pigs or goats or some such, disturbed in their sleep by this most unorthodox intrusion.

"Here," Thorgrim said and led the way into the dark area between two of the buildings. He paused there and the others paused as well and they listened. There were men approaching. They could see the light of torches dancing on the earthen wall and the sides of the buildings. They could see men running, but all was still in confusion.

"They're looking for us," Harald said in a whisper.

"Yes," Thorgrim said, biting off the word as he realized that the black mood was enveloping him, the consuming and inexplicable fury that would sometimes grip him in the dark hours. It was odd that it should come on so late into the night, but many things about him were changing as he grew older, and this was one of them.

And there was no denying it; he could feel the mood creeping over him like the first hints of a coming illness. Soon, he knew, he would not be able to tolerate anyone speaking to him. They had to finish this business quick.

"Harald, with me," he snapped. "The rest of you, go. There." He pointed with Iron-tooth to a knot of men-at-arms fifty feet away. They were advancing cautiously, torches in left hands, swords in right, searching for the intruders.

"Twenty minutes, no more," Thorgrim added and the men were off, Starri Deathless once again leading the rush, running, screaming, axes swinging. Thorgrim saw the men-at-arms stop, toss their torches aside and spread out, standing ready for this renewed attack.

And that was all the time Thorgrim could spare for them. "Let's go," he said to Harald and he ran off in the other direction, his senses sharp as he moved through light and shadow. He could see men running toward the place where Starri and the others were fighting. Fighting and making all the distracting noise they could before they once again disappeared into the dark.

The bonfire was no more than fifty feet from the big hall and it cast its dancing yellow light on the tall building. There was a door at the far end of the hall and two guards there, men charged with securing the entrance, men who would not be lured away by the sounds of a fight. And inside the hall, cowering as his men fought his battles for him, was the Irishman, Kevin. Thorgrim knew it. He could feel it.

They came out of the shadows and into the great circle of light cast by the bonfire and ran the last hundred feet across the open ground for the door to the hall. Thorgrim could see the guards react as they caught sight of the running men, could see them tense up, take a step in his and Harald's direction. They would guess these two were not friends, but they could not be sure.

Thorgrim was still fifty feet away, running hard, Iron-tooth held high, when the guards finally understood that they were in serious peril. Their spears, held upright at their sides, came down to the horizontal, the tips slightly raised and aimed directly at the chests of the men coming at them.

Twenty feet, ten feet, and then Thorgrim slowed, coming to an awkward stop, sweeping Iron-tooth down with a backhand stroke, connecting with the wooden shaft of the spear and knocking it aside. He went for the man's chest with a straight thrust, but the guard was quicker than Thorgrim thought he would be. He dodged aside and swung the spear like a club, hitting Thorgrim on the upper arm and knocking him off balance.

Thorgrim stumbled sideways as the guard tried to pull the spear back to a place where he could thrust it into Thorgrim's gut. But it was an awkward weapon, too long for such close quarter fighting.

You should have dropped that spear and pulled your sword, Thorgrim thought, even as he thrust Iron-tooth into the man's neck.

He pulled Iron-tooth free and the guard went down on his knees then toppled on his side, kicking and making a strangling noise. Thorgrim turned to see what Harald was up to, found him standing over the body of the second guard, blood glinting on Oak Cleaver's blade.

Thorgrim stepped up to the door and pushed and he could feel that it was barred on the other side. He could feel the fury boiling up and he cocked his leg and slammed his heel into the door, waist-height. He felt the door move, a fraction of an inch, and he heard something start to break. He kicked again and the door moved even more. Then Harald stepped up and delivered a powerful blow with the bottom of his foot and the door swung open with a wrenching, shattering sound.

The hall was spacious, bigger than his own at Vík-ló, with the roof peaked so high that even the light of the big fire burning in the hearth could not reach it's very top. There was a great table running down the length of the hall, and at the far end of the table stood the Irishman, Kevin—and he looked very afraid.

Thorgrim stepped through the door and moved slowly around the table. Kevin was wearing mail, a sword hanging from his belt, but they looked more for show than for actual fighting. Then Thorgrim noticed there was another man there, by Kevin's side. He recognized the man, but could not place him. Then he remembered. It was Kevin's translator. What was his name? Eoin, that was it. Thorgrim was surprised he could recall that.

He walked around the table toward the two men who watched him the way deer will watch a hunter approach, not sure if they should bolt or remain perfectly still. Kevin whispered something to Eoin and Eoin stepped away, came toward Thorgrim, arms open as if to show he held no weapons. He began to talk.

He was talking in Thorgrim's native tongue and Thorgrim could have understood the words if he had bothered to listen, which he did not. Instead he continued to approach and Eoin continued to talk and when Thorgrim was close enough he darted Iron-tooth out like a snake striking and drove the point right into Eoin's heart.

Thorgrim felt the tip pause, just for an instant, as it hit the mail. He felt it tear through the metal links, deflect off bone and then go straight in with hardly any resistance after that. Eoin's mouth and eyes went wide, as men's did when stabbed in the heart. Thorgrim had seen it often enough. Eoin made a gurgling noise, but Thorgrim suspected he was already dead. He jerked Iron-tooth free and Eoin fell with no other sound.

Kevin had taken a step back from the table and now he was talking, fast and urgent, but he did not speak Norse and Thorgrim could not understand the words. Despite the black mood, the hint of a smile played on Thorgrim's lips.

This, he realized, was why he had killed Eoin.

Without Eoin, Kevin could not use words, and words were Kevin's most lethal weapon. They were the weapon with which he had killed nearly all of Thorgrim's men and nearly killed Thorgrim, too. Kevin used words the way other men used swords and axes, and now Thorgrim had taken that away from the man.

He had not done so because he thought Kevin's words might have some effect on him. They would not. He had done it to see the terror in Kevin's eyes when he realized that no matter what he said, his words could not possibly do him any good.

And Thorgrim was not disappointed. He saw the realization dawn on Kevin's face and then the unabashed fear. He saw the very moment when Kevin realized that he would not talk his way out of this.

Thorgrim guessed that Kevin would now try the only option left to him, and he was correct. Kevin jerked his sword from its sheath, took a step forward and brought the blade down like an ax, right at Thorgrim's head.

He was fast, faster than Thorgrim would have thought, but not fast enough. Iron-tooth was up, held horizontal, and Kevin's blade stopped dead as it connected. Kevin whipped his blade around and tried a slashing attack at Thorgrim's legs, but once again Iron-tooth was there to stop it.

The panic was now plainly visible on Kevin's face. Thorgrim was tempted to keep this up, to toy with him, cat and mouse, until Kevin collapsed in exhaustion. But he knew he did not have time to indulge himself that way.

The next attack was clumsier, more desperate than the first two, an awkward lunge right for Thorgrim's belly. Thorgrim flicked Kevin's blade aside, stepped in, and drove Iron-tooth's bloody steel into Kevin's heart just as he had Eoin's.

Kevin's eyes bulged; his mouth gaped open. Thorgrim pushed the blade harder, and this time he felt it tear though the mail on Kevin's back. He stepped up close so he and Kevin were just inches apart, and the only thing holding Kevin upright was Thorgrim's sword.

He saw Kevin's eyes shift, just a hair's breadth, until he was looking into Thorgrim's eyes, and Thorgrim had the satisfaction of seeing that the man was still alive, that the last thing on earth he would see would be the satisfied face of the man he had wronged, getting his final vengeance.

And then the light in Kevin's eyes went out and his body shook with a death rattle. Thorgrim tipped his sword down and Kevin's corpse slid off and fell in a heap at his feet.

Kevin was still gripping his sword, but Thorgrim did not mind. Kevin was a Christian, like all the Irish, and Thorgrim did not think Christians would be welcome in the corpse hall, no matter how they died.

And even if they were,Thorgrim was certain that the Valkyrie would not choose a lying, cowardly pathetic maggot like Kevin to sit at the table of Odin. Kevin was gone, and Thorgrim was satisfied that he would never see him again, in this world or any other.

Chapter Thirty-Seven

A slaughter was inflicted on the foreigners
at the islands of eastern Brega…
The Annals of Ulster

Harald Thorgrimson kept his ears on the open door and his eyes on the back of the hall. A wattle wall separated the big room from some others back in the shadows—sleeping chambers or storerooms he guessed, perfect for armed men to conceal themselves and come rushing out with weapons drawn.

As he watched for movement at the far end of the space, he listened to what was going on out in the night. He heard Starri shriek two or three times in quick succession, he heard orders shouted back and forth, he heard the distinct sound of blades hitting blade, blades hitting shields. If the others were doing what they were supposed to be doing, they were leading Kevin's men-at-arms on a merry chase through the dark. And they would keep it up for another few minutes, no more.

Harald kept near the door, Oak Cleaver in hand, as his father advanced on the two men in the room. One was Kevin, the object of their visit; the other was the translator, Eoin. It was Eoin who was stepping toward Thorgrim, hands out. He was speaking their Norse language, welcoming Thorgrim to Kevin's hall, offering him food and drink.

Harald shook his head. That was pathetic, even for the desperate ploy that it was. Then, to Harald's relief, Thorgrim drove Iron-tooth through Eoin's heart.

It was Kevin's turn next, and much as Harald would have liked to concentrate on this final act, he did not take his eyes from the far wall or his ears from the grounds outside the door.

Now Kevin was talking, and Harald half listened to the words. He heard offers of silver and gold, slaves, promises to aid the Northmen in lucrative raids. Harold could not tell if Kevin, in his panic, had forgotten that Thorgrim could not understand him, or if he hoped Harald would translate, or if he just could not stop himself from talking. The latter, Harald guessed.

Translating would have been pointless, and Harald did not bother. His father had no interest in Kevin's words, and there was nothing that Kevin could offer that Thorgrim could not simply take. What's more, Harald knew that the black mood was working on him. It was odd that it should happen at that hour, but after a lifetime of experience Harald knew the signs perfectly well. They had to finish this business with Kevin and be out of here soon.

There were few things that Harald Broadarm feared, but one of them was having to deal with his father when the black mood was on him. He swallowed hard, working himself up to say something about the need to hurry, when Kevin drew his sword and took an awkward swipe at Thorgrim's head.

Oh, thank the gods, Harald thought. Now it would be over soon, as long as Thorgrim was not tempted to prolong Kevin's misery.

Kevin attacked again, and then again, and Thorgrim parried the blows. Harald was just starting to worry that his father would indeed draw this out when he saw Kevin die on Iron-tooth's long blade. Harald gave his father half a minute to savor the vengeance, and then he hurried over to him, across the big room.

"Father," he said, laying a hand on Thorgrim's arm. "We have to go."

Thorgrim turned and looked at him with that expression Harald knew well, the one that said his father only half recognized him, half knew who he was. But the black mood had not taken hold entirely, Harald could see that, and so he was not surprised when Thorgrim nodded, then bent over and wiped Iron-tooth clean on the tail of Kevin's tunic. He slid the blade into the scabbard and followed Harald out into the dark.

They paused just outside the door to Kevin's hall and listened. The bulk of the noise was coming from around the other side of the building, coming from some place deep within the ringfort.

"Let's go," Harald said and he took off running toward the sound, glancing back to make certain that his father was following behind, relieved to see that he was. They ran around the far side of the hall, where the tall building shielded them from the light of the bonfire, and raced off into the dark. There was fighting up ahead, which was good, because without the sound of battle like a horn in the fog Harald did not think he would have ever been able to find his fellows. The ringfort was much bigger than it had seemed from the outside.

They came around the side of a small building that looked to be a smithy of some sort and Harald could see them, fifty paces away, by the ringfort's outer wall. They were all but surrounded by men-at-arms. They were outnumbered, but not wildly outnumbered, and not yet overwhelmed.

"Here we go!" Harald shouted. He drew Oak Cleaver and he picked up his pace and he yelled as he ran at the fighting men, yelled as loud and manic as he could to surprise the Irish men-at-arms and throw them into confusion.

And it worked. He saw heads turn, men turn, then turn back as they realized there was danger on all sides. He saw one take a sword thrust in the shoulder, courtesy of Thorodd Bollason, on whom he had foolishly turned his back.

Harald came in with sword swinging, knocked a spear shaft aside, thrust and missed, but he was more concerned about sewing panic, and in that he was successful. He saw men backing away, unsure what threat was the greatest, the men they had been fighting or the new arrivals at their backs.

And then Thorgrim was among them, Iron-tooth scything the air. His father had abandoned his usual subtle, skilled sword craft and now was slashing and hacking, but the effect was what they sought: the collapse of the Irishmen's will to fight. Spears and torches were flung aside and the men-at-arms bolted off, running in half a dozen different directions, wanting only to get clear of the Northmen who had so taken them by surprise.

They would regroup, they would come again, but it would not matter. Thorgrim and the others had done what they had come to do. Now it was time to go.

Godi stepped up, a grim sort of smile on his face. He looked at Thorgrim, opened his mouth to speak, then stopped. He shifted his eyes to Harald and Harald gave a little shake of the head, and Godi gave a little nod, an all but imperceptible gesture. Godi had been with Thorgrim for a year or more and he recognized the black mood and knew what it meant.

"Here," Harald said, sheathing Oak Cleaver and nodding toward the wall. "We'll go over the wall here." Starri was there, breathing hard, coming out of his temporary madness even as Thorgrim was lapsing into his. Starri scrambled up the earth wall. He took one of his axes and drove it into the palisade four feet above the earthworks and drove the second in three feet above that. One by one the men went up the sloping wall and, using the axes as steps, went up and over the palisades. They dropped to the wall on the other side, then slid down to the ground.

It took no more than a few minutes before they were all on the outside of the ringfort once again, lost in the dark. From the far side of the wall Harald heard a cry of alarm. It was followed by more voices and then the sound of running feet and he guessed that the body of the late rí túaithe of Cill Mhantáin had been discovered.

"Let's be gone," he said in a low voice and headed off at a quick pace over the open ground, back the way they had come. They walked for ten minutes before they saw a flicker of light off to their left, though how far off it was impossible to tell. It flashed and then flashed again, a striker on flint, then remained steady as the flames took hold. It made a fixed point in the dark and Harald altered course to make for it.

They walked for ten minutes before they reached the point of light, which was the flame of a torch held by Cónán's man, Cerball. Behind him, barely visible, were the horses Cerball had brought, twelve in all, all once the property of Kevin's men-at-arms. The Northmen mounted up and Cerball and another of Cónán's men led the way, torches in hand, casting just enough light that they could find their way past the hill, through the little valley with the lake and the woods, and finally to the place where Cónán's men were secreted away.

Cónán was there to greet them. He was smiling and looking smugly pleased with himself. He approached Thorgrim's horse and was ready to start telling the tale of his exploits leading the Irish warriors on their wild goose chase when Harald slid down from his mount and intercepted him.

"My father's not really in the mood for talk," he said in a low voice. Thorgrim, in fact, had said nothing since they had come back over the ringfort's walls. He had just ridden in silence a few lengths' distance from the others.

"Is he all right?" Cónán asked and there was genuine concern in his voice.

"He's fine," Harald said. "It's just a thing that happens to him. Kevin mac Lugaed's not so fine, however, and you'll be happy to know it."

And Cónán was indeed happy to hear the news. He and Harald and the others went off to where a small fire burned and the Northmen were given meat and ale and they told their story and Cónán told his. And somewhere, out in the dark, unseen, Thorgrim Night Wolf sat on the grass and let the black mood, the wolf dream, steal over him.

By the time Ottar Bloodax staggered into his tent that night and lay down on the furs heaped on the ground, he was very drunk and very pleased.

Jorund's news had been the most welcome thing he could hear. Not about the deaths of Galti and Einar, of course; they were good men, and he was sorry to lose them. But the news that the wolf was not real, that it had all been the doing of the traitor, Aghen. And the further news that rather than having to go fight Kevin, Kevin was coming to him.

Ottar had been suspicious at first. He had to be. A man did not reach the position Ottar had reached, and remain alive for very long, if he was not suspicious. But things had indeed turned out as Jorund said they would.

On Jorund's word alone Ottar had put his men on a battle footing: weapons, armor, helmets, shields. He had sent scouts out ahead, and they had soon come back to report men on foot and men on horseback coming their way, and coming fast. Ottar arranged his men in a shield wall and waited.

He had not waited long. The men on foot came tearing over the crest of the hill and Ottar called for the shieldwall to stand ready, but those men had turned to the left and seemed to disappear into a creek bed that was all but hidden from where Ottar and his men stood. He was about to order his men to chase them down when the horsemen came over the crest of the hill. That was when the real fighting started.

Normally the mounted warriors would have had a great advantage, but not this time. They seemed entirely surprised to find Ottar's shieldwall standing in their way. They were disorganized and winded from what Ottar realized was a long chase across country. They were in no position to attack; they were hardly able to defend themselves when Ottar's shieldwall advanced.

It had not been a slaughter, but something close. The horsemen fought well as they tried to get themselves into some kind of order, but there was not much they could do. The shieldwall hit them and drove them back and put them into even greater disarray. Orders flew back and forth, knots of riders formed and charged in and out with their deadly spears and even managed to wound and kill some of Ottar's men. But in the end they had been overwhelmed and they used the speed that their mounts afforded them to turn tail and race for the hills to the west.

When it was over Ottar looked around the field of battle, the wounded, the dead, the bloody weapons held high, and he saw it was good. "Tonight we feast!" he roared. "And tomorrow we go to Kevin's ringfort and cut that sorry bastard's heart from his chest!"

The men cheered. They cheered loud and with enthusiasm, the cheering of men who had just fought a battle and lived and won. Men who would fight another on the following day with the expectation that they would win again, and in victory gain great plunder. They were men who would now follow Ottar Bloodax with the loyalty he expected and deserved.

The eating and drinking had gone on late into the night, the black and moonless night, until Ottar could feel his eyes closing, his body slumping. He knew he had to get to his tent before he passed out by the fire, because passing out was a sign of weakness and he could show no weakness. He stood, staggered off, pulled the flap of the tent back.

A small oil lamp sat on a barrel, its flame dancing in the draft made by the moving tent flap. Like most Northmen, Ottar did not like the dark and those things from the other worlds that might lurk there. It was worse in Ireland, where strange and foreign spirits might resent the intrusion of the men from across the sea. So Ottar ordered his slave to keep a lamp burning and the slave never failed because he understood the price of such failure.

Ottar had energy enough to unbuckle his sword belt and set it on the ground by his pallet, where he always kept it while he slept, ready to be taken up in an instant. That done, he fell on the pile of furs and a moment later he was asleep.

It was still night when he came awake again. It was black as death in his tent save for the one tiny flame. His head was still swimming with drink so he knew he had not been asleep very long. But something had woken him. He was not sure what it was, but he felt a chill of fear on his flesh.

And then he heard it—a growl, low, ugly, menacing and close. Ottar gasped, sat up, his hand falling on the hilt of his sword.

The wolf was no more than five feet away, right at the entrance to the tent, crouching low, ready to leap. It was black and its eyes shone in the light of the oil lamp and its teeth were white and bared and it was looking directly at him.

"Ahh!" Ottar shouted. "Ahh!" He leapt up, drawing his sword as he did. He took a wild swing at the beast, but the animal tilted its head, just the tiniest of moves, and the tip of the sword sailed past, finding only air.

"Ahh! Bastard! Son of a whore!" Ottar shrieked. He felt his bladder give out, the warm urine soaking his leggings. He slashed again with his sword and again the wolf dodged the blow easily, growling, keeping low.

"Come and get me, you bastard! Kveldulf!" He held the sword in front of him, two-handed, tip pointing directly at the spot between the wolf's eyes. He could hear men running and someone shouting his name, but his eyes were locked on the wolf's eyes and he did not reply or move even an inch.

Then the wolf took a step toward him, a slow, careful step, still in its crouch, still ready to spring. Ottar saw the tip of the sword wavering as his hands and arms shook. He heard his own breath, shallow and rasping.

"Ottar! What is it?" Ketil's voice. He was approaching Ottar's tent, more men with him. But Ottar did not dare call out, and he was not even certain he could. He did not trust his voice. He heard little whimpering sounds, barely audible over the wolf's growling, and realized they were coming from him.

"Lord Ottar?"

And then the wolf leapt. It came right off the ground, jaws open, eyes wide, leaping as high as Ottar's throat. Ottar screamed, a shrill, high-pitched cry of pure terror and he threw up his hands and dropped his sword. Then the wolf was past him, leaping by so close it brushed Ottar's arm and he could smell the fetid canine scent, a scent like death. The animal came down at the far end of the tent and did not stop. It pushed through the flap and disappeared just as Ketil pulled back the flap at the front.

Ottar whirled around and looked at Ketil, and Ketil and the men behind him looked back at Ottar. Ottar could see on their faces that they did not know what to make of all this. They looked bewildered, maybe a little frightened, their expressions mirroring his own reaction.

He wanted to ask if they had seen it, had seen the beast that had come to his tent, but he did not, because he knew they hadn't. The wolf had come for him and him alone, just like it always did.

But now it had to end. He could endure it no longer. There was a limit to how long a man could live with terror such as this, and Ottar had reached it.

"Tomorrow," Ottar said, and he hoped his words would carry some authority, but when he spoke his voice cracked and the one word came out weak and pitiful.

"Tomorrow, lord?" Ketil asked.

"Tomorrow it ends."

Chapter Thirty-Eight

A great dissension among the foreigners…
and they became dispersed
The Annals of Ulster

Thorgrim woke, groggy and sore in the middle of a field. The sun had not quite come up above the hills to the east, and the field and the country around were swathed in early-morning gray. The sky above might have been an unbroken dome of clouds or it might have been perfectly clear; it was hard to tell in that light.

Only part of the sky was visible to him. Most of Thorgrim's field of vision was taken up by Starri Deathless, who was shaking his arm and saying his name, over and over.

"All right, Starri, I hear you," Thorgrim said irritably as he pushed himself to a sitting position. The black mood had been on him the night before. He remembered that, and he was sure the others had sent Starri to wake him in case the mood was on him still.

"Listen," Starri said, cocking his head to one side and remaining silent for a few seconds. "Do you hear him?"

Thorgrim listened. He could hear something, or thought he could, but he was not entirely certain. "Someone yelling something," he ventured.

"Ha!" Starri said. "Yes. But not 'someone.' That great dung pile Ottar Bloodax! And he's calling for you. And you were not so easy to find, let me tell you. In the future I'd be grateful if you would pass out closer to the camp."

"I'll do my best," Thorgrim said and he stood, pressing his lips together to avoid groaning from the stiffness in his limbs. He straightened and looked around. He was in the middle of a great stretch of grassy country, with a smattering of woodlands to the east. A thin plume of smoke was rising straight up in the still air a couple hundred yards away near the trees.

He could better hear now that he was standing and facing the source of the noise. He could hear the clear cadence of a voice calling the same thing, over and over, though he still could not make out the words.

"Come, come," Starri said, and he indicated with a nod of his head that Thorgrim should follow him. The two of them set off through the knee-high grass toward the smoke and the sound of one man shouting.

A few minutes later they arrived in the camp, with its fire rings and iron pots hanging over the flames and the women bustling around and the men staggering here and there. It was as familiar now as a home in which one had lived for some time, and only the ground on which it was laid out seemed to change.

As Starri and Thorgrim came into the camp, the other men turned and a few nodded their greetings. There had been some talk among them of his wolf dreams and what they meant, Thorgrim could tell. He recognized the look.

I woke up on the same stinking patch of Irish sod I fell asleep on the night before, he thought to himself. *I went nowhere, nothing changed.* But he had long ago given up trying to explain that to anyone. Men would believe what they chose to believe.

Harald came hurrying over and he nodded toward the field beyond the camp. "Do you hear him, Father? He's been at it since before dawn."

Thorgrim frowned and turned his head toward the sound and wondered if his ears were going as quickly as the rest of him seemed to be. But no, he could hear it, and he could make out the words now. Two words. *Night Wolf.* Over and over. The voice of Ottar Bloodax, but there was an odd sound to it.

"Come," Thorgrim said. "Harald, Starri, Godi." He looked around. Cónán stood ten feet off, arms folded in a casual way. "Cónán, care to come with us?"

"Always up for a bit of fun," Cónán said, trying to sound as if he did not really care one way or another.

The five of them headed out in the direction of Ottar's voice. Harald walked at Thorgrim's side. "When we heard him, Father, we sent some men out to see what was going on. See if this was some sort of trap. They said Ottar was just up here, just around that stand of trees, alone in the middle of a field. None of his men with him. No weapons."

They rounded the patch of wood that Harald had indicated, pausing before they came out in the open. From where they stood they could see Ottar a couple hundred paces away. As Harald had said, he was standing alone in the middle of the open ground. The countryside stretched away for hundreds of yards in any direction before rising up to a series of hills beyond. There was no one else to be seen, just Ottar by himself.

"Night Wolf! Night Wolf!" he cried and his voice sounded as if it was near giving out.

Cónán stood at Thorgrim's side. "My men have been all around the country here," he offered. "Ottar's camp is a few miles off to the east. This is not a trap. There's no one but Ottar here; they're sure of it."

Thorgrim nodded. "And what of Kevin's horsemen?"

"Rode off yesterday," Cónán said. "After Ottar's men bloodied them up some, they headed for home. Once they find that Kevin's dead I don't reckon they'll have much fight left in them."

Thorgrim looked back at Ottar, standing alone in the field, calling for him. It was pathetic, really. There had to be some trick here, something he did not see. But he could not imagine what it was, and he could think of only one way to find out.

"Let's go talk to the man," he said. He headed off across the field and the others fell in behind him. They had not gone more than ten feet before Ottar saw them coming. He stopped yelling and stood perfectly still, watching their approach.

Thorgrim kept his eyes on the big man, waiting for him to make some move, pull a weapon, do something to suggest what he was about. But he did nothing. He just stood there and let them come closer.

Ten paces from Ottar, Thorgrim stopped. For a long moment they just looked at one another.

He looks bad, Thorgrim thought. It was the only word he could think of to describe Ottar's appearance. His hair was a tangled mess and there were bits of something—food, straw, leaves—in his long beard. The wicked scar on his face seemed to throb; it looked red and swollen in a way Thorgrim had not seen before.

But Ottar's expression was the worst of it. He looked broken. Frightened. Like a man who had given up, just given up.

"Yes, Ottar?" Thorgrim said at last.

Ottar did not reply, not right off. He squinted at Thorgrim and cocked his head, as if studying some curious thing. "You were abroad last night, but you were not…you," he said at last.

"I was asleep last night," Thorgrim said. "In my camp. Surrounded by these men." He jerked his thumb over his shoulder. That was not entirely accurate, of course. He had been off on his own, not surrounded by the others. But it was close enough to the truth for the likes of Ottar, accurate enough to serve as an answer to so strange a question.

"No matter," Ottar said, waving the question away like he was waving away a bee. "It's time for us to end this, Thorgrim Night Wolf. You and me. Time to end it."

Thorgrim nodded, though he had no idea what Ottar meant. Thorgrim had every intention of ending Ottar's rule of Vík-ló, and his life as well. That had been his plan since Glendalough. But Ottar seemed to be referring to something else. What, Thorgrim did not know.

"Yes, Ottar. That's why I came here," Thorgrim said.

At that Ottar seemed to brighten a bit, as if Thorgrim was granting him some favor. "A *hólmganga* then," Ottar said. "Tomorrow, when the sun is over the hill there. You and me."

Hólmganga. A duel, single combat, an organized fight to settle a difference, to end a feud. Two men would fight to first blood, and then if both parties agreed, the wounded man could pay off the other with three marks of silver and the affair was finished.

But that was not how it would end with Thorgrim and Ottar, that much was clear. Their hólmganga would not be over until one man's body lay bleeding and lifeless in the grass.

Thorgrim shook his head. "I didn't come here just to kill you," he said. "I came here to kill you and kill your men and drive whoever is left into the sea. To take back Vík-ló." And to his surprise, Ottar seemed to panic as he said those words.

"Vík-ló, then," Ottar said. "The man left alive will be Lord of Vík-ló."

"I will be left alive," Thorgrim said, "and you'll be dead. And then I'll still have to fight your men to take my longphort back."

Once again Ottar gave a dismissive wave of his hand. "Most of these swine have no loyalty to me. They'll join you, if you can kill me. Those few who are loyal, I'd ask you to let them sail off, if they choose. The other whores' sons can do as they wish."

Thorgrim considered this. If Ottar's words were true, they offered the simplest means of taking Vík-ló back. A battle would mean more of his own men dead. Nor was he at all certain the Irish bandits could stand up to Ottar's Norse warriors. But if the whole question came down to a fight between him and Ottar, then he did not have to worry about any of that.

"You say these things, Ottar," Thorgrim replied, "but how do I know that you speak for your men, and not just yourself?"

"I will send a delegation to you," Ottar said, a bit too quickly. "The captains of my ships, the lead men. Those men that the bastard Aghen didn't murder. They'll tell you."

"Very well. Send them today. And if I agree, I'll send word back with them."

An hour later they saw the delegation approaching over the grassy field, a dozen men walking straight for the camp.

"Ottar wastes no time, does he?" Starri said.

"No," Thorgrim said. The two of them, and nearly everyone else in the camp, were standing and watching their approach. "He's very eager for this, and I don't know why." He turned to Aghen, who was standing a few feet away. "Aghen, come with me," he said and the two of them walked out to meet Ottar's men.

The one heading the delegation was a man named Ketil and he threw a look of pure loathing at Aghen but addressed himself to Thorgrim alone. He more or less reiterated what Ottar had said. Some of Ottar's men would sail away. Some would likely join with Thorgrim. But they would not contest the rule of Vík-ló. That would be decided by the hólmganga, and nothing else.

"Give us a moment," Thorgrim said. He led Aghen back to the camp where the two of them and the other leaders gathered and talked.

"Do you believe him?" Thorgrim asked Aghen.

"Yes, I do," Aghen said. "Ottar has done nothing to make the men love him. If you kill him in the hólmganga then Ketil, I guess, will be their leader, and no one has respect for him, and they don't fear him like they do Ottar. They'll have no one to lead them in a fight to defend Vík-ló."

This made sense. The others agreed. Thorgrim returned to Ketil and the men of Ottar's delegation. "Tell Ottar he'll have his duel," he said. "Tomorrow, where we met before. Once the sun has cleared the hills."

Thorgrim had fought duels before, three of them, and two of them he had won. They had been fought to the point where first blood had dripped on the ground, as the law stated, and then the duel ransom had been paid. The reasons for those disputes had not been so great that they were worth killing for, or being killed. Thorgrim could not even recall why he had fought the first one.

But this fight would not end with a duel ransom. This was for the rule of Vík-ló, and the lives of the combatants.

A hólmganga was as far from a wild brawl as a fight could be. The rules were laid down by the law, and they would be obeyed, or the man who broke them would forfeit honor and likely his life.

There would be no mail, no helmets. Just a sword for each man and three shields apiece. Each man would have a second who would hold the shield for him and deflect the other combatant's blows. When the shields were battered to splinters there would be no more.

The question for Thorgrim, then, was who would serve as his second, who would hold his shield. There were several men, good men, from whom he might choose. Godi, big and strong as an oak tree was a logical choice, as was Starri Deathless, so quick and completely without fear. But really there was no choice at all. There was only one man there whom Thorgrim wanted at his side at that moment, only one in whom he believed entirely, and that was Harald Thorgrimson. Harald Broadarm. His boy.

The sun went down and Thorgrim ate and he went off on his own and lit a small fire in front of the little statue of Thor he carried with him. He prayed to the gods that he might be victorious, and prayed that if he was not, he would die well and the gods would continue to bless Harald and keep watch over all his people. Then he returned to camp and lay down and once again Failend came and lay down beside him. He slept deeply and he did not dream.

Chapter Thirty-Nine

"Here will you lie down
And breathe your last with me,'
Said the Hild of the rings.
Gisli Sursson's Saga

It was well before dawn when Thorgrim woke, and for some moments he lay there, motionless, feeling Failend's warm body pressed close to him and trying to recall what important thing was happening that day. And then he remembered, and he stood and worked the kinks out of his muscles.

No matter how early Thorgrim rose, it seemed the Irish women were always up before him, and now one of them approached with a bowl of water. Thorgrim nodded his thanks and rinsed his face and ran his fingers through his hair. He stepped over to the fire that was just gaining strength and savored the warmth of the flames, though the morning was not particularly cold.

Soon the others were stirring, and the smell of breakfast bubbling in the iron pots stole over the camp. They ate in silence, and then they donned mail and helmets and strapped on swords and hefted shields. They would go to the hólmganga ready for battle, if need be. All save for Thorgrim, who, if things went as planned, would be the only one among them who would actually fight.

The first gray light of dawn was showing itself in the east as they headed out of camp, Thorgrim's men and Cónán's men and Aghen and the men who had come with him, and the women as well. They made a long line as they snaked over the fields, Thorgrim in the lead, Harald, Godi, Starri, Aghen and Cónán all walking by his side like a house guard around their jarl.

Ottar's people were already at the dueling ground when they arrived, nearly two hundred men clustered around the two sides of the space marked out for the fight. They were not arrayed for battle but rather for the best view of the coming action. Their own fate, and not just that of

Thorgrim and Ottar, would be determined that morning. And beyond that, a hólmganga was always grand entertainment.

Thorgrim approached from the corner opposite Ottar's men. He looked over the fighting space. A wool cloak about eight feet square had been pegged to the ground. Around the perimeter of the cloak was a space three feet wide that was marked off at its outer edge by strings, known as hazel poles. The hazel poles were the limits of how far the combatant could go. Put one foot over the hazel pole and you were thought to be retreating. Two feet and you were running away.

As long as the seconds had usable shields, the fighting could take place in any part of the hazel pole square. Once the shields had been shattered, and it was sword against sword, all the fighting would take place on the cloak itself.

"This looks right," Thorgrim said to Harald, who was at his side. "Put the shields there," he added, indicating the corner nearest them. He looked up. The sky was growing lighter and he could see the cloud cover had broken up and the sky was all but clear. It would be a fine morning.

That's a good omen, he thought, but then he remembered that it would be a fine morning for Ottar as well as himself, and he was not sure how to read the sign.

"You'll stay mostly to this corner of the square?" Harald asked. He was nervous, Thorgrim could hear it in his voice, but he was not sure if the boy was afraid that his father would be killed or that he himself would do his part poorly and help bring that about. Both, Thorgrim guessed.

"I'll start out on this side," Thorgrim said. "It's where Ottar wants me. When the sun comes over the hill it will be in my eyes. That's why he laid the hazel poles out as he did. So I'll work around as we fight."

Harald opened his mouth to ask another question, but then Ottar's men began to part and Ottar himself came pushing through the crowd, a couple of men bearing his three shields following behind. He was dressed in a new tunic, a clean garment, and his hair and beard were combed.

"Thorgrim Night Wolf," he said as he stepped over the hazel pole. "You came. I wasn't sure you would. Thought I'd have to drag you out of bed, or out of whatever hole you were cowering in."

Thorgrim regarded the big man as Ottar told his second where to put the shields down. This was not the beaten, cowed, despairing Ottar of yesterday. This was Ottar as Thorgrim had come to know and despise him: arrogant, loud and insufferable.

What has happened with you? Thorgrim wondered. Was yesterday's attitude a ruse, a trick to get him to fight? No, Thorgrim did not think so. Ottar would know that a ruse was unnecessary, that Thorgrim was unlikely to refuse a challenge to a hólmganga.

And then Thorgrim realized that it was the hólmganga itself that had buoyed Ottar's spirits, the chance to fight and to end whatever it was that Ottar wished to end. Their rivalry, the rule of Vík-ló, the grudge Ottar had long borne him, Thorgrim did not know what it was, but Ottar was clearly glad for the chance to finish it, one way or another. That was why he had nearly panicked when Thorgrim wavered in his decision to fight this duel.

Thorgrim blinked as the edge of the sun broke free of the hill to the east, sending its brilliant light over the country around them and the hazel pole square at their feet.

"I'm here, Ottar," Thorgrim said at last. "So let's get on with it. I'm hungry and I wish to have breakfast in my hall at Vík-ló."

Ottar laughed at that. "And you'll die hungry, you pathetic shit! I would say you'll have your next meal in Odin's corpse hall, but miserable cowards the likes of you don't go there. And if they eat in Niflheim, I don't know. Whatever they feed on there, it will be good enough for such as you!"

Behind him his men laughed, but not all of them, not nearly all of them, and the laugher did not sound as genuine as Ottar might have wished.

"Come along, Ottar," Thorgrim said, stepping toward the edge of the cloak. "All you've ever been able to do is talk, like some old woman. That and watch while your men die. Let's see if you even know how to do anything else."

Ottar stepped forward too, and by his side was his second, a big man, nearly as big as Ottar himself.

Good choice for a second… Thorgrim looked the man up and down, taking his measure. He did not look fast and he did not look smart. *You're doing me a favor, Ottar,* he thought.

Thorgrim unbuckled his sword belt, drew Iron-tooth, and tossed the scabbard and belt aside. There was no need for that encumbrance during the hólmganga. And when it was over he would have all the time he needed to buckle it on once more, or else he would never have the need to again.

"All right, Harald, you know what you're about, here?" Thorgrim asked, and Harald nodded. He was standing at Thorgrim's left side, one of the three shields in hand. The nervousness was still there, Thorgrim could see it, but the boy was calmer now. The waiting was always the worst of it. Once the sword blows began, Thorgrim knew that his son would do what needed doing.

"Listen here," Thorgrim said to Harald, speaking softly, too soft to be heard by any of the others. "I picked you to be my second because there's none I trust more, and no one who can do this work better than you. If I'm killed, it will be the doing of the gods, not you. You'll have done your best and no blame should ever fall on you. And by that I mean you should never blame yourself. Do you understand?"

Harald nodded. Thorgrim put his hand on the boy's shoulder and squeezed it softly. "If I die, I die with honor," he said, "and I'll wait for you in the corpse hall."

Harald nodded again. Thorgrim could see he did not dare speak.

Then Ottar's voice roared from the other side of the cloak. "If you are done with your goodbyes there, Night Pup, let us get on with it."

Thorgrim stepped forward, stepped onto the cloak, facing Ottar, Harald at his side. "I challenged you, Night Pup," Ottar said, "so you may strike first. You had best kill me with this blow. It's the only chance you'll get."

That was how the hólmganga was fought. Blow for blow, with the seconds deflecting the attacks until one man was wounded or dead, or the shields were all shattered. And then it was weapons alone on the confines of the eight-foot square cloak.

Thorgrim stepped forward and to his right, shifting around so the sun was not directly in his eyes, until he was within striking distance of Ottar. Ottar's second, like Harald, was on his man's left-hand side where he would not interfere with Ottar's sword arm. He held the shield partway up, taking a half step closer to Ottar as Thorgrim approached.

Then Thorgrim brought Iron-tooth back over his shoulder and chopped down, an awkward strike at Ottar's head. The second raised the shield and took the blow on the painted wooden surface, leaving a deep cut in one of the boards. Ottar laughed at the weak effort, but Thorgrim was not bothered by that. He had never intended to strike Ottar. He wanted instead to gauge the speed and skill of the second, to understand how best to get past the shield.

Harald was braced for the return blow, his shield held ready, but the blow did not come, not at first. Instead, Ottar took a step back and he lowered his sword and looked Thorgrim in the eye.

"You know, Night Wolf," Ottar said, and his tone was more formal, less mocking than it had been. "Before you die, you should know why you're going to die. So I'll tell you. And the funny thing is, it's not even about you. Not really." He paused, as if getting his thoughts straight in his head, then went on.

"There's only one man I have ever been frightened of, in all my life. Only one man who scared me so much I shit myself sometimes just to hear him coming. This was years ago, mind you. And that man was my father.

"He was a big bastard. So big he makes me look like a child. And mean. Meanest son of a whore I ever knew. That anyone ever knew. Everyone in our village was scared of him. Terrified, and with good reason.

It didn't seem he could be killed, not ever hurt. But do you know how he died?"

"Did you bore him to death with all your talk?" Thorgrim asked and to his surprise Ottar actually smiled at that.

"No, Night Pup. He was killed by a wolf. Out in the forest. Maybe several wolves, I don't know. I saw his body. I was…ten years old? They made a mess of him. Ripped him apart. And I always figured that it couldn't have been a real wolf, not a flesh-and-blood wolf, because no flesh and blood wolf could have killed that bastard. So I reckoned it was something else, something from the gods, some spirit of the forest, maybe. And I figured if this thing came for him, it would come for me, too. All my life I've waited for the wolf to come for me.

"And then I meet you, and you're not afraid of me, though you should be. And they call you Night Wolf. And they say…things about you. About what you are. And part of me might have believed it. But no more. I don't believe it any more. It's not true, what they say. And so now I must kill you, so I can end these thoughts I have about you and the things they say about you. I have to kill you so I can show everyone that you are just a weak and pitiful man."

Thorgrim nodded. He could hear the change in Ottar's voice as the man talked. The more words that came from his mouth, the more he sounded as if he was trying to convince himself that he was speaking the truth.

"You say you want to kill me, Ottar, but still you just talk and talk," Thorgrim said. "Do you not have the courage to actually fight?"

Those words seemed to have struck their mark. Ottar frowned as he came forward, readjusting the grip on his sword. He shot a quick glance at Harald and a bit of a smile played over his lips.

Thorgrim looked to his left, toward his son, a darting glance. Harald's eyes were wide in fright and he held the shield awkwardly, as if he was as likely to drop it as hold it up in front of Ottar's blade.

Thorgrim forced himself to look grim, despite his wanting to smile. Harald might have been nervous before, but now he was perfectly calm. The look of terror on his face was a sham, designed to lure Ottar into thinking this would be easy. And it worked.

Ottar lifted his sword, cutting straight down as Thorgrim had done. Then, with the blade in motion, he twisted his arm to send the attack in low, to get under Harald's shield, to slash Thorgrim's belly or his legs. And Harald followed the move with ease, slamming the shield down on Ottar's blade and knocking it nearly to the ground as Thorgrim leapt forward, thrusting too fast for Ottar's second to react.

The tip of the blade ripped through Ottar's tunic and Thorgrim felt it bite flesh. Ottar bellowed and leapt back as his second brought the shield up in time to knock Iron-tooth aside, but too late to stop it from delivering a shallow but painful wound.

"Idiot!" Ottar yelled and cuffed his second on the side of the head, hard enough to knock the man nearly off balance. Thorgrim and Harald took a step back, watching and waiting. Thorgrim had struck the last blow. Now it was Ottar's turn and there was nothing Thorgrim could do but brace for it.

Ottar stepped to his left, hoping to bring Thorgrim around so the sun was once again in his eyes, but Thorgrim did not move, so Ottar stepped up quick and brought his sword down hard, no subtlety this time, just a powerful blow at Thorgrim's head.

Harald raised the shield and caught the blow, but the force of it jarred his arms and the sound of steel hitting wood was mixed with the sound of wood splintering under the impact. Ottar stepped back, his second close by in case Thorgrim tried his fast reposte once more, but Thorgrim remained where he was. He and Harald looked at the shield. The center board was buckled and cracked.

"That will be good for one more blow," Thorgrim said. When it came to shattering shields, Ottar with his great strength would have an advantage. But Thorgrim knew he would have to match Ottar shield for shield if he hoped to live through the morning.

"Come on," he said and they stepped back onto the cloak. Thorgrim had a pretty good idea that once he struck at Ottar, Ottar would try a fast counterstrike, and he hoped Harald was ready for it.

Let's be rid of that shield, Ottar, Thorgrim thought. He slashed down hard, hitting Ottar's shield with a powerful blow, nearly as powerful as Ottar's had been. He saw the wood on the face of the shield crack and then, as he had guessed, Ottar was on them, clubbing down with his sword, striking the face of the shield Harald held aloft and shattering it.

But Thorgrim did not hesitate. He darted forward, leading with Iron-tooth. Ottar's second was there, shield in front. Thorgrim drove Iron-tooth's tip into the broken board and levered it sideways, praying to the gods that the blade did not break. But Iron-tooth was a well forged weapon, blessed by the gods, and rather than breaking the blade, the leverage tore Ottar's shield apart.

The four men stood on the cloak, breathing hard, the shields in the hands of the seconds no more than shattered wrecks. The blood from Ottar's wound was spreading over his tunic. Thorgrim looked down. There were splatters of blood on the cloak on which they stood. That, according to the law, meant that the duel could have ended there. But no one suggested they end it, and no one would.

Harald and Ottar's second tossed the ruined shields away and took up fresh ones and returned to the combatants' sides. Thorgrim pointed to Ottar with the tip of his sword.

"Your stroke, Ottar, if your wound isn't hurting you too much," he said. Ottar did not smile, did not respond to the ribbing. The wound was no doubt causing considerable pain, but more than that, it would have shaken Ottar's confidence, an even greater advantage. He stepped up and swung his sword hard, a sideways blow that Harald deflected. Thorgrim went next, stepping forward with two quick steps before Ottar had even brought his sword arm back, striking Ottar's shield, knocking the second off balance.

But Ottar was there again, just as fast, and Harald barely had time to get the shield in front of Ottar's weapon. *Bang, bang, bang.* Six blows in quick succession, the shields suffering from the impact of strong blades wielded by strong arms. Ottar and Thorgrim stepped back at the same time, heaving for breath, their seconds doing the same.

Then Ottar, still winded, came at Thorgrim again, taking Thorgrim and Harald by surprise, a fast, bold move. He slashed low and Harald brought the shield down quick but not quick or low enough. The tip of Ottar's blade scythed under the edge of the shield and Thorgrim felt it rip across his shins, a dull pain, like being hit with a club. And then an instant later came the sharp agony of rent flesh, the warm spurt of blood.

Ottar had moved so fast his second failed to keep at his side. Thorgrim lunged and his sword found Ottar's left shoulder, the tip sinking an inch deep. Ottar bellowed and swung his arm around and knocked the blade free. If it had been Ottar's right shoulder, and if Thorgrim had not been slowed by his own wound, the hólmganga might have ended there. But in truth the wound to Ottar's shoulder was a minor thing. The wounds to Thorgrim's legs were not.

Thorgrim staggered back. He could feel the blood running down his shins and soaking into his leggings. He looked at Harald and Harald was looking at him with horror and shame and anger and Thorgrim shook his head, hoping to convey what he was thinking. *Not your fault, not your fault.*

He took a step forward, gritting his teeth, trying not to show the pain because he did not want Harald or Ottar to see it. Ottar was gasping for breath now, head back. It was his turn to strike a blow and he was drawing it out, using the moment to suck air into his lungs. Then a growl built in his throat and as it lifted in volume he came forward, sword up, and his second was at his side.

Ottar was shouting in rage when he reached Thorgrim and Thorgrim was shouting as well and once again the blows hammered down, sword, shield, sword, shield, all nuance abandoned in their mutual fury. And then they staggered apart once more, and the shields, which had borne the brunt of the attacks, were no more than ruins in the seconds' hands.

Both Harald and Ottar's man took their time in discarding the broken shields and taking up the last of the three. They were sweating, red-faced and breathing hard, but the men for whom they held the shields were in worse shape yet.

Thorgrim was grateful for the brief chance to breathe and let his arms fall at his sides. He could feel the blood running into his shoes now, and the pain was like a burning brand pressed to his legs. But the blood on Ottar's tunic, at his side and shoulder, was spreading. Thorgrim could see that Ottar, too, was fighting to not show pain, which meant he must have pain in abundance.

I need to end this soon, Thorgrim thought. It would come down to which of them had greater endurance, which was least wounded, and he did not know the answer.

Then Harald was at his side once more, the last shield in his hand, and Ottar's second was also in place. The next strike was Ottar's and he circled in, moving forward and sideways, trying to work Thorgrim around so the sun was in his eyes. And this time Thorgrim obliged him, turning as Ottar turned until the sun was full in his face.

Ottar stepped up and made a powerful stroke, right at Thorgrim's head, coming in high and sideways. Harald raised the shield up to catch the sword, but Thorgrim was moving even before Harald had the shield in place. He ducked low, under Ottar's sword, under the edge of the shield, and launched himself forward. He came down, shoulder on the cloak, rolled, and used the momentum to his regain his feet, now at Ottar's back.

Thorgrim shouted in pain as the weight came on his wounded legs. He heard Ottar bellow with rage as he spun around, too fast for his second to follow, and the brilliant sun hit him in the face like a solid thing. Ottar squinted and threw up his arm to shield his eyes and Thorgrim thrust. Iron-tooth caught Ottar's neck just as Ottar realized his mistake and tried to jump clear.

The blood was bright welling up from the wound, and it stood out dark against Ottar's blonde beard. But Thorgrim had not killed him; he had done no more than goad the bull. Ottar shouted again and slashed at Thorgrim, but the sun was still in his eyes. Thorgrim turned the weapon aside and thrust again, and with his left arm Ottar managed to knock the blade out of line.

Harald rushed up to take his place, having recovered from the quick shift in the men's positions, and Ottar's second did the same. Then Ottar stepped up and raised his sword over his head, holding it in a two-handed grip, and brought it smashing down on the shield Harald held aloft.

There was only one purpose to such a blow, and that was to shatter Thorgrim's one remaining shield, and in that Ottar was utterly effective. The power on his striking sword forced Harald halfway to his knees, and with a rending sound the shield burst into its component boards, leaving Harald gripping the iron boss to which clung a few broken bits of wood.

Thorgrim did not hesitate. He stepped in and thrust, but Ottar's second was there and Iron-tooth bounced off the flat surface of the shield. Then Ottar struck again and Thorgrim was just able to turn the sword aside.

Shield…Ottar's shield… Thorgrim thought stupidly, his mind clouded with exhaustion. He had to destroy Ottar's last shield. Then, with weapons alone, he might use skill and speed to overcome Ottar's brute force. He stepped up and slammed Iron-tooth down on the face of the shield, felt the wood give, then stepped quickly back and to his left, putting Ottar's second between him and Ottar just as Ottar tried for a killing stroke.

"Idiot!" Ottar roared as he stumbled against the man who held his shield. He stepped back and once again struck his second on the side of the head. The man staggered under the blow and Thorgrim thrust and once again found Ottar's left shoulder, driving the point in at nearly the same place he had wounded him before.

"Bastard!" Ottar roared. With the blood running bright though his beard and staining the front of his tunic, his eyes wild, his mouth hanging open, he looked like the madman he was. His second came hurrying back to his side, but Ottar hit him again and jerked the shield from his hands and tossed it away.

"Come, Night Wolf!" Ottar screamed, his voice nearing hysterical. "Kill me, or let me kill you!" He slashed at Thorgrim, and Thorgrim parried the blow, their swords ringing out like bells in the morning air. Then Thorgrim slid Iron-tooth forward and thrust once more, but this time Ottar leapt back, clear of the attack.

With shields gone, so too was the need for an orderly exchange of blows. It was a brawl now, and the fight would go to the fastest and most skilled blade, or the luckiest. The two men circled one another, stepping around the perimeter of the cloak, eyes holding eyes, blades ready. Ottar lunged and Thorgrim parried and lunged in return. Ottar tried to knock the blade aside with his left forearm, but Iron-tooth tore through his sleeve and Thorgrim could feel the weapon's edge ripping through flesh and scraping bone.

He expected Ottar to scream, to jerk his arm away, but instead Ottar did the one thing that Thorgrim did not expect at all: he stepped forward and kicked Thorgrim hard in his wounded shins.

The pain shot through Thorgrim's legs and into his gut and he felt his knees buckle under him. He shouted with the agony of it, despite himself, and fell to the cloak, coming down on hands and knees, Iron-tooth slipping from his grasp.

Take up the sword, take up the sword! he thought, his mind in a desperate panic. In the next instant Ottar would deliver the killing blow and he could not die without a weapon in his hand. He had to reach the corpse hall. He had promised Harald he would wait for him there.

Thorgrim looked up. Ottar was looming over him, sword raised above his head, nothing but air between the blade and Thorgrim's skull. A look of triumph was already showing on his face as their eyes met. Thorgrim wanted to curse him, to die with defiance on his lips. He opened his mouth, but the words did not come. In their stead came a growl, deep and guttural.

It was a savage sound, a feral sound. Where it came from Thorgrim did not know. It came from his bowels, it came from his soul, it vibrated in the morning air. And Ottar froze, sword over his head. His eyes went wide and the look of triumph dissolved into terror and he backed away fast, step by step, until he was off the cloak then over the hazel pole.

And there he stopped, realizing what he had done, stepping out of the square. A murmur ran through the watching men, a low, ugly noise. Ottar looked side to side, the terror gone, humiliation in its place. He lifted his sword once again and bellowed his wounded bull bellow and charged over the hazel pole, running at Thorgrim who was still on hands and knees on the cloak.

Thorgrim's hand lashed out and his fingers wrapped around Iron-tooth's grip. He was aware of the burning agony in his legs, but the pain seemed unreal somehow. He pushed up with his arms, pushed off with his feet, and launched himself into the air like an animal leaping at its prey, Iron-tooth held straight out in front of him.

He leapt just as Ottar came onto the cloak with sword raised, and he struck with the force of their combined momentum. Iron-tooth's point hit Ottar in the chest and kept going without the slighted hesitation, ripping out the big man's back and stopping only when the cross guard fetched up against Ottar's body.

The two of them slammed into one another, the impact engulfing Thorgrim in a wave of agony, and they went down in a heap. Iron-tooth slipped from Thorgrim's grip once again and his every instinct cried for him to get the weapon back in hand. He rolled to the side, came up on his feet, his knees nearly buckling again with the burning pain in his legs.

Iron-tooth was standing upright just in front of him and he grabbed the hilt and pulled, and only then did he realize that it was upright because it was sticking up from Ottar's chest.

Thorgrim held the blade at his side, the blood bright on the steel and dripping on the cloak at his feet. He looked down at Ottar. His eyes were wide and stared unblinking at the sky above. The blood was spreading over his new tunic, a great swath where Iron-tooth had gone through his heart, and lesser pools of blood where he had been wounded in the shoulder and the side.

Thorgrim took a small, staggering step and he heard the blood in his shoes making a liquid sound. He thought he might collapse again, but then Harald was there at his side, holding him up, and Starri Deathless was on the other side, and the hazel pole square was filling with men coming forward.

He looked up at the sky overhead. It was blue, a thing he had not seen in a long time. He felt the sun warm on his face. It was an omen. A good omen. And now he knew it was an omen that the gods had meant for him.

Epilogue

"And here, my warrior,
You will rule over all this wealth
And have dominion over me,
And we will have riches
Beyond gold's measure."
Sisli Sursson's Saga

The men-at-arms had had enough. Lochlánn could see that just in the way they rode, the way they held their weapons. From the moment they first sallied out of Ráth Naoi things had not gone well, and they had only gotten worse from there. They had driven the Irish and the heathens over the countryside, had come to what they thought was the triumphant end of a long chase when they had run headlong into Ottar's shieldwall.

They had behaved like warriors, and Lochlánn was proud of his men, and Niall's as well, but they had been disorganized and worn out after the lengthy pursuit. They gathered as best they could, charged the heathens, taken some down with their long spears. But they were tired and their mounts were tired and the heathens were ready for them, fresh and eager for a fight. It had not lasted all that long, in the end.

The horsemen had been driven back, then driven back again, and then one of Kevin's men had blown a horn, the note long and loud as it sounded over the field of battle. Lochlánn did not know what the horn meant, but he had a good idea, and when the men under Niall's command began to retreat, and quickly, he knew he was right.

"Back! Everyone back!" Lochlánn shouted, riding back and forth across the field, calling to his own warriors. "Senach, get the men back! We'll meet up on that hill yonder!"

Once he had his own men in motion, Lochlánn wheeled his horse and rode after them, leaving the jeering heathens behind. Down the sloping hill and then up the other side, where Niall's horsemen were milling around. Lochlánn rode up to the high ground, pulled his horse to a stop, and turned. The heathens were lining the crest of the hill they had just abandoned, but they showed no inclination to keep coming. The hour was late and the heathens doing battle on foot would have a hard time pursuing, and a more difficult time attacking once the riders were able to organize. The fighting for that day was over.

Lochlánn looked around at the men slumping on their horses, their near-dead expressions. Senach's face was smeared with blood and his arm was hanging limp from a wound in the shoulder, and the men around him did not look much better. There was no fight left in them, and Lochlánn knew the fighting was over not just for that day but for the foreseeable future.

Louis de Roumois came riding up and reined his horse to a stop at Lochlánn's side. There was a rent in his mail shirt and his tunic under the mail was torn and bloody. For a moment he just sat, wide-eyed and trying to catch his breath. Then he said one word.

"Niall?"

Lochlánn frowned and looked around, but he could not see Niall anywhere. "Echach," he called to one of the men-at-arms from Ráth Naoi. "Where is Niall?"

Echach looked stunned, but he shook his head and then said, "Killed. In the second charge. Spear through the heart."

Lochlánn felt sick. He liked Niall and had come to respect him. He respected the man's courage, and he had no doubt that it was that courage that had gotten him killed. And that made him think of Kevin mac Lugaed, safe back at the ringfort. His proper place was here, at the head of his men. It should have been him dying in the grass, not Niall.

I might just kill that coward myself, Lochlánn mused.

"There's nothing more for us to do here," Louis said, breaking in on his thoughts. "The men are spent, the horses are spent. We must ride back to the ringfort and make our plans there."

Lochlánn knew that Louis was right, but the rage born of the day's events was still boiling in him and his anger and suspicion with Louis had not dissipated. In fact, it had only become worse with Louis's haughty behavior and his ingratiating himself with Kevin and Niall. But now Niall was dead and Kevin probably would be soon, once Ottar reached Ráth Naoi, and Lochlánn had had enough.

"Do not tell me what we must do, you Frankish whore's son," Lochlánn said. "You're still my prisoner, pray do not forget that. Once we've resolved all this we'll be going back to Glendalough and there you can explain yourself in a law court."

And that was all he had to say to Louis de Roumois. He reined his horse over, called an order to the men, and in a long and weary line they rode back to the ringfort at Ráth Naoi.

There was no smoke they could see rising from the gable end of the hall as they crossed the open pastureland that surrounded the ringfort. No men on the walls. Nothing moving. It was not until they reached the big gate that they saw someone at last, one of the handful of men-at-arms who had stayed behind to guard the place. He was standing by the palisade, right above the gate, waiting for the riders to approach. He seemed to be weary and holding himself up with his spear.

Lochlánn stopped ten paces from the gate. He expected it to swing open, but it did not. He looked up at the man on the wall.

"Will you open the gate?" he asked.

The man looked down to the ground behind him. He looked left and right. There was apparently no one there to open the gate. Echach rode up to Lochlánn's right side.

"You've seen us coming for a mile at least," he said. "Did you not think to open the gate? Kevin mac Lugaed will hear of this, depend on it."

"Kevin mac Lugaed's dead," the guard said. "And Eoin."

"Dead?" Echach asked.

"Dead. Killed by the heathens."

Echach and Lochlánn exchanged glances. "Where are the heathens now?" Lochlánn demanded.

The man on the wall shrugged. "I don't know. Run off? They aren't here."

"Well, damn you, open the gate now!" Echach said with greater volume and urgency.

"There's nothing left," the man on the wall said. "The rest of them, the other men-at-arms, they looted this place clean. All Kevin's hoard, clothes, weapons. They loaded it all on carts and then they were gone, off to the north."

Echach looked to the north, as if he might see the others riding off with the wealth of Ráth Naoi. Then he looked to the east as if he might see Ottar's heathens coming up over the hill. He turned to his men, the remnants of Kevin's mercenary army. "Off to the north, then," he called. "We'll have to ride hard."

"What?" Lochlánn said. "Where are you going?"

"You heard what he said," Echach replied, nodding toward the guard on the wall. "Bastards plundered the place and now they think they can ride off and keep it all for themselves. Not if I can help it."

"But the heathens, they'll be coming this way," Lochlánn said, and even as he said it he realized how ridiculous it sounded.

"Another good reason for us to ride north," Echach said. "No one's paying us to fight heathens now." With that he turned his horse to the north and kicked his heels into its flanks. The tired beast managed to work itself up to a trot, and the rest of the late Kevin mac Lugaed's men rode after him.

Lochlánn looked to his left, where Senach was sitting his horse. "No point in us staying," Senach said. "Even if the men weren't ready to drop in their tracks, we couldn't beat the heathens on our own."

He was right, and Lochlánn knew it. It was over. The hunt, the fighting. They had come within a hair's breadth of finishing the work begun at Glendalough, but in the end that achievement had been snatched from them.

Then Lochlánn recalled that there was one thing they could still accomplish, one important issue they might yet resolve. He looked around at the gathered men. He looked again, his eyes sweeping from man to man, his panic growing as he searched their faces.

"Senach," he said, "where the hell is Louis de Roumois?"

Louis de Roumois was about four miles to the north of Ráth Naoi. He had been riding hard, but he could see that his horse might well die of exhaustion, might drop dead right under him as he rode. He had seen that before, had even had two of his own mounts die that way.

The difference now was the degree of trouble he would be in if that were to happen. The chances of his getting another horse in that country—a place that so many considered a land blessed by God, but one he was sure was cursed—were practically nonexistent.

So he slowed his horse to a walk and looked back over his shoulder and saw nothing that he did not expect to see. There were fields and stands of trees and birds circling high overhead. There were a few faint columns of smoke on the horizon. There were no shield-bearing heathens, no horsemen riding hard in hopes of running him to ground.

Seeing that, he reined the horse to a stop and swung himself down to the ground. The horse stood there, too tired even to eat, and Louis stretched and worked the kinks out of his muscles. He looked around. He had only the vaguest notion of where he was.

Getting clear of Lochlánn and the rest had been easy enough. Defeated men, exhausted men were not terribly vigilant as a rule. Lochlánn, conscientious leader that he was, would always insist on riding at the head of the column, and Senach could be counted on to ride at Lochlánn's side. Louis had slowed his pace as he rode, and slowed it some more, falling back so gradually that no one took any notice.

Finally he was at the end of the column and it was just Kevin's men around him and they did not give a tinker's damn what Louis did. They were passing the stretch of woods by the pond when Louis told the man beside him that his horse had picked up a stone in its shoe and he had to stop and clear it. The man only shrugged and said nothing, as if wondering why Louis thought he would care.

So Louis stopped and dismounted and lifted his horse's foot to clear the imaginary stone and the column of riders moved on without him. And then he mounted again and walked his horse toward the woods and disappeared from the view of the other horsemen. He waited until they were up and over the crest of the far hill before riding hard in the opposite direction.

And now, for the first time in a very, very long time, he was alone. No monastery, no men-at-arms, no Failend, no heathens, no Irish bandits. Just him and his horse. He sighed and ran his eyes over the great green empty country around him.

He was alone, but he was not without resources. In the night, at the ringfort at Ráth Naoi, he had managed to get to Lochlánn's saddlebag and withdraw the small silver chest that had once belonged to Colman and then, after Colman's untimely and unnatural death, had passed to Failend and now to him.

Louis felt no guilt about that. The heathens were the enemy of mankind. He had fought them in Frankia and now he had fought them in Ireland. They were doing Satan's work, and Failend had joined them, and that, to Louis's mind, meant she forfeited anything of worth. Particularly as this silver, if it had stayed with her, would most likely have found its way into the hands of Thorgrim Night Wolf.

So Louis had his horse and he had his silver hoard. He had his sword and his considerable skill and experience in the use of it. He had his courage and his wits. If he kept on in the direction he was riding he was pretty sure he would find his way to Dubh-linn.

Dubh-linn. This whole country of Ireland was nothing but a smattering of ringforts and the seats of ridiculous puffed up farmers who thought themselves minor kings. There was nothing like the cities he knew in Frankia and Frisia. He had never been to Dubh-linn, but as he understood it, it was the only city of any note in all of Ireland, and it had taken the heathens to build it.

There was one thing he hoped to find in Dubh-linn, one thing he thought it likely he would find, and that was a ship. The Northmen sailed their vessels of war, their longships, to that place, but there were merchants there as well, tubby ships from the lands of the Saxons and the Picts, and from lands further over the seas. There was money to be made in Ireland and that brought the ships and the merchants as well as the raiders and the slavers. And there Louis hoped to find passage back to his home, back to Frankia. He had debts to settle and they would be settled with blood. It was the coin in which his brother would pay.

Louis put his foot in the stirrup. He hoisted himself up into the saddle and turned his horse's head north once again, toward Dubh-linn, toward Roumois, toward home.

There were over a hundred men and two dozen women in the army that Thorgrim Night Wolf had accumulated since shoving *Sea Hammer* back into the Avonmore River at Glendalough. Now, with the Northmen who had served Ottar and now chose to serve him, he had another seventy five or so.

The rest, who made up the crews of two ships, had been given leave to return to Vík-ló, to put to sea and sail off to anywhere they wished. It was the agreement he had made with Ottar and he meant to honor it. Thorgrim also gave them leave to take Ottar's body so they could send Ottar off with a proper funeral.

For all the good it will do that miserable bastard, he thought.

It was an impressive number of men and women making for Vík-ló, but there were just two dozen horses, and most of those were carrying camp equipment and supplies, and one was bearing Ottar's stiffening corpse. Under normal circumstances Thorgrim would never have ridden when everyone else was forced to walk, but these were not normal circumstances. On foot he could not have made it half a mile.

While Ottar was still bleeding out on the cloak, Harald and Starri and Godi had lifted Thorgrim and carried him off and laid him on the grass. They cut his leggings away and Harald had called for Failend, self-proclaimed Irish healer, to come and tend to his wounds. As Failend stood there, wide-eyed, muttering something, Cara pushed past with her basket and expertly dressed the deep slashes that Ottar's blade had made in Thorgrim's legs.

With his wounds dressed and his shins cleaned of blood and his blood-soaked shoes removed, Thorgrim was lifted to his feet, wincing as he took his own weight. They brought a horse around and helped him up in the saddle and the whole strange parade headed off in the direction of Vík-ló.

In the many times that Thorgrim had come or gone from the longphort it had nearly always been by sea. He realized, as the brown walls of the earthworks and the high palisade hove into view that he had only seen the place from the land side on a few occasions.

Strange, he thought and he wondered what this meant. He had not been in Vík-ló so very long, he concluded, not long enough to have seen it from every angle. It was not his home. His farm in East Agder in Norway, that was his home. Vík-ló was a temporary thing, and soon, soon, the gods would let him return to his real home. Or so he prayed.

As they approached, the gate swung open as if by magic, like arms spread in welcome. Thorgrim walked his horse down the trampled road that ran through the heavy oak doors and into the longphort. Now things began to fall into place, sights as familiar to him as Iron-tooth or the slightly bewildered look on Harald's face. His hall, and the hall that belonged to Bersi, dead at Glendalough. The houses, the bakery, Mar's smithy, the rise of ground that hid the river from view. Places where men had lived and men had died.

There was a great scorched place just outside his hall where Ottar had burned Valgerd alive. Aghen had told him the story.

Starri was next to him now, looking up at him. "You're not home, Night Wolf. Don't think that," he said.

"No," Thorgrim agreed. Starri understood. This was not home. But where was home? Norway? East Agder? The sea? All of Midgard?

Starri Deathless knew where his home was—Valhalla, Odin's corpse hall. And like Thorgrim struggling and failing to return to his farm, so Starri struggled and prayed and fought to reach that place.

And maybe he was right to do so; maybe the mad berserker alone among all of them understood what this struggle was about. Valhalla. It was the one place they knew they might reach, the one place where they knew they would be welcome, where they would be happy until the coming of Ragnarok.

Maybe that was the home they sought. Maybe that was the only real home they would ever find.

Would you like a heads-up about new titles in The Norsemen Saga, as well as preview sample chapters and other good stuff cheap (actually free)?

Visit our web site to sign up for our (occasional) e-mail newsletter:

www.jameslnelson.com

Other books in *The Norsemen Saga*:

Glossary

adze – a tool much like an ax but with the blade set at a right angle to the handle.

Ægir – Norse god of the sea. In Norse mythology he was also the host of great feasts for the gods.

Asgard - the dwelling place of the Norse gods and goddesses, essentially the Norse heaven.

athwartships – at a right angle to the centerline of a vessel.

beitass- a wooden pole, or spar, secured to the side of a ship on the after end and leading forward to which the corner, or clew, of a sail could be secured.

berserker - a Viking warrior able to work himself up into a frenzy of blood-lust before a battle. The berserkers, near psychopathic killers in battle, were the fiercest of the Viking soldiers. The word berserker comes from the Norse for "bear shirt" and is the origin of the modern English "berserk."

boss - the round, iron centerpiece of a wooden shield. The boss formed an iron cup protruding from the front of the shield, providing a hollow in the back across which ran the hand grip.

bothach – Gaelic term for poor tenant farmers, serfs

brace - line used for hauling a **yard** side to side on a horizontal plane. Used to adjust the angle of the sail to the wind.

brat – a rectangular cloth worn in various configurations as an outer garment over a *leine.*

bride-price - money paid by the family of the groom to the family of the bride.

byrdingr - A smaller ocean-going cargo vessel used by the Norsemen for trade and transportation. Generally about 40 feet in length, the byrdingr was a smaller version of the more well-known *knarr.*

clench nail – a type of nail that, after being driven through a board, has a type of washer called a rove placed over the end and is then bent over to secure it in place.

curach - a boat, unique to Ireland, made of a wood frame covered in hide. They ranged in size, the largest propelled by sail and capable of carrying several tons. The most common sea-going craft of mediaeval Ireland. **Curach** was the Gaelic word for boat, which later became the word

curragh.
derbfine – In Irish law, a family of four generations, including a man, his sons, grandsons and great grandsons.
dragon ship - the largest of the Viking warships, upwards of 160 feet long and able to carry as many as 300 men. Dragon ships were the flagships of the fleet, the ships of kings.
dubh gall - Gaelic term for Vikings of Danish descent. It means Black Strangers, a reference to the mail armor they wore, made dark by the oil used to preserve it. *See* ***fin gall.***
ell – a unit of length, a little more than a yard.
eyrir – Scandinavian unit of measurement, approximately an ounce.
félag – a fellowship of men who owed each other a mutual obligation, such as multiple owners of a ship, or a band or warriors who had sworn allegiance to one another.
fin gall - Gaelic term for Vikings of Norwegian descent. It means White Strangers. *See* ***dubh gall.***
Freya - Norse goddess of beauty and love, she was also associated with warriors, as many of the Norse deity were. Freya often led the **Valkyrie** to the battlefield.
halyard - a line by which a sail or a yard is raised.
gallows – tall, T-shaped posts on the ship's centerline, forward of the mast, on which the oars and yard were stored when not in use.
gunnel – the upper edge of a ship's side.
Hel - in Norse mythology, the daughter of Loki and the ruler of the underworld where those who are not raised up to Valhalla are sent to suffer. The same name, Hel, is given to the realm over which she rules, the Norse hell.
hird - an elite corps of Viking warriors hired and maintained by a king or a powerful jarl. Unlike most Viking warrior groups, which would assemble and disperse at will, the hird was retained as a semi-permanent force which formed the core of a Viking army.
hirdsman - a warrior who is a member of the **hird**.
hólmganga – a formal, organized duel fought in a marked-off area between two men.
jarl - title given to a man of high rank. A jarl might be an independent ruler or subordinate to a king. Jarl is the origin of the English word *earl.*
Jörmungandr – in Norse mythology, a vast sea serpent that surrounds the earth, grasping its own tail.
knarr - a Norse merchant vessel. Smaller, wider and sturdier than the longship, knarrs were the workhorse of Norse trade, carrying cargo and settlers wherever the Norsemen traveled.
league – a distance of three miles.
leech – either one of the two vertical edges of a square sail.

leine – a long, loose-fitting smock worn by men and women under other clothing. Similar to the shift of a later period.
levies - conscripted soldiers of ninth century warfare.
Loki - Norse god of fire and free spirits. Loki was mischievous and his tricks caused great trouble for the gods, for which he was punished.
longphort - literally, a ship fortress. A small, fortified port to protect shipping and serve as a center of commerce and a launching off point for raiding.
luchrupán – middle Irish word that became the modern-day leprechaun.
luff – the shivering of a sail when its edge is pointed into the wind and the wind strikes it on both sides.
Midgard – one of nine worlds in Norse mythology, it is the earth, the world known and visible to humans.
Niflheim – the World of Fog. One of the nine worlds in Norse mythology, somewhat analogous to Hell, the afterlife for people who do not die honorable deaths.
Njord – Norse god of the sea and seafaring.
Odin - foremost of the Norse gods. Odin was the god of wisdom and war, protector of both chieftains and poets.
oénach *–a major fair, often held on a feast day in an area bordered by two territories.*
perch - a unit of measure equal to 16½ feet. The same as a rod.
Ragnarok - the mythical final battle when most humans and gods would be killed by the forces of evil and the earth destroyed, only to rise again, purified.
rod – a unit of measure equal to 16½ feet. The same as a perch
ringfort - common Irish homestead, consisting of houses protected by circular earthwork and palisade walls.
rí túaithe – Gaelic term for a minor king, who would owe allegiance to a high king.
rí ruirech – Gaelic term for a supreme or provincial king, to whom the **rí túaithe** owe allegiance.
seax – any of a variety of edged weapons longer than a knife but shorter and lighter than a typical sword.
sheer strake – the uppermost plank, or strake, of a boat or ship's hull. On a Viking ship the sheer strake would form the upper edge of the ship's hull.
shieldwall - a defensive wall formed by soldiers standing in line with shields overlapping.
shroud – a heavy rope stretching from the top of the mast to the ship's side that prevents the mast from falling sideways.
skald - a Viking-era poet, generally one attached to a royal court. The skalds wrote a very stylized type of verse particular to the medieval Scandinavians. Poetry was an important part of Viking culture and the ability to write it a highly-regarded skill.

sling - the center portion of the **yard**.
spar – generic term used for any of the masts or yards that are part of a ship's rig.
strake – one of the wooden planks that make up the hull of a ship. The construction technique, used by the Norsemen, in which one strake overlaps the one below it is called *lapstrake construction.*
swine array - a Viking battle formation consisting of a wedge-shaped arrangement of men used to attack a shield wall or other defensive position.
tánaise ríg – Gaelic term for heir apparent, the man assumed to be next in line for a kingship.
thing - a communal assembly
Thor - Norse god of storms and wind, but also the protector of humans and the other gods. Thor's chosen weapon was a hammer. Hammer amulets were popular with Norsemen in the same way that crosses are popular with Christians.
thrall - Norse term for a slave. Origin of the English word "enthrall."
thwart - a rower's seat in a boat. From the Old Norse term meaning "across."
Ulfberht – a particular make of sword crafted in the Germanic countries and inscribed with the name Ulfberht or some variant. Though it is not clear who Ulfberht was, the swords that bore his name were of the highest quality and much prized.
unstep – to take a mast down. To put a mast in place is to step the mast.
Valhalla - a great hall in **Asgard** where slain warriors would go to feast, drink and fight until the coming of **Ragnarok**.
Valkyrie - female spirits of Norse mythology who gathered the spirits of the dead from the battlefield and escorted them to **Valhalla**. They were the Choosers of the Slain, and though later romantically portrayed as Odin's warrior handmaidens, they were originally viewed more demonically, as spirits who devoured the corpses of the dead.
vantnale – a wooden lever attached to the lower end of a shroud and used to make the shroud fast and to tension it.
varonn – spring time. Literally "spring work" in Old Norse.
Vik - An area of Norway south of modern-day Oslo. The name is possibly the origin of the term *Viking.*
wattle and daub - common medieval technique for building walls. Small sticks were woven through larger uprights to form the wattle, and the structure was plastered with mud or plaster, the daub.
weather – closest to the direction from which the wind is blowing, when used to indicate the position of something relative to the wind.
wergild - the fine imposed for taking a man's life. The amount of the wergild was dependant on the victim's social standing.

yard - a long, tapered timber from which a sail was suspended. When a viking ship was not under sail, the yard was turned lengthwise and lowered to near the deck with the sail lashed to it.

Acknowledgements

Thanks, as usual, are due to a great number of people. Thanks once again to Steve Cromwell, to whom this book is dedicated, for his on-going help in making the series so eye-catching, and to Alistair Corbett for his magnificent photography. Thanks to Dmitry Burakov, of BDSart Jewelry for the use of the pendant, his original creation, on the cover. My sister, Stephanie, provided aid and comfort in so many and varied ways. So, too, do my children, Elizabeth, Nathaniel, Jonathan and Abigail. Thanks to George Jepson, Helen Hollick and Cindy Vallar for all their good work in promoting not just my books but those of so many worthy authors. Thanks to David Mullaly for all his help and for planting the idea for the ending to this book and to fellow mariner Carol Newman Cronin for her help as well. Thanks to Alicia Street at iProofread and More for her fine work bringing her keen editing eye to this book.

And, as ever, thanks to Lisa Nelson - partner, shipmate, wife of twenty-three years and counting…

38253551R00197

Made in the USA
San Bernardino, CA
02 September 2016